WHISPER
ON THE
WATER

EARL MURRAY

A TOM DOHERTY ASSOCIATES BOOK
NEW YORK

This is a work of fiction. All the characters and events portrayed in this book are either products of the author's imagination or are used fictitiously.

WHISPER ON THE WATER

Cover art by David Wright

A Forge Book
Published by Tom Doherty Associates, Inc.
175 Fifth Avenue
New York, NY 10010

Forge® is a registered trademark of Tom Doherty Associates, Inc.

ISBN: 0-812-53887-0

First Forge edition: January 1998

Printed in the United States of America

0 9 8 7 6 5 4 3 2 1

Spirit Woman

The Blackfeet covered their mouths in amazement. "Aiee, she comes to kill us! She has a spirit's powers!" A woman with such strong medicine was seldom seen. And such powerful medicine that she possessed, even for a warrior, was rare. She went among them, chanting the verses to her song, swinging the club and killing them. Their lances and arrows would not touch her. Some of the warriors had firesticks, and even the balls shot with powder could not find her. The Blackfeet ran from her in fear. She fought like five warriors, and with the strength of as many, also. Her eyes were like fire. "Aiee! She is a spirit! She seeks revenge!" From that day forward, she would be called Spirit Woman.

"Murray skillfully weaves period detail and Native lore to create an engrossing tale featuring an uncommon heroine."
—*Publishers Weekly* on *Spirit of the Moon*

"Today there are possibly a scant dozen writers of the Native American experience who really understand and feel it's spirit. One who must be included on that short list is Earl Murray."
—Don Coldsmith, author of *Ruin* and *The Spanish Bit*, on *Thunder In the Dawn*

By Earl Murray from Tom Doherty Associates

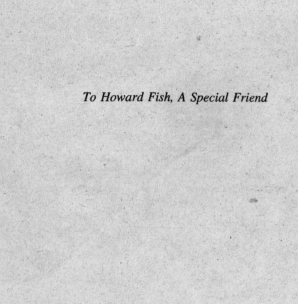

To Howard Fish, A Special Friend

Prologue

It was July, the Moon of the Serviceberry. It was the time of the Salish Celebration Festival. All gave thanks at this time for the gift of life. In times past, those who had lived through wars and hard winters gave a special thanks.

Now night was falling and the third day of celebration was nearly over. Drums were beating and the dancing was beginning. Near one of the fires a small girl was proudly showing her parents her winnings from the contests of the day. She had been the best among the children of her age in all the footraces, the arrow throwing, and the swimming. She had ridden a winning horse in the races of that morning. Now she owned many new necklaces and rings; brightly colored cloth with which to make new dresses, as well as new buckskin with which to make a coat.

"You have done well, my daughter," her father said with pride. "You bring honor to our family."

Soon there were other young people near the fire, seeing what the girl had won. Then they were gone to show others and the father settled back to smile at his wife. Their daughter was indeed gifted in her abilities to compete against others her own age, and even those older.

From the darkness came an old Indian woman. "I would like to talk," she told the young girl's father. She spoke through a mouth that held no teeth and her eyes were small dark circles in a face wrinkled as worn lodgeskin. Yet the eyes were bright and they shone in the light of the fire.

The young girl's father offered the old woman a seat near his wife and watched as her eyes grew ever brighter. A bony hand came up from under a worn blanket and pointed into the darkness after the young girl.

"She is a gifted one," the old women said. "You should be proud."

The girl's father nodded. "We are indeed proud."

"Yes, she is a special one, as was one of her ancestors of many years past," the old woman went on. "It is not often that such a person is born. And to be a woman is a special thing." She looked closely at the father. "This ancestor I have just spoken of, do you know who she is? She would also be an ancestor of yours, for your daughter is of your blood."

The father hung his head. "No, I do not know the story. I'm sure I must have heard it as a child, but I do not remember. I am ashamed, for it is a story I should know."

"Yes," said the old woman. "It is a story you should know."

"There are many such stories I do not know," the girl's father confessed. "I was of the generation who, as a boy and a young man, listened very little to the stories of our people. This was because we did not wish to know. But now things are different. We all wish to know about our ancestors; and many of our elders are gone, so many of the stories are lost. Yes, it is nearly too late."

The old woman shook her head. "It is not too late. When your daughter has passed her twelfth winter, go to the Lake of the Flathead. Look for large rocks on the same shore where Sun rises. On these rocks you will find a story written in pictures. Find these rocks. Your daughter will know what to do."

Then, without another word, the old woman arose and was lost in the darkness.

During the same month, the Moon of the Serviceberry, after the daughter had passed her twelfth winter, the father took her to the Lake of the Flathead. Together they searched among the rocks on the shore where Sun rose each day. They were there many days and saw only those pictures and stories which they had already seen in years past and knew. "What did the old woman wish that I should see, Father?" the young woman asked many times. "There is nothing here we have not seen before." And each time she spoke, her father would say, "Let us keep searching for new stories."

Then one evening a thunderstorm came over the Lake of the Flathead. Lightning flashed many times across the sky and rain fell. The two, father and daughter, took shelter among a group of large rocks just above the shoreline. As the lightning flashed, the young woman saw carvings in the rock. It was almost dark and her eyes could not make out the drawings. But when Sun came again, it was easy to see many things carved in the stones.

"There are many stories here, Father," said the young woman. "See, she must have been a woman warrior. She must have owned a truly beautiful horse. And, look! Some of the carvings look like lightning, such as that which came with the storm last night."

Her father looked at her strangely. "How do you know these things, Daughter? It is hard to see many of those symbols, and even harder to understand them."

"Oh, yes! Yes, it is all here! There was a man in her life. A white man, one of those called Long Knives by our people during those times. See, it goes up and down, all over the rocks."

"What strange thing is happening here?" her father whispered to himself.

His daughter went on reading the symbols. At times her

eyes would fill with tears. Sometimes she would laugh.
Once she sang a song. At this her father drew back, for he
had never heard her sing it before. It was a song he had
heard long ago as a child. It was a woman's song of childbearing.

When the young woman was finished, there was a
strange light in her eyes. "I have a story I must tell our
people, Father. It is a story of long ago that was somehow
lost. This story must be told again for all our people to
hear. My children and their children, in turn, must tell this
story."

Her father studied the rocks. "How did you see so
much?" Then he remembered the old woman's words.
"Find these rocks. Your daughter will know what to do."

"I will begin the story tonight," the young woman said.

Her father nodded. Yes, his daughter was indeed a special person. "Let us return to our people," he said to her,
"so that you may begin the story tonight."

Part One

BLACKFEET AND LONG KNIVES

Chapter 1

SIKSIKA!

The still waters of the mountain lake mirrored a face, young and pure. She was a member of the Willow Cutters band of Salish people. She smiled and watched a waterbug dance its way through her reflection as she rouged her cheeks with red ochre. She rubbed fragrant blossoms of horsemint under her ears and along her neck, and carefully arranged the soft doeskin dress around her shoulders. In her heart and upon her lips was a song of joy, for this was the day of her warrior, Sun Bear Standing.

Though this small mountain lake was close to her heart at this time in her life, her favorite waters was the great lake of the mountains far to the north, the lake of her people —the Flathead. It was at this great water that she had been given life, and a name that had stayed with her throughout her days as a child growing to womanhood. It was to this giant water that her mother had taken her infant daughter and knelt upon a grassy bank. She had touched the clear waters with her fingers and put them to her baby's lips.

"May you always know the eternal gift of life," she had said, as tiny beads of water formed on the child's lips and cheeks. "And may Sister Water always look upon you with kindness and fill your years with happiness and peace." Gently, she had placed her baby's toes and fingers against the cool freshness of the mountain lake. Like the leaves of the quaking aspen that fell into the water near them and made gentle ripples, so had the infant child as her tiny body touched the water. Like the soft voice of life, a whisper.

Whisper on the Water.

And now Sun Bear Standing would come to her and make these waters close to her heart. He would tell her how she was the prettiest of all Salish women and how his lodge would have sun the whole night through. He would tell her how he had given her father twenty-three of the finest horses, along with many furs and robes of the finest kind. Also, one of the big firesticks called Hawkens that had come with the Long Knives, the men with white skin who looked for the beaver. With the horses and the Hawkens firestick her father would ride proudly in war against the Blackfeet, the terrible raiders from the flats beside the mountains. The robes would keep her father the warmest of all warriors during the cold winters and make him look the finest in council and meetings of society among men. Sun Bear Standing would tell her all this and make her happy.

As Whisper thought of these things, she stood up from the banks of the lake and smoothed her dress once again. She was troubled. Sun Bear Standing should have appeared by now. She began to gather berries, for this was the reason she had given her mother for going to the lake. Her trouble grew deeper and turned to cold fear, for the birds began to fly out from where they had been singing in the trees and the little sounds in the woods ceased. The forest became deathly still. Whisper crouched and hid in the brush along the trail. Then, from the camp just back of the lake came the sounds of wild shouting and yelling. The screams of women and children pierced the quiet air and brought a sickness to the pit of Whisper's stomach. Mixed with the yelling were Blackfeet war cries.

Siksika—the terrible Blackfeet! Whisper remembered well her first encounter with them and the horrors of years past overwhelmed her. That day they had swept down on her people's small band. The men had been away hunting and those left were only women and children, tended by the young men and the very old. Many had died under the war clubs and lances of the raiders. Whisper, eleven winters at the time, was subjected to a cruelty that would forever scar her mind. She would never forget those faces, painted and laughing, as they chased her among the lodges. They had caught her and torn her doeskin dress off, laughing harder. Then they had pushed her to the ground and forced themselves on her. There had been five of them before the pain had taken her senses from her and sent her into blackness. She did not know how many there had been after that. Perhaps they had quit once her screaming stopped. She had awakened to find an old woman, who had hidden outside of camp during the raid, tending to her bleeding. An older brother had been killed and her mother, too, had been cruelly treated and left for dead.

She could remember her father coming home with fresh buffalo meat and throwing it on the ground, then crying out in his anguish and hate. There had been a singer with the hunt, and he had made a special song for that day:

> We have come home from the hunt.
> Aiee, our people all lay dying!
> Many of our people dead.
> Aiee, their spirits are wailing!
> Against Siksika we make war!
> Aiee, Siksika all will die!
> Their blood will fill all the valleys;
> And wolves will find them every one!

Whisper had heard this song and had formed in her mind the main words; words she would never forget:

Against Siksika we make war!
Aiee, Siksika all will die!

In the days that had followed the raid, Whisper and her mother had had many tearful nights together. Her father had told both of them many times, ''Though our lodge is changed, we must live on as before.'' But in his heart a sickness had formed he could not hide. And after the revenge raid he had come home with his left arm badly broken. Crooked Arm had become his new name; and though he would still be known as a respected warrior of the band, he would always have pain and his usefulness in war and on hunts would be limited.

With both her brothers dead and her father with a near-useless arm, the lodge had become poor in horses and meat. Whisper had been forced to learn some of the skills usually left to young men. She learned to hunt and fish, and she had learned these skills well. Yet, these were things reserved for men and Whisper's father did not take the great pride in her he would have if it were a son killing deer and elk, and spearing fish in the shallows. No, things would never be the same around their lodge for Whisper's mother was past the child-bearing age and her father did not care to take another woman. This part of their lives had been changed before when her aunt, also a wife in the lodge at the time, had run off with another warrior. Her father had never gotten over the shame. Now his sons were gone.

Into the eyes of her mother and father, Whisper had seen a great change come gradually over the years. Happiness had flown away like the summer birds before the snow. Their faces never laughed. Their eyes showed only sorrow and their mouths never spoke of happy things. Over the years Whisper had come to be very sad. Then, finally, in her womanhood she had found happiness with Sun Bear Standing.

Whisper reached the edge of camp, fighting the fog that covers the mind in times of great fear. The terrible cries of dying people filled the air. Blackfeet men were tearing scalps from the heads of the fallen, and screaming loudly as they waved them in the air for the others to see. In the midst of the fighting was Sun Bear Standing's finest horse, riderless and confused. Sun Bear Standing lay among the dead, his body filled with Blackfoot arrows. Near him lay her father, being scalped in death.

Whisper's mind turned over and over at the sight. She cried out loudly and began to wail. Then her wailing ceased. The face of the woman took on a strange, hard stare and her fists closed tight. She charged into the middle of the camp, screaming at the top of her lungs. All around her were the Siksika; their bodies black and crimson, their faces streaked and spotted. She found a war club near a fallen warrior and turned to face three Siksika who were stripping the clothes off a young girl. The words to the song the singer had made that terrible day of her childhood came back to her. She began a low chant that rose higher and higher as she repeated the verses:

> *Against Siksika we make war!*
> *Aiee, Siksika all will die!*

She screamed in much the same fashion she had heard the Flathead men do when preparing for war, and brought the club down against one of the warrior's heads. Her arms were strong and the club moved swiftly. Her aim was true and the skull cracked like a large egg.

One of the others turned on her in surprise. Again she screamed and swung the club flush into his face. His eyes popped out of his head and he became a writhing form among those already dead or dying. The third one lunged at her with his knife, reaching a hand out to grab her by the hair. She swung the heavy club hard into his chest cavity. His ribs cracked like dried twigs and he sank, screaming, to his knees. Her next blow caught him full against the side of the head, covering the stone with paint and blood.

The other Blackfeet saw this and covered their mouths in amazement. "Aiee, she comes to kill us! She has a spirit's powers!'' A woman with such strong medicine was seldom seen. And such powerful medicine that she possessed, even for a warrior, was rare. She went among them, chanting the verses to her song, swinging the club and killing them. Their lances and arrows would not touch her. Some of the warriors had firesticks, and even the balls shot with powder could not find her. The Blackfeet ran from her in fear. She fought like five warriors, and with the strength of as many, also. Her eyes were like fire. ''Aiee! She is a spirit! She seeks revenge!'' From that day forward, she would be called Spirit Woman.

Though Whisper fought as fiercely as any warrior who had ever lived, it was a bad day for the Willow Cutters band of Salish people. The Blackfeet had come ready for war, and they were too strong in numbers. Salish men fell before the enemy and yelled for their families to hide in the forest. The women and children cried as they ran, for their fathers and husbands would all die this fine day. It would be a time of great mourning for those who escaped. But they would still have life, and thereby would give life in time to more Salish people.

As the battle drew to a close and the last Salish warrior lay dead, all Siksika eyes turned to the Spirit Woman who had made war against them with fire in her eyes, killing many of their number and wounding still others. She stood, exhausted, in a circle of Blackfeet whose eyes were wide and whose mouths spoke to each other in low tones about this woman of great medicine. ''Who is she that comes to make war? Who is this Spirit Woman?'' She had come from out of the forest, with a chant of war that had put fear in their hearts. Never had a woman been so bold before them, fighting against numbers she could never win against, yet scattering them like deer before the wolf. No one would kill this Spirit Woman. No one would dare, for the spirits would look upon them with displeasure.

Whisper stood holding the club, too tired and weak to raise it again. She had fought and fought, and now she wondered what they would do with her. When it was plain she would fight no more, some of the Siksika came forward and touched her, as if to get some of her strong medicine to have for themselves. But most just stood in awe.

From the group came a Blackfoot warrior with his head held high. He was dressed as a war chief, a high honor for someone his age. He looked to be about as many winters as Whisper, but his confidence was that of a tribal elder. His eyes were dark and heavily masked by a coat of black paint, streaked through with vermilion. His body was also a mass of paint, coated over with grease. White ermine tails lined his war shield and decorated his hair around three eagle feathers that fanned out about his head. His own medicine was strong and it was clear he thought highly of the Salish woman.

One of the other Siksika began talking to her in sign and Blackfoot tongue about the young warrior who stood before her. Whisper could not speak Blackfoot, but she could read the sign used among the plains tribes well.

"This man is Walking Head, war chief of the War Dancers band of Siksika peoples. He will tell you how it is in his heart."

The young war chief, with his arms folded in front of him, eyed the Salish woman with a stone face. After a time, he brought his arms out to make sign.

"You have a fighting spirit in you this fine day. Are you a woman chief among your people?"

Whisper shook her head. "Kill me now, for my people are all dead. I wish to live no longer."

The young Blackfoot war chief grunted. "It is not so. Our warriors wish the words you speak were true. It is because of you that many numbers of Salish women and children ran off into the forest. It is because of you that your Salish men fought harder than I have ever seen them fight."

"Some of my people escaped?" Whisper asked, hardly believing.

Walking Head nodded. "They will be found."

Whisper's spirit lit up at the thought that maybe her

mother had escaped death. Her mother, whom she loved so and to whom she owed so much.

Walking Head sensed her sudden alertness. "Does the Salish woman think her warrior has escaped?" he asked mockingly. "If he was a man, we now have his scalp stretched out to dry. If he is in the forest, then he is a woman and belongs with the women."

"He could have killed you with one blow hand-to-hand!" Whisper spat. "You stinking dog!" Her club came up and Walking Head quickly grabbed it and wrenched it from her.

"You have some fight left, Spirit Woman," he laughed. "That is good. You are a strong woman. You will bear me many sons who will some day become great Siksika warriors."

Whisper's eyes were flashing as she formed her sign swiftly and plainly for Walking Head to read. "I will be dead before I lie beneath a dog such as you! Kill me now, for if you don't I will surely kill every one of you and slit your bellies open for the wolves before we reach your lodges. You are all dogs!"

There was a silence while Walking Head studied her. Her breath came in short gasps and her eyes were fire. He studied her up and down, his own face etched in iron. "It is not us, the powerful Siksika, who are dogs," he said. "It is you, the Salish, and your brothers, the Pend d'Oreille, who howl when the moon rises and eat stinking flesh. You come to the land of the Siksika and our brothers, the Pikuni, to kill our buffalo and take the berries that grow from the bushes. You sneak along the ground like the snakes you are, hiding in the rocks and holes in the ground, for you are cowards and you are afraid. And it is good that many such dogs have died this fine day."

"It is you who are afraid," Whisper told him. "It is you, the Siksika dogs, who must have three and more the numbers of each of our Salish warriors. If there had not been so many of you, the forest would have been red with Siksika blood and all the mountain peoples would have cried for joy. The wolves would have laughed with their bellies full and the black raven that caws in the sky would have picked your bones. Yes, you would all be dead now and my people would have danced the scalp dance for many suns in a row.''

Walking Head glared at her through eyes that were slits. ''It is we, the Siksika, who rule over all others, who will dance over scalps, Spirit Woman. And if you had not been in the grace of the spirits, you too would have been slain and left to rot. But now, since you have shown yourself to be of powerful medicine and to have the strength known only to warriors, now you will come to my lodge and raise plenty sons for me who will learn to war in the Siksika way. I have spoken.''

Chapter 2

HENRY'S LAKE

Ravens flew cawing and flapping overhead, just above the tips of the high trees. Whisper knew the big birds would find her people before the wolves, but would have to depart to branches and wait their turn at the leavings when the wolves did come. Whisper cried softly to herself, for the souls of her people would surely wail, lost forever in the Land of Eternal Snow now that they were without heads and arms and legs. They would have to be avenged; their spirits would have to be released, for now they would never reach the Land of Eternal Summer, where the days are always bright and happy, and meat is always in the pot.

"It would be well to forget you were ever Salish," she remembered Walking Head saying. "You will learn Siksika ways and teach my sons."

It was then she had spat in his face. His eyes had become fire but he did not strike her. Instead he had laughed. "The Spirit Woman wished me to gain disfavor with those inside her body. It is not for me to hit you now. It will be best to wait until the spirits have left and you once again return to the woman you really are."

It had then been Whisper's turn to laugh. "You are a fool. I will never return to the woman I once was. I will always be the Spirit Woman."

The strange look Walking Head had given her had made her laugh again. The look had been one of surprise, then almost fear. It had been as if Walking Head had seen something in what she had said, a vision perhaps. He backed up a step and the strange look lasted another moment. Then he had come forward and touched her, and the look had vanished. "You may always have the spirits with you," he had said, "but you will learn the Siksika way. You will forget your old people."

As she rode, hands bound, in the middle of the column, she held the hope deep within her that her dear mother still lived. When Walking Head had told her that many of the women and children had escaped, it had made her heart glad. It had given her new strength. It had made her raise her eyes to the sky and believe, once again, that the Great Spirit did care for her. The Blackfeet had looked for her people, as Walking Head had said they would do. But they had found nothing. They had spent their time cursing and raising their voices in anger. The search had wasted their time and made this journey back to their camp less joyous for them than it would have been before, had they left and not tried to find those who had escaped.

Whisper was happy for this. No one could find mountain Salish when they did not wish to be found. She, herself, had learned as a small child never to make a sound while in hiding, and never to look upon someone hunting for you so that the spirit of that person could not feel you there. She had remembered her lessons well and had many times hidden by the waters of a stream or lake and watched the beings of the forest drink without them knowing. Once she had almost touched the side of the big-antlered elk, the monarch who calls to the forest in the Moon of Grass Curing, September, when he forms his band of she-elk. He had been drinking deeply of lake water, his ivory antlers counting seven points to a side. He had never known she was there. She had not been there to shoot him with her bow, for his meat at this time of year would smell and taste of the mating excitement that ran in his blood. No, she was content to just watch. She had learned the skills of hiding and stalking game well. And if there was any reason she would feel glad that her father had been injured on the Blackfoot raid, it would be for this. It was good to put down the work of a woman at times, to hunt and be alone in the forest.

Now she felt better for those who had escaped. Well she knew they could care for themselves until finding others to live with. And well she knew no band of Siksika, or their brothers the Pikuni, would ever find them. Whisper smiled to herself. A day would come when she would again be with her band, with the woman called Little Grasses, her mother; once again they would all live together in happiness.

The Blackfeet took her northward, along the waters the Long Knives called Henry's Fork. Toward where Sun rises each day were high rock peaks that still held the snows of winter, the high peaks called *Tetons* that the French Long Knives said looked like the breasts of a woman. Behind was the broad valley that fell away from the mountains and spread far in all directions. The trail along the waters called Henry's Fork led back down to this valley and to the great rushing waters called the Snake River, which made deep cuts in the flats below. Whisper looked back in sadness, for it was here that her people had wished to go. They were to meet first with the Long Knives at their rendezvous in the place called Pierre's Hole, where they would trade furs to these white men for the firestick, and would be pleased with vermilion and knives for war against the Blackfeet. Whisper herself had gotten many pretty things and was happy when talk of the summer trip was once again heard in all the lodges. From the rendezvous in Pierre's Hole they would have traveled with other Salish bands into the Snake River country for the summer hunt. It would have been a time of great joy and feasting, for the buffalo were plenty in this land.

But now she would go with the Blackfeet, up over these high mountains and down into another valley to the north called the Three Forks. "You will come with us to our summer hunting grounds at the Three Forks," Walking Head had told her. "And when the snows of winter send the geese down to the warm lands, you will be with me in my lodge far to the north on the Big Muddy. You will be a Siksika in Siksika land." Already she could see herself trailing on foot behind Walking Head's horse with a rope around her neck. The Siksika would all have black faces and be yelling, showing Salish scalps on their coup sticks and running Salish horses around camp in a circle in a demonstration of glory. Yes, the Three Forks put fear in her heart.

Whisper knew the country of the Three Forks well. Her people had followed trails through the mountains to this place many times at the end of the winter to hunt the buffalo and gather the roots and berries of many wild plants that grew in the hills and on the flats. The elders told lodge tales of the old days and how there was always war with the Blackfeet over these hunting grounds. There were many raids back and forth to steal horses, and women and children. There was always war with the Blackfeet.

Whisper tried not to think of the day that had just passed, nor the terrible time ahead of her at the Siksika camp on Three Forks. Her head was down as the horse carried her farther up into the mountains along Henry's Fork. Perhaps she could escape, she thought, for there was still much country between them and the Three Forks. Not far ahead was *La Roche Jaune*, a place called Yellowstone by the Long Knives. This was a broad land of the high mountains, where waters formed that would flow both toward the giant waters called Pacific by the Long Knives and also into the land of the plains to the east. It was a place where the air smelled of sweetness during each of the warm moons, and there were many of the trees called lodgepole pines by the

Long Knives because of their use by the Indian peoples. These trees grew thick and it would be an easy thing to become lost among them, if only she could find the chance. And it would have to be here, in the Yellowstone, that she made her chance, for this country took them to the waters of the Madison. Once at the Madison, her chances of escape would be almost hopeless, for the Three Forks would be just below.

"You will lie beneath me in my lodge, and each time that I want," she remembered Walking Head saying to her. This made her even more determined. Escape, or die trying. But she would escape; and it would be this day, she thought, for the spirits were with her.

Henry's Fork carried them up to the broad waters she knew the Long Knives to call Henry's Lake. It filled a giant meadow with a deep blue that shimmered in the light Sun put upon its surface. They were getting ever closer to the Yellowstone now and Whisper knew she would soon be watching Walking Head tell of his brave deeds while he watched the women dance around the scalps of her people. As she watched the Siksika water their horses and those stolen during the raid, she knew this would be a time they would try to rest before continuing their journey. Many would be off their horses for a time, laughing and talking of the raid. But Walking Head knew her thoughts and was not to be fooled. "You watch this woman closely," he told a warrior. "Do not let her have a horse until we are ready to leave." He had then given her a sly smile and left.

"I cannot drink, nor can I wash the dust and sweat from my face with ropes on my hands," she told the warrior watching her.

The warrior stood with his arms crossed and shook his head.

Whisper let out a small laugh. "The bold Siksika is afraid of the Spirit Woman. He is afraid she will prove him less than a man and cause the others to laugh at him."

The warrior narrowed his eyes.

Whisper laughed again. "What I say is true. Why are

you not tending the horses with the other young men?
Maybe you should be in camp with your women.''

The warrior sucked his breath in hard. He started to raise
his arm, but thought better of it. It would not be good to
strike this woman on this fine day when the spirits were
with her. After a moment, he untied the bonds.

The warrior watched her carefully while she knelt at the
water's edge. Then loud shouting behind him took his attention from her. Long Knives. A large body of them on
their way to rendezvous. Whisper quickly jumped into the
cold waters of the lake.

Behind her the shouting and yelling became intense. The
Blackfeet began singing their war songs and adding fresh
paint to their bodies. The Long Knives were yelling,
''Bug's boys! Bug's boys!'' and making their way to cover.

Soon the fighting began. Though the Blackfeet far out-
numbered the Long Knives, the Long Knives had the big
Hawken firesticks that were deadly in their hands. The
Blackfeet screamed and fell dead and dying all along the
banks. They could not get close to the Long Knives and
their arrows could not kill from so far away. But the Blackfeet had fought many times and would not be discouraged
so easily. They sang their war songs even louder, as many
of their number had fallen and had to be avenged. They
waved their weapons and shouted at the Long Knives, then
moved out to surround them.

The Long Knives showed that they, too, had fought before. They chose a stand against a steep bank of rock and
slag timber that came down to the water's edge, and laid
their heavy packs down in a circle to face the Blackfeet.
From there the Hawken firesticks could slay many Blackfeet before they themselves were reached.

Whisper knew these men who wanted the beaver. She
had learned much about the Long Knives during the times
her people had traded at rendezvous. For two winters her
best friend had taken a Long Knife for her husband and
they had shared a lodge in camp. Now she was with him
and Whisper saw her only at rendezvous each year. Whis-

per had learned much of the Long Knife tongue during this time and also many things about the differences between their ways and her own.

Whisper was now far out from the shores of the lake. She had seen the opportunity to escape and she had taken it. She swam with strong strokes, rejoicing in her freedom. But behind her was the Siksika warrior who had been left to watch her. He knew he would be shamed as a warrior if he let her get away from him. Whisper knew, with a smile on her lips, that he would pay for his pride with death. For she knew well the ways of the water; she had learned them as a child and could swim better than anyone she had ever been tested against. Even the best warriors themselves could not beat her. She had learned the secrets Sister Water had told her in the giant waters of the Flathead. Her people had watched with their mouths covered in amazement at the things she could do and the stamina she showed while swimming. While all the young girls were having their childhood names changed, she kept the name her mother had given her, for she was indeed a child of the water. She would always be Whisper on the Water. And now she would use what she had learned from Sister Water against her enemy.

The warrior swam up to her and reached out a hand to grab her by the hair. Whisper caught his wrist and dove hard into the depths of the cold lake, hauling the Blackfoot along with her. Once under the water he became a thrashing, churning form, with eyes that popped out in fear. He tried to wrench loose from her, but her grip was too tight. He tried to grab her with his free hand, but she was too agile. She was like a fish, sliding through the water with ease and grace. There was no way he could touch her, or free himself from her. She played with him while he fought for his life.

She let go of his hand and followed him to the surface to fill her own lungs with air. Now she could go under for a long time while the Blackfoot would soon feel the pain of no air to breathe. She watched him gasp for breath, then once again took hold of him to lead him to his death. In her mind was the face of Sun Bear Standing, her two young brothers, her father saying, "Our lodge is changed . . . Our lodge is changed . . ."

She had him by one foot and was dragging him down again. He fought, but had no control. She tugged and pulled him down into the dark water while he strained his lungs to save himself. With one last burst of energy, he turned and caught her arm. He was strong; he was desperate for life. Now, Whisper thought, these waters will take a Blackfoot to the bottom when he no longer lives in this world. Whisper drew the knife from the Blackfoot's breechclout and stabbed the arm that held her. He jerked back in pain and turned for the surface. She was behind him, pulling the head back with a handful of hair. The knife blade slid across his throat and his whole body seemed to pour out black into the lake. He jerked for a moment, then grew limp. She made a quick cut around the forehead, from ear to ear, and pulled hard. She made another cut at the back and the scalp came free. Whisper turned for the surface while a dark form sank into the depths of the lake.

Chapter 3

THE LONG KNIVES

Whisper made her way to the surface of the lake, feeling a weakness trying to overcome her. She had fought hard in the ice-cold water and her muscles were beginning to stiffen. It was lucky she had not eaten, for she surely would be fighting the stomach knots that come when the belly is full.

She slipped the scalp down into her dress and the knife through the material at her neck. Ashore, the fighting was getting heavy. The yelling of the trappers and the war cries of the Blackfeet could be heard above all else. She set her course for the edge of the lake where the Long Knives were making their stand. She breathed heavily as she swam and fought the numbing cold of the water and the weariness that told her body to quit. The Long Knives never seemed to get any closer as she swam; but she fought ahead, knowing that to stop meant death.

The shore seemed a haze to her when she reached the Long Knives. She heard one of them yelling about Blackfeet swimming after them as the ball from a Hawken rifle made a zipping splash near her left shoulder. Another voice quieted the shots coming toward her and strong arms pulled her from the lake. She collapsed in a heap, breathless and shivering from cold.

Whisper lay hugging the shore, sucking the life giving air in long gasps while the shouting and the fighting went on around her. Again strong hands took hold of her and pulled her from the bank, where arrows were driving themselves into the mud and shallow water around her. She found herself wedged in under a fallen log behind the breastwork of trapping gear and furs. There life finally came back into her lungs and spread throughout her body.

Once again the fever pitch of the Blackfeet echoed in her ears. Their red and black bodies slithered and bobbed through the layer of trees between them and where Whisper lay under cover with the Long Knives. They moved in and out of the shadows and crawled as close as they could. They screamed and shot what guns they had and maneuvered to shoot their bows. All the while the Long Knives' Hawkens were booming and Blackfeet were singing death songs while others pulled them back through the undergrowth to die. But the Blackfeet were many and they kept fighting, yelling oaths of revenge and hatred. Behind the breastwork was a continuous zip of feathered arrows and a whack or dull thud when they hit a tree or the ground, and a scream or curse when one struck a man.

Whisper saw a Long Knife grab the shaft of an arrow that stuck from both sides of his arm and snap it in half, pulling the feathered end out toward him. His face showed the dull look of pain and columns of sweat washed trails through the black powder that covered his face. Two others lay still. In their buckskin coats they looked like lumps of fur with arrows sticking up from each one.

Whisper made her way to one of the fallen and found his Hawken. She knew the big gun well. She had shot such a gun many times when the Long Knife who was the husband of her friend had lived in camp those two winters. She knew how it shot and how the blast sent a ball as big as a man's fingernail deep into an enemy's body. She had killed Siksika with such a gun before and now she would use such a gun once again to take revenge on her hated enemy. The blood in Whisper's veins began to run fast, for now she could avenge many of her fallen people. Now they would reach the Land of Eternal Summer and know true peace. And now many Siksika would die—maybe even Walking Head if she could find him in her sights. "You will lie beneath me . . ." once again came back to her. The Blackfoot dog!

Whisper yelled her people's war cry and waved the scalp she had taken. She saw a Blackfoot who was working his way around the rock face above them. Her Hawken boomed and a charge of powder and ball slammed into the warrior. He screamed and fell with a crash into the trees below, bouncing through the boughs before thudding onto the forest floor. The trappers yelled and laughed, charging their own guns with a new vigor.

"Die, Siksika dogs!" Whisper screamed.

Again the trappers yelled and sent rounds into the trees where the Blackfeet were now backing out with their hands over their mouths in amazement. It was the Spirit Woman! Again she had been sent by the spirits to avenge her people against the Siksika. They had guided her across the cold waters of the lake to the shore where the Long Knives were. She was indeed of the spirits, for no human being could have swum so far in water that cold. And now she was killing them as she had in her camp during the raid. They were falling before her gun, and they could hear her haunting chant, her war song:

> *Against Siksika we make war!*
> *Aiee, Siksika all will die!*

This was not a day in which the Siksika could fight against her and win. Their numbers were falling under her strong medicine and the firesticks of the Long Knives. It was not a good day to fight for the Siksika.

The arrows and shots from the timber quit coming and the death songs of wounded Blackfeet were heard as warriors loaded them on horses for the trip back to their camps on the Three Forks. Their camps would not be so loud and the scalp dance would not hear as much drumming, Whisper thought. The Siksika would not paint their faces black and sing their victory songs this fine day, for they had lost many of their number. Much wailing would be heard from the Siksika women when Sun was once again high in the sky. And there would be no Salish slave woman in the lodge of Walking Head.

When the Blackfeet were gone, one lone figure moved his horse into the open just out of rifle range. It was Walking Head. He was showing a medicine pipe, a sign of peace, and motioned that he wished to talk. Talk! Whisper knew the Black-foot word for talk—it meant the same as war to them. She knew how Walking Head would tell the Long Knives that his heart was now good and that he wished no more war with the Long Knives, who were now his brothers. It would be a foolish thing for these Long Knives to believe that the Siksika wanted peace.

"That's Walking Head for sure," one Long Knife spoke up. "He's sportin' more white ermine than would fill a whiskey keg." He raised his Hawken. "One good shot and I'll have Blackfoot hair."

"Wait!" said a young Long Knife next to Whisper, putting his hand on the barrel. "Let's find out what ails him."

Whisper saw that this young Long Knife was the one who had pulled her from the water and found safety for her on the bank. He was younger than most of the others, and taller. He had a fine, strong face with piercing blue eyes. His hair was red and blonde mixed and it curled up around his wolfhead cap. He looked at Whisper and back out to Walking Head. "We sure must have some special Flathead woman here," he told the others. "It's not like Walking Head to be out makin' palaver. He'd rather fight than talk."

Walking Head turned his horse sideways and spoke to the Long Knives in sign and Blackfoot. "My brothers, it

is not right for us to fight. We are as one. It saddens my
heart that blood has been shed between us this fine day.
This has happened only because of the woman who is now
among you. She has escaped from us. She is a Spirit
Woman and can only bring you all bad fortune. Send her
out to me and I will go in peace.''

The young Long Knife pulled himself up on a fallen log.
He spoke in sign and Blackfoot tongue, making sure that
Walking Head understood every word. ''There is no peace
in Walking Head's heart. And there is no peace in the Long
Knives' hearts. We are not fools. You would have made
war upon us even without the Spirit Woman, who is now
one of us and does not wish to see you again. Now go
crying away to your women. These are my final words.''

Walking Head sat up on his horse so that his loud voice
would carry even better. ''Spirit Woman, the Long Knife
dog has the last word this fine day. But other days will
come. Some day you will be in my lodge, Spirit Woman,
and the Long Knife dogs will be meat for the wolves!'' He
turned and galloped off after the others.

''Ayers!'' yelled one of the others as he pulled the young
trapper off the log. ''Why'd you do that? He just wanted
this squaw here. Now we'll lose our hair for sure.''

The young trapper shook the older man off and told him
sternly, ''Beeler, you don't have the brains you were born
with. There's nary a Blackfoot alive that wants peace.
They'd find a way to take our hair no matter what. As for
this woman here, she don't go to no Blackfoot. Not after
she helped run them off like she did.''

A few of the others cheered. Beeler turned his grubby
face into a scowl. He was a big man and had scars on his
arms and face to prove he had fought many times before.
He took off his buck-skin top and squared around in front
of the young trapper. ''Look, Ayers. You've gone too far
to suit me. This child don't see the need to lose hair over
no Injun squaw. Now, I say we send her out of here and
save us a heap of trouble.''

''Jim, maybe he's right,'' one of the others spoke up.

The young trapper pulled his own shirt off and took a deep breath. "She don't leave here with no bunch of Bug's Boys," he said flatly. "God Almighty, can't a one of you tell when his hair's been saved? And she's got Blackfoot hair of her own to boot!" He held up the scalp Whisper had taken from the warrior in the lake. "So I say she stays." He gave the scalp back to Whisper and turned again to face Beeler.

"You've got no call givin' orders, Ayers," Beeler said. "We're all free trappers here. Nary a one takes orders. See?"

"No one's out to give you orders," said Ayers. "You do what you want, but the Flathead woman stays."

"You're one who don't care about his hair," Beeler argued.

"Beeler, you never did have a lick of sense. Those Blackfeet have high-tailed it out of here singin' death songs. They're whipped good for today. Besides, it's damn near dark and you won't see them hangin' around a place of death at night. Especially with this Flathead gal here they're callin' Spirit Woman."

"Just what do you plan to do with her then?" Beeler questioned. "Maybe make a soft spot in your bedroll?" Beeler laughed mockingly and his men joined in. "She's got no kin that I see," Beeler went on. "Odds are good you'll get her without givin' up nary a horse or gun." The laughing continued.

Jim Ayers grunted. His blue eyes were calm and a sardonic grin worked across his lips. "No call for that, Beeler. Just because God never made a woman that would want you. Guess you'll have to stick to pluggin' mules."

Beeler stiffened and a Frenchman named Courchene spoke. "Ed, it is best to go and forget. *Oui*, it is best we leave now."

Beeler sized up the young trapper, standing tall and strong with his ruddy face drawn up firm, waiting for a move. Beeler was a hard man in his own right and was not known for backing down. But the young trapper had the advantage of age.

"You done as much as everyone says you have, Ayers?" Beeler asked. "This child don't think none of it's true at all."

Jim Ayers stood firm, without answering.

"*Non*," said Courchene again to Beeler. He put his small eyes on Jim and squinted. "It is finished for now. *Oui*, it is time to leave. And maybe the Blackfeet, they take the hair of this man, Ayers. *Oui*, and maybe the others with him."

"I aim to see if there's blood in this hoss," said Beeler, his eyes suddenly darkening.

"We wait," Courchene persisted. "Another time, she come soon."

Beeler curled his mouth up. "Another day then, Ayers. How's that?"

Jim nodded. "Whenever you feel like loosin' teeth."

Beller put his buckskins back on and grouped his men up. They took the two dead trappers and moved out into the dusk. Jim Ayers watched Beeler eye him viciously and knew the other time and place would not be long in coming.

The fire leaped and licked at the wood the Long Knife, Jim Ayers, put on it. He had nice eyes, Whisper thought, even though her sorrow for Sun Bear Standing was still great. His eyes were the kind that looked into you and reached to the roots of your very being, much the same as a wise medicine man when he searches to see what you are made of. This Long Knife's eyes were the same. Yet they were gentle eyes that showed not hatred but a confidence that made a person feel the strength in him.

They were the same as any man's eyes. They saw the full breasts that pushed out the doeskin from her shoulders, even more so now that the dress was still wet from the lake; they saw where the lean thighs brushed against the skirt. These eyes admired all they saw of her, but not as the eyes of the other Long Knives. The eyes of Jim Ayers were not the eyes of pure desire. They studied her as a being as well as something for pleasure. They looked into her own eyes and sought to know what was beyond them; to reach back into her mind and to know what she was thinking. This young Long Knife was a man of power and dignity.

"Do you speak the Long Knife tongue?" he asked her in sign language.

Whisper nodded, keeping her eyes averted from him as an Indian woman does out of respect for a man.

"Then you know all that went on out there about givin' you back to the Blackfeet?"

"Yes," Whisper answered. "But I would have died before I would have gone with them. They are dogs!"

"How did you end up with the likes of them?"

Whisper took a deep breath. "They killed my people this morning. I do not wish to speak of it."

The trapper was silent for a moment, piling more wood on the fire. Little sparks danced into the sky and the light gave the darkness around them a soft glow. The other trappers that had stayed with Jim Ayers sat around the fire, feeling its warmth and glow, and feasting on fresh elk. They laughed over tales of days past and the battle that had just been fought. Jim Ayers sat back from the fire and looked into it as he spoke.

"Are you the only one that didn't go under?"

Whisper shook her head. "There are others who ran into the forest. Some day I will find them."

"If Walking Head don't catch up with you first. That Injun wants you bad."

"I will die first," Whisper repeated. She took a deep breath to release her hatred and spoke once again. "Will you and the others travel to where the furs are traded and the Long Knives come from far in the direction where Sun rises to bring presents?"

"We're all headed for the rendezvous," Jim answered. "You must have known as much from the furs we've got with us. Maybe you'd like to ride with us. There will be plenty of Flatheads there.''

Whisper nodded. "I will be of no burden to you."

Jim laughed. "No, that's a sure thing. Not the way you swim and fight Blackfeet."

Whisper got up and moved away from the fire. Her thoughts would not get away from the Blackfeet. Her heart was sad and she wished to be alone, away from anything that brought her mind back to this bad day in her life. Once again she sought the sanctuary of the forest.

The night was still around her. All that broke the silence was the voices of men cursing and laughing around the fire. The breeze was cool and it made her think again of the fresh morning air she had breathed not long ago. Then that sweet morning air had been fouled by the smell of blood and the sounds of her people screaming as the Blackfeet killed them one by one. But which ones had they killed? Whose were the faces she would never see in this life again?

Her warrior, Sun Bear Standing, would never again tell her of his love for her. He had been the only warrior who understood her. Of all the young men in the band, and even other visiting bands, he alone had understood that she was indeed a woman and needed the things a woman needs, even though she had been forced of necessity to do some of those things a young man learns. Maybe since she had learned the skills of hunting and fishing better than most, she had become a figure of embarrassment to the other young men. Maybe because of this they felt she would always be demanding more of them and telling them she could do better. Only Sun Bear Standing understood that this was not her way; this was not how she would be with the warrior who took her for his lodge. But then Sun Bear Standing had been special. He could do everything well; and even though there were things he knew Whisper could do better, he would just laugh and say he didn't believe it. It would have been a wonderful thing to see the smile on the face of her father at the number of horses and fine furs he was to have received in exchange for his daughter; and he would know well that his daughter would give him fine grandsons from such a warrior as Sun Bear Standing. Now that could never be.

And what about her mother. Where was the small woman they called Little Grasses? This was the woman who had loved Whisper so dearly and who had held Whisper to her breast when she was little so many times during the loud thunder in the sky that brought rain, and for warmth against the cold at night during the Moon of Continuous Snow. Was she gone forever? Was her soul wandering lost in the forest, crying out to be avenged? No, it could not be. Though she could count on two hands twice the number of friends she had seen lying dead near Siksika feet, she would never believe her mother lay with them.

She sat down on a log far back in the timber, her back against a tree and her moccasins planted in the fallen needles that made a thick mat on the ground. She began a low song of mourning. Though she was strong in spirit, the heavy burden of a day such as this had been almost too much.

With the knife she had taken from the Blackfoot in the lake, she made a long gash in her left forearm. Then she switched hands with the knife and did the same to the right forearm. As the wounds flowed, the lines of blood were dark against her skin.

From afar came the cry of a wolf, then one who answered. They were down below where her people had fallen, calling in all those who wished a feast this fine night. They would have full bellies for many suns to come. She thought of making her way back, but that would be of no use. Those dead would be nearly bones by the time she would get there and it would only serve to make her grief worse. And it would not be good to go back, for the spirits of her people would be all around her crying out for her to help them when she could not. She had killed Blackfeet with the Long Knives, but had been able to take only one scalp for dancing over. One Blackfoot scalp was not enough.

She lifted her eyes to the dark sky that showed glittering dots where the stars were. She held her arms above her, as if reaching out for someone or something. She spoke softly, barely above a whisper. "What is it, Amótkan, that makes these bad things happen? I cannot live without my people. I cannot live with the loss of Sun Bear Standing and my father. I cannot be happy when all my heart ever knows is sadness and pain. The days will all go by without the light that shines from Sun; my heart will always be in darkness and my eyes will not see for the wetness that is forever in them. My wrists and arms are only scars from my many times of grieving." She hung her head and once again began her low song of sadness.

Then a strange feeling came over her. She stopped her sad song and looked around her. The moon had risen so that it made a round white ball above her. Its light came down through the trees and made the forest seem like early day. She felt a closeness near her and looked to see the tiny owl of the forest sitting at the end of her log, his small body perched up on a dead limb in the full light of the moon. He was a silent little warrior who hunted in the dark of night and went away from the day into the holes and hiding places of the forest. He was no bigger than her fist, but was stout of heart and a wonder to see. There were not many whom he let look upon him. For this Whisper felt he had come to be just with her.

She sat still and watched him for a time while he looked at her out of eyes that seemed to cover his whole face. She knew there was a reason for his being here, for his coming to her in the moon of this fine night for her to see and, yes, for her to hear. Now it was for her to listen. She could hear him saying that the forest and the hills and the plains go on while all those who live in these places must die some day. Those who live fashion new life for others; and all must go on living, even as death comes near. That is the way it must be. It is not for the living to understand the ways of death. It is but for the living to rejoice in life and rejoice with those who live around you. The gift of life is something those who are born will always have, even after they are called from life as it is known here. It is for the living to be strong and go on living.

Whisper looked down at her bleeding arms and back to the dead limb. The limb was bare, with only moonlight reflecting from it. Somehow the little owl had melted into the night; was gone in silence. The tiny warrior of the forest. Whisper felt the warm wetness of tears on her cheeks. She had known a tiny warrior in their band. She had seen him in death near his mother just that morning. Little Fox had been but a small child who had shown the makings of a brave warrior in manhood. All the men in camp had talked that he would grow up to be a great Salish warrior. His little black eyes had been those of a smart child. When he had seen but four winters, he had lost his mother to the sickness that sometimes comes with bearing children. He had been strong and had shown a love for his tiny sister that made all in camp wonder at his courage. He would have, indeed, been a fine warrior.

Now Whisper would be strong herself, for the spirit of Little Fox had come to her in the tiny owl and had given her courage. He had come to be her guardian. She would grieve no more over those now dead, but be happy for them in the life beyond; she would give thanks to Amótkan that she, herself, had been spared. She would envoke Amótkan to help her find the woman called Little Grasses, her mother, for now Whisper felt sure this woman had been spared so that some day they could again share the life that was in them both.

This was the way it must be.

Chapter 4

RENDEZVOUS

It was a sight to behold. The eye could not take it in all at once. Though Whisper had seen it before, each year it seemed to grow greater in size and bring in many more people. It was the time of year when the Long Knives came together to be as one. They came from catching the beaver to trade with other Long Knives who had journeyed from far toward where Sun rises. It was when all the Indian allies of the Long Knives, mainly the Flathead, Nez Percé, and Shoshoni peoples came together to trade their own furs and play games of chance and race their ponies. There was much singing and dancing, much drinking of the spirit water called whiskey. It was a time of much goings-on.

Rendezvous.

The valley was filled with horses, loose or on picket, while all around was the sound of drums and dancing. Again the tall peaks called *Tetons* showed themselves high above them, the jagged humps reaching father into the sky than an eagle could soar. Campfire smoke carried high into the evening sky and melted into thin clouds above hide lodges.

It was the young Long Knife, Jim Ayers, who had led
the way down into camp. It seemed the yelling would never
stop, and the laughing and clapping on the back went on
for a long time. It had been an entire winter, and sometimes
longer, since many of the Long Knives had eaten buffalo
together and told tales of the daring things they had done.
The tales were told of warring on Black-feet, and of the
terrible things the big white bear had done in his anger
toward other Long Knives. He was Old Ephriam to them,
the grizzly. As terrible an animal that ever lived and hunted.
He feared nothing and crushed those in his path. His jaws
were large and held teeth that could tear the smoke-
hardened hide from a lodge into little pieces, and crush the
skull of an elk like the egg of a small bird. This was Old
Ephriam, the grizzly, ruler of the forest. The Long Knives
knew him well.

In the distance, Whisper saw a band of Indians approaching. They were Salish. Some of her people! Maybe they
knew of her mother, or the others in her band. While the
Long Knives went on with their talk, Whisper went out to
meet them. She waited until they had stopped the drums,
until the chromes they were chanting were complete.

"It is good to see my people again," she said, "for I
have been lost from the Willow Cutters band, the band of
Crooked Arm, my father."

One of the elders stepped forward. "Where is Crooked
Arm?"

"I cannot speak his name."

"How many others have gone?"

"All but some women and young children. And me. I
wish to find my mother, the one they call Little Grasses."

The elder thought a moment. "How is it you have lived
and are not with the others?"

"I would be a slave now if it were not for the Long
Knives." She pointed to where Jim Ayers and the others
talked. "Siksika! As many suns ago as are on one hand."

Some of the others in the band began to talk. Another

elder approached and asked, ''Were these Siksika of the Horse Runner band?''

''They were.''

''And their war chief was Walking Head?''

''How is it that you know?''

The elders and the others in the band who had crowded around to listen backed away from her and held their hands over their mouths in surprise.

''How is it that you know this?'' Whisper cried.

The elder who had first approached her motioned for silence. He turned to Whisper and looked upon her as if she were a ghost. He came toward her cautiously. She stood while he reached out and placed a hand upon her doeskin dress. His hand felt her hair, finally her face.

''I am real. I am Whisper on the Water, of the Willow Cutters band. Why do you treat me this way?''

The elder stepped back. The grey brows above his eyes pressed down heavily as he studied her. The wrinkles on his face grew deeper. ''I have never looked upon one such as you,'' he said. ''Never before did I think it possible that a story such as the one told about you could contain truth. You indeed must be the Spirit Woman.''

Whisper steadied herself. ''How is it that you know?''

''See!'' one in the band hissed. ''See, it is her! She even says that it is so!'' The others broke out in talk again.

Once more the main elder silenced them. ''The story I tell you passes the lips of truth,'' he said to Whisper. ''For such a story could never be dreamed up in the heart of any man. It was a Nez Percé who told it.''

A Nez Percé. A dying one, Whisper learned, one who had crawled off to die from a raid by Walking Head upon his small hunting party. It was a mad and avenging Walking Head, for he had not only lost the Spirit Woman, but many of his warriors because of her. He had been out to kill and take scalps; to go back to his lodge in defeat would bring shame upon him and his war party. The Nez Percés had not been painted for war. And Walking Head's terrible cries about spirits and the woman who possessed them had

caused great fear among them. Some had been tortured and
asked if they knew where this Spirit Woman might be; if
they knew where the Long Knives had taken her. Were
there other Salish bands that she might have gone to? The
dying Nez Percé had told much in his last breath.

"But I am Salish, one of you," Whisper said. "I only
want to be with my people."

"We are afraid of you," said the elder. "And you will
bring the Siksika to our land."

"Is there any among you who have seen or heard of
those from the Willow Cutters band?" Whisper asked.

There was silence.

"It would be best that you go," said the elder. "There
are many here who fear you; there are many who wish for
your powers. You could never be one of us."

"But I *am* one of you."

The elder shook his head. "I have spoken."

"Fiddler! You crazy old hoss!"

Near a fire a large group of Long Knives were clapping
their hands and stomping to the music of a small stringed
box that an older Long Knife played. The box had a small
handle that the older Long Knife fingered strings on and
another slimmer stick that he pulled across it. Whisper had
seen them before and had heard them referred to as fiddles.
Beside him were other Long Knives with other stringed
boxes Whisper knew to be banjos and guitars. The Long
Knives used these boxes to make their music, and they all
drank whiskey and yelled.

The older Long Knife had twinkling eyes that shone from
under white eyebrows and a grizzled beard of the same
color. The whiskers parted for a spit of tobacco and a smile.
Then the old Long Knife pulled off his wolfskin cap and
flung it high in the air above him.

"Jim Ayers! By the Jesus! What a sight for a poor old
gaunt-bellied 'coon."

Jim and the older Long Knife hugged each other and
clapped each other on the back. They danced around the

fire and wrestled each other like bear cubs. Soon they stopped and drank whiskey from a jug.

"How's the beaver business, Fiddler?"

"Cain't complain. No siree. Got plew that'll shine with any." The old Long Knife spit again and drank from the jug, his eyes seeing Whisper.

"You with a brigade?" Jim asked.

He shook his white-whiskered head. "No sense trappin' in a crowd. Makes more sign for Injuns to read. Me and Joe Marker come off Siskadee two days back. And you?"

"I come over from Three Forks with a bunch."

Fiddler whistled and drew from the jug again. "That's Blackfeet grounds. You'll lose your hair for sure in that country."

"Good beaver pickin's, though," Jim said. "Those streams shine with fur."

"Good for those with hair they want to part with, or those who already have," he chuckled. Again he looked at Whisper, his white beard closing down over the mouth and the smile leaving. "So it was you, Jim, who put the run on Walking Head at Henry's Lake."

Jim motioned toward Whisper. "It was really this gal here. Took hair in the lake and all. Damndest thing you've ever seen."

"So I heard," Fiddler said with a nod. "The story is around. That Walking Head is as mean as they come. Good fighter, too. It takes big medicine to mess with him and make it stick."

"She did it," Jim said, like he was bragging. "And right well."

"You aim to keep her?" Fiddler asked.

Jim shuffled his feet some. "Well, Fiddler, she's not really mine to keep. She'd like to find her band. Her ma especially."

Fiddler winked and picked up his fiddle again. "I expect you'll stick around her until she does."

The old Long Knife went back to playing and the others broke from their stories and back into yelling and stomping.

It was a festive time for the Long Knives, who had just this one time of each year to be together. It had come to be such a time for the Indian allies also, for many different bands came and they saw others of their own people only during that time of year. But for Whisper, these first few days had been ones of disappointment, for many of the Flathead bands she had spoken with shared the same feeling as the first band she had seen. She was not a relative to any of them and it was felt she would only bring trouble to the band, even if her medicine was great.

"Damn, Fiddler," Jim broke in again. "I see you're still playin' *Turkey in the Straw*. A man would think you'd learn somethin' new by now."

"This ol' hoss knows other songs," Fiddler came back.

"Yeah? Let's hear one then," said another Long Knife in the group, laughing and tipping a jug.

Fiddler put the bow to his instrument. "This ol' hoss shines best at *Turkey in the Straw*." He started in while the others laughed and joked about it.

Fiddler finished the tune and spat and laughed with the rest. His eye went to Jim, then Whisper and back to Jim. He noticed Whisper always was close to Jim, no matter where he was. He smiled to himself, as if thinking Jim hadn't told all when he said he was just helping Whisper find her family and nothing else. But Fiddler didn't know that Whisper was not welcome among those of her people that were not relatives, and that her people had come to be afraid of her.

Soon a Long Knife came to the group with a big stick of buffalo hump meat and laid it across the fire. "Fresh kill today!" he yelled, which set the others to cheering and cutting chunks from it. They laughed and drank through greasy mouths, as one story after another was passed around the fire.

"We've heard lots about that squaw with you, Jim," one said. "How's about we hear it from you firsthand?" The others cheered.

Jim looked to Whisper, who was starting to get up from

her seat near him. "Don't go," he said, putting a hand on
her. "No need to." He turned back to the others. "There's
not much to it except we put the run on them. About the
same as when old Fiddler here, chased that Gros Ventre
down with his big grey stallion. That was way up on Big
Muddy, at the mouth of Arrow Creek. Remember, Fiddler?"

Fiddler washed down a chunk of meat with a pull from
his jug. "Wagh!" he said, wiping his mouth with a buckskin sleeve. "Wished I still had that grey rascal. He could
run a heap faster than any wind that ever blowed."

"You sayin' you lost him?" Jim asked.

Fiddler got himself comfortable near the fire and pulled
a pipe out of his pocket. "Yep," he nodded. "Wasn't stole
by Blackfeet, neither." He tamped tobacco into the pipe,
letting the silence settle in around the campfire and the eyes
of the men fix themselves on him. "It was up on the Beaver's Head. A bunch of us pulled in late last fall, just before
the snow set in. Damned if there wasn't this one greenhorn
in the bunch." He lit his pipe with kindle from the fire
while a few chuckled and settled in for the story. "Well,
this greenhorn up and decides he wants to ride ol' Sagebrush. And there's nary a hoss that was ever born was more
touchy than Sagebrush."

Fiddler puffed on the pipe and blew a ring of smoke
above his head. He took another swig from his jug and let
it settle through him while the fire crackled and the others
waited. "Well, this greenhorn feller keeps pesterin' me
about how he wants a ride on old Sagebrush. I told him
this hoss don't ride like any other hoss there's ever been.
You don't say 'Giddup!' to make ol' Sagebrush go and
'Whoa!' to make him stop. No, you say 'Holy shit!' to get
him started and 'Hell's bells!' to hold him up."

Again the chuckles came, more and louder. Fiddler went
back to his story. "Well, this greenhorn keeps at me and
says he can remember all that. So I let him on ol' Sagebrush
and off he goes. He didn't do too bad for a time, there,
rememberin' to say 'Holy shit!' when he wants him to go

and 'Hell's bells!' to get him stopped. But then that young greenhorn must've got cocky. I seen him a high-tailin' it along the big flat that leads to the buffler jump just this side of ol' Block Mountain, and he's headed for that jump lickety-split. I figured he must've forgot what to say. Then right at the edge of that cliff I heard him yell, 'Hell's bells! Hell's bells!' and ol' Sagebrush come to a grindin' halt.''

"Good thing he remembered when he did," one trapper put in as the others laughed.

Fiddler puffed on his pipe again and rubbed his grizzled old chin. "But then he peered way over that cliff, and I heard him say, 'Holy shit!' '' The group broke into a roar and went to whooping and drinking again.

From the shadows came the forms of three other Long Knives. Ed Beeler and the Frenchman, Courchene, had come with one other. None of the three looked in a pleasant mood.

"Sit a spell," said one Long Knife. "The stories are just startin'."

Beeler looked around. His eyes came to Whisper and Jim, and stayed. The three newcomers sat and took large pieces of hump from the fire while one of the others told a story.

Fiddler talked low under his breath to Jim. "This hoss feels a change come in over camp."

"Things don't set good between us," Jim said. "When all was said and done up at Henry's Lake, Beeler was all for givin' this Flathead gal up to Walking Head. And after she's taken hair and all. I couldn't see the right of it."

Fiddler grunted. "Sounds like him. But he's a mean one, come one-to-one kickin'. Best watch him close and get your licks in early."

Beeler finished a mouthful of meat and came over next to Whisper. He took a bag from his side and fished out a handful of blue beads. "You Flat-head squaws like blue beads," he said, leaning into Whisper's face. "Let's go for a walk."

Whisper turned away.

"I got mirrors, too. Fix your face pretty."

"Leave her alone, Beeler," Jim broke in. "Go out with the mules and horses."

Beeler's eyes were like coals from the fire. "Ayers, you broke in before agin me at Henry's Lake. Twice will cost you blood."

This time Courchene said nothing. He just watched Jim with hard eyes.

Jim stood up and took off his cap and buckskin vest. He unbuttoned the red cloth shirt he was wearing and threw all to one side. "Winner gets hair. That how you want it?"

"Hair and balls both!" Beeler retorted.

With sudden speed and quickness Beeler drove straight ahead, grappling for the neck. Both men went down and Beeler was on top, driving his thumbs into Jim's throat, his eyes bulging with hate. Long Knives moved from other fires, crowding to see. Many yelled for Jim while a few could be heard for Beeler. Fiddler had rekindled his pipe. His eyes were serious and the smoke came out like lodge fire, but he said nothing.

Jim arched his back, but Beeler's weight was like that of a horse. He pressed harder into Jim's throat and Whisper's hands doubled tight into fists as Jim's breath started to rattle. Jim's arm came up hard and the palm of his hand cupped under Beeler's chin, forcing his head up. His fist drove wrongly into Beeler's throat and sank deep. Again Jim arched his back and Beeler rolled off with a bag, his eyes popping from his head.

"Get up, Jim, get up!" many of the Long Knives screamed.

Jim lay sprawled, wheezing. Beeler lay nearby, his hands holding his throat, his tongue flapping in and out.

"Get up, Jim!" Whisper said. "Up! Quickly!" Fiddler puffed on the pipe and chewed it like a peace of old bull, but still said nothing.

Jim came to his knees and shook his head. His chest heaved. Again he shook his head. He made himself rise to his feet and staggered. He caught himself and breathed deeply as his strength returned in full. Then Courchene stepped behind Beeler.

"Knife!" Whisper screamed.

Beeler had gotten to his knees. His face was as red as if painted and the firelight showed the whites of his teeth. He snarled like some bear and lunged at Jim, the knife gleaming in his hand.

Jim turned sideways and a scarlet line showed along his ribs. Again the big man's weight pushed Jim down, but Jim rolled on through, kicking Beeler up and over. The fire in Jim's side was clear on his face as he moved atop Beeler like a savage cat. His fists were quick and heavy. Beeler's eyes and face soon showed the same red that covered Jim's side. In no time, the nose of the big man lay crooked and his snarls grew to be grunts of pain. But he, too, was strong and would not be done in easily.

A big arm found Jim's head and Beeler quickly tightened down a neck lock. Jim would not go to his back and found Beeler's kidneys to be soft to heavy punches. Beeler let loose and staggered to the ground, then found the knife again.

The sound was a crack, and it made the stomach sick to hear it. Jim had taken Beeler by the wrist and, in fury, had twisted the whole arm in a circle. The shoulder had popped from its socket. Beeler lay writhing, trying to scream. But he had no air and his mouth was wide open with only gurgled noises coming out. Jim had the knife.

"Don't do it, Jim!" It was Fiddler.

Jim turned. "He would have done the same!"

"No. You showed him how it is. Leave it!"

"I'll take hair!"

"No! Leave it!"

Jim dropped the knife and took a deep breath. Whisper was quickly there, seeing to the gash along his ribs. Beeler, in blind pain, lay writhing. Jim's eyes found Courchene.

"How would you like the same, Frenchman?" he said, his eyes hard. "I ought to cut your lousy throat with your own knife."

"Jim, enough," said Fiddler.

Courchene glared at Jim, then he and the other trapper went over to Beeler and knelt beside him. "Hold him," Courchene ordered the other. "The shoulder, I'll pull it back in place."

Bones popped and Beeler's body jumped like fire had been placed under it. He arched over and fell into blackness.

Fiddler looked at Jim's cut. "You'll take a stitch or two," he said. "That little gal of yours will fix you up smart."

"We have made enemies," Whisper said to Jim, watching the cold eyes of Courchene and the other trapper as they took Beeler away. She looked up at Jim and found him smiling.

"You know what?" he said to her. "You sure are pretty."

Chapter 5

SPIRIT WOMAN

The days passed and the rendezvous continued—the giant feast and drinking time of the Long Knives. The nights were as long as the days and it seemed no one slept, only drank and ate and gambled their money and supplies on races and games of chance.

There were other games played, also. Games with the Indian women who had come to the rendezvous with their people. Games by the Long Knives for their affections. Would it take two mirrors? One mirror and beads? Maybe brightly-colored cloth of many different kinds from the land of the Long Knives and from far to the south where Sun puts his heat out much more than here, and for many moons of the year. For the prettiest Indian women the price was high. But nothing was too high for these Long Knives who had been out in the mountains without a woman. Even those who might have been with women not long before acted as though crazed. It was though there were not enough women in all of the mountains to do for them.

Beeler had left with his men soon after Jim had beaten

him. He had sold his furs quickly and was in no mood to
stay. Now the fight seemed a thing faraway in Whisper's
mind, for she had again gone to thinking of her mother and
her people. The cuts on her arm had begun to heal and she
again opened them, crying out for her father and Sun Bear
Standing, the warrior she would have married. The nights
had become long and full of sorrow, the days without sun-
shine. Always her eyes were open for new Flathead bands
coming to rendezvous, and always she went away fighting
tears. Sometimes anger and disgust almost made her shout
out loud or strike out against them. She wished to hear,
"Your mother is with us. See, she comes now to be with
you." Instead it was, "We know nothing of your mother
or the Willow Cutters band," and, "You are too powerful
to live among us. Our men do not wish a woman in their
council." At times there were kind or understanding faces
among them, but they were always the faces of other
women and, therefore, had no voice to speak.

Now it was a day when she had again found a new Salish
band at the rendezvous and had heard the same words from
them: "Go away!" She went into the forest to be alone,
far up and away from the main camp. It had taken a whole
morning's journey to reach this place. Here the *Tetons* rose
up gigantic before her, the patches of old snow gleaming
on the high rock tops and in the deep gorges along the
sides. The forest was deep green from summer rains and
the flowers painted the meadows in splotches of red, blue,
and yellow. The wind was still and the birds sang midday
songs. Not even the sounds from the rendezvous below
found their way up here. Then she heard footsteps. He wore
a wolfskin cap with reddish-blond hair that curled out from
under it. His deep blue eyes were soft and questioning.

"You're a hard one to find," Jim said.

"You know the skills of tracking well, Jim," Whisper
said. "There are many, even fine warriors with many coup
to their names, who could not have found me."

Jim sat down next to her and pulled a grass stem. He
rolled it in his fingers as though studying it and stuck the

end into his mouth. "I thought maybe you'd left for good."

"I would if only I knew where to go."

"Don't fret. There's bound to be more of your people come in before this thing is over."

Whisper took a deep breath. "I do not know if that is bad or good. All I see is wide eyes and hands held over mouths in amazement. All I hear is 'Spirit Woman! Spirit Woman!' wherever I go. Through all of this, my sadness grows deeper."

Jim continued to chew on the grass. "All this will pass," he said. "Could be they like to build on a good story. It will all pass over and things will get back to normal."

"You do not understand," Whisper said. "My name is on everyone's lips. Even the elders speak my name and tell each other how they have seen me. To many I now seem greater than a Spirit Woman. It is said I have counted coup on hundreds of enemies and that I am the head of a lodge, with many scalps lining the doorway. These stories are as many as the birds who fly south for the cold moons. They are like the stars in the sky, too many to count. These things do not go away. They are told by the elders to the young, to be told in turn when they become old and have lived many winters. No. I am someone alone. I have only my mother who knows me and will not believe these things—if she still lives."

"Your ma will turn up. Maybe not here, but some place. Just give it time."

"I have no time. I have no one."

Jim took the grass he had been chewing on from his mouth and threw it to the ground. "You've got all the time in the world. You're young. You're pretty—real pretty. And you've got someone. That is, if you want someone."

Whisper got up and moved off a ways. Jim Ayers had told her he cared for her. She turned not get his blue eyes out of her mind. He was behind her now. She could feel him there, waiting. She turned to look at him, his face rough from wind, and his body firm and hard from life in the mountains. A strong man for having walked so far and climbed so high to find her, with the wound still fresh in his side. He must indeed care for her. He was close to her now. He would have put his arms around her had she not moved away again.

"I feel as though life is playing tricks on me," she said. "It is all so strange, all that has happened. The raid on my people's camp; Walking Head; the fight at the waters of Henry's Lake. My mind cannot see it clearly. It is like the fog that covers the high peaks in early morning." She turned to him. "Was it real? Did it all truly happen? Are you real?"

"You are here," Jim told her. "I am here." He pointed up to the *Tetons*. "Everything around us is real. You've got to live with life the way God made it. Good or bad, it's there."

"But I did not cause these things to happen to me."

"A lot of things just happen," Jim said. "That don't mean you're at fault because of it. They just happen." He looked off toward the *Tetons*, like he was remembering something in his own past. He took a deep breath. "You can't change what has happened. You can only hope you learned somethin' by it."

How true those words are, Whisper thought. They are the words of wisdom. Things happen that cannot be controlled. Sometimes a life can be forever changed by them. Whisper thought back on the raid by Walking Head and the Blackfeet, and what Walking Head had said to her: "It is not for me to hit you now. It will be best to wait until the spirits have left and you once again return to the woman you really are." Whisper remembered herself laughing and saying, "I will never return to the woman I once was. I will always be the Spirit Woman." She remembered Walking Head's face; the strange look that had come over him. He had seemed in a trance for a time. It had been as if her words had struck something deep within him. Perhaps he had been realizing a vision, as she had first thought. Perhaps she, herself, had been in the vision. Maybe he felt he would realize that vision at a future time, for he had said to her, "You will learn the Siksika way. You will forget your people."

It was all too strange. And now the words that Jim had just spoken seemed like those of a wise elder: "You cannot change what has happened. You can only hope you have learned from it." What, Whisper asked herself, will this all bring? Where will my life go now?

"And another thing, you don't have to be afraid of me," Jim said.

"I'm not afraid of you."

"You act like it. It seems lately you've changed." He pointed to the reopened gashes on her arms. "I see you're back to grievin' again. What good will that do you?"

"It is a custom of my people. You know that."

"Yes, but why keep it up? I wasn't sure you could stay on that horse when we broke camp back at Henry's Lake, with all the blood you'd lost. When we got down to rendezvous, you started fixin' yourself up with that same stuff you used on my knife wound the other night. It seemed then like you were sorry you'd cut yourself all up like that. Now this. Can you tell me why?"

Whisper turned her back. "I have not yet completed my time of sorrow."

"Why?"

"I do not wish to speak of it."

Jim took Whisper by the arms and turned her around to face him. "What is the matter with you?"

Whisper looked up into his eyes. "Why did you follow me up to this place? Why are you not with the others below, drinking with them and taking part in the shooting matches and telling stories? I am not a happy person. I am not a person you can laugh with, as the others are. Why is it that you waste your time here?"

"I came up to see you," he said. "If I liked their company better, I'd be down there now."

Whisper knew he wished to take his hands from where they were on her arms and put them around her. His eyes said so. His mouth moved like he wanted to kiss her. Instead, he let her go and stepped back.

"I can't figure why you've got to act this way. I know you lost family, but did you lose a man, too?"

Whisper hung her head. "We were to be married that very day." Whisper looked at him a moment. "Why is it that you care for me so? Do you not have someone yourself elsewhere? Do you not have a woman?"

"Sure, I've had women," Jim said. "Some white, some red. One even black."

"That is not what I mean."

"Well, never anyone special, if that's what you mean. Bein' tied down just don't suit me."

Whisper frowned. "Your answer is strange for one who has followed me to this place. And with pain in his side. Is it that you want me once just to say you have had me?"

Jim shook his head. "I made you a promise to help find your people and your ma. I aim to keep it."

"But your promise has been kept. I have found my people. I can stay with them and look for my mother."

"You just told me they're all afraid of you. Why do you think you can find someone to stay with?"

Whisper was silent for a moment. "But why is it you want me with you?" she finally asked. "It was you that just told me you wished to have no woman tie you down."

"I meant that about ordinary women." He started back down the hill. Turning, he said, "Just remember, you're not alone. You've got somebody if you want." He turned again and was soon lost among the trees, following the steep trail back down to the valley floor.

Whisper watched him leave, and her thoughts trailed after him for a time. Why had this young Long Knife come into her life? Why must he look at her like that with those piercing blue eyes? From where she stood, she turned, as if beckoned, and looked upon a dead tree standing nearby. A dead pine that had once been of gigantic height and width in life, with gnarled grey branches and trunk. Upon one of the lower branches there appeared a small feathered body with two eyes that seemed to cover his whole face. The tiny owl of the forest. He sat still as a small brown stone, watching Whisper. Suddenly she felt a dull itching in the skin of her arms. She looked at them and noticed that the long wounds were once again beginning to heal over. Do not reopen the wounds, she told herself. They are to heal over. Your grief is over. She looked up to see the branch was bare. The little owl was gone. But Whisper knew he would be back again. Another time, another place. The little owl, the spirit of the child warrior, Little Fox, had been there all the time she had been talking to Jim Ayers. He had been there to put the words into Jim Ayers' mouth. The little owl would follow her, Whisper knew. He would follow her always. He would be there to strengthen her; to make her remember the meaning of life.

It made her feel good, for she knew now someone watched over her.

Chapter 6

THE PALOUSE HORSE

The rendezvous went on with each day being much the same as the last. There was drink, dance, and gambling. But Whisper's days were somewhat different. There would be days when she would look at Jim through eyes which seemed to want him for herself. Then those eyes would change to sorrow or uncertainty, and she would make herself distant from him. There were times when she slept away from camp by herself. Since that first time, Whisper never did see Jim follow her on her frequent walks into the high country for solitude. He had told her what was in his heart. Now he spent his time with the business of furs and was joining in with the others in the games and drinking, leaving her to sort things out for herself.

It was the old Long Knife, Fiddler, who now seemed to be watching her, maybe caring for her in some strange way. Though there were many Long Knives who desired her, none would take the chance of possibly answering to the wrath of Jim Ayers. What he had done to Beeler had reached every lodge and campfire before Sun had moved to first light. And with Fiddler always seeming to be some-where near, most everyone held back from even speaking to her.

Among her own people and the other Indian peoples, the stories continued to be told. Each time they grew with the telling. She was a symbol. A singer from a Bannock band made a song, a prayer that was soon adopted by others:

> *See her walk among the lodges,*
> *Spirit Woman, medicine woman.*
> *She comes among us with her power,*
> *And mighty warriors watch her pass.*
> *Oh, Spirit Woman, medicine woman,*
> *Keep the Blackfeet from our lands.*

Whisper had become the best-known Indian at the ren-dezvous, yet the only person to be around her was a griz-zled old Long Knife whom she wished would go away.

"Why do you make a shadow of yourself?" Whisper asked Fiddler one day.

"Maybe we just take a likin' to the same things," he answered with a laugh. "I like horse races and you must, too, or you wouldn't be here."

Fiddler was much the same as she remembered an old medicine man, Elk Chaser, to be. Old eyes always looking, seeing. Old mouth always working around a smoking pipe. Talking little, only smoking and watching. Men like these chose their words wisely and needed few of them. There was always a sense of calm about them, even when all others ran about in confusion. They always seemed to know how things would turn out. They always seemed to know the right things to do and when to do them.

Whisper remembered well how old Elk Chaser had more than once led them to game in the snows of winter when every belly was shriveled from hunger. Once there were a few buffalo trapped in a snow-filled canyon, a place old Elk Chaser said he had been before, during another such winter. Another time he had showed the hunters where an-

imals become stuck in pools of sticky black liquid that
smells strong and runs out of the ground. During the winter
moons the snows cover the black and the animals cannot
see the trap they are walking into. This old Long Knife,
Fiddler, seemed to be the same sort of man. Whisper had
seen this the night Jim Ayers had fought the evil Beeler in
her behalf. While others yelled and moved around and worried for Jim, the old Fiddler just watched all that happened
with only a puff from his pipe and a glint in his eyes, like
one hawk who watches another fall from the sky onto his
prey.

"Fine set of horses out there," said Fiddler. He lit his
pipe and puffed out a big ring of smoke that floated above
his head and melted into the air. "You can't find a better
man than Jim. No, siree. That young hoss shines with the
best of them."

"I do not want a man."

"Cain't live by yourself. No, siree. That's no good."
Fiddler blew more smoke rings into the air. "Sure some
nice horseflesh out there."

A column of horses was lining up out in front. Drums
pounded and all around was laughing and betting. The race
was to begin soon. Already many people lined the course
along the valley floor the racers would follow. Both Indians
and Long Knives were to ride in the race. Their horses were
all gaily decorated with feathers and paint, a custom of the
Indian peoples adopted by the Long Knives. It was one of
the first races of the day, with the top five in each race to
go on to a final race late that afternoon. Whisper looked
out into the group of men and horses. Her eyes suddenly
went wide and she put her hand over her mouth in amazement.

"You like that Palouse horse, do you?" Fiddler asked.

"Appaloosa!" Whisper said. "A horse of the Nez Percé.
And the most beautiful I have ever seen."

Near the middle of the column was a big stallion, as deep
red as the sky when Sun leaves to let nightfall come. His
mane and tail were pure white scattered over the rump and

lower back. His head was high. He pranced as he awaited the time when he could run loose with the wind and carry his rider across the lush green bottom.

"That greenhorn Wyeth from back in Boston just won that horse in a game of hands," said Fiddler.

"He is beautiful," said Whisper. "The Long Knife is very lucky."

The race began. Shouting and yelling was heard the length of the course as the riders stretched their horses out over the bottom. Many cheers and yells went up at the finish line. Nat Wyeth finished third with his red appaloosa stallion.

Fiddler puffed hard on his pipe. "That big red should show heels to the rest without so much as a deep breath. My thinkin' is young Wyeth's got more horse than he's been under before." Fiddler puffed again on his pipe. "Yep, that horse could shine with the best. He just needs someone who can ride him."

"He is truly a beautiful horse," Whisper said again. "The Long Knife has much luck to own him."

Fiddler turned to Whisper. "If I was to tell young Wyeth he could make a heap of money lettin' you ride his horse, I'll bet he'd listen."

Whisper's eyes got big. "Would that be possible?"

Fiddler chuckled and puffed on his pipe again. "Young Wyeth's a greenhorn sure enough, but he's got a head for business."

Whisper stood patting the big horse's neck, her eyes seeing every line of the appaloosa's body. She rubbed his nose gently and he nickered softly to her. Whisper told him, "I like you, big horse. You are a friend of mine. You are Red Thunder." The big horse nickered again and Whisper gave him a handful of sweetgrass, which she had picked especially for him along one of her secret trails she had used during these past days of her disillusion with life. Sweetgrass, the powerful medicine and purifier. She had used it often in her own ceremonies, the ceremonies of women.

Surely this day it would be good medicine for the big horse, the Red Thunder. He would now run swift with her upon him.

"I'm new in this country," Wyeth told her. "And I'm told you ride very well. I can also see he likes you. I'll let you run him and I'll make the bets."

The final race had come. The best were here; the very best. She had taken him through two earlier runs; had held him back, as Wyeth had wished. But now she could let him loose. She would feel his power at its best. Never before had she seen or ridden such a horse in her life. This was, indeed, a great day.

It was nearly day's end and the air spoke of night with its coolness coming in. Many had come to watch. Almost the whole camp. The winners of the whole day were in this race, and the winner would surely be riding the fastest horse there was in the mountains. The line had formed and Sun cast a late-day gold down into the valley. Horses pranced and riders tensed, waiting for the signal. Along the side were bettors, yelling for the race to start and cheering their riders. Campfires with sticks of fresh buffalo hump awaited the laughing and yelling to come afterward, where stories of the race would be told along with stories of other races on other grounds. But for now, the fires burned low and all the camp stood watching.

Many eyes watched Whisper and the big red. Much talk was going on about them. Other horses were thought to be faster, other riders better. But she was the Spirit Woman. Many of the Indian peoples there now looked upon her as a legend just beginning. She was maybe a powerful spirit living in a woman's body. Some believed she would use her great medicine to make her horse win. Most of the Long Knives were not so much in awe, though. They thought it all just a lot of talk, a result of Indian ceremony and religion. There were bets placed against her and there was shouting that she was just a woman and could not win in a hard ride against the men.

''We are ready, my Red Thunder,'' she said into the horse's ear.

She fell in with the motion of the stallion as if she were a part of him, a motion so smooth and fluid that Whisper felt she was sitting on something still. But underneath, the powerful legs made the grassland a blur all around her. She bent low to the neck and let the white mane whip into her face. The wind carried her own hair out behind her and brought water to her eyes. She could hear other horses on both sides of her, their heavy breathing and the clomp of their hooves against the grassy valley floor, now packed down from the many races. Their riders yelled for them to move faster, faster. Red Thunder surged ahead and soon the shouting was further and further behind her. Red Thunder had poured out his strength for her and had carried her across the finish line well ahead of the rest.

But she did not stop at the finish line. Instead, she urged the big horse even faster on down the valley. Those at the finish shouted after her when they saw what she was doing. She was stealing Nat Wyeth's horse!

She was well out in front of those who came chasing after her. None would ever catch her, she knew, for the speed of Red Thunder was too great and she had already put a lot of distance between herself and her nearest pursuer. Still they would try, for a horse such as Red Thunder was too valuable to lose and Wyeth had many friends who would help in the chase. Whisper did not worry, though. She had Red Thunder, and all they had was their anger and nearly three miles of valley to make up before they could catch her.

She rode on, slowing the big stallion as the shouts grew distant and finally silent. She was alone with Red Thunder, the Palouse horse she had fallen in love with.

She took a trail that led high up among the peaks overlooking the valley. The mountain air was still in late evening and all that could be heard was small birds singing roosting songs. Ever higher she went, ever higher with her friend the big horse, the only one who understood her. She followed trails she had come to know well since the beginning of rendezvous, trails she had walked and shared her loneliness with. Now she would have this beautiful horse to talk to and he would care.

She found one of her favorite spots. Here, well-hidden in a little pocket surrounded by trees, she built a fire in the darkness. It cheered her. And the little spring of water that bubbled from rocks nearby sang to her of peace.

She talked to the big horse and fed him handfuls of lush grass. Only a small breeze rustled in the tops of the trees, not touching them down in their safe hideaway. All was quiet.

The big horse lifted his nose to smell and Whisper turned from talking to him. Across the fire a lone figure was standing, watching her. She jumped in fright.

"You sure are one for pullin' crazy stunts," said Jim Ayers.

"How did you find me?"

"I think I know you pretty well by now." He walked around the fire toward her. "You sure are a feisty one."

"But, how were you able to sneak up on me like that? Why is it that Red Thunder did not sense your horse?"

"I'm as much Injun as you are in some ways," said Jim. "I keep to the best side of the wind when I track and I teach my horses to be still when I put my hand over their muzzles. Now let's go back."

Whisper hung her head. Big tears formed in her eyes and rolled down her cheeks. "This has been my only happiness for many suns," she said. "I do not want my happiness to be over."

Jim took her in his arms and held her. Whisper did not resist. She laid her head against his shoulder and wrapped her arms around his middle. More tears came and her body trembled with sobs. It was a while before her crying stopped.

"You sure took off on that horse," Jim finally said.

"There wasn't one set of eyes that wasn't bugged out that whole race."

"I did not want that time to end," she said, drying her eyes. "I did not ever want to get down from his back."

"I know," said Jim. "He's quite a horse. But he's not yours."

"No one would ever find Red Thunder and me if I did not wish it."

"I did," said Jim. "I found you. Besides, half these mountains know who you are by now. No sense in ridin' a horse that's not yours. Especially one like that."

Whisper took a deep breath. "If that is the way it must be."

"That is the way it must be."

Chapter 7

COLTER'S HELL

It was getting close to the end of rendezvous. Whisper and Jim had again become closer. She spent most of her time with him now and had come to find the other Long Knives more willing to accept her than her own people, even though she had in fact stolen Nat Wyeth's red appaloosa. This Red Thunder was a horse Whisper could not get out of her mind.

The Long Knives did not call her Spirit Woman, nor did they touch her to try and get some of her big medicine. They were a straightforward bunch who took her for what she was. They admired her for her ability to ride horses well. They cheered when she won a shooting contest with bow and arrow. Of course, the others in the contest, mainly warriors of different Indian peoples, thought she was performing magic by her accurate shooting. Whisper had come to accept this from Indian peoples now and it did not sadden her as much as it once had.

Now that rendezvous was nearly over, Jim was intent on selling his furs. Most of the other Long Knives had sold their plews of beaver right away and were making ready for another winter's trapping season. But Jim was among a number of free trappers who were holding out for better prices. And as there was great competition among those Long Knives who owned fur companies, it seemed Jim would get the prices he desired.

Jim had told Whisper how all the Long Knives considered each other friends, but were hard-hearted when the business of furs was discussed. Would the best price come from the American Fur Company—the Company as most Long Knives called it? Maybe the Rocky Mountain Fur Company had more money they wished to spend. While with Jim, Whisper had met Jim Bridger, John Gervais, and Tom Fitzpatrick, who was called Broken Hand by the Indian peoples. These men were partners in the Rocky Mountain Fur Company and had been among the first to get to rendezvous. They had broke out the whiskey early and had succeeded in getting a great number of furs. They wanted Jim's furs badly. Henry Vanderburgh and Andrew Drips of the American Fur Company also poured much whiskey down Jim, wishing his furs for themselves.

"Some of these men have more money than the number of all the Indian peoples in the mountains," Jim had told Whisper. "This fur business will make a good businessman rich." But most of the Long Knives were not rich and never would be, Jim had gone on to say. Most were not in it for money. "Trappin' furs means freedom. No orders from anybody. A man comes and goes as he pleases. He's only got bears and Blackfeet to worry about."

Although Jim was busy with furs, he had not forgotten about Whisper's mother. Finding her had become part of his plans for the upcoming trapping season. He told Whisper he and Fiddler would take her along and they would join forces with a large group under Milton Sublette and Henry Freeb, who were taking members of the American Fur Company to trap south on the Humbolt. They would be following the Snake River and would see many bands of Flatheads in their journey. Whisper once again felt a surge of joy and the hope of finding the woman called Little Grasses was renewed.

While Jim talked of the upcoming trip, Nat Wyeth came over to where they sat by the fire with a jug and two tin cups. The moon was high and it looked as though Wyeth had emptied the jug and filled it again more than once since sundown.

"Care for a snort?" Wyeth asked.

"Don't mind if I do," said Jim.

Wyeth filled a cup for him and asked, "Have a good year, Jim?"

"Damn good. Next year will be even better."

"Did you decide to put in with the Company? Word has it you plan to head for the Humbolt with them."

Jim broke out in a small grin. "No. I don't aim to put in with anybody. I'm goin' with Sublette for the ride."

Wyeth filled Jim's cup again. "I've heard a lot about you, Jim. Good things. I know you're a good man or you couldn't have talked that little squaw of yours into bringin' my horse back."

"She was just on a spree, that's all," said Jim, looking into the fire. "Can't blame her for that."

Wyeth grunted and finished his cup. "I mean to start up an outfit of my own, Jim. I'll be with Sublette, too. Only I plan to go on to the Columbia. The beaver shine out there. What you say you put in with me, Jim? I'd damn sure make it right by you."

"No. I'm one hoss who's happy the way he is."

Wyeth poured again, setting the jug down harder and slurping loudly from his cup before he spoke again. "Jim, I wish you'd take me up on this. You know you can't get a good deal for furs on your own."

"Good enough for me."

Wyeth took a deep breath. "God, I wish you'd listen to reason. There's good money for both of us."

"Save your breath, Nat. I've heard it before. How's about another cupful? That's good stuff."

Wyeth poured, frowning. "Beeler joined up with me,

Jim. He's got a passle of friends. Better to be with a man like him than agin him.''

Jim turned to Wyeth. "You a friend of his, too?''

"I only said I hired him. He gets beaver. Business is business, Jim. You've got that to learn yet.''

"I like things the way they are now," Jim said evenly. He drained his cup. "More.''

"This hoss wishes you'd change your mind. I'd sure hate to see a man of your caliber go agin the grain.''

"I've been trappin' free all along. No call to change now. But if you're hankerin' for a deal tonight, Nat, I can sure as hell make you one.''

Wyeth perked up. "What do you mean?''

"I mean I still got furs. Might you be interested?''

"I might," said Wyeth.

"What say we go take a look at them. Even if I don't plan to join you, I can still make fur deals with you.''

"I can't pay you money," Wyeth said. "I'm not set up for business yet.''

"This hoss didn't say anything about money," Jim retorted. "You've got other things besides money, ain't you?''

"As a matter of fact, I do," said Wyeth. "Let's look at them beaver pelts of yours.''

Whisper was asleep in her robes when she felt a gentle nudge.

She sat up and rubbed the sleep from her eyes. "Jim, what is it?''

The fire flickered still, though it was nearly morning, and she could see clearly what Jim was showing her. Before her was an appaloosa horse. A big red one with a white rump, and white mane and tail. The big horse nickered when he saw her.

"Red Thunder!''

"This child don't have a beaver plew to his name," said Jim. "But you've got yourself that Palouse horse.''

Whisper looked at Jim. Her mouth was open, but no words would come out.

"We've got ourselves a few days to see how he rides," Jim went on. "I know a spot up on the Yellowstone that's really pretty this time of year. If we leave now, it'll give us time to get up there and back by the end of the week."

Whisper's mouth was still open.

Jim tugged on her. "Get your things together, Whisper. We've got a ways to go."

They crossed the pass of the *Tetons* as Sun broke full in the east. Below them was a broad valley called Jackson's Hole, a huge blanket of green nestled in the forest floor. They made their way down from the snow-streaked rocks of the high country into a lush basin of flowers showing their brilliance of red and blue and yellow. Birds were flitting among the quaking aspen in the draws and along the creeks, singing morning songs and welcoming Sun's first light for another day.

They moved north, keeping the giant *Tetons* on their left and following a long valley through which the waters of Lewis's Fork of the Snake River flowed. Elk and deer stood in large herds along the banks, watching them as they passed. Beaver slapped their tails against the water, and dove under into mud and stick houses that stuck up as mounds all along the banks. "This country shines with beaver," Jim said.

Again they began an upward climb, though gradual, past a huge body of water named Jackson's Lake. They were at the back door of *la Roche Jaune*, the Yellowstone.

"Ever hear of Colter's Hell?" asked Jim.

"Yes," Whisper answered. "The Indian peoples ear that place. Devils live under the ground here."

Jim laughed. "There's no devils in the ground, just hot water. The whole country up there is called Colter's Hell. There's no place like it I've ever been. Old Colter was out to make palaver with the Crows, is the story they tell."

"That is true," Whisper said. "The Crow people, with whom the Salish hunt and trade, tell the story of the white man who came among them nearly thirty winters past to ask for furs. They told this white man of the trails used by Indian peoples through this country and he found the Stinking Waters. Devils live in the ground there, also.''

Jim laughed again. ''Whisper, as long as you're with me, you won't have to worry about no devils.''

They reached the geyser basins along the giant waters of *la Roche Jaune*—the lake of the Yellowstone. Sun had just left the sky and a vermilion red light shown out across the water. Nighthawks were darting about and the cries of loons echoed across the still lake. The air held a pleasant coolness that relaxed both the body and the mind. Off from the lake, the trees opened into a large meadow where the ground lay barren and white with minerals. The area was covered with sink holes, some too large to jump across and others so small a body couldn't fit down into them. Vapor rose in steamy clouds and mixed with the red dusk. A small band of elk that had bedded down at the edge of the trees got up and stared awhile before disappearing into the forest.

Jim jumped down off his horse with a laugh. ''We're just in time for a late evening swim,'' he said. ''These hot pots make mighty fine swimmin' holes.''

''What about the devils?'' asked Whisper.

''Wagh! Devils don't care for hot pots. They can't swim.''

Whisper giggled as he pulled her down from the big stallion. She touched the ground lightly at his feet and found herself in his strong arms, looking up into those deep blue eyes. A warmth spread through her, a warmth that made her want to press closer to him. She let her arms encircle his thick chest and she moved her feet between his.

''A flower of the forest,'' he said to her softly. ''You are the spring beauty of the mountains.'' He gently touched her lips with his own. Then the touch became a soft kiss that sent a feeling running deep into her body.

Whisper's body surged with warmth and she felt herself being pulled against the big trapper's body. His arms were so strong, yet gentle in their caress. His lips moved against her own, bringing alive in her the fires of a woman. It happened so suddenly that it startled her.

She moved away and looked at him an instant, her heart pounding. A smile moved across his face and he again told her of the small flower of the high country, the spring beauty. Then he was carrying her. He had picked her up and was taking her toward one of the sink holes.

"Got to be sure and pick the right ones," he said with a laugh. "There's a few of them here that'll boil a man's bones clean."

Then he set her down and, quicker than she could do it herself, he had pulled her doeskin dress up over her head. In the same quickness, he too undressed, and they stood facing each other with the rising vapors on all sides of them. Her heart seemed to pound louder than before as she looked upon the lean form of the mountain man. The muscles of his broad shoulders and chest curved inward to his waist and on to trim legs, coiled with the springing power of the mountain cat. In that same moment, he saw her also, and whispered to her softly that she was beautiful.

Then she was with him in the small pool of steaming water, the bottom feeling like warm sands. They were laughing and splashing like children. Whisper let herself feel free as she never had before. This carefree man who lived but a day at a time had torn her loose from the trials of her past life. His secret strength was a power so great she could do nothing but yield to it. Never before had she been able to forget all and enjoy a fulfillment such as she was feeling this night.

He kissed her again and she felt him as he pressed against her and encircled her with his warmth. She held him close and his breath found her ears and her neck.

"Oh, yes. You are ready for love," he said.

They left the pool and took their buffalo robes to a grassy spot at the edge of the basin. The moon was shining through the trees and a bright glitter of stars filled the sky above them. Jim lay Whisper next to him on one of the robes and covered them both with the other one. Whisper smiled at him and he planted soft kisses along her cheek, small and simple touches of the lips that left the skin warm and tingling. He traced a gentle line with his forefinger along her thighs and up across her breasts, stopping at the back of her neck to mingle his fingers with her long black hair and press his lips to hers. "You are even more beautiful than the spring beauty," he told her.

"I am afraid," she told him.

"Afraid of what?"

"I only remember the Siksika. Even with Sun Bear Standing I was afraid. I could not do it."

Jim kissed her gently. "Touch me," he said, "and forget your fear." He guided her hand to him. "Forget the past. I am no Blackfoot."

Whisper moaned when he kissed her again. The fires of a woman came stronger now that she was touching him. His lips found her ears and her neck. He pushed her down on the robes and she opened her arms to him.

In their love he was gentle. For the first time in her life she came to know the complete fulfillment of passion. Her whole body trembled with the gentle strength of the blond trapper.

When it was over, there was no sound but the steaming pots nearby and a soft breeze that was moving through the trees. Whisper and Jim lay in each other's arms, sharing the warmth they had created between them.

"Whisper," Jim said to her, "I want you to be my wife. I want you to be with me always. My words come from my heart and can never be taken back."

Whisper took a moment to answer. "I wish for that to be, Jim. I would someday like to be your wife. But now I must find my mother. My heart cannot rest until then."

"We can look for her together."

"Your path will not always lead to the land of the Salish. There are more beaver in other lands."

"We'll find your ma first," Jim said. "We'll find her, then go up for beaver."

"It may take many moons to find her, Jim. It may take

even as long as from the snows of one winter to the snows of another.'' She took a deep breath. ''I do not know if it would be right for me to be your wife at this time. I do not know if the spirits of my people would smile upon us. Maybe it would make them angry. I cannot say. Until I learn of my mother and know that the spirits of my people are resting in the Land of Eternal Summer, I cannot stay with you.'' She got up and put on her doeskin dress. ''We must go now,'' she said. ''The Long Knife, Sublette, and the others will be leaving for the waters of the Snake soon. We must be back in time to leave with them.''

Chapter 8

WHEN WARRIORS MEET

Sun had just broken over the high *Tetons*, pouring light down on the large traveling body of Long Knives and Indians. Jim rode silent in the column of men, Whisper behind on her appaloosa. It was the second day of the journey and he had said very little to her since they had left the rendezvous. She was lucky even to be riding with them, Whisper thought, for Jim had seemed angry during the ride back from the hot springs. Fiddler rode just ahead of Jim, puffing his pipe. When he had asked Jim what the trouble was, Jim had remarked, "A man can't get nothin' for his furs, that's all." But Fiddler knew there was more to it than just the business of getting fair pay for beaver. He had only to look at Whisper to see that.

Other things had happened, also. Whisper had overheard Jim telling Fiddler about a little owl he had seen sitting on the barrel of his Hawken the night before. He had laughed about it and had told Fiddler what a cute little ball of feathers the owl was. Whisper did not wish to speak to Jim about it because of his mood, but she had begun to wonder what was happening. Surely Jim did not know of the spirit of Little Fox that lived in the tiny owl's body. Whisper thought if she were to tell him he would only laugh it off as he did many of the Indian beliefs. But why would the little owl want to see Jim. What could that mean?

Another strange thing had happened. Whisper had seen a bad omen that morning. A raven had come to her bed and awakened her with his sharp cawing. He had been sitting on the ground by her robes, his black feathers shining in the early light. It meant a bad thing would happen. Whisper was frightened. She wished she did not have to travel that day, for staying in one place would be safer. But she would have to face the day and only hope that the omen passed her by, for she had to travel with the Long Knives to the place where her mother might be.

Now, as she traveled, Whisper was among the first to see a very large band of riders coming down onto the flats from the forest nearly a mile away across the valley. She told Jim and Fiddler of them, who in turn sent the news up to the Long Knife leader, Milton Sublette. One of the riders across the valley carried a Union Jack and there was talk that some of those from the American Fur Company had come late for rendezvous. Whisper shook her head no and Fiddler took a spyglass from his pack.

"What do you make of them?" Jim asked.

"Blackfeet!" Fiddler answered. "Plain as day."

Those across the valley had spotted them also and were grouping themselves up for talk. Whisper took the spyglass from Fiddler.

"Blackfeet sure," said Jim.

"Atsina," Whisper said. "They are called Gros Ventres, Big Bellies. They are the same as Blackfeet. They live with them; they do murderous things as the Blackfeet do. They are all dogs!"

"Looks for certain like they mean war," Fiddler remarked. "We'd best get ready for a set-to sure enough."

Jim nodded. "Looks like we'll see blood today, all right."

The Long Knife leader Sublette grouped them up and ordered a few of them to ride back to the rendezvous camp for help. Already the flats across the way were swarming with Atsina. Many were women and children, which would make the warriors even more dangerous. Soon war songs started from both the Atsina and the numerous Flatheads and Nez Percé with the Long Knives. As Whisper watched Jim help the others form a breastwork with their trapping gear, a cold fear came over her.

"Must we stay here?" Whisper said to him. "This is not a good day for fighting."

Jim took it as a joke. "What's the matter, Whisper? Are you tired of takin' Blackfoot hair?"

"This is a bad day for fighting! You must listen to me! I have seen the raven by my bed this morning. He was laughing. It is not a good day."

"Don't worry about me," Jim said to her, looking up from his work. "There's a pile of Gros Ventres who'll go under before night settles in and I plan to take as much hair as anybody."

Whisper turned to Fiddler. "You are of more age. You have seen and learned much. Tell him we must go now. It is not a good day for fighting."

Fiddler was ramming a fresh charge into his Hawken. "Young pretty, you've got nary a thing to worry you. That young hoss can take care of himself and then some."

"Why do you not listen?" Whisper said. "Why do neither of you believe me? It is a bad day!"

The Atsina were painting themselves and yelling at the top of their lungs. Their numbers were over one hundred in fighting warriors alone. They knew the Long Knives were but half as many. They would take their time and they would sing their war songs for well they knew that the Long Knives could not last long once the fight began. Yes, blood would flow before Sun had crossed straight above.

"How'll those Gros Ventres go about this?" Jim asked Fiddler. "Will they come straight on?"

Fiddler shook his head. "This ol' hoss sees a good

chance they'll try to pull a sneak on us. They'll try to get us closer so's to come in quick and take our hair without loosin' too many of their own. There's nary a one of them cares to come on straight to powder and ball.''

"They are like the fox who lives in the brush of the bottomland,'' Whisper put in. ''They sneak about with their backs low to the ground. They cannot be trusted. See? See what I have said?'' She pointed to the clearing between the two groups.

One of the Gros Ventre chiefs had paraded to the middle of the clearing wrapped in a scarlet blanket. He was waving a medicine pipe above his head and making the sign of peace. Whisper spoke again of lies and deceit.

The Long Knife leader, Milton Sublette, addressed the group in general. ''We all know that Gros Ventre wants our hair and him wavin' that pipe out there won't make us think any different. We can stall for time, though, if we send somebody out to palaver. My brother Bill and Robert Campbell should show up here with their men before too long. The thing is, we need time.''

Whisper's eyes flashed. ''I would like to go,'' she told Jim. ''It would be good to shoot out the heart of a dog.''

"That is for me to do,'' said a man near her. ''I have waited long for this moment. Do not take it from me.''

"Who are you?'' Whisper asked.

"My name is Antone Godin. My father was killed by those dogs on the Big Lost River two winters past. Those waters are sometimes called Godin's Fork because of his death. Today I will avenge that death.''

"I, too, have lost family to the Siksika,'' said Whisper. ''I will go with you.''

"I have heard much of you, Spirit Woman,'' Godin said. ''Save your magic for the Siksika. I wish to face the Atsina with my own medicine.''

Godin rode out from the group and took a Flathead brave with him. The two rode defiantly toward the Gros Ventre chief who awaited them with the medicine pipe across his arm and the red blanket draped over his shoulder.

"They'll splatter that Gros Ventre all over the meadow," Jim said. "Don't that chief know that?"

Fiddler puffed on his pipe. "I reckon he thinks his medicine will protect him. He looks to be one solid blotch of paint from here."

"His paint will soon be blood," said Whisper. "And this whole valley will be blood." Again the cold fear returned to her and she cringed with the thought she may have just missed sealing her fate. If the Iroquois half-breed Antone Godin had not been more vengeful than she herself was, she might have fulfilled the raven's prophecy of doom by meeting the Gros Ventre chief and possibly losing her life for it. In her hatred for the Blackfeet and their allies, she had forgotten for a moment that this was not a good day for fighting. She could not afford to forget again. It is time to leave, she told herself.

Whisper gripped Jim's arm and pulled him aside. "Will you not listen to me? We must not fight this day. The raven was laughing."

"You were sure in a hurry to knock off that Gros Ventre chief," Jim reminded her.

"I had forgotten about the raven. He was laughing. We must leave."

"There's no need for all this," Jim said in disgust. "We've got plenty of guns and more on the way."

"That does not matter. We are marked. It does not matter how many fight with us. This day we are marked."

Jim blew out his breath. "Leave if you have a mind to, but this hoss aims to take hair today."

Antone Godin and the Flathead stopped their horses near the Gros Ventre chief. Their hands went up in greeting. The Flathead's rifle spoke and the Gros Ventre chief tumbled backward off his horse and lay doubled over on the ground. Godin began singing a victory song and quickly pulled the red blanket out from under the dying Gros Ventre, then ripped the scalp from his head. Holding the scalp and blanket for all to see, the two men rode hard back to the Long Knives.

The Gros Ventres were screaming. Their war songs became louder and their drums filled the valley with a steady rhythm of war. They taunted and jeered and showed themselves obscenely in hopes of bringing the Long Knives out into the open to fight. They screamed insults and mocked openly to make their enemies mad and foolish enough to leave the safety of their breastworks. The Long Knives would not move. The longer the Gros Ventres carried on, the sooner the rest of the men from rendezvous would show up. But there was not much time left. The Gros Ventres were vile with hatred; they would charge soon.

Sun moved higher in the sky and the Gros Ventres finished their final ceremonies for war. They would come now, and they would fight as hard as warriors can fight, for they had taken the time to invoke strong medicine upon themselves. They would go into battle with weapons that were swift to kill and they would be untouched by the firesticks of the Long Knives. There is no warrior more fierce than one who is prepared for battle.

Then, from the direction of rendezvous, the valley filled with men. The Long Knife leader, Milton Sublette, led the cheering as he watched his brother, Bill, and Robert Campbell lead a party of trappers and Indian allies into the middle of the clearing. There were many Flathead and Nez Perce warriors along and the group numbered over three hundred strong.

Jim laughed. "I told you, Whisper. That raven of yours can't laugh no longer."

"He did laugh, though. It is still a bad day."

It was now the Gros Ventres who were looking at numbers much greater than their own. It was a day for blood; a good day to die. The Gros Ventre women began singing death songs for there was no escape. Their mortal enemies, the Nez Percé and the Flathead were coming down the valley now and would count coup and line their lodges with scalps this very day.

It was then that some of the wiser Gros Ventres began to think of their lives and build themselves a fortress to defend from, much the same as the Long Knives had. They pulled fallen trees and logs into a tangle of willow and brush in the swampy bottom. Soon they, too, had a breastwork. If it was a good day to die, many of those who dared come in after them would also sing the song of death.

The Long Knives with their Indian allies split into two groups to charge the fortress. The Flathead and Nez Percé took one side and the Long Knives went across to fight from the other direction. They would have the Gros Ventres trapped between two forces and kill them all easily. It would be a very big battle with many men on both sides and the day would see the most blood of any day ever in the mountains.

Whisper, her eyes wide with fear, clung fiercely to Jim's buckskins but could not hold him back. The Gros Ventres lay ready and waiting in the thick tangle of brush.

Bill Sublette raised his Hawken and yelled, "Let's ride to Blackfoot hair!"

Whisper yelled to Jim as he joined the others in the charge to the willows.

A volley of arrows and rifle fire poured from the Gros Ventre fortress. Long Knives and Indian allies fell screaming and jerking. Whisper's breath left her as she watched men fall on all sides of Jim while he surged ahead on his horse, into the tangle of brush, killing a screaming Gros Ventre with his Hawken. He pulled back to reload, but did not see two mounted warriors rush out from the tangle after him. Whisper screamed and jumped on Red Thunder.

"Take this with you," yelled Fiddler. She caught his Hawken and turned her appaloosa for the willows.

The two warriors rushed Jim. One was swinging a war club while the other tried to drive his lance home. Both were covered with red and black stripes from head to toe, screaming war chants at the top of their lungs. Jim swung the heavy Hawken into a war shield and felt the blow of the war club against the barrel, knocking it from his hands. His horse reared and he slid off backwards to the ground. He rolled to miss the thrust of the lance, but took a glancing blow from the war club off his back. He let out a heavy grunt and slumped over onto his side, arching his back in pain.

Whisper had worked herself into a frenzy. Her eyes were slits of hate and she screamed while waving the Hawken above her head. She drove her big horse past Jim between the two warriors, firing the Hawken through a medicine bundle and into a paint-covered chest. The Gros Ventre screamed and dropped his club, clutching a chest where blood ran red over black paint. In a moment he was in a lifeless pile beneath the horses. Whisper turned Red Thunder to face the lancer. There was no time to recharge the Hawken; the warrior was upon her.

She swung the gun by its barrel, knocking the lance away. As his horse went by, the warrior jumped, grabbing Whisper by the arm and shoulder. They fell to the ground in a tangled heap.

Whisper was strong, but no match for the Gros Ventre. She struggled to get out from under him while he reached for his knife. His face was painted hatred and from his mouth came a slur of war songs.

His knife was out when Whisper saw the eyes go large and the mouth fall open, big and round. His breath caught in his throat and he jerked forward, arching his back. Whisper heard the dull ripping sound of a knife pushing through ribs again and again, and saw Jim's large form over the back of the Gros Ventre. The warrior coughed up and Jim pushed him sideways off Whisper. He gave her the knife.

"Take yourself some hair, Whisper. I'll get the other one."

It was hard for Jim to mount again, and hard for him to stay on. All around the fighting continued. Screams and war cries seemed to be getting louder since the trappers and their Indian allies were having trouble getting in to the Gros Ventres. The willows and fallen logs made a tight fortress and the Gros Ventres had killed a good number of those who had tried to get in. Whisper's worry now was for Jim.

"You handled that well, Little Pretty," said Fiddler, taking the Hawken from her and helping Jim off the horse.

Jim got himself over to a tree and sat back against it, taking a long gulp of whiskey from Fiddler's jug. "Damn, he got me square in the back."

"I thought you'd gone under," said Fiddler.

Jim winced as he set the jug down. "I'll piss blood for a week."

"We're gettin' ourselves pretty well shot up," said Fiddler. "Bill Sublette caught a ball in the arm and Campbell just drug Sinclair in. It appears he'll go under. How many more you see down out there?"

Jim shook his head. "It didn't look good. Maybe we should have planned a little better before we charged off like that."

"Why did you not listen to me?" Whisper asked. "If I am to be your woman, you must listen to me."

Jim sat up. "Did I hear that right?"

Whisper nodded. "I have thought about it. I wish to be with you. Our medicine will be good. I know your words are true when you speak. I know you think of how I wish to find my mother. With you, I know I will some day find her."

Jim, forgetting the pain of his back wound, grabbed Whisper and hugged her close. "Whisper, I'll never make you sorry. You'll be cared for the best way I know how."

Fiddler laughed and fired up his pipe. "Who's been takin' care of who?"

"You must not fight any more today, Jim," Whisper said. "It is time you heard the words I speak to you about such things as when and when not to fight. There are other things I will tell you about myself in time, and also some of the things that I have been taught to believe. You must learn these things too, for if you do not, there will be much about me you will not be able to understand and our life together will be difficult because of it."

"Don't worry about that, Whisper," said Jim. "I'll listen to anything you have to say. But, just one thing," he added with a laugh. "Keep that damned raven away from us, will you."

Whisper smiled. "The raven will bother us no more, for I have a brave Long Knife who does not care what the raven says. Because of that, the raven cannot make his words come true and he must leave in shame."

"It looks to me like this fight is about over," Fiddler put in. "I see some boys settin' fire to them logs and willows full of Gros Ventres. Things ought to go pretty fast from here."

"Let them fight," said Jim. "I've got myself a little Salish gal and I can't take care of her full of holes and Gros Ventre arrows." He gave Whisper a hug.

Whisper smiled. Yes, her life had changed since the raid on her people by the Siksika. She herself had known it would. But she could never have imagined that a Long Knife would play an important part of her new life. Now, as she looked at Jim and the happiness that showed in his eyes, she was glad for it.

Part Two

INDIAN WIFE

Chapter 9

JACKSON'S LAKE

Sun was red-gold in the far western sky, moving toward high peaks where snow lay deep over rocks and scattered pines. Below, along the waters of the Snake, the leaves were gone and the river fought against ice that built up along the banks. It was during the Moon of Late Autumn—November. A flock of geese flew in a long V, coming down from high above onto the waters called Jackson's Lake. With a great flapping of wings they broke in flight and landed in a long, splashing line across the water. Whisper and Jim were just off shore, wrapped in buffalo robes, watching from a group of pines.

"The birds are truly beautiful," said Whisper. "It makes my heart sad to see them going to the warm lands far to the south. It means the snow moons are here."

"Winter has a beauty of its own," said Jim. "There's times I've seen you wrapped in a colored blanket standin' in the snow with the green of the woods behind you and your black hair trailin' clean down your back, and I thought to myself God never made a prettier picture for a man to see."

Whisper smiled. Her dark eyes were soft and loving. "I have never known such happiness," she said. "The seasons pass so quickly since I have found your arms."

The snows of winter were coming for the second time already since their meeting at the waters of Henry's Lake and the rendezvous that followed. Their time together seemed to move as fast as the pronghorn, the creature known to many as Antelope, who lives where the forest ends and the grass plains begin. Their lives had been as close as two lives could be. They were always together. She hunted with him and he gathered berries and dug roots with her. She learned to wade icy streams and set the foot-catching irons for the beaver. He could now cut poles and build a tepee that would withstand any storm. Though other Long Knives shared little in the work of their Indian wives, Jim helped Whisper with even the smallest of chores. She in turn could pack beaver plews as high as any Long Knife and knew the business of furs equally as well.

And Whisper had taught Jim the ways of the Salish hunter. He now had a bow and arrows of his own, and could send them straight and true to their mark. He had found them as deadly as the Hawken when shot from close range, and had learned from Whisper the stealth of the mountain cat in getting close to his prey.

From Jim, Whisper learned the secrets of the deadly fire-stick. His Hawken now fit well in her hands and her aim was as steady as that of any Long Knife in the mountains. Even the old Fiddler puffed on his pipe and nodded his head when the Hawken spoke in her hands. Jim was proud of her, and she of him. It was a union of body and spirit.

Jim was watching the geese on the lake. He shook his head and remarked, "Those young geese sure do grow up in a hurry. They no more than popped out of an egg a short time back."

"It is the way of all wild creatures," said Whisper. Her eyes had suddenly begun to sparkle.

"What makes you so happy?" Jim asked.

She smiled. "You wait here. I will return in a little while."

Whisper got up and went to where Red Thunder stood grazing in a nearby meadow. She had known many good times with her big Appaloosa since that day at rendezvous when Jim had traded his furs to the Long Knife, Wyeth, for him. Well she knew that her happiness with this horse was because of Jim. Her life had changed greatly since she had met this young Long Knife. She had learned the true meaning of deep love. Though a cool breeze came into her face from the lake, she felt warmth inside.

Whisper took a small pack from the saddle on Red Thunder and went over to sit beneath a tree. She combed her hair with a brush of porcupine quills, singing a song of joy. She made a part in the middle and, using a small mirror Jim had gotten for her at rendezvous, she put a streak of vermilion from front to back. She smiled. The red part made her hair look its best. She took fragrant herbs and rubbed them on her face, neck, and arms. Horsemint was Jim's favorite. She smiled again. She would please him the best way she knew how, for he had surely pleased her.

Still singing, Whisper went back over to Jim and sat down.

"Why are you all dolled up?" he asked.

"I wish to please you, for you have pleased me greatly."

He smiled and looked back out across the lake. "We're mighty lucky," he said. "There's a heap of beaver in these parts and no one to bother us."

Whisper took Jim by the arm and pointed out on the lake. "The geese seem truly happy," she said. "They swim together as a family."

Jim nodded, looking across to where more geese were coming in against the red sky of evening. "That's a pretty sight if ever I saw one."

Whisper pulled him close to her. "Jim, there is something I wish to tell you."

He was looking at her with his eyes narrowed. Usually when she said she wished to speak to him in that way, she wanted something. Or sometimes it meant trouble, maybe a skunk in camp, or no beaver in the traps. "Can't it wait until after the sunset?" Jim asked.

"It will make the sunset better," she said.

Jim waited a moment. "Well, what have you got to tell me?"

Whisper smiled. "I am with child."

Jim's mouth dropped open. "What? You are?" He grabbed her and hugged her tightly. "You mean it?"

She nodded. "I am in my second moon now. I am sure of it."

Jim let out a yell. "Good! I got me a boy to teach beaver to."

"What if it is a girl?"

Jim shrugged. "Hell, she can learn beaver, too."

They laughed together and Jim kissed her softly. "You have made me happier than any man alive. Any man, any-where."

"You know how much I love you," she told him. "But how much do you love me?"

"More than you could ever know." His eyes got big and he raised his hand and waved it in a circle above their heads. "It's a love way bigger than this country around us. It fills these here mountains. It spills over them peaks to the west and clear on down the Columbia to the big Pacific. It runs east, out across the flats and clay hills to the land of the Sioux and Cheyenne, then clean on to that other ocean called the Atlantic. It's a mighty big love, Whisper."

Whisper was listening intently. "Do many huge waters flow far to the east also?"

Jim nodded. "And there's oceans of ice to the north, and people who wear heavy fur all seasons of the year. There are oceans far south where there are only people with black skin. They live among strange animals bigger than three lodges together."

Whisper laughed. "You tell more stories than the old men in camp."

"They are true," Jim insisted. "It's all true, by God, and this hoss swears to that."

"You do speak truth?"

"You have seen black men. That one hoss, Jim Beckwourth, you know who he is."

Whisper nodded. "Yes, I have seen the black white men. What you say must be true. But I have never heard the stories of these animals you speak of—the ones bigger than three lodges."

"Some day we'll see all these lands," said Jim. "You and me and the little one."

Whisper put her arms around his neck and rubbed her nose against his with a giggle. "You are some man, Jim Ayers. You have dreams and visions as big as those giant waters called oceans you speak of."

"We'll see all that some day," Jim repeated. His lips touched hers. "We'll do it all."

She felt his strong arms drawing her in close to him. A warmness welled up in her. His big hands were under her doeskin dress and she felt her breasts swell to his gentle touch.

"You make a cold evening warm," she said.

He drew the buffalo robes in close around them and they lay in the warmth of each other's arms. She pushed his buckskin pants down and brought a rush of breath from him. In their time together they had learned the ways of deep passion. "I'll never get tired of your touch," he told her. "There has never been a man like you," she said back.

They held each other for a time after it was over, and the desire came again to both of them. Their love was more heated than before, and in the middle of their passion they were jolted and bumped heavily by something above them. The robes were knocked off them and they sat naked in the cold, laughing. Red Thunder was anxious to get back to camp.

Along the banks of the Snake sat two buffalo-hide tepees, their doorflaps facing Sun to the east. Whisper had drawn signs of love with paint and a charcoal stick all around the outside of one lodge. The inside smelled of fragrant herbs. There were things women used for cooking and everyday work. And there were soft robes for sleeping.

Fiddler's tepee was plain and without frills. It was a place of work, also, but the work of catching beaver. The inside smelled of castor and traps, and was scattered with his bucksin clothes.

When Whisper and Jim got back from the lake, Fiddler was seated crosslegged next to a fire. His whiskers broke into a little smile.

"You two must have found somethin' of interest out there. It's been a passel of time since you left." He lit his pipe.

"That was a mighty fine sunset," said Jim quickly. "We had to see it all."

"It was mighty fine at that," Fiddler agreed. "The whole day went plumb fine to suit me, but for one thing." He took a deep breath.

"Well, what?" Jim asked.

"Old Ephraim."

"What?" Jim's eyes were large.

"White bear," said Fiddler. "Seen fresh sign all along the stream. A mighty big one from the looks of it. Half the trees got claw sign."

"He is telling us he owns this part of the river," said Whisper. "He wants us to know this is his land."

Fiddler sat and puffed his pipe. "He's not one to argue with. Them claw marks reached twice as high as any two men."

"Where'd you see the sign?" Jim asked.

Fiddler got up and pointed. "Just downriver." He grabbed a burning stick for a torch.

The trail broke out from the trees and brush along the river and into a little park on a sidehill. High up along the trunk of a big pine was a set of claw marks, white and deep where they had ripped away the bark.

"Damn, he must be huge!" said Jim.

Whisper looked at the claw marks and shuddered. She knew the big white-tipped bears for what they were— dangerous and unpredictable. There were many of these bears throughout the mountains and valleys. Other animals lived in fear of them. One day this creature would be afraid of a man, the next he would charge and kill with a fury and hatred that was unmatched. They could kill with one swipe of their paws, their paws being as big as both the hands of three men. Yes, Whisper had watched them many times from a tree. There was usually safety from these bears in trees, she had been taught, for their claws are not made for climbing. It was known, though, that a tree with low branches was dangerous to climb, for the bears would pull themselves up on these branches if they were big enough to support their weight. Whisper knew it was always best to keep out of the bears' sight. To avoid them was to avoid the chance of death.

"He rules much of this land," said Whisper. "He must be truly powerful."

"Maybe we'd best move on," Fiddler suggested, his pipe a cloud of smoke. "A bear that size has got no equal."

"Hell, we can't," said Jim. "This country shines with beaver. We can take plew this year that will put them all to shame. This is the best luck we've had in a long, long spell."

Fiddler frowned. "You think loosin' your guts is a spell of luck?"

Jim shook his head. "Fiddler, there's no sense in goin' way overboard on this thing."

Fiddler's frown deepened. "Jim, if you had a lick of sense you'd hear me out. Damn, you've seen what them bears can do to a man. Remember Jim Brier over on the Platte? His ribs on both sides was without a lick of meat and his skull was crushed like an egg. And you know about Hugh Glass. There's one hoss who's lived to tell the tale. Just listen to him a short spell and you'll shy away from any talk of bear after that."

Fear spread through Whisper. She knew the words Fiddler spoke were a clear warning, and she knew the fate of one so foolish as not to fear the great white-tipped bear—the grizzly. The sight of this creature made even the bravest warrior draw quick breath. The black bear of the forest was a deadly foe when provoked, but the grizzly was certain death. The small, dark eyes, mostly unseeing, sat in a dish-shaped face lined with long teeth. The ears were stubby and rounded, and would flatten back against the head at the slightest unnatural sound. These bears had a strange savage alertness about them that put ice in the blood. They were known to show an intelligent fighting sense when in brush or thick cover, often attacking a foe from ambush, leaving nothing but partial remains for the relatives to mourn over. They feared nothing, these bears, and went unchallenged as rulers of the land. Whisper hoped Jim would not value the beaver more than he valued their lives.

Jim thought a moment. "Maybe we could move down or up the river."

Fiddler nodded. "I'm for either one."

"He is indeed a mighty ruler," Whisper put in. "It would not be good to challenge one so powerful. One blow could kill any creature alive. And I could not live without you, Jim."

Chapter 10

ABSAROKA

Sun crossed the sky three times and there was no new sign of the great bear. There were no fresh tracks, nor leavings from animals killed by him. "He was just passin' through," Jim said with gladness and relief. "He's gone now. We can stay and cash in on these beaver." Fiddler said little. He consented to staying, but his old eyes were always looking. He set his traps always facing the shore while Jim laughed and told him he was getting nervous in his old age. Jim kept saying the bear was gone. But, like Fiddler, Whisper could not sleep well at night.

One other thing bothered her even more, though. She had yet to find her mother. In the moons that had passed, she had looked often; she had listened for stories or talk. She had listened for the name Little Grasses on passing lips. There had been neither talk nor stories. During the warm moons, when the beaver's fur was thin, both Fiddler and Jim would join in the search. Many times they would split up in order to cover more country and visit more Flathead bands at once. There had been no word.

Still Whisper would not give up hope. It was the work of evil spirits that kept her from finding her mother. Whisper had told herself many times she would have found her mother along the waters of the Snake after the rendezvous two summers past if only they had left the big group of Long Knives led by William Sublette and not fought the Gros Ventres, as she had wished. News of that fight had traveled fast and all the Indian peoples along the bottomlands had moved together in big groups for fear of vengeance by the Gros Ventres. Many of the bands had even moved back up into higher country for safety. Whisper felt her mother had, indeed, been living with a band along the river but had moved back into the mountains to hide.

That great fight was now called the Battle of Pierre's Hole by the Long Knives. The story had been retold many times around campfires and was now famous in the hearts of all who had been there. Jim would smile at Whisper with each telling, for she had saved his life at that battle. He had proof in a jagged scar along his ribs. There were times yet when he would get up in the night and walk, holding his back in pain, for he had been hurt inside and the wound would never fully heal.

Yes, the evil spirits had been working against her that day. She had known this, but no one would listen. Whisper knew that the raven who had come to her bed that morning two summers past had indeed laughed for what was to happen. It was true that neither she nor Jim had been killed in the battle, but the battle had ended in a very strange fashion. It had been decided that the Gros Ventre stronghold would be burned. The Gros Ventres then began yelling vengeance oaths, which made many of the Long Knives believe that the main rendezvous camp was being attacked by their brothers, the Blackfeet. Almost all of the Long Knives and the Indian allies left to defend the camp. As darkness fell, the Gros Ventres escaped. Only their dead and wounded were left. Later the other Long Knives returned with bowed heads. There had been no attack on the main camp; it had either been a trick or someone had listened with ears that could not make the right words of the Gros Ventre tongue.

Because of this the scalp dance drums were not so loud and all the land was in fear of Gros Ventre vengeance. After nearly three moons of searching the bottomlands, Whisper had raised her voice to a raven who flew cawing over the treetops. "Raven, I will seek vengeance on you!" she had screamed. "Because of you the Gros Ventres live and my mother has gone into the mountains to hide, where I cannot find her. Now, Raven, since you are a brother of the Gros Ventres and the Blackfeet, you will some day lie in death on the forest floor!"

Since that time, there had been no more Gros Ventres. Other Long Knives told stories of fights with them after the Battle of Pierre's Hole, but Whisper and Jim had seen no more of them. It had been nearly two winters with no fighting; a time spent in peace with each other and the old Long Knife, Fiddler. Once a war party of Piegan Blackfeet had traveled through a valley below them and Whisper had wished to do battle. But the Piegans had been many in number and fighting them would have been foolish.

Yes, there had been peace, but Whisper knew it could not last. There had been too many recent omens. Around every Long Knife campfire there was now beginning to be much talk about Blackfeet. Some had been nearly killed by them; others had seen them and had managed to avoid them. Still others talked of seeing death at their hands. The talk was of a large war party of Siksika, led by a young war chief whose medicine was the Weasel. Walking Head, a name Whisper knew too well.

Whisper had not seen or heard about Walking Head since the fight at Henry's Lake. He had no doubt traveled back with his people far to the north, above the waters of the Big Muddy and into the high, cold grasslands that were the home of the Siksika. Only now was his name being spoken again. The talk was of his quest for the Spirit Woman, and his hatred for the Long Knife, Jim Ayers, who had possession of this woman without right. He had come back down to the forested lands to take this woman. His power was great and his medicine was good. He had gained many coup in destroying a Cree stronghold on the waters of the Saskatchewan. There were many who followed him. His war party numbered over one hundred warriors.

Now, as the Moon of Late Autumn drew to a close, a recent omen troubled her. The little owl of the forest had appeared. Once again he had come to be her strength. She knew well this could only mean the time of peace now was gone. He had not spoken to her, but only sat long enough for her to see him before disappearing into the forest on his tiny wings. Then Sun had crossed the sky but twice when she and Jim met a large war party of Absaroka while setting traps. These were the Crows, who lived in the mountains and valleys along the waters of the Yellowstone. They, too, were mortal enemies of the Blackfeet and had joined together many times with the Flatheads to do battle.

They had been led by a great war chief among the Crows, a chief well known for his courage in battle. He was called Rotten Belly, and his coups were many. His words to her had been a warning.

"It is you, Spirit Woman," he had begun. "I have heard much of you, and of your brave deeds in battle against the Siksika. There is much talk of your powers among all the Indian peoples of the plains and forest. And now, Spirit Woman, the Siksika are here and you will have to show that your medicine is great."

"Have you seen the Siksika?" Whisper had asked.

Shaking his head, Rotten Belly had answered, "Had I met the Siksika, my hands would be red with their blood and I would now have many scalps to blacken my face over and show my people. But it is well known that Walking Head, war chief of the Siksika, has journeyed back down from the cold lands to the north. It is known he no longer lives in the valley where the waters called Belly River flow. Instead he and his war party have moved their lodges among a band of Pikuni—Piegans—near the Great Falls of the Big Muddy. It is well-known he vows to find you someday and take you back north among his people.

Yes, and all this has made the wives in his lodge angry.''

"He is not a man and cannot keep his wives happy,''
Whisper had commented while the Crow warriors laughed.
Then she had added, "He will not get me. Instead that dog
will get my knife across his belly, and the wolves will sing
feasting songs.''

Rotten Belly had then smiled and said, "Yes, Spirit
Woman, you have the fire that is seen only in truly great
warriors. But you will have to find Walking Head before I
do, for I also wish to have his scalp hanging on my coup·
stick for all to see.''

"Our wishes are the same,'' Whisper had told him.
"Some day one of us will see that wish in truth.'' She had
then made the signs of those who fight as brothers. "I will
stand by Rotten Belly against the Blackfeet. I will fight to
the death.''

The Crows had shouted her name as a chant. Rotten
Belly had nodded his approval. "You are now a sister of
the Absaroka people. Your name will be spoken with
honor. He who is the enemy of the Spirit Woman is the
enemy of Rotten Belly also. So let it be.'' With that the
Absaroka had departed and Whisper had gained a powerful
ally. These were a people well known for their fighting
ability, and their hatred for the Siksika and other Blackfoot
tribes was as great as that of the Salish. Yes, the return of
the little owl and the meeting with Rotten Belly had given
Whisper a strange feeling. Now she knew that blood would
flow again before another moon was full.

The red line of light in the west had given way to the heavy
blue that signals darkness to the forest. A lone wolf knew
this and howled long and high. Another one answered
somewhere far off and the sound drifted through the cold
stillness.

"They must have had a good hunt today,'' Jim remarked,
putting wood onto a fire that roasted a leg of elk.

Fiddler grunted. "They've found meat no doubt. Alive

or dead, they found somethin'." He rosined his bow and set into a tune.

"This can't compare to good buffalo hump," Jim said, cutting a slice off the elk. "But I've tasted lots worse fixin's."

Whisper nudged Jim and pointed to the edge of camp. Three deer watched from the shadows, curious at the strange sound of Fiddler's music. Then they turned their heads and sniffed the air behind them. In a few quick bounds they had again disappeared into the forest

"Something close by has frightened them," said Whisper. Fiddler stopped playing and took up his Hawken. Jim and Whisper moved apart, getting low to the ground, looking out into the darkness at the edge of camp. Horses snorted. Then the fire shone on three riders.

"The wind, she is a cold one," said a rider. "*Oui*, a cold one. It makes the belly very empty."

Fiddler frowned. "You make a late camp, Frenchman. A man would think you're out to roust him."

Whisper felt a sudden uneasiness as the three men got off their horses and came over to the fire. She remembered these men. They were Beeler's men. The Frenchman, Courchene, was one of them. He was the one who had slipped Beeler the long butchering knife that night at the rendezvous when Jim had fought. Whisper knew these men to be as evil as Beeler himself. She looked at Jim and could tell his memory was also good.

"What do you want, Courchene?" Jim asked, his Hawken resting across his arm. "Beeler send you?"

Courchene raised his hands. "*Non*, that is not it." He pointed to the other two. "Jakes and Bolman, they are with me only. We trap for the beaver ourselves. *Oui*, for ourselves. Beeler is not one who is good to work for."

"Courchene is right," Bolman quickly said. "Beeler's never done no good by us. We all feel the same."

"What do you say, Jakes?" Jim asked.

Jakes nodded that he agreed, but his eyes did not meet Jim's.

"Where are your pack animals?" Fiddler asked. "A hoss with saddle and man carries mighty few beaver plews, I'm thinkin'."

The three looked to one another. Courchene spoke. "The pack mules, they are below on the river. It is too far to bring them."

Fiddler broke into a lopsided grin. "Then there's more than just you three, to be sure. A man in his right mind don't run off without his pack string, unless he's got no care about Injuns stealin' him blind."

"Oui," said Courchene. "A man without the traps cannot get the beaver." He laughed nervously. "Maybe a man could find a drink. *Oui*, a drink would be good."

"It's poor fare lyin' to a man, then drinkin' his liquor," Jim said.

Courchene's eyes hardened. "There is beaver enough for all, is there not? We only come for the beaver, to trap for ourselves. We come as friends. *Oui*, friends." He motioned to one of the other men. "Jakes, show them. Bring the present we would share with them."

Jakes got up and started for the horses. Whisper saw Jim cock the hammer on his Hawken. Fiddler, too, brought his gun up.

"Non!" said Courchene, putting his hands up in front of him. *"Non,* we do not wish for trouble. We are friends." When Jakes came back he had a parfleche. Courchene took it from him and held it up. "See. We are friends. Eat."

From the parfleche Courchene pulled three fresh buffalo tongues. "Good fixin's," Bolman said from behind. "Mighty good fixin's."

"Where did you find the buffler?" Fiddler asked. "We ain't seen nary a sign in a long spell."

Courchene's face had a tight little smile on it. Whisper knew the look to be the one of that night by the rendezvous fire when he had slipped the knife to Beeler. "Ah," he said, "it is the secret. We have many good things. See, we share with our friends." He fashioned a stick through the buffalo tongues and hung them on the spit over the fire to roast.

Whisper moved over next to Jim and talked in a low voice. "I do not like these men," she said. "They are like snakes who live under rocks and come out only to strike and spread poison. Be careful."

Jim nodded. "Beeler sent them. I don't care what they said. They're liars."

Bolton and Jakes began arguing over one of the buffalo tongues, tearing the meat from each other's hands. Courchene yelled at them. "We bring the choice buffalo for our friends and you two fight like wolves."

"We're entitled to our share," Bolton said. He was cutting on one of the tongues and stuffing large pieces of meat into his mouth as he spoke.

Fiddler had moved over to Whisper and Jim and was talking while Courchene and the other two argued. "Might be some hair raised before the night's over," he said. "Maybe their own if they don't step lightly."

"I'd wager some other bunch had them tongues," Jim said. "I'd say Courchene killed for them. There's nary a one of them three got the know-how to take tongues and cut them proper, like those were cut."

Whisper nodded. "They are snakes."

Courchene had gotten the other two to quit fighting. "It is a silly thing," he said. "They fight like children." He glared at the two men as he cut a piece off one tongue and shoved it out to Whisper. "Eat."

Whisper shook her head for a long while, making it plain she did not like the men or their offerings.

Bolman spoke up, grease running from his mouth. "Word's around that the hills are crawlin' with Blackfeet. They're out lookin' for a Flathead Injun woman." His eyes went quickly to Whisper before returning to the buffalo tongue he was chewing on.

"What else did you hear?" Jim asked.

"This is just what we heard," Bolton said quickly. "We heard it from Bridger and his men. It seems that young hoss, Walking Head, is back down here and he's got a mighty hot fire for that Flathead squaw. He's got a bunch of fighters from his own band. Piegans and Bloods are in on it, too. Lots of horses and robes for whoever gets her." He looked quickly at Whisper again. "Catchin' that squaw would make some Injun buck rich in short order." He laughed.

While he talked, Courchene and Jakes had both been watching Jim and Whisper. Courchene still had the tight smile that made him look like he knew something and was enjoying his secret. The muscles in Jim's face grew taut, like the sinew of a bowstring.

"I don't suppose there's a white hoss around that's got the same notion?" He eyed Courchene hard.

Courchene laughed nervously again. "*Non.* There is not a smart man who would try and bargain with the Blackfoot, Walking Head. *Non.* He likes the hair of the Long Knife." He drew a circle in the air around his head with his knife, then pulled his fur cap off like it was a scalp. He laughed and the other two laughed with him.

"That Injun gal's got some scalps of her own," Fiddler put in. "She handles a Green River knife with the best of them. And I hear French scalps are bringin' a premium these days."

The laughing stopped. Courchene's face lost the little smile. His features were hard, now, and his mouth had turned into a tight line. "It is not trouble that we wish," he said. "We come only for the beaver, and to share the buffalo tongue. *Non*, not for trouble. We come as friends. But now you talk of French scalps."

"You bring trouble, you get trouble," said Fiddler. "Here's a hoss that can still scrap with the best of them."

While the talking went on, Whisper searched the forest around them. She knew Courchene for what he was and felt certain he would have others sneak in behind them while they talked. Courchene's eyes told her this, also, for he took quick looks into the forest himself. Only his face had begun to show small signs of worry, like whoever was supposed to come from behind should be here and was not.

Then off in the forest a sound of men yelling could be heard. Horses were snorting and they could hear the sound of brush and wood breaking. Jim put his Hawken into Courchene's face.

"Come as friends, did you? I'll blow those weasel eyes off your face if someone else shows up here that knows you."

Then the horses in camp began snorting and pulling against their reins. "Hold them, Jakes!" Courchene ordered.

"Stay put!" Jim yelled.

Jakes stayed where he was and the horses reared, snapping their reins and running off into the night. Whisper's breath caught in her throat. At the edge of the camp was a huge shape that came into the light of the fire, reared up high on hind legs, and roared.

Chapter 11

RULER OF THE FOREST

Courchene jumped to his feet, ignoring Jim's Hawken in his face. He screamed and ran out of the camp, following Jakes and Bolton, who were already trying to find their horses.

"Holy Lord A'mighty," Fiddler said in a half-whisper. "Head for the trees!"

The huge bear was still on hind legs, towering high above the fire. His mouth was dripping froth and the light of the fire caught the blaze of hate that shone from back within small eyes.

Jim pointed to the grizzly's left side. "He's got an arrow in him! He's blood mad!" As he turned to leave camp, he yelled at Whisper, "Let's find a tree. What are you waitin' for?"

Whisper picked up Jim's Hawken where he had dropped it. She leveled it and pulled back the hammer, keeping the fire between herself and the bear. One good shot was all she needed.

Jim yelled again. "Whisper, get away from him! You can't stop him with one shot!"

The bear came back down on all fours. A low, heavy growl came from the throat of the bear, a deep sound that rumbled from within and made Whisper's hands shake. Jim continued to yell at her while the bear again roared in anger.

Whisper kept the Hawken leveled. "Rise again on your hind legs, mighty ruler," she said to the bear. "I need to see your heart."

Whisper moved to the left, then right, as the grizzly tried to circle the fire to get at her. He was crouched and his back was one huge hump where the white-tipped hairs bristled like the quills on a porcupine. His jaws popped open and shut, like the snap of a large trap, exposing yellow-fanged teeth longer than a man's fingers. His head swayed back and forth and foam dripped from his mouth like water. At times it seemed as if he were ready to spring over the fire, but then he would claw furrows in the ground as does a mad buffalo, and roar loudly with his head held up. Whisper waited for the chance to shoot. It could only be once, and it had to kill. "Stay back!" she yelled to Jim and Fiddler many times as they started to come to where she was. If the bear saw them, he would surely charge and the safety of the fire would be lost.

Then the grizzly rose to his hind legs once again, towering as high as the two lodges. Whisper's breath left her. Just across the fire, not a full man-length away, was the most powerful creature she had ever seen. She brought the Hawken to her shoulder. Now was her chance to shoot.

The Hawken boomed just as the grizzly began to lower himself back to all fours. Instead of reaching the heart, the ball passed through the front of the bear's nose and blew a gaping hole just under his left eye. The grizzly roared with a fury matched not even by the loudest of thunder. Then the camp was showered with burning wood and embers. The grizzly had charged through the fire at Whisper.

Whisper found herself on the ground, being dragged like a doll. She screamed. She tried to pull away. Then she heard, "Stop fighting me!" It was Jim. He was pushing her up a tree. She had been numb with fright and he had grabbed her and pulled her behind Fiddler's lodge just as the bear had come through the fire, swinging wildly with huge claws. Now Jim was climbing a nearby tree himself.

Below was the bear, nearly blind with rage. He was tearing Fiddler's lodge to small bits with his teeth and claws. The teepee poles snapped like kindling wood and the buffalo hide covering ripped like a cloth torn by a woman. Blood flowed in streams from the bear's nose and eye, and flew in all directions with each rip and tear. Underneath mounds of shredded hides and shattered wood lay the Hawkens. There was no chance to find them.

"Where is your horse pistol?" Whisper yelled to Jim.

Jim shook his head. He hoped the bear would either bleed to death or run out of the camp in blind rage. Whisper hoped someone could shoot the bear from behind while he was tearing up the lodge. She did not think a bear that size would die very soon from a wound to the nose and eye.

Then the bear was standing under her tree, growling and roaring up at her in rage. He had heard her yelling to Jim. She climbed higher in the tree, for his massive claws nearly reached her. The grizzly roared and began shaking the tree with all his might. Cones and needles showered to the ground. Dead limbs snapped as Whisper lost her balance and caught herself once, then twice. The tree swayed and jerked like a small sapling in a windstorm. All Whisper could see beneath her was a mouth full of teeth opened wide.

"Hold on, Whisper!" she heard from below. Jim had gone into their lodge and had found her lance. He was carrying a burning stick from the fire and in his eyes was the look of a creature who would fight to the death. He clamped his knife between his teeth and took firm hold of the lance in one hand, while holding the burning stick up in the other. Then he was beside the grizzly, thrusting the fiery torch up under the huge jaws. The flames brought a deafening roar as the greasy fur around the bear's nose and mouth caught in a sudden burst of fire. The grizzly stumbled back, pawing at the burns that covered his nose and ears. He dropped to all fours again, rubbing his face in the dirt and swinging his powerful claws in blind rage.

Again Jim charged the bear, yelling wildly and swinging the burning stick. The grizzly reared and started for Jim on his hind legs, swinging his claws in front of him and roaring in rage. Jim held the torch high to blind the grizzly. The grizzly swung wildly at it, knocking it from Jim's hands. Jim took firm hold of the lance and studied the bear's massive chest. His chance had come. With all his might he hurled the lance. The steel point struck home with a slicing thud.

For an instant the grizzly stood still in shock, holding the long shaft that stuck out of his chest with his paws. The bear coughed up a mouthful of blood, then another. Red foam dripped from his jaws and the growls and roars gurgled in his throat. His lungs had been ripped apart by the lance.

The bear staggered, as if to fall, then lunged at Jim with all his strength. Jim scrambled sideways and fell among strewn tree branches. A rush of air above his head told him that the claws had missed him by inches. Then Jim was up as another blow scattered pine cones and needles in a spray over his back. He could hear the grizzly's labored breathing and the blood that rattled in torn lungs. Still the bear had awesome strength.

Jim was up a tree, the bear tearing chunks of bark and branches off below him. Jim climbed higher. The grizzly began shaking the tree, as he had with Whisper. He heard Whisper shouting below, saw the arrow she shot into the bear's neck. Then came another arrow that went deep into the chest. Again the grizzly was on all fours, refusing to die. Whisper was chanting, shooting more arrows. Finally, with a tremendous roar, the bear stumbled and fell sideways. The pointed end of the lance stuck high above the grizzly's back, pushed through from the chest in the fall. There was no more roaring or snarling, only labored breathing that died down lower and lower as each moment passed.

Jim and Fiddler came down from the trees and stood beside Whisper. The grizzly's eyes had turned glassy and his huge legs twitched for a moment. Then there was only stillness.

It took most of Sun's next passing to sing the strength and victory songs. It had been a double victory, for the grizzly had killed one of the enemy. The arrow Jim had seen in the bear's side had been that of a Blackfoot, and in the stomach they had found the warrior's remains. The arrow had been painted to gain great medicine from the bear. But the Blackfoot had failed in his quest and paid for it with his life.

Whisper thanked Amótkan for giving Jim strength and courage. "But it was you, Whisper, not me," Jim had said, to which Whisper had replied, "My arrows only made him die sooner. If you had not come to where I was falling out of the tree, I might have also found a place inside the bear's stomach, much the same as the Blackfoot."

In her songs to Amótkan, Whisper asked Him to put the grizzly's strength into the child she carried within her. She ate a portion of the bear's heart, so that her own child would have the same courage. This would be especially good if she had a boy-child, for a heart with such strength would make a truly great warrior of which all the Salish peoples could be proud. She ate portions from the bear's front and hind legs, so that her child would be strong of limb, and a piece from the tongue so her child's voice would be strong. Yes, a bear such as this could give her child unusual power, if it so pleased Amótkan.

Also, the bear would provide items that would be useful to them now. There was the skin with all that long hair, which would be of much warmth during the upcoming cold moons. The fat would mix well in cooking and be a cover on the body for warmth in the cold, and for protection against flies and mosquitos during the warm moons when the air is filled with their buzzing. Whisper would use the teeth for decoration. Her dress and leggings would look as fine as any that could be found.

Best of all, though, were the claws. She would make a necklace for her husband, Jim, the bear-slayer. It would symbolize his strength and courage. He was now a warrior of great honor, to be looked up to by not just Whisper's people, the Salish, but by all Indian peoples of all lands. In hand-to-hand fighting, he had killed the great white-tipped bear. "You are an honor to me and my people," she would tell him when she put the necklace on him. "Those who see you wear it will treat you with honor. Other women will look upon me with envy to have such a brave man for a husband. They will know I live in a lodge that is safe by day and night."

All these things she would say to Jim after her baby was born, for she could not put anything around her or her husband's neck while she carried the child. To do so could mean strangulation for the infant at birth. After her baby was safe from the womb, she would honor her husband.

Whisper's thankfulness and joy was shared by Jim, but still his face did not show the true happiness that should come with a victory over a bear of this size. He was listening to Fiddler talk about Courchene and the other two who had come to camp the night before.

"It seems we just plumb weren't meant to trap beaver hereabouts," Fiddler was saying. "If it ain't bear problems, it's skunk problems."

"Why don't you suppose they stole our horses?" Jim asked.

Fiddler grunted. "Can't see that they would've had time, bein' they all hightailed it so fast and left us to reckon with Old Ephraim here ourselves. Yellow-bellied varmints is what they are!"

"Beeler's out for us, no doubt about it," Jim said. "But I'd just as soon fight them as run. There ain't enough of them to scare me."

"There's plenty of them," said Fiddler. "Now we find

new beaver ground or risk loosin' our hair. Maybe you loosin' your woman.''

"Damn, Fiddler! I said Beeler don't scare me!"

Fiddler had taken a map he had drawn of the mountains and surrounding country out of his pack. He opened it and looked at Jim with a hard eye. "You'd best listen up, Jim. It ain't Beeler that puts a scare into me. He'll work the Blackfeet agin us, you wait and see.''

"Beeler don't make friends with Blackfeet. That's crazy, Fiddler!"

Fiddler looked up from his map. "You just can't see the nose you got on your face, can you, Jim? Beeler's got a score to settle with you, plus Walking Head wants your gal. Now you heard them talk about rewards of horses and robes to the man who'll bring your gal to him. And you know damn well that Courchene's got a Piegan Blackfoot for his squaw. You seen her yourself just this summer at rendez-vous on New Fork.''

Jim nodded. "That's a fact.''

"Well, it don't take no school-learned dandy to see that all Beeler's got to do is have Courchene and his squaw let on to the Piegans that they know where the Spirit Woman is and that Walking Head will give many presents for her. Then, by God, we've got Blackfeet on our tail in no time!''

Jim thought a moment, then nodded. "I never thought of it that way.'' He looked over to Whisper.

"Fiddler speaks truth,'' she said. "It is not good for us to stay in this place. There have been too many omens.''

Jim nodded again. Omens. He had come to believe in Whisper's inner feelings. He never questioned her now, not since that day in Pierre's Hole when she tried to tell him it was not a good day to fight. Now he had a bad back from a Gros Ventre war club to prove she had been right.

"Where to then, Fiddler?'' Jim asked.

Fiddler went back to the map, tracing a finger north toward Crow country. "I'd say the Yellowstone. Crows don't mix with Blackfeet and we've got Rotten Belly on our side now. We'd have a fairly safe winter.''

"Could be hot grounds down there, too," said Jim. "Not Blackfeet. I mean there's Company men all over that country."

"American Fur don't put the scare into me Blackfeet do," said Fiddler. "You're right, though. We'll have to keep a sharp eye." He shook his head like there was no hope for a good trapping season, then got up and went over to his pile of gear.

Whisper watched Jim. He was also looking heavy-hearted. She knew the reason for their feelings, for Jim had told her many times how it was in the mountains now that so many Long Knives had come to trap the beaver. There was much competition for trapping grounds and the wealth that came from selling the beavers' fur to those people far toward where the Sun rises. She knew that the American Fur Company had many holdings on the Yellowstone and that any but Company trappers would be looked upon with disfavor by the Long Knife leader, McKenzie, who lived where the waters of the Yellowstone and Big Muddy meet. Jim had told her also that things were much the same with Old Gabe and Broken Hand, the names given to the Long Knives Jim Bridger and Thomas Fitzpatrick. They were part-owners of the RMF, the Rocky Mountain Fur Company, and were equally as determined to take the beaver for themselves. The Sublette brothers, Robert Campbell, and the black Long Knife, Jim Beckwourth, were all members of the RMF, and would surely be seeking the best waters also. There was much hatred between the two companies and fighting was a common thing. Whisper was glad she had come to know Rotten Belly of the Absaroka people. Now the Crows were her friends and she could help Jim trap the beaver on their lands and know they would help her if she needed them.

Fiddler had come back from his pile of gear with a jug and was drinking from it between puffs on his pipe, now and then offering it to Jim. His gaze went alternately from watching Whisper work on the grizzly to far out over the mountains, like he was looking at something that might not be there much longer.

"These hills ain't the same as they once was," he said. "No sirree, not when I first come. And last night showed it plain as day." He took a long drag from his jug. "This old hoss would just as soon be born again someplace else."

"There's good beaver around yet," said Jim.

Whisper saw Jim also looking out to the mountains as he spoke. He hadn't meant what he said. He just didn't want Fiddler to sink into one of his low moods again. Fiddler was feeling low often now that there were getting to be more and more Long Knives in the forest.

"There's beaver yet," Jim repeated. "We'll have ourselves a good year, Fiddler. You bet."

Fiddler had taken another long drag from the jug, and the whiskey had spilled down his front. His eyes were watery and sad-looking. "Maybe so," he said. "Maybe we'll have a good hunt yet before the snow melts come spring. But it can't last. You know it can't, Jim. You're as good a young hoss as I ever set trap with. But, damn, there ain't many days left we can do as well as we once did. Not with men takin' each other's scalps just over good beaver diggin's."

"We'll make a go of it on the Yellowstone," said Jim. "Maybe there'll be Blackfeet, and Company men, and Beeler, and Old Gabe's bunch all at once." He patted his Hawken. "But, by damn, we'll get our share of beaver!"

Chapter 12

SHAHAPTIAN

Buffler!'' said Fiddler, peering through his spyglass at the broad flat below. "They be buffler all right!''

Whisper sang a song of thanks and praise to Amótkan. Their journey to the Yellowstone had begun, and already Sun had crossed the sky seven times. They had traveled over much ground and the nights were showing the chill that bit deep in the high mountains now that the Moon of Late Autumn was nearly gone. Now their fires would cook plenty of meat and their stomachs would not be empty during the upcoming cold moons. They would also have hide to replace the lodge destroyed by the bear, new hide that would be strong and resist the cold wind that would come before another moon passed.

Whisper was also thankful that the meat would be buffalo, for it meant her child would now be nourished well within her and would know the meat from the great beast that fed her people.

The buffalo looked black and large against the brown and red of the meadow below. Their noses were buried

deep in the cured grass, searching out the green shoots at
the base of each plant that always come when the air cools
and brings storms of mixed snow and rain to the foothills
and mountains. Jim and Fiddler both looked a long time
through their spyglasses, counting the animals and figuring
the best way to get close to them without them knowing.
Whisper, too, studied the herd intensely. It would take careful planning to make a good number of kills and insure a
plentiful supply of meat. Buffalo were hard to find this far
from the bottomlands, where they lived during the cold
moons.

Whisper said the prayers needed before the hunt. Then
they moved down to the flat, staying behind the cover of
trees as much as possible and keeping the wind to their
faces. The buffalo were not keen of ear or sight, but would
become quickly alarmed at a strange smell. The herd was
not big, but there would be plenty of meat if they were
patient and chose each kill carefully.

Whisper knew Jim and Fiddler also were wise in the
ways of the buffalo. Fiddler told stories of how many of
them would fall to the power of the Hawken rifle before
the herd became alarmed and ran. A good shot could kill
an animal where it stood while the others grazed without
notice. Many could fall in this manner until a change in
wind and the smell of blood sent them stampeding away.

Whisper watched while Jim and Fiddler prepared their
Hawkens for the hunt. They would select cows from the
herd, for they were the best to eat this time of year. Cows
that had not raised a calf during the year were the fattest
and were preferred. They would not take any bulls, for they
would not be as good until the spring when the warm
moons made their meat more tasty.

They were close now, hidden in a patch of timber on a
hill above where the buffalo grazed. Fiddler cursed, wishing
they were on the same level as the herd. A killing shot a
hand above the brisket was going to be hard from where
they were. But there was no way to get closer. The hunt
must begin here.

Whisper held her bow and two arrows, a quiver of more arrows slung over her back. She held the horses ready. Most of the hunt would be from horseback, for they were close and the herd would surely run as soon as they heard the sound of the big Hawkens. She patted Red Thunder on the nose and neck and talked to him in a low voice, telling him to run swiftly and to show the courage of a good buffalo pony. She fed him sweetgrass and let him smell it, much the same as she had before the races in Pierre's Hole. He would need all his speed this fine day.

Fiddler and Jim each shot and two of the herd fell. The buffalo did not run, but stood for a moment with their tails raised in alarm at the noise. Then they went back to grazing. Jim and Fiddler recharged their Hawkens and fired again. This time Jim's animal stumbled into a lumbering gait, bellowing wildly and running into others. The herd broke and ran.

"We must hurry!" Whisper yelled.

Whisper was already on Red Thunder and Jim and Fiddler had both jumped on their own ponies. The buffalo made a mad dash out of the small meadow and down onto a larger flat just below. Whisper had a good feeling as she rode Red Thunder through the tall brown grass at full speed. The wind whipped through her hair, and she felt as though she had wings as her big horse ate up the ground between them and the stampeding herd. Whisper looked across to see Jim and Fiddler gaining ground on the opposite side of the flat. She smiled. They both were yelling and whooping, scaring the herd into a tight column between them and Whisper. Like Whisper, they knew the ways of hunting on horseback. Soon they would push the herd so tight the buffalo would fall and turn into one another. Then they would mill about in confusion, grouping into a mass that had no leader. Whisper, Jim, and Fiddler could then move their ponies in a circle around the confused buffalo, choosing the ones they wished to kill. This was the method of hunting buffalo used by most Indian peoples with horses. It was called the surround.

The herd was grouping tighter and the surround would soon form. Whisper fitted an arrow to her bow and picked a big cow. She leaned way over to one side of Red Thunder and moved him in close to the cow, then away again as sharp horns just missed the pony's belly. They moved in close again and the cow bellowed in fear as she ran, froth running heavy from her mouth. Whisper leaned over and shot an arrow low, just behind the animal's shoulder. The cow bellowed again, her eyes rolling in her head, and lurched into a cartwheel that left her kicking in death behind the herd.

Jim had killed another cow on the other side with his own bow. He whooped loudly and raised the bow in a sweeping arc over his head. He then held his horse back as Whisper and Red Thunder forced the lead cow into a sharp turn that sent the rest of the herd into a confused tangle. The surround was complete now, and well-placed arrows and Hawken fire brought more buffalo down. When they had finished, seven had fallen and awaited skinning. Meat and robes would be plenty.

Whisper sang the Good News Song—the buffalo song of her people. Her knife worked swiftly on one of her kills while Jim and Fiddler started on two others. Again she thanked Amótkan for their success in finding the buffalo and downing them. She said prayers and recited chants so that the surviving buffalo in the herd would not look upon the kills this day with disfavor. She prayed they would understand that she and those with her needed this meat to live. The buffalo were sacred and to disregard their feelings would mean great misfortune—maybe even death.

She built a fire to roast some of the parts while she butchered. The best parts were the heart, tongue, and kidneys. These parts were worthy of being eaten raw. It was a good way to feast, cutting choice parts and dipping them in the juices of the gall bladder.

During the entire morning, Whisper butchered and packed meat. Though the air was cool, it was a happy day. She sang songs of joy as she built up her fire. Both Jim and Fiddler had eaten much already and were getting lazy. They were seated next to a fire, using a fallen buffalo for a backrest. From the sound of their laughter, they were telling stories. Whisper smiled. It was good that Jim's happiness had spread to each one of them, for it made the day even brighter.

Sun had nearly crossed the sky when Whisper crouched behind the buffalo she was skinning and fitted an arrow to her bow. Jim and Fiddler had seen also, and had their Hawkens ready. Coming down the hill was a column of riders. But they were not coming fast and they had their hands raised in peace.

"Shahaptian," Whisper told Jim and Fiddler. "Nez Percés."

"I'll be damned," Fiddler remarked. "They're a far piece from home. And travelin' the wrong side of the hills to get back, too."

"It is strange to see them here," Whisper agreed. "They are hunters, but also wear the paint of war."

Whisper greeted them in sign and in their own tongue. The Nez Percés were neighbors and brothers, and it was common for such tribes to know the tongues of each other. They were happy with the offer from Whisper to share in a feast of fresh buffalo meat. Then their leader put his hand over his mouth in surprise.

"Spirit Woman!" he said to the others. "It is the Spirit Woman!" They all backed away.

"The Nez Percés are brothers of the Salish," Whisper assured them. "There are only good feelings between us."

It was their leader who spoke. "That is good to hear, Spirit Woman. I, Little Hawk, am a brother to the Salish, as are all the others here. But there is much talk of you since the gathering of the Long Knives in Pierre's Hole. It is said that you are a wild person who hates everything and everybody. It is said that you are more powerful than any warrior who has ever lived, and that you can kill many with one stroke of the hand."

"It is only the Blackfeet I wish to kill," said Whisper.

"The Siksika, the Pikuni, and the Kainah are all dogs. They crawl like the snake and live in holes. Death to them all!" Whisper raised her fist.

The Nez Percés screamed their war cries. The word Blackfeet brought hatred to their faces.

Little Hawk spoke again. "It is true. I, Little Hawk of the Nez Percé, hate them. They kill my people and burn our villages. And for this we have taken revenge." He yelled and raised his lance. It was lined with fresh scalps.

"Aiee!" said Whisper. She looked at the scalps closely. "They come from the Pikuni! Are they here?"

"Pikuni—the Piegans!" Little Hawk hissed. "Three suns past. They are now dogs lying dead, with wolves cleaning their bones." He raised his head to the sky and yelled again. "It is Piegan meat the wolves fill their bellies with!" The other Nez Percés yelled war cries. Little Hawk went on speaking. "It was my wish to kill them all, but there were Long Knives and other Piegans that came and they were many in number."

Jim turned to Whisper. "Did he make the sign for Long Knives?"

Whisper asked Little Hawk, "Is it true there were Long Knives with the Piegans?"

Little Hawk nodded. "It is true. It was a strange thing to see Long Knives among warriors of the Blackfoot peoples. But it was that way."

"How many?" Whisper asked.

Little Hawk held up three fingers. "There may have been more. I do not know. We were few in number and did not wish to fight."

"Looks like you called a bull's-eye on what Beeler had in mind," Jim said to Fidder. "He had Courchene hightail it with his squaw to the Piegans right away, didn't he?"

Fiddler grunted. "I'd lay odds Courchene had them Piegans with him the night he came to our camp on the Snake. Them Piegans were back in the trees waitin' until dawn when they could come in and get us. We had luck with us that Injuns don't fight at night, and then that bear comin'

into camp. It's a funny way to look at it, but like as not
that grizzly saved our hair.''

Whisper knew now that Fiddler's words were true. She
could remember the strange feeling she had had that night
that eyes were watching from the trees. She remembered
Courchene's eyes looking past them into the night and
growing impatient. Now she knew he had been waiting for
dawn to come. But the grizzly had come instead.

"That grizzly saved both our hair and our horses," Jim
said. He turned to Whisper. "Ask the Nez Percés where
they saw the Piegans and the Long Knives."

Whisper spoke and Little Hawk raised his arm and
pointed north.

"There were many lodges of Pikuni, the Piegans, north
of here. They are less than a sun's ride from the Burning
Mountains, the place called Colter's Hell by the Long
Knives. This is where we killed this many Pikuni." He held
up both hands and left two fingers down on one hand.
"This is where we saw the Long Knives and more Pikuni
riding together." He laughed. "But that was after we surprised the small hunting party and made them meat for the
wolves!" He screamed a war cry. Then he showed with
pride three nearly dry Piegan scalps that hung from his war
shield. He singled one out and held up the coal-black lock,
stained with bear grease and blood. "This Pikuni dog told
me before I cut his head off that many more of his people
were near, and that many of their Siksika brothers had journeyed down from their homelands far to the north. He said
that these Siksika were led by Walking Head, a fierce and
brave warrior. He said I should sing a good song of victory
this fine day, for the other Pikunis and their Siksika brothers
would soon avenge his death. Then I would sing my own
death song. I laughed as he spoke, but now I know the
smoke of many Siksika lodges rises above the river of the
Stinkingwater. The words were true. Walking Head jour-
neys with many Siksika warriors to join their brothers, the
Pikunis."

Whisper cast her eyes to the northeast, to where the river

of the Stinkingwater flowed. "I have heard that Walking Head is now in these lands," she said to Little Hawk. "You say he is camped on the Stinkingwater?"

Little Hawk nodded. He pointed to some of the other Nez Percés with him. "Rising Deer joined us with his own hunting party one sun after we met the Pikunis. He spoke of many Siksika lodges, a journey of seven suns from here, on the river of the Stinkingwater where it meets the river of the Bighorn. There were as many lodges as the fingers of ten hands twice. The center lodge was painted with the sign of the weasel—it is Walking Head's medicine."

Whisper nodded. "Yes, the weasel is Walking Head's medicine."

Little Hawk continued. "That is why we travel these trails instead of those that would take us to the Three Forks, then on over the High Divide and into our own lands. There are too many Pikunis. There are too many Siksika. Together they are more than the buffalo. We cannot fight so many. Yes, we will follow the trails that take us farther south and into the valley where the waters of the Snake flow. Then we can turn back north and cross the mountains into the valley of the Kamiah, our homelands. It would not be wise for us to stay in these lands of the Yellowstone, not when there are so many Pikunis and Siksika."

"Yes, you are wise to travel these trails and stay away from the Pikunis and the Siksika," Whisper said. "But they are many suns from here and now is a time for rejoicing, for you have many Pikuni scalps to dance over this fine day. We will feast and tell stories of war."

Fires were built and the feasting began. The Nez Percés were happy to share in their victory over the Pikunis. It meant the Spirit Woman and her Long Knife husband were brothers of the Shahaptian peoples. They were also happy that Whisper had offered them meat to show that her heart was good. They had found buffalo themselves, but the Spirit Woman had told them to save it. She knew that it was a long journey to the valley of the Kamiah and that the cold moons would begin before they once again saw their people.

The dancing and singing went on past sundown and into the night. There came howls from the wolves off in the forest in answer to the cries of the Nez Percés. Moon—the Sun of the Night—had risen full when the dancing stopped and more feasting began. The pipe of peace was offered back and forth from the Nez Percé leaders to Whisper, Jim, and Fiddler. Soon it was time for sleeping. Sun would come before long and it would be time for the Nez Percés to begin a long journey back to their homelands.

Whisper knew that their own trails to trap beaver on the Yellowstone would be longer now. They could not travel north along the edge of the mountains, for this would take them to the Stinkingwater. They would surely meet Walking Head and the Siksika if they went that way, and Whisper knew that going straight north would take them to where the Pikunis camped with Courchene and the other two Long Knives. Now, before they slept, Whisper would talk with Jim and Fiddler. It would be a hard journey.

"No sense in travelin' the east slope to the Bighorn," Fiddler was saying. "With Walking Head and all them Blackfeet, we'd go under for sure."

Jim was looking at Fiddler's map. "Why don't we just go straight north up over the top, Piegans or no Piegans? Just go smack over the top, the shortest way."

"That's hard country this time of year," said Fiddler. "Snow can be over a man's head."

"Not this year," said Jim. "Not yet."

"It only takes one storm," Fiddler argued. "Just one pile of clouds up there and we'd go under for sure."

Whisper knew Fiddler's words to be true. The Yellowstone was high snow country. It was not a place to be when the cold moons came. Whisper knew the Pikuni were only traveling the high trails because they wished to find her. But there were surely more Pikuni traveling to the west, also, to make sure that their numbers covered all the trails. They wanted the Spirit Woman to have no escape.

"We'll hit Blackfeet no matter which way we go," said Jim. "The hills are full of them. I say we go the shortest way, over the top. We travel by night and hide out by day, and maybe miss them."

"Don't you think our hair would be safer with the Nez Percés?" Fiddler asked. "Maybe we could stick with them until we hit the lower Snake, then head straight north into the Gallatin. Then we could cross the mountains east into the Yellowstone."

"My God, we'd lose half our trappin' season! Besides, that's all high country too. The snow settles just as deep in the Gallatin as it does anywhere in these mountains."

Fiddler lit his pipe and puffed. "Maybe we should go south for beaver. Forget the Yellowstone. Hit the Siskadee maybe."

"What? And stand elbow to elbow with half the fur brigades in these hills? Hell, that's worse than no beaver at all!"

"We must worry about Walking Head," Whisper told them both. "He is in these lands and he will travel until he finds me, no matter where we are. But if we stay in the land of the Abaroka, the Yellowstone, we will have Rotten Belly and his people to fight with us. Yes, he has told me this and you both have heard him. The Crow are a good fighting people who hate the Blackfeet. And they are many in number."

"Yes," Jim nodded. "She's right, Fiddler. Rotten Belly wants Blackfoot hair worse than anybody I know." He glanced over at Whisper. "Well, maybe not everybody."

Fiddler nodded. "For a pretty lady, she sure does have a powerful cravin' for Blackfoot blood." He winked at Whisper and gave her a smile through his grey tangle of beard. "You wouldn't miss a chance at Blackfoot hair no matter what, would you? I'm thinkin' you'd vote to go over the top even if Rotten Belly wasn't in on this thing with us."

"It is not something that is funny," Whisper told Fiddler. "Those dogs have killed many of my people. I shall hate them as long as I live."

"Well," said Fiddler, "it won't be a cinch whichever way we decide to go. Maybe you two have something. Maybe our best bet is to make Crow country for the winter." Then he puffed hard on his pipe. "My guts are crawlin', though. We're headed smack into a hornet's nest."

Chapter 13

AT THE FIREHOLE

A streak of grey broke into the black sky in the east. The horses breathed heavy steam and ice covered the hair around their mouths and noses. The snow was crusty and crunched beneath their hooves. It had not fallen nearly as deep as it sometimes did when the cold moons came to this place, but it covered the leggings above the knees. Frost coated the lodgepole pines that stood tall and close together on this high plateau. The trees grew thick here, high up where the waters of the Yellowstone began, and broke open into large meadows that were good grazing for elk and their brothers, the moose. This high land was a sparkling sea of white that Sun would bring little warmth to this fine day. Whisper brought the buffalo robe up tighter around her neck while a wolf, far off on a hill somewhere, howled long and deep into the still air.

"Mighty high country," said Fiddler. "And mighty cold."

Fiddler's words were true, but the memories of times past warmed Whisper's heart. Just behind was the giant lake of

the Yellowstone, where Whisper and Jim had spent their
first night of love in the warm water pools along the shoreline. "Hot pots" was the name Jim and Fiddler had given
them, a name most all the Long Knives used. Yes, her first
time with Jim as a man had warmed her greatly, and the
memories of it warmed her now. She smiled to herself.
Now she carried Jim's child within her; it too made her
feel warm, though the air swarmed with crystals of ice.

In the east, Sun had turned the sky red. It was time to
stop traveling and hide out until night once again mixed
them among the shadows of the forest. Their journey had
been slow, and Sun would cross the sky again as many
times as the fingers on one hand before they reached the
safety of the Absarokas in the valley below. Yes, it would
be many more nights of eating cold meat and sleeping without the warmth of a fire.

"How much further to where we stop?" Jim asked Fiddler.

"Four, maybe five miles."

Jim cursed. "It's light, Fiddler. We're sittin' ducks for
Blackfeet."

"We'll make it," Fiddler said. "Just keep your eyes
peeled."

Ahead was a valley that spread out from a river called
Firehole by the Indian peoples. It was a place where the
ground rumbled and steaming waters sprayed high into the
air. Bubbling holes of mud were scattered among the pools
of boiling waters. It was a place where voices spoke from
the earth, a land of demons and spirits. It was part of the
country called Colter's Hell by the Long Knives. This was
the place Fiddler wished to go until darkness once again
returned, for there was not a Piegan alive that would risk
meeting the bad spirits there.

Whisper had never been to this place, but had heard
many stories from the elders in her village. It was a legend
among all the Indian peoples of the forest and plains that
Firehole was once the home of fire spirits. Long, long ago,
when fires and burning rocks burst forth from far beneath

the surface, they made all the land a sea of liquid rock with
flames as hot as Sun that killed all the living things that
were once there. The fire spirits conquered all the land and
were very powerful for many, many years. Then the Great
One—whom Whisper and her people knew as Amótkan—
made these evil fire spirits go back far below the ground,
so that trees and flowers and birds could once again live
on the surface. But the fire spirits did not live quietly in
the middle of the earth where the Great One sent them.
They make loud noises and cry out in endless roars from
below, saying they again wish to live above the ground.
Their anger makes boiling waters shoot high into the air
and the ground soft and unsafe to walk on. They cover the
ground with their spit, which comes out of the holes of hot
water. It is white and yellow and makes a hard crust over
the ground so that trees and grasses cannot grow well. Yes,
this was the land of the fire spirits, the bad spirits that hate
all living things.

Whisper knew if they made it to this bad place, they
surely would be safe until nightfall. This was a place feared
by all Indian peoples, for the Great One warned of the bad
and evil things that happen there. It was told that all those
who go near were at the mercy of the fire spirits. The air,
thick with hissing steam and strange smells, hid holes of
hot mud and water that would swallow a man or woman
whole and drag them far below.

Whisper did not wish to go there, but Jim had told her
she must either live among the fire spirits for a short time
or see death at the hands of the Piegans. So she told herself
not to be fearful, for Jim had powerful medicine against
evil spirits. He mocked them and laughed at them. It was
not a good thing to do, but Jim was powerful and the spirits
left him alone. Whisper had known this to be true the night
they had first come to the warm waters and had shared their
love. She had been afraid that night and he had calmed her.
She smiled again with contentment. Her husband, Jim, was
more than a man.

Sun rose above the trees and put a bright shine onto the

snow. Off the trail a small band of elk watched them pass by. The trees were full of birds and squirrels making morning sounds. Whisper watched and smiled as a number of blue grouse flew from high in the branches of a nearby pine. Then her heart stopped. In the sky was smoke from Piegan lodges.

"It's not much further now," said Fiddler. "But we ran smack dab into them, didn't we? Couldn't have done better with an escort."

They crossed the river called Firehole and the horses drank deeply of the warm water. The shores were lined with elk feeding on grass kept free from snow by the warm steam. Ducks of different colors and sizes fed on green shoots that also never saw ice. Farther down, a flock of Canada geese honked and flapped their wings along the shore. Now only a short distance lay between them and the rumbling ground. Already they could see clearly the steam and stinking gases that clouded the air and made the trees along the Firehole hang heavy with ice.

Suddenly the forest was filled with the scolding of squirrels and jays among the trees. The elk looked up from their feeding and began wading across the river, looking back into the thick timber along the shore. A feeling came over Whisper, a feeling she had had just before the raid on her village by Walking Head and the Siksika. Jim and Fiddler both had their Hawkens ready. Whisper fitted an arrow to her bow.

"No use lollygaggin'," said Fiddler. "Let's roll for the hot pots!"

In a few jumps the horses were at full speed. The trees seemed to come alive with screaming Piegans. "Hang on!" Fiddler yelled. "The hot pots are just over the hill!"

The pack horses trailed behind Fiddler, struggling against their ropes and the treacherous footing in the snow. The Piegans gained on them easily. Whisper and Jim took positions on either side of Fiddler and got ready to meet the first charge. Whisper and Jim were both yelling Salish war cries. It was a good day for fighting.

The Piegans were not surprised by this, for they knew the Spirit Woman would be fierce and hard to capture. They knew her man, Jim Ayers, to be a bold Long Knife who would not be easy to kill. The Piegans knew this and had prepared themselves. No doubt they had danced around fires of war to make themselves ready. Their warriors were painted and ready for battle. Screaming war cries of their own, they rushed forward and crowded close on both sides. They, too, felt it was a good day for fighting.

Just ahead the trail wound its way through a thick grove of trees. Fiddler was yelling for them to hold on. If they could keep the Piegans off them until they reached these trees, they would find safety. It would be hard for the Piegans to fight in the heavy timber, and the geysers and boiling mud lay just beyond the trees.

Whisper's arrow found its mark in a Piegan. He fell sideways from his horse and bounced in the snow. She heard Jim's Hawken explode and saw another of her hated enemies fall. She fitted another arrow to her bow and waited for others to crowd in close. They did not come. Instead they were riding hard up the trail. They yelled and screamed as they rode by, making obscene signs and laughing. Then Whisper saw the reason for their happiness. They were closing off the trail where it led into the trees.

Red Thunder was running full speed when they hit the line of Piegan warriors, who had been trying to get out of the way. Red Thunder crashed into a Piegan horse and rider, knocking them sideways and causing a pileup with another horse and rider. Whisper lurched forward, but caught herself as Red Thunder stumbled to his knees in the pile of kicking horses and screaming Piegans. Fiddler rushed by with the pack string and on into the safety of the trees. She saw Jim fire his Hawken at a warrior who was jumping onto one of the pack horses. Then, as Red Thunder regained his balance, Whisper was met by three Piegans.

One of the Piegans clutched his neck as one of Whisper's arrows went clear through and out the other side. He gagged and choked, coughing blood down his front and

onto his horse. He tried to sing his death song, but it was
drowned out as his horse threw him face first into the snow.
The other two fell upon her with screams. One held Red
Thunder's bridle while the other tried to pull her onto his
own horse. She hit him several times with her fists, one
blow drawing blood from his nose. But his eyes were crazy
and he would not let go of her. His medicine was strong.
He tugged at her but she would not let go of Red Thunder.
She was, herself, wild-eyed and crazy. She kicked and
pulled hair, and freed one arm long enough to pull her
knife. It went into his ribs and he yelled. His eyes became
crazier then before. Whisper held her knife ready to strike
again when a heavy blow to her middle doubled her over.
The other Piegan who was holding Red Thunder had his
war club raised again when a ball from Jim's Hawken
spilled his brains over his face and neck. Without a sound,
he fell forward onto Whisper and smeared her with blood
and matter as he flopped into the snow.

Whisper was doubled over Red Thunder's neck, struggling for breath. Her lower body was exploding with pain
that seemed to burn her in half. Nausea came and her mouth
filled with stomach fluids. Her vision became shot with
stars and black streaks, and she clung to Red Thunder more
by instinct than by conscious effort. She could hear yelling
and screaming, and more Hawken fire. Once or twice came
the whisper of an arrow. There was a blurred green and
brown around her. Trees. More yelling and rifle fire. It was
all a haze. The only thing that was real was the pain from
her abdomen that flooded her mind and tried to force her
legs into letting go of Red Thunder. The hide covering on
her saddle was wet and sticky beneath her. The wetness
traveled down the inside of her thighs and soaked her leggings. Each lurch and jump that Red Thunder made brought
stronger stabs of pain that shot through the constant burning
inside her. The stars and the blackness became more intense. "Whisper! Whisper, hang on!" she heard Jim shouting. "God damn, we made it! We made it!" Fiddler was
yelling. She heard the voices and the words, but her mind

made something else of them. "Pikuni! Pikuni! They are killing you as you ride! You will fall and the Pikuni will have you!" She felt hands upon her, tugging at her. "They have me! They will not take me from Red Thunder!" She cried out in anger. She tried to strike her enemy. "Whisper, it's me! Stop it! It's Jim!" But her mind said "Pikuni! Pikuni!"

The arms pulled her from Red Thunder. No, they could not take her. How could they have taken her from the horse? She must have had a moment of weakness. She lay on the ground; her breath was a series of gasps.

"Whisper? It's Jim. Can you hear me?"

The pain came on strong again. She screamed.

"Whisper. It's me, Jim. Whisper? God, she's all blood!"

"She's hurt inside, but she ain't coughin' it up."

"Her dress, her leggings. They're covered. Where's it all coming from."

"Below, I'm thinkin'. Down below."

"Below? Oh, God!"

"She's quit bleedin'. She won't die."

"Oh, God. She was so happy. . . . No. No!"

"Jim, it's happened. Thank the Almighty she ain't dead. Thank the Almighty we all ain't dead."

"Pikuni!" Whisper sobbed. She tried to rise. Jim and Fiddler held her down. "Pikuni!"

Then all was blackness.

Chapter 14

ANGRY WATERS

Whisper leaned against the trunk of a dead fir tree, drinking a herb tea she had prepared for herself. "I cannot remember what happened," she said. "I only remember fighting with two Pikunis, then a fire in my stomach. A fire that still burns."

Jim turned to Fiddler. "How did you know to breathe into her like that? I thought she'd gone under for sure."

"She needed air," said Fiddler. "She was hurtin' so bad she couldn't breathe right. An old coon on the Musselshell done the same thing to me once when I was even younger than you. We'd best worry about them Piegans now."

Sun had passed to the west and the air had taken on the afternoon chill that came in the cold moons. Still the Piegans circled the geyser basin and screamed war cries. They knew the Spirit Woman was hurt and could not ride for a time. They knew it would now be much easier to capture her and kill the two Long Knives with her. But there could be no fighting where the bad spirits lived.

"They'd like us to come out in the open and away from

these hot pots," said Fiddler. "There ain't nary a one of them cares to risk his hair in here among the bad spirits. No siree." He laughed. "The Devil's always been on my side."

"I'll fight with them all right," Jim said through gritted teeth.

"Jim, don't go bein' foolish," Fiddler warned. "All we've got to do is wait them out."

"They're pretty cocky now," said Jim. "They'll get careless here before long and I'll pick one of them off." He turned to Whisper. "I know someone besides me who'd like a few Piegan scalps right now."

Whisper nodded but said nothing. Except for the nod, she had shown no sign of having heard what Jim had said. The shock was still strong within her. But now the shock was not because of the blow from the Piegan war club; it was knowing the baby she had dreamed of holding in her arms would not be there. Her eyes were blank.

"She'll come out of it," said Fiddler. "She needs time."

From the forest beyond the geyser basin came the sound of drums. Smoke rose in columns from three different fires. There were shouts and war cries. There was dancing. The Piegans wished to fight very badly.

"Makin' medicine," said Fiddler. "Maybe they figure to come in here after us."

"I aim to see to it some Piegans go under," Jim said. "One way or another."

Fiddler thought a moment. "There's ways to have us a little fun and get some Piegan hair at the same time." His face was serious. "But only if you was to tell me you'd do it my way, Jim. This old hoss just about went under once today. That's a plenty."

"You lay it out, Fiddler." Jim was already checking the charge in his Hawken. "I'll follow and do what I'm told. Blackfoot hair is what I want."

At the edge of the geyser basin was a small meadow surrounded by trees. From here the Piegan dancing and war songs could be heard plainly. Their fires were just over a small hill.

"Stick to cover here in the trees," Fiddler instructed Jim. "Don't blink or they'll see you. I'll go out a ways and get their attention and we'll work it how we planned."

Whisper then appeared. Her pain showed with each step she took, but her eyes were hard and determined. "I wish to fight also."

"You ain't in no shape for that," said Fiddler.

"I wish to fight."

"You need rest," said Jim.

Whisper shook her head. "We fight together. All of us."

"Stick with your man, Jim, then," Fiddler said. "Seems a fact you want hair worse than either of us."

Whisper and Jim nestled down into the snow behind a clump of willows. They waited there while Fiddler walked out into the meadow. "This ought to be slick," said Jim, as Fiddler fired his Hawken, recharged it quickly, then lay face down in the snow.

They did not have long to wait. Piegans appeared in the trees across the meadow and gathered to talk about the Long Knife lying still in the snow. Whisper smiled to herself. Yes, it was a good trick. There would surely be a warrior among them who would come out to strike the first coup. There would surely be one who wished to gain honors for himself so that he could boast to others of his bravery. Yes, there would be one who would come soon.

One of the Piegans kicked his horse and moved out to the edge of the meadow. He looked all around at the trees and the brush. His eyes stopped on the willows where Jim and Whisper hid. Whisper smiled again. He could not see them, she knew, for she had made sure there was plenty of snow over them for covering. The Pikuni dog could look, but he could not see.

The other warriors were chanting now. Then another warrior moved his horse out from the group. Whisper's breath caught in her throat. The two Pikunis were going to race to see which one would reach Fiddler first and strike first coup.

"I wonder if Fiddler figured there'd be more than one?" Jim's voice was filled with concern.

The two Piegan warriors started across the meadow to Fiddler, their horses at a dead run. They were both yelling with their coup sticks stretched out in front of them. Fiddler's game with death was now Piegan sport.

"Fiddler!" yelled Jim. He was up and out of the willows and down on one knee. His Hawken spit smoke and fire.

One of the Piegans slumped forward over his horse and dropped his coup stick into the snow. The red of blood mixed with the white and brown spots on his horse and he tumbled off and lay doubled up in agony. The other jerked his horse to a stop just before he reached Fiddler and looked across to where Jim was recharging his Hawken. Then Fiddler rose to his knees and again the smell of gunpowder filled the air. Two dead Piegans and Jim and Fiddler were laughing.

Whisper did not laugh. She rose from her hiding place among the willows and shot an arrow into the Piegans. It was a long shot and traveled in an arc, but it hit the warrior she had aimed at. He yelled and tugged at the shaft that went through his upper leg and into his horse's ribs, pinning him. Whisper got ready to shoot another arrow but she did not. The warrior had dropped the trade rifle he had been aiming at Jim. In their joking and laughter, Jim and Fiddler hadn't noticed the Pikuni with the trade rifle. Either one or both of them could have died the same way as the two Piegans lying in the snow.

The wounded Piegan was still tugging at the arrow that had pinned him to his horse. The horse had become terrified and was running circles in the meadow. The Piegan screamed at the others to help him as the horse began bucking and jerking sideways. But the others had fear in their eyes. Strange things were happening to them here. Men jumped up out of the snow from nowhere to kill their numbers with the firestick. The Spirit Woman had survived a blow to the stomach that would have killed some warriors and surely wounded most others badly enough to make them lay in blackness upon the ground. But now she shot arrows and made horses crazy. It was not a good day to fight anymore. They moved back out of arrow and rifle range.

Then other Piegans came. They yelled war cries and showed painted shields and lances. Whisper knew they were not from this village that had attacked them. They were from a different village and led by a different war chief. Whisper's eyes narrowed. Now she knew why they were here. Among their numbers was Courchene and the other two Long Knives.

"Come on Courchene!" Jim was yelling. He was pointing to the wounded Piegan, whose horse had stumbled to its knees and was slowly bleeding to death. The Piegan had broken the arrow shaft and freed himself from the horse. He was now crawling toward the yelling Piegans, leaving a trail of blood in the snow. "Show them Blackfeet your medicine, Courchene. We've been waitin'."

The wounded Piegan tried many times to rise to his feet, but always fell back down. He was losing blood from his wound and becoming weaker as the snow and cold worked to fill him with shock. Jim continued to mock Courchene and the other Piegans. Courchene even took a shot, but the ball fell harmless in the snow ahead of them. Then for a time, all the Piegans did was yell.

"If they won't come on and fight, why don't they leave?" Jim asked.

"They're figurin'," said Fiddler. "They don't hanker to lose any more warriors if they can help it. But Courchene's got them riled again and talked into gettin' revenge one way or another."

"It is I that will take revenge!" said Whisper. She had just returned from scalping the two dead warriors and was holding her bloody trophies in the air for the other Piegans to see.

This brought the Piegans charging in closer. But as soon

as Jim and Fiddler raised their Hawkens they moved back again. Their screaming became intense and they showed themselves obscenely, yelling every form of mockery they could think of.

Fiddler laughed. "It sure fries them when they lose their dead and wounded to the enemy. Then to see their kin lose hair before their eyes, that's a thing that's hard for them to stomach."

"There's more hair left to take," said Jim.

He walked over to where the wounded Piegan struggled in the snow. Though the warrior was nearly breathless with exhaustion, he pulled his knife and lunged at Jim. With a laugh, Jim kicked him flush in the face, nearly knocking him out. The other Piegans screamed in rage.

Jim made sign for them to come ahead and save their brother, though they would get death from the firestick as a present. "You are all dogs!" he told them in sign. "You should be gathering wood with your women. You are all children. You fight like children. I will now give you something to remember me by."

Whisper was by Jim's side. "Let me kill him."

"No. I've got a present for this one." He took the wounded warrior by the hair and pulled him across the meadow and to the edge of the geyser basin. The warrior tried to struggle but could not find the strength to overcome Jim. He again was kicked in the teeth.

Steam rose in a dense cloud from a large pool of boiling water. It was bubbling violently and had just sent up a tall spray that had turned to a white mist high in the air. Small rivulets of water pushed over its top and hissed as they ran down to join other hot waters in a stream below.

Jim again made sign. "You are dogs to hurt my wife, the Spirit Woman. For this you will pay. You are going to lose one of your brothers to the bad spirits who live far below in the ground. Yes, the fire spirits will have your brother."

The Piegans screamed and rode up as close as they ever had, before once again retreating for fear of the rifles. It

would be a terrible thing for their brother to be taken by
the fire spirits. It would be hard for them to return to their
village and tell his widow she would never see her husband
in the Great One's Land because he now belonged to the
fire spirits who lived in the ground in the Burning Mountains.

"This is bad medicine, Jim," said Fiddler. "You could
have them on our tails from here on in to get revenge for
this."

"This is their payment for what they did to Whisper."

Fiddler turned to Whisper. "How about you, pretty lady?
Their guts will boil every time they think about you."

"I wish it were all of those dogs who were going to the
fire spirits this fine day."

Jim made more sign, telling them they all had black
hearts and that they all had black hearts and that they had
been foolish to try and capture the Spirit Woman for Walking Head. He told them their greed for robes and horses
had cost them many warriors this fine day and that it would
cost them many more in time. Yes, the fire spirits would
want more of them once they had the taste of Piegan blood.

The Piegans were yelling again, but now their voices had
a quiver of fear in them. Courchene began shouting at them,
trying to arouse the fever to fight back. But this was an evil
land and Jim's words were those of a man possessed by
the spirits that dwelled below in the ground. They were still
mad but they did not all wish to die.

Jim pulled the warrior closer to the boiling pool. "It is
time. You will now see this dog you call a brother go into
the ground. And you will see that he has a child's heart."
He made a circle around the warrior's head with his knife
and ripped off the scalp. He held it high in the air and
waved it. "I have the hair of a dog!"

The Piegans screamed again. Courchene was yelling at
them with a fervor even greater than he had shown earlier.
The wounded warrior was now singing his death song in
high, shrill tones. Jim pushed and there was a splash.

The wounded Piegan would not cry out at first for he did

not wish to have the heart of a child. The terrible waters soon ended his silence, for the meat was boiled from his bones and rose to the surface around him. The rivulets of water that spilled out over the pool turned dark with blood. The Piegan warrior cried out and sank below the surface. It had happened in the time it takes to blink the eyes twice. He was now with the fire spirits that rumbled deep in the ground.

Whisper shouted loud and long at the triumph over the Pikuni warrior. "Dogs! Dogs! You terrible dogs!" She doubled over in pain, still yelling.

Fiddler came and took her back in among the geysers. "Hey, now. You've got to rest easy!"

"They are dogs!" she sobbed, pounding her fists on the ground. "They have killed the child in my body. They are dogs!" She sat up cross-legged and raised her head to the sky. She began a high, wailing song of mourning.

Jim went back out to the Piegans. "Do you hear my woman, the Spirit Woman? Do you hear the sounds she makes? It is for you Piegan dogs to know that the fire spirits that live here are speaking through her voice. Now that they have your brother and like his blood, they say they want more of you. Yes, they want to take more of you into the rumbling ground." He began to laugh. "And they are saying they will come out of the holes of boiling water to take you!" Then he screamed a loud cry that was eerie to hear. "Ha, I see them now." He pointed to a pool of boiling water that was turning into a geyser. As the water sprayed high into the sky, he yelled, "Yes, they are coming out to get you. Ha, ha! They will get you all!"

The Piegans turned their horses and rode them hard in a broken formation through the trees, yelling chants and calling upon their own guardians to save them. They would ride as fast as they could; they would not listen to Courchene and the other two Long Knives. No, the fire spirits would not get them.

Jim came back and threw the scalp he had taken hard against the ground. "Damn, I wish I had the whole bunch of them to pour down them hot pots." He laughed. "Did you see the look on their faces, Fiddler, when that geyser went off?"

"We ain't out of this yet," said Fiddler. He picked up his Hawken and looked around. Whisper was still singing her song of mourning and as Fiddler looked through the steam and mist, his face fell to a deep frown. "Best get set for more trouble, Jim. My guts just cramped up on me. And there's bad medicine crawlin' up my back."

"Courchene?"

Fiddler nodded. "He and those other two will be a sight worse to fight than all them Piegans put together. They won't let no hot pots stop them."

Jim looked around again, pulling the hammer back on his Hawken. "But, God, we can't see a thing in here for the steam."

"Yep," said Fiddler. "That's why my guts are so tight."

Chapter 15

WOMAN WARRIOR

More of the day passed and they did not see Courchene and the other two. But that did not mean they would not come. Those who knew them knew that the things they would do to others, just to get the fur of the beaver, made them snakes. And Beeler, the man they worked for, was even more of a snake. His hatred for Jim would drive him to do anything. Whisper thought back on the strange things that had happened. Beeler had used Courchene well in his plot to kill Jim and have her captured for trade to Walking Head. Beeler knew Walking Head and his band of Siksika were now in these lands looking for her. And he knew Walking Head would pay many robes and horses to anyone who brought the Spirit Woman to him. Since Courchene had a Piegan wife, it was easy to make contact with that tribe of the Blackfoot nation, the brothers of the Siksika. It was easy to tell the Piegans that the Spirit Woman was in these lands and could be captured easily. It would mean much wealth and honor for them. Yes, Beeler's trick to send the Piegans after her and Jim had almost worked.

Whisper knew the danger in leaving the geyser basin for the lower Yellowstone lay not in the Piegans now, but in Courchene and the other two Long Knives. But where were they? Maybe they had left with the Piegans, content to wait and fight again another time. But surely they must think that now was a good time to come, for they knew if they succeeded in killing Jim and Fiddler, they would have no trouble with her. They knew she could not resist them for long; the pain within her was too great. And they would also have the advantage of the steam in the geyser basin for cover.

These things weighed heavy on her mind. She did not know if Courchene and the other two would be smart enough to attack them again while she was still weak. But even the danger of fighting in a place where she could not see her enemy could not take Whisper's thoughts from the sorrow she now felt. Losing the child she had carried and loved even before its birth was almost more than she could bear. She had spent many days in dreams of caring for the little one. She had spent much time planning for the arrival of her newborn sometime in the Moon of the Camas. It was to be a great moment in her life, a time of rejoicing and happiness. She would then be able to give Jim, the man she loved so much, the most meaningful thing they could ever posses together: a child of their own flesh and blood.

Now all that was gone and her heart was sad, sadder even than when she had realized she might never see her mother again. After all the searching and praying and asking, she had finally told herself that Amótkan had taken her mother to the Land of Eternal Summer. It was at the time they had found the herd of buffalo, and joy had spread through them for finding meat, that she had told herself she would no longer think of her mother. Whisper had asked Amótkan for His help in taking her thoughts from the woman called Little Grasses, for now she had a good husband whom she loved dearly and she was carrying his child. For this reason she must be always happy and cheerful. Thinking of her mother could only rob her of the joy she would need to share with Jim over the little one inside her. All had been well then, until this bad day, this day that had cost her a child. Whisper's head hung heavy with grief.

Jim came over and held her closely. She put her face into his shoulder and cried softly.

"I know it's bad now," he said. "But another time will come and things will work out."

"Jim, I am so sad. My heart is heavy and I feel like dying."

"No, no." Jim held her even tighter. "Don't think that. We'll have another child."

Whisper continued her mourning, singing low songs of sadness and drinking herb tea to reduce the pain and swelling in her abdomen. They would not travel that night, she told Jim and Fiddler, for she must have more time for mourning. The night hours would be spent praying for the spirit of the child lost from within her. Jim and Fiddler both told her they would stay as long as she wished. Jim blamed himself for what had happened.

"All because of my greed," he said. "I was so all fired set to trap fresh grounds on the river below that I plumb didn't care about anything else. Now look what's happened. Well, it's no more for this hoss. I don't aim to set another trap as long as I live."

"Do not say those things," Whisper said. "It is because of you that I am alive. This trail through the Burning Mountains was the shortest way to cross over. And this place where we are now has saved our lives. Maybe if we had taken any other trail we would all have died. No, Jim, do not say that you caused this bad thing to happen."

"We could have gone south," said Jim. "Even west. I just wanted beaver on the Yellowstone. The best beaver. Now I would settle for anything else, if only this hadn't happened."

"No, Jim," Whisper argued. "Walking Head would have come no matter where we looked for the beaver. The Yellowstone is the best place for us. We have even talked at counsel fires about this. Yes, it was decided we would journey to the Yellowstone to find the beaver. Rotten Belly and the Absaroka have spoken to us as brothers. These are their lands and they will fight with us. We all spoke in agreement to journey on this trail. Jim, do not blame yourself for what has happened.''

Sun had traveled far over in the sky. A glow of gold evening light shone through the frost in the air. As Whisper lay resting in her buffalo robes, she heard the sound of horses nearby. She quickly motioned to Jim and Fiddler. It was surely not the Piegans who had come back, not after the scare Jim had put into them earlier in the day. If it were the Siksika, or another band of Piegans, they would not have come so late in the day. Morning was the best time for fighting.

Whisper listened closely. The men were off their horses and she could hear the sounds of rifles being cocked. There was no doubt who it was. She could hear their footsteps, though faint, as they walked slowly through the steam. Courchene and the other two had decided that sunset would be the best time to attack. It was the hardest time of the day to see, and shadows took on strange forms.

Whisper heard them stop. Then the footsteps began again. They had split up and were coming from three ways. Though her pain was great, Whisper slowly got to her feet. If she was to die this fine day, at least it would not be lying like a rock on some buffalo robe. But her thoughts did not linger on her death. Nor did she think that Jim and Fiddler would meet death this day. It was anger, not fear, that helped her get to her feet and make ready to fight. Courchene and the other two had caused the death of the child she had carried. It was they who had led the Piegans to this place. This would be the last time, Whisper thought, they would ever again sneak around trying to kill someone. Courchene and the other two would sing their death songs before Sun left the sky.

Whisper gave the sign to Jim for bow and arrow. They must be silent. Though the men would surely cry out when they were hit, there would be no noise from the Hawken firesticks to give away their location.

Whisper's pain was great, almost unbearable. But the anger she had once again charged herself with put strength in her body and cleared her mind for thinking. She fitted her bow with an arrow and set out into the heavy steam and mist, while Jim did the same and took another direction. Fiddler would stay with the horses where they grazed at the edge of the geyser basin. He would use his Hawken and get the first shot at anyone who came near. It seemed strange that Courchene had not come with more men to fight. But there was no doubt the Piegans had told him they would fight no more this day. And it was likely they would never fight in the Burning Mountains again, for the fire spirits had caused them to lose many of their numbers. It was a good day for the fire spirits, Whisper thought, for the bones of three Long Knives would soon join those of the slain Piegan in the boiling waters.

Whisper was out in the geyser basin now, her bow ready, her eyes peering through the heavy steam for movement of any kind. The boiling pots bubbled and hissed. Mud popped in some of them, while others were deep caverns where the waters growled and the stinking breath of the fire spirits came up from below. Whisper made herself forget her thoughts of the evil spirits that lived in these pools and caverns. Her thoughts must be kept strong and ready for the moment she met Courchene or one of the other two. The steam was thick and another person could be seen only if they met face to face. That would not be good, for surely the gun could be fired more quickly than the bow.

Then Whisper saw an opening ahead. The pools here had once contained stinking, boiling waters like the others, but were now only empty caverns that were black and deep. In the middle of the opening stood a group of stunted fir trees. They grew crooked and were covered with a thick layer of frost. Here was the spot she needed to gain an advantage on her enemy. The air was clear and the trees gave her good cover. It was a place where she could see those coming before they saw her.

The moments passed slowly and the pain again fogged her mind. She could not let this happen. She took a handful of frost from a limb above her and rubbed it on her face and neck. It took her breath away and made her skin tingle, but it also cleared her mind. She must keep her eyes extra sharp now, for Sun had fallen nearly level with the trees and the light was leaving the forest.

Then to her left, she saw a form in the steam. It showed only for a moment before it was again lost from sight. Then the form appeared again, a form that was cautious and moved slowly. Whisper crouched low and held her bow ready. Now she would wait and see who the form was.

After endless moments, the form stepped out into the clearing. It was Bolton. His face looked as mean as the night he had been in their camp on the Snake with Courchene. He was quiet when he walked and careful of the sounds he made, but that would not save him now. Whisper carefully pulled her bow and aimed it through the branches.

The arrow caught him full in the chest, passing almost clear through until only the feathers could be seen. His mouth dropped open in shock and surprise. A rush of breath escaped his lungs, but he did not cry out. He just stood with his mouth hanging open, looking at the arrow in disbelief. He did not see Whisper until the second arrow went into his chest next to the first one. Only then did he look up in his last moments of life and see the Indian woman standing with her scalping knife in her hand, waiting for him to fall.

The Long Knife died on his feet without a word. His Hawken made a thud as it hit the ground. His eyes rolled back in his head and he pitched forward onto his stomach. From his back, the two arrows stood up straight with heads pointed skyward. They made a raw, rasping sound as Whisper pulled them through the Long Knife's body. They were good arrows and she would need them again. With a quick twist of her wrist and a sharp tug, the scalp came free and she placed it in her belt. She would have shouted a cry of victory, but it was still not safe in the geyser basin. There was plenty of time for the scalp dance after Courchene and the other Long Knife were also dead.

The shadows were very long now and Sun was partially hidden by the tree tops. Vision in the geyser basin was very difficult now. Things that moved were not easily seen. With the coming of night, an eerie silence fell over the place where the fire spirits lived. Whisper could hear them hissing and spraying water, but it was hard to see anything. Again she fought the fear that crept into her, a fear taught since early childhood. Evil spirits liked the darkness and this was the time they liked to prey on those still living. Whisper prayed to Amótkan to protect her now that night was falling. She must not give in to her fears; it could mean her life.

Then Whisper heard the loud blast made by a Hawken. She heard footsteps, running footsteps, and then a loud splash. More screaming began and died out as it was muffled by boiling water. Again all was silent. Only the bubbling geysers and the hiss of steam was heard. Then came a man's voice from nearby. It was Jim.

"Courchene! Drop your rifle!"

Suddenly a man was right next to her. It was Courchene. His eyes were wild and crazy, and his hands clutched at his blood-covered chest. He saw Whisper and screamed, then turned and ran into the steam.

Another shot sounded and another scream was heard that quickly died into moans.

"Whisper? Whisper, where are you?" It was Jim's voice again.

"Here," she answered.

Then Jim was there, holding her tightly. "Thank God! I thought one of them had put you under."

"Have you been hurt?" she asked.

"Just a little burn from hot water is all," he said. "I got one of them and he fell into a hot pot."

Behind them, in the steam where they could not see,

Courchene lay dying. He was calling for his mother, and praying to the Virgin Mary for mercy and forgiveness. His eerie cries and moans caused the fear to come back into Whisper.

"It is his spirit crying out! We must leave here!"

Jim laughed. "No, it's just a dead man breathing his last. We've got one more to find yet."

"He lies somewhere behind me," Whisper said, pulling the scalp from her belt. "He fell to my arrows."

"I should have known you'd get your licks in," said Jim. "Let's get back to Fiddler."

"Is he hurt?"

Jim shook his head. "That old buckskin is as tough as they come. He caught Courchene sneakin' up on the horses and planted a knife right in his brisket. Courchene must have had a thick hide to get way over here." He laughed.

Courchene was dead when Whisper and Jim reached him. He lay in a pool of blood that looked dark and lumpy in Sun's last rays. Jim pried his Hawken from his stiff fingers and took the powder and ball.

"That hoss won't have any need for these where he's goin'," Jim said. Then he quickly pulled Courchene's lifeless body over to one of the boiling pools and pushed it in. Whisper covered her mouth so that her own spirit would not escape as she watched the body seem to come back to life before the boiling water cooked it apart and left only small pieces of buckskin floating on the surface.

Fiddler was waiting by the horses. "Damned if you two didn't scare me some. What with all that noise out there, I thought maybe you'd both gone under."

Jim laughed. "This gal of mine here is too tough for that. She put Bolton under herself, without nary a sound."

"It takes a heap to put you down, I'd say," Fiddler told Whisper. "This old hoss could never fight like that after takin' a Piegan war club in the guts. No sirree, you're somethin', you are!"

Jim and Fiddler found the horses and supplies the other two had left on picket. In the supplies was the firewater the

Long Knives called whiskey. Jim and Fiddler drank and told stories to one another of this day and others past. Whisper could not share in their victory and happiness. Fiddler's words about the Piegan war club, and the pain within her, once again returned her to deep sorrow. She told Jim and Fiddler she must spend time by herself. Jim was not happy that she was leaving the safety of the geyser basin, but did not try to stop her.

Whisper took Red Thunder and rode to a place where she could be alone. The light of a cut moon shone into the forest and the air stood cold and still. Far off wolves began howling and others began answering from closer by. Now she was away from the fire spirits in the geyser basin and could pray and sing songs of mourning without them hearing. This was the kind of place that would be best for her. It was a lonely spot by a small creek that was nearly covered over with ice.

"Please do not come, Little Fox, little owl who is my guardian," she said. "I wish to be alone this night, for no one can lessen my sadness."

She took out her knife. Her long black hair fell into the snow, and when she had finished cutting it off, she also cut her arms and legs. The voice of the creek running its icy waters over the rocks in the channel became mixed with the high wails of a woman in mourning.

Chapter 16

A MEDICINE SHIELD

The cold moons passed and the warm moons came, bringing a green to the valleys and parklands. Sun shone warm and brought grass and flowers to the meadows and fields. The buffalo shed their hair and calves appeared among the herds in great numbers. On all the waters ducks and geese led their broods among the rushes and cattails along the shores. Spotted fawns came to the deer, and wobbly-legged calves followed their mothers as vast elk herds began their summer migration to the high country. All the land was filled with joy, for this was the time of new births and rejoicing.

This was also the happy time of year for all the Indian peoples. The hard moons were past, and once again the lodges would need no fires to keep them warm when Sun left and darkness came. Whisper knew her people, the Salish, would soon be performing the First Roots Ceremony. This was a special and honored ceremony, for it marked the time of food gathering. They would be thankful in this time of Earth's greatest fruitfulness. They would pray for a good year of gathering the bitterroot and the camas, the most cherished of plant foods among the Salish people. Yes, the women would sing happy songs as they journeyed to the hills and fields with their root-diggers and their hide gathering bags. Small children would romp and play among the grass and flowers, their laughter bringing joy to all who heard them. It was a time of newness, a time of freshness, and for all the many lands that Amótkan watched over, it was a time of rebirth.

Whisper felt none of the happiness which usually came to her when the warm moons arrived. Her heart still weighed heavy from the loss of the child she had carried within her. Though her body had healed and her wounds of mourning were now scars that no longer bled, her mind still went back to that time in the Burning Mountains when the Piegan war club had ended her childbearing songs. Neither Jim nor Fiddler could help her. She had gone within herself and would let no one break the shell she had closed around her.

It had made Jim's days heavy as well. He had hoped the coming of the warm moons would ease her sadness. Nothing he did or said seemed to help. Though he and Fiddler had had as good a year at trapping as anyone in the mountains, it was hard for Jim to rejoice over their good fortune with Whisper as sad as she was. Neither the Siksika nor the Piegans had ventured near, for the Absaroka were powerful here, and Rotten Belly's warriors were always ready to defend against the raiding Blackfeet.

One day as Jim made ready to set his traps, he found Whisper sitting at the edge of the river. The sky was dark and a late spring rain had begun to fall. Whisper saw him come over to her and she knew it was time for them to talk.

"It is an unhappy day," she told him as he sat down beside her. "My heart is grey, like the sky."

Jim cleared his throat. "You've been this way for a long spell, Whisper. I've tried to help you every way I know how. It's time you told me straight out if you'll ever be the same as you once were.''

"Have I not been a good wife?"

"You have. You've been good that way. But you're not yourself and I can't make myself happy when you just mope around and won't talk."

"I am afraid things have changed forever with me," she said. She bit her lip and tears flooded her eyes. "I fear I cannot give you another child." She hung her head.

"Why not?"

"Because of the Piegans. They have hurt me inside. I have not conceived a child since that time we fought in the geyser basins."

Jim took her hands in his. "Now, Whisper, that don't mean a thing. You've got to stop this. You'll ruin your whole life, and mine. We'll have children in time. Nothin's wrong with you, it just takes time."

"No, time cannot heal me." She wiped the tears from her cheeks and sniffed. "Time cannot change what has happened. That part of me died during the fight with the Pikunis. Yes, they killed the childbearing part of me."

"That ain't true," Jim argued. "How can you feel that way when you always have to care for yourself at the woman's time of the month? Those are crazy words."

"Do not call me crazy, Jim!" Whisper shot back. "I am not crazy." Again she broke into tears.

Jim took a deep breath and rubbed his head through his hair. "Damn, don't be so touchy. I didn't mean you was crazy. I only said you don't have to worry about yourself."

"We have slept together many times since the fight at the geyser basins. Still I have not conceived. I should be with child again by now."

Jim threw up his hands. "Hell, we was together more than a year before that night at Jackson's Lake, when you told me you was carryin' a child. It ain't been half that long now and you're worried. I can't figure you out."

Whisper got up. "Maybe some day a part of you will

die. Then you will understand." She turned and was lost in the forest as the rain began to come down harder.

Sun crossed the sky many times and Whisper still did not change. Jim kept trying to bring happiness back but each time he spoke, or brought a present, he failed. He failed even to bring a smile anymore, for Whisper seldom smiled now. She was changing. She thought less and less of her duties as a wife, and did not care for the lodge or keep the camp neat and clean like she had in the past. The nights of love became fewer and fewer. "How can we have any little ones this way?" Jim would ask her. He never got an answer. It was as if he was living with a different woman, a woman he did not know. Her eyes had become hardened and the light within them was not bright. Now she often journeyed off by herself. Sometimes she was gone overnight. Jim had quit worrying about her; there was nothing he could do. He knew she was preparing herself for something.

Then one morning she showed up at camp with a hoop covered with stretched deerhide. She hung it on her lance near the entrance to their lodge and looked straight at Jim.

"Is that a medicine shield?" he asked her.

"It will be a medicine shield some day," Whisper said. "After the proper prayers and fasting, I will know how to paint it. Then it will be a medicine shield."

"Why? What is all this?"

"This is a bad time in my life," she told Jim. "It is a time of trial. It is a time of war for me. I must kill Walking Head."

"What?"

"Yes, I must kill Walking Head. It is the only way in which I can avenge those things which have happened to me in the past. It is the only way I can once again achieve happiness. And I must do it myself. It is the only way."

Jim shook his head. "You can put up a fight with the best of them, no doubt about it. But that hoss ain't about to sit still and let you put him under."

"It will take strong medicine," said Whisper. "It will take much preparation. I will need the blessing of Amótkan. I will need a time of fasting and praying. I must do the things a Salish man does to become a warrior. I must make a vision quest. This must be done in the homeland of my people—the Bitterroot. Yes, I must visit the Medicine Tree."

Whisper had talked before of the Medicine Tree, the sacred tree of her people. She had told Jim many times before that she wished some day they would journey across the High Divide into the Bitterroot, where she could again pray beneath the Medicine Tree, as she had in her youth. Now it was not a matter of wishing she could go; it was something she had to do.

"I must leave soon," Whisper said.

Jim was silent a moment. "I can't figure all this. Did you ever think of what I might say?"

"I will wait until the season for trapping beaver is finished. I will help you with your work until then. After that, I will go."

"I mean what if I don't want you to go, Whisper?"

"I must go. You must not try to stop me, Jim."

"This is crazy!"

"It has to be!"

Jim blew out his breath in frustration. "Why? I mean, can't I at least go with you? Can't we at least round up some Flathead warriors maybe? Why go alone?"

"This is to be a sacred mission," Whisper explained. "Walking Head is the son of Emptép, daughter of the Evil One. Walking Head is on this earth to ruin my life. I know this now. I know I must find him and end his life; I must send him back to Emptép, where he and his spirit can no longer kill and destroy those things which I treasure in life. This must be done in a sacred manner. There can be no others there to make it a bad day for fighting. No, I must go alone."

Jim was still not able to understand. "I know how you live, Whisper," he said. "You have ways of doing things to keep you in good favor with your spirits. That's fine by me. I can even see where some of those things would be good for me now and then. But I can't get used to an idea that might take your life. Do you understand? I don't want to lose you. You mean too much to me!" He grasped her shoulders with his big hands. His eyes were half angry and half sad. "You might not come back!"

"That is something I must also face," she said firmly. "But I must do this thing. Voices have told me."

"The little owl?" Jim asked.

Whisper shrugged. "I do not know. Maybe. But, yes, voices have spoken to me. I must end Walking Head's life. It is for my peace in the rest of this life. It is for our peace. I do not care so much for my own peace as much as the happiness we will lose if Walking Head continues to make each day a bad one. This cannot go on. You must understand."

"But why can't I help you?"

Whisper's eyes flashed. "I have told you! It is a sacred mission!"

"Sacred, hell! You'll be killed!"

Tears flooded Whisper's eyes. "Jim, you and I have come to know each other as well as any woman and man ever have. But there are things that you as a white man will never understand about the Indian peoples. Please do not say what I have to do is not sacred."

"What do you want me to do, Whisper, just sit back while you run off and let them Blackfeet put you under?" He threw his fur cap against a tree. "I'm worried about all this! Why can't you understand the way I feel?"

"I will return to you after I have made my vision quest," Whisper promised. "I will not look for Walking Head until I have spoken to you."

Jim relaxed a little. "How long will this trip to the Medicine Tree take?"

"I will come to the place where the Long Knives are to meet for trading. The Siskadee—the Prairie Hen River. I will meet you there for the rendezvous of the Long Knives.''

"That's a long ways from the Bitterroot," Jim said.

"Red Thunder is strong. He can carry me many miles while Sun crosses the sky but once."

Jim looked at the shield. "So you've decided to become a warrior. When will you go back to bein' a wife?"

"I will always be your wife. After Walking Head lies dead, things will be as they always were."

Fiddler walked into camp, just back from the stream with fresh beaver skins. "Damn, the beaver shine here!" he laughed. The silence quickly took the smile from his face and he looked from Jim to Whisper. He threw the skins in a pile and started from camp. As he was leaving, he said, "I figured this day would come, and I don't aim to be a part of it. There's more traps to check."

"Wait!" Whisper called. "Fiddler, do not go."

"This is none of my concern."

Whisper went over to him. "Yes. You are a friend. Hear my words, Fiddler, that you might understand why these days are hard for me."

"I'd just as soon see you two patch things up."

"You do not understand," Whisper told him. She pointed to the shield. "I am leaving for a time. When the beaver's fur is no longer thick and the trapping is finished, I shall return to the Bitterroot, the land of my people. There I will go on a vision quest. I will not see Jim or you until the rendezvous of the Long Knives."

"She aims to get medicine," Jim put in. "She's out for Walking Head's hair."

"That's a tall order, Pretty Lady," Fiddler said. "It wouldn't be fittin' for you to go after that mean hoss on your own."

"You speak the same words as Jim," said Whisper. "No one understands."

After a moment, Fiddler said, "Understand is a mighty big word, Pretty Lady. This old hoss understands that all folks are different and they all figure there's things they've got to do. There ain't always a way to understand what they do or why they do it. A man has just got to accept those things and still be friends."

"You do not think that I am an evil wife? You do not think it is wrong for me to leave Jim?"

Fiddler looked over to Jim and then back to Whisper. "There ain't nothin' can compare to the two of you in the eyes of this old hoss. You're the same as my own flesh and blood, the two of you. But things happen a man can't be set for, things that ain't always good. You two got things to settle between yourselves and I've got traps to set."

When Fiddler had left, Jim turned Whisper to face him. "Stay with me until after rendezvous. We'll go together."

Whisper shook her head. "I cannot. I must do this thing myself. I must go soon. I can only hope time is on my side."

Jim stepped back from her. "I can see there's no use talkin' sense to you." His eyes had become dark and full of anger. "Go paint up and fight every day for all I care. Hell, you want to be a man, go ahead. But as for me, I don't roll with no man in my bed!" He turned and walked from camp.

Whisper sank to her knees in front of the fire. Her head hung down and tears dripped from her cheeks to the ground. She took a deep breath and settled herself. She knew she would have to leave now. She could not wait until the trapping was over; things would only become worse between Jim and herself. Now she was alone and it would be a good time to start on her journey, for she must be alone throughout her vision quest. She would meet Jim and Fiddler on the Siskadee after her visit to the Medicine Tree. She could only hope Jim would be happy to see her. She could only hope he understood by then. If there was no understanding in his heart by then, their paths would surely part. With or without Jim, she had a mission to complete. That was the way it must be.

Part Three

THE TRAIL TO WAR

Chapter 17

THE MEDICINE TREE

Sun was high and Whisper had good feelings. They were warm feelings that brought a mist to her eyes, for she was now back in her homeland. She was in the Bitterroot, the home of the Salish, and she was traveling familiar trails. She could remember times past when she played as a child along the flowing waters called Bitterroot, while her mother gathered the roots of the plant that had given this land its name. The Bitterroot was truly a beautiful place, a place where high mountains surrounded a long, open valley covered with grass and flowers of all kinds. It was called the Land of High Trees by other Indian peoples because of the beautiful forests that grew there. From under the trees flowed streams that were lined with bushes of every sort that provided berries each year for gathering. It was a land of plenty. Here the summer winds sang songs of joy while the meadows fed deer and elk and moose, and waters from sweet springs flowed through every draw.

During her journey, Whisper had seen Salish villages and had watched the people dig roots from the ground and pass the day in song. But she did not stop to visit. This was not the time to visit, for this was a mission she hoped would give her strength and independence. It would not be good to become involved with others at this time.

Whisper knew this would be the hardest thing she had ever done. It would take all of the strength in her being. She would need to give herself fully to the spirits, to walk among the clouds and be unafraid while they spoke to her and showed her things beyond human existence. She knew if she fasted and prayed in the right manner, she would learn much about the Great Mystery and the Universal Plan. She knew some of what she learned would make her happy; some things would frighten her. She could be feeble of neither mind nor heart during this time, for it could mean bad things for her. She would have to take time to know the meanings of the things she would see and hear. And she would have only herself to question on these things, for she did not now live in a Salish village among others who had made this journey. She would not have the privilege of discussing these things with a shaman or one of the elders. But she had known she would be on her own before she had started her journey. Because of this, she knew she must be doubly strong.

Whisper hoped Amótkan would tell the spirits to receive her and show her the things she wished to see. Though she had taken the tiny owl of the forest as her guardian, this would be the first time she had ever sought the spirits themselves. Salish children were sent to obtain guardians at an early age. But as a child, Whisper had never sought a guardian. This had not been important to her at the time. And since she was a female, it was not thought important to the elders.

The land where the spirits dwelled was far different than anything found on Earth, Whisper knew. She also knew that the spirits did not wish that everyone speak with them. There were Salish warriors who had gone out many times on a vision quest and had seen little or nothing. Then there were others who had received messages on their first or second mission. This was not a thing that was easily understood by human beings; it was only important that they accept the way things were. Those who were chosen to see and hear beyond the range they knew as human beings had to be wise in the use of this new knowledge. Good things could come to them only if their hearts were good; if their hearts were evil, they would surely be sorry.

Now that the time had come, Whisper knew there could be no hurry to this thing she must do. She would now take time to clear her mind and become ready to learn things she could not even dream of. To do this, she must first spend time seeing and feeling the things around her. She must remove all other things of this world from her thoughts. That would mean forgetting, for a time, about Jim and Fiddler. That would mean forgetting about the awful things she had known as a child and, now, as a woman. She could not let herself think of her hatred for the Siksika and the Pikuni, who had robbed her of happiness in times past. No, her mind must have time to readjust to Earth, to once again feel the things so close to her very being, without thoughts of pain and hate.

There were days spent watching herds of deer and elk feed and care for their young. She felt the cold water that flowed in the streams and the rich, black earth that sifted through her fingers. She lay in meadows of grass and flowers, gazing up at the sky and letting her mind wander with the clouds. There was time spent studying the blossoms of shrubs and flowers. She felt the hard bark of an old tree and wondered what a creature of such age must know about time and all the changes that time brings.

Then she journeyed north from the Bitterroot to the giant waters of the Flathead. It was on the banks of this big lake that she had been given birth. She had breathed the first air of her life on Earth here, and it would be good to once again touch the ground of her past. She must try not to think of times past here, but let her mind flow freely and enjoy the places of her beginning and namesake.

Sister Water was cool and clear, and felt good. Whisper

swam far out into the lake and climbed upon an island. There she gave thanks to Amótkan for allowing her the privilege of strength in the water. The island was far out from shore and there were many who would not even dream of swimming such a distance. Yet it did not seem far to Whisper, and her body was not tired.

As she looked all around the waters and marveled at all she saw, she felt good. The breeze off the lake relaxed her and the smell of pine and fir gave the air a wild freshness that made the skin tingle. For a time she watched ducks and geese move about on the lake, and shore birds bob and dip in the shallows as they searched for food. A pair of chickadees flew over her and settled on the lowest branch of a tree just above her. Their tiny bodies moved constantly as they bounced up and down on the branch, watching her curiously. They made their little "dee-dee-dee" sounds, tiny black eyes shining from under the patch of black feathers on their heads that made them look like they were wearing caps. Soon they had seen enough of her and flitted away among the branches, zigging and zagging off into the trees on the island.

Whisper knew these were the things she must see and feel to make herself ready for the vision quest. She must get as close to her surroundings as possible. She must see all the things in life that are meaningful. Here it was easy to feel close to Earth; this was the place of her birth. And though this place was the most special of places to her, she knew she must see many more things if her mission was to be fulfilled.

Sun crossed the sky many more times and Whisper continued to prepare herself for her vision quest. She went high up among the peaks of the mountains, where the wind always blew and the air was thin. She touched the snow that stays there all moons of the year and watched the eagle soar out from the rocks to make circles over the forest and meadows below. His piercing scream echoed from high rock walls and carried into the clouds. She saw white-haired goats jumping among the high crags and cliffs, never once

loneliness is to know there are things we can be doing that will make our hearts glad. Then loneliness cannot enter.

"We must feel others, for only by feeling others can we feel ourselves. This is important to know. Those who turn around when others are in need are building a cavern within themselves. This cavern is called loneliness. When we do good things for and with others, this cavern is filled up with the good feelings that come from the heart. Then there is no place for loneliness."

Whisper built up the fires and sang more songs of prayer. Her hunger and thirst did not bother her now as they had in the first few days, for her mind had separated from her body and the mind did not feed on the things the body needed. Her mind became open to the heavens. She heard more words from her brother, who had told her these words from the elders many winters past:

"Each human being is something special. Amótkan made them all the same, yet set each apart from one another. Human beings are like the leaves on a tree, all alike, yet all different. Each one grows on a different fork of the tree, yet all are fed from the same trunk. All receive nourishment from the roots of the same tree but each one receives this food separately. Each human being must learn which branch he or she grows on, and whether Sun faces them most in the morning, at midday, or in the afternoon. Each human being must learn that like a leaf, he or she has two sides. These two sides are part of the same whole, but are different in the things they are meant to do to help the being live and grow. It is hard to see these two sides, for we think of ourselves as one. Yet, we are not one. We are a mixture of the things found on both sides. And we are also mixed with the beings that exist in the others around us. Like the leaves, we touch each other as we live. Much the same as a wind brushes the leaves of a tree together, our lives are mixed with one another and we are allowed to grow together—to take nourishment from one main trunk. These are things we must learn and understand."

Now, as darkness was complete, Whisper began to hear rumbling in the sky. Until now she had not heard or seen anything evil. She had not even remembered that it existed. But now the sky was dark and clouds blocked the light of the moon and stars. Whisper fought fear as a jagged spear of lightning forked down into the forest.

Another bolt flashed through the night, and a deep rumbling followed. She set about to gather pam, the leaves of the fir tree, and made the fire burn high and bright. She would burn pam and the smoke would ascend to the sky and chase away the thunder. Yes, in time the storm would leave.

The thunder and lightening did not leave, but only became more intense. Was Amótkan mad at her? Was "He who sits at the top of the mountain" angry that she wished to speak with the spirits? Was He sending evil to visit her? Her heart pounded as she gathered more pam and sang songs as the smoke rose to the clouds. Still the thunder rolled, and still the lightening shot down from the sky. Behind each flash she now saw a face. Once her mother. Then Walking Head! Again Walking Head!

Whisper began to tremble. "No! No!" she shouted. She prayed to the Medicine Tree. Its high top swayed in the sudden violent wind. The thunder grew louder and the flashes brighter and more jagged. The faces became more horrible. Walking Head's mouth was open; he was screaming. There were more warriors. They, too, were all screaming. "No!" she yelled again. She ran down the hill. She fell in the darkness. She ran further and fell again. Everything was spinning. There were colors. They too were spinning and whirling, mixing together and forming odd bands of new colors. She could not get up. She tried to cry out, but couldn't. Then, all the colors were gone. All was black.

Chapter 18

THE FACELESS WARRIOR

Rain fell from the sky in large drops. It came fast and the wind blew it in sheets into the forest and meadows. Each bolt of lightning poured light into the forest as if, for a moment, day had returned.

"Whisper on the Water," came a voice. "Rise from your sleep. There are things you must see this night, many things, and the time is short."

Whisper got up from where she had fallen and looked into the darkness. Though she heard the rain falling around her, she could not feel it. Nor did the loud claps of thunder come to her ears. But thought, it is not light from the storm. It must be light from the thunderbolts, she thought. But it was different in some way. No, she thought, it is not light from the storm. It is a different kind of light. It is Light.

"Whisper on the Water," came the voice again. "Hurry! The time is short."

Whisper began walking toward the Light, which was becoming brighter. She did not feel fear; she did not wonder at the voice. Her footsteps fell as if she needed no effort to climb the hill through the trees. Though she kept walking, it seemed the Light never got any closer. She kept going, passing through thickets of tall, skinny trees as if they did not exist. She passed over deadfall timber, where naked branches and fallen trunks lay sprawled over one another in heaps. Still her progress did not slow. It seemed as though she walked above it all. Finally, she came to the Medicine Tree.

"Follow me," the Light ordered.

The Medicine Tree turned white as the Light spread completely around it. Then a large opening in the trunk appeared, as if the skin flap on a giant lodge was pulled back so that she might enter.

"Follow me," the Light repeated.

Without hesitation Whisper walked through the opening and found herself on a high hill overlooking a broad valley below. A long line of people were marching through the valley on foot. Dogs pulled travois heavily loaded with food and belongings. The people wore animal skin clothing that was plain and without decoration. Their hair, even that of the men, had few adornments and their weapons were clubs and lances with stone points. They looked more pitiful than any people Whisper had ever seen. But, as they marched, the people were all singing at the tops of their voices.

Whisper looked up from the valley. Beside her was a warrior dressed in the finest elkskins, whose hair was adorned with many feathers and trinkets. She could not tell who he was or to what tribe of Indian peoples he belonged. His dress was the same as many different tribes, for he represented all those Indian peoples who had adapted the plains culture. This made it possible for Whisper to relate to him as a person. But he was not fully a person. There was one distinct thing that made it clear he was not of this world: his face was a blur.

"What do you see below?" he asked. His was the voice she had heard coming from the Light.

Whisper continued to stare at him. "Who are you?"

"That is not important. It is important that you see and listen."

"You speak Salish. You must be Salish."

"Do not be foolish, Whisper on the Water. In any other tongue you would not understand my words. Where I live, Salish words do not exist. Nor does the language of the Siksika, the Pikuni, or the Shoshone. All peoples understand one another and live as one. Think about this during your time with me.

"Another thing I will tell you. There are many things you will see and hear during your time with me. These things will be happening to people—human beings such as yourself. Your eyes will perceive them as Indian peoples so that you will be better able to understand the meaning of what you see. But you must understand that where I come from human beings are not separated by color and tongue, as they are where you live. Now, what do you see below?"

Whisper again looked down into the valley. "I see Indian peoples singing a journey song. I hear them all singing and, look, the children are playing as they travel."

"Then you would say they are happy?"

Whisper thought it a foolish question. "It seems they are very happy."

"Good," he said. "That is what is important. Let us now travel to another valley. Turn around."

Whisper turned and šaw another valley below, much the same as the first valley. There was a column of Indian people moving camp, much the same as the others had been doing. Only many in this group were riding horses. These were mostly men, with eagle feathers in their hair and war paint on their faces. Both men and women wore clothes made from tanned skins. These clothes were fringed and Sun's rays danced where trinkets and shells had been sewn into place. The men carried lances with sharp metal points and wore quivers of arrows across their backs. They watched the hills around them and signaled to scouts who

were riding off from the main column. The women kept
the children close and quiet, so they might travel as silently
as possible.

The warrior spoke. "What do you see in this valley that
is different from the last valley?"

"There are many things," Whisper answered. "It seems
these people are traveling through enemy lands and,
therefore, they cannot sing journey songs or enjoy the
day."

"Is there anything else? Can you find a reason why this
has happened?"

Whisper looked puzzled.

"What is the main thing these people now have that the
other people did not have?"

"Horses."

"What would you say was different about these people
with respect to time?"

Whisper studied the people in the valley for a short
while. "It would seem they are a people of a later time.
They have finer clothes and have developed their tools and
weapons to a higher degree." She looked back to the warrior. "Do you mean these things are true because of the
horse?"

"Think about your own people," he said. "They could
very well be those people down there. Does the horse not
allow you greater freedom to travel and hunt farther from
those places you once hunted before the time of the horse?
Are you not able to kill more game from horseback than
on foot? And since there is more meat in the pot, does that
not allow you to spend more time on other things besides
hunting? Things like making clothes and shaping better
weapons? Yes, but the horse also brings you in closer contact with your enemies. There is more fighting among enemy tribes since the horse."

Whisper thought a moment. "Then there is always the
chance bad can come from good?"

"You have perceived well," said the warrior. "The
horse was a Gift sent from Amótkan to make the lives of

the people easier. However, the horse has also made the lives of the people harder. Now there is more chance of raids by enemies."

"Would it have been better if the horse had never come?" Whisper asked.

The warrior shrugged. "That cannot be answered. What you must think about is how you use each Gift you receive. The horse is but one Gift. There are many others. Now I will take you to still a later time."

Once again Whisper was asked to turn around. Below was another valley, but the scene was far from peaceful.

"Again, tell me what you see below," said the warrior.

Whisper was horrified. She looked upon an Indian village where many of the lodges were burning. There was screaming, and rifle fire of a different sort than any Whisper had ever heard.

"I see Long Knives raiding a camp of Indian peoples. But the Long Knives are dressed in blue, and wear strange markings on their arms and legs. One of them is blowing on a strange horn. They shoot strange firesticks, not like the Hawken that my husband, Jim, has. They have strange knives that are very long and curved. They are using them to hack and cut at the Indian people. There is much killing. But why?"

"Turn around again."

"I do not understand."

"Turn around. Our time together is growing shorter."

Another valley appeared below. It was filled with dust and war cries. Many warriors on horseback were closing in on an enemy.

"This time the Long Knives in blue are being killed," said Whisper. "But what can all this mean?"

"We will go again to a place of peace," said the warrior. "We do not have much more time and there is still much more you must see and hear."

Once again they were overlooking the valley where the first group of people journeyed on foot in simple clothes. Their singing was as loud as before.

Whisper sat down and looked out over the valley, watching the children and hearing the laughter and song. She took a deep breath. Soon her nerves were settled and she began to push the horrible things she had just witnessed out of her mind. She was soon absorbed in the peaceful scene below.

"Is this valley not more enjoyable than the other valleys?" the warrior asked.

"Why do you ask questions that have an answer so easy to see?" Whisper returned.

The warrior grunted. "Maybe you think the answer is obvious. And the answer should be obvious. But if you will now remember what you just saw in the other valleys we have visited, you will know the answer is ignored. Even though peace is the best for men's hearts, it is something they will never know."

Whisper turned back to the valley, thinking on his words. It was true all people were most happy when there was peace. Yet no people lived very long in peace. It was a strange thing to understand. After watching the people in the valley a while longer, she turned back to the warrior. "I have never seen such peace as exists in this valley. Is this the Land of Eternal Summer?"

The warrior shook his head. "No. That is a place of far greater peace than this. No one can go there unless they truly want to. That is something you must think about as your life goes on. Gifts will come and you will benefit from them, much the same as you did with the horse. But bad things will also come with the good. People will decide how it is they want to live. They will decide what they want to do with their lives. But you must decide what is best and what is right for you. You must use each Gift wisely. Come, we have other places to visit before our time is over."

Then, in a matter of moments, Whisper saw many things she could not explain. She saw more valleys, each filled with different kinds of lodges where different kinds of peoples lived. Some were Indian peoples, some were Long

Knives. Many of these lodges were very strange looking and were built in funny shapes such as she had never seen before. Many were made of wood or stone, and others from materials Whisper had never known existed.

She saw many strange things carrying these peoples. There were strange looking things that moved along the ground and put smoke out from behind. There were even huge silver eagles that carried many people inside their bodies and flew far above the clouds.

Then, in each valley, the warrior would say, "Now I want you to look upon this valley in a much later time."

Each time he said this the lodges would disappear and the huge silver eagles would be gone from the sky. Sometimes there would be nothing left but an empty valley with a river and trees. Sometimes, remnants of the lodges would be there, crumbling into pieces with age. Other times the valley would change to burning rock, much the same as the legends described the Yellowstone when the fire spirits lived there. Never did any of the valleys remain the same.

"This should tell you something about time and change," the warrior said.

"Does all of this mean that what we do as human beings on Earth means little in time?" Whisper asked. "Am I to believe that however great a people become, they will surely pass away in time?"

"You again have perceived well, Whisper on the Water," the warrior said. "There are many more truths that will come to you as your life goes on. Never forget what is important in life."

"But how do I make my life happier when there are others who do not wish for my happiness?"

"Our time is over," said the warrior. "We must go back now."

"Wait!" Whisper cried. "I have many questions."

"They are for you to answer yourself," said the warrior. "You have seen that time leaves nothing the same. You have seen how time can bring both good and bad things to all peoples. Now you must learn how time can be used for good things.''

"But what about Walking Head? I came because of Walking Head.''

"Time will answer your question. You can see that in the Universal Plan those who are happy are those who are at peace, at peace with themselves and at peace with others. There are times when only fighting will bring peace. But fighting for fighting's sake will only bring sorrow. You can see that those who are truly happy do not wish to have anything more in life than happiness. They are content with what they have. They give thanks for each Gift, and use it wisely. You have seen that new things can mean an easier life, but an easier life is not necessarily good. Also, you have seen that war is part of man's nature. But war does not bring happiness. Only you can decide what will bring happiness.''

"I came to the Medicine Tree to gain strength, for I wish to make my life happy. I thought I could only do this by war—war against Walking Head. Now you tell me war will not bring happiness.'' Whisper threw up her arms. "What am I to do?''

"All human beings are born to live with burdens. Some are small, some are great. It is part of the Universal Plan. And it is for human beings to choose how they will live with these burdens. Sometimes things happen that lessen or eliminate these burdens. If you think about it as you continue to live your life, you will see that some choices are made for you. But some choices you make yourself, for human beings have free will. Then it is important to accept what has happened and choose the right way to live. These are the tests of life. You have a good mind. Use it.''

"Then I am to fight Walking Head?''

"That is your own decision.''

"I have already made the decision to fight. Why do you not show me the right way to fight him?''

"You wished to gain greater knowledge,'' the warrior said. "And you have gained greater knowledge edge. If what you have seen today does not help you with your burdens on Earth, then your mission has failed."

"But I came for more power."

"You have more power. It will take time for you to learn how to use it. How you use it will then be up to you. Maybe then you will understand some of life's secrets. The time for everything in your life comes only when it is right, and if it is right. You cannot make things happen that do not fit into the Universal Plan. Those things will not happen. You cannot change that. When things do happen, maybe you will know why. Maybe you will not. Your choice to act will govern your happiness. This is the way it must be."

Whisper turned and looked down again at the peaceful valley where the people were singing. "I do not wish to leave this place," she said.

"You must," said the warrior. His voice and his form were fading. "Our time together is finished."

Chapter 19

DREAMER

Whisper awoke and Red Thunder was standing above her, nudging her with his nose. Morning had come and the forest was wet. She was soaked, but the warmth of Sun filled her with a fresh new feeling. She went to a nearby spring and drank of its freshness. With her knife, she dug up a number of yampa plants growing in the meadow. She built a fire and took dried meat from a parfleche on her saddle. She mixed the roots of the yampa with the meat and made a stew.

Her strength slowly began to come back to her and, as she ate, she took time to reflect on what she had experienced. She had awakened far down the hill from the Medicine Tree. She did not know why. She could not remember coming down the hill. But she could remember the storm vividly, and the images it had brought. The faces of her mother and Walking Head had seemed real. Then her thoughts had seemed to take off on their own into a world she had never seen before. Yes, the warrior had seemed real, and so had all the things he had shown her. But she

could not visualize herself as flesh and bone when all this
had happened. Perhaps that was the way of a vision.

The day passed and Whisper continued to build up her
strength. She ate as she had never eaten before. As she
thought back on what she had heard from the faceless warrior, she began to wonder how she would use this new
knowledge in her life. It was still hard to understand some
of these things but, as the warrior had said, perhaps their
meaning would become more clear in time.

Whisper passed the night in a deep sleep. Her brain
turned over and over as those many things she had seen
and heard settled into her sleeping mind. Some of what she
had seen reappeared again as dreams. Though the dreams
were not nightmares, they were vivid and she could again
see the turmoil that exists in all parts of Earth. Then, as her
dreams continued, she saw herself at the head of a group
of warriors. They were Salish, and were all wearing war
paint. She, herself, had stripes of red and yellow down her
face, and her forehead was completely black. There was
much cheering and yelling. There were chants of bravery.
There was a singer, and his song was the same as she had
heard at the rendezvous two winters past:

> *See her walk among the lodges,*
> *Spirit Woman, medicine woman.*
> *She comes among us with her*
> *power,*
> *And mighty warriors watch her pass.*
> *Oh, Spirit Woman, medicine woman,*
> *Keep the Blackfeet from our lands.*

There were many warriors and they were waving fresh
scalps. They were Siksika scalps! And she was yelling the
loudest of all. It was the war cry she had screamed before.

> *Against Siksika we make war!*
> *Aiee, Siksika all will die!*

"We have waited long," one of the warriors was saying. "We have waited long, and now the time of the Spirit Woman has come. The spirits have told her now is the time to kill our enemies. This day the Siksika will die!"

There was much more yelling and screaming of war cries. There were many more chants to Whisper, who would now lead them against their hated enemies. Then, with her lance pointed forward, she led them in a charge down a long hill. At the bottom was a large meadow. From the hill on the other side of the meadow came screams and war cries from another people—the Siksika. They, too, were charging down the hill toward the open meadow.

The two sides met at the bottom. The dust and blood of war began. Whisper was screaming, driving her lance into Siksika warriors, slamming their heads with her war club. It was a good day for the Salish. None of their number was lost, while many Siksika warriors lay still in the blood of the meadow. Salish arrows went true to their marks and, even though the Siksika had the dreaded firesticks from trade with the Hudson Bay Company, they had no magic. The brave Salish warriors wrenched these firesticks from their enemies and laughed. The Siksika were not so bold this day. Many of them ran like children. But then another band of Siksika came charging down the hill. Again the Salish warriors followed Whisper in yelling war chants. There would be more blood before this day was through. As the Siksika came down off the hill to avenge their fallen brothers, an even more bloody fight began. This time warriors fell on both sides and the screaming deafened the ears. The dust boiled thicker while horses and men piled into each other in an explosion of hatred. The time had come to kill all Siksika! As she yelled and fought, Whisper knew this would be the hardest battle she would ever see. With her war club raised, she charged a figure on horseback. It was the war chief of the second band that had charged down the hill. It was Walking Head!

Whisper awoke with a start. Sun had broken over the High Divide to the east and the land was bathed in gold.

Again Red Thunder had nudged her, and he stood with his nose in her face as if to tell her it was only a dream. She laughed and patted her stallion's nose. "You would not let me finish the battle," she joked. "Now I will have to find Walking Head again."

Whisper ate more food and continued to think on the things that had happened. The dream had shed new light on her thoughts. Surely she would meet Walking Head sometime; the dream had made that much clear. Someday they would meet face to face in battle and one of them would walk away. But now she knew that day would have to come according to the Universal Plan. She could not plan that day herself, for it would have to come when the time was right. Yes, she would have to wait, and go when the signs told her to go.

The dream had told her another thing; she would not be alone. Until now she had thought it would be necessary to carry out her mission against Walking Head on her own, but the dream and the words of the faceless warrior convinced her this was not true. From the words of the faceless warrior, she had learned that it was not good to close out others. Maybe she would someday meet someone who wished to kill Walking Head as badly as she herself did. Maybe she would receive a Gift, something or someone who would help her against Walking Head. Maybe it would be her husband, Jim. Maybe it would be someone else. If it was not in the Universal Plan, she would not meet with anybody. Nor would she be given a Gift of any sort. These were all things she would find out in time. She must learn how to use time. "There are times when only fighting will bring peace. But fighting for fighting's sake will only bring sorrow." She remembered these words from the faceless warrior. "If you think about it as you continue to live your life, you will see that some choices are made for you. . . . You have more power. It will take time for you to learn how to use it. . . . The time for everything in your life comes only when it is right." The faceless warrior had said many things that she must remember.

Whisper would now spend the rest of the day with a special purpose. Because of her dream, she now knew how she would paint her medicine shield. She had seen her shield in the dream, and it had been painted in the way of the storm. Yes, that was now the source of her power. The spirits had been telling her that on the night of her vision. She remembered Sun, shining in a yellow ball below the dark clouds. She remembered the jagged flashes of lightning coming down on both sides of Sun, showing the great power that was contained in the storm. She remembered the Medicine Tree swaying in the wind and the sound of rain coming from the sky. Yes, her shield would have Sun in the middle, with streaks of lightning on both sides. Her colors would be red and yellow. Red, for strength. Blood was red and it was the strength of the body. Yellow, for Sun. Sun was the power of all Earth. These colors and signs she had seen on her shield in the dream. Also, there would be eagle feathers lining the shield. The eagle was also the symbol of strength and courage. She had seen some in her dream, flying in the breeze as she led the warriors in the charge down the hill against the Siksika. Yes, her shield would be a symbol of strength and courage. It would show all others that she had seen the sources of power and that they had spoken to her. The storm was now her medicine.

When Whisper finished with her shield, Sun sat far over in the sky. The birds were singing evening songs and the streams were lined with deer and elk. It was a time of peace in the forest. Whisper did not know if she would take this peace with her back to the Siskadee, or never again know the meaning of the word. This she would know in time. It would depend on what lay ahead for her in the Universal Plan. She would now live her life with Jim as she had lived it before, and would wait for the signs that told her what she must do. Jim would be glad to hear she was not going to find Walking Head, that is, if he still wished her to be with him. He had become very angry with her recently. She knew her love for him would never die; she could only hope his feelings for her were the same. She could only hope that her life with him had not ended because of her journey to the Bitterroot. If he truly loved her, he would understand that it had been necessary for her to do what she felt she must do. This man, Jim, had made her happier than she had ever been in her life, and she wished him to be the source of her future happiness. Now she would go to the Siskadee and meet him. Then she would learn how her life would be from now on. Yes, her life would change now because of the things she had seen and heard since the beginning of her vision quest. If Jim still loved her and waited for her coming, then he would also understand when she told him her mission against Walking Head was not over. It would depend on the signs. It would depend on the Universal Plan.

Now she would sleep. Maybe more dreams would come and tell her how her life was to be. But she hoped these dreams would wait for her to reach the Siskadee. She now had Jim on her mind and it was a good feeling.

Chapter 20

SISKADEE

Sun was straight above and the land was hot. Along the water's edge tall cottonwoods grew and gave shade in a land where no other shade existed. It was the Siskadee— the Prairie Hen River. There were no forests in this land, for it lay below where the forests grew. It lay between those mountains topped by the three giant peaks called *Tetons*, and those mountains which gave birth to the waters of the Wind. It was an open, rolling valley where prairie hens in vast numbers made their homes on sagebrush slopes and in the greasewood that covered the salt-crusted bottoms. The Long Knives were calling it Green River now, and it was a good place for the beaver. This was the place Whisper was to meet Jim, for it was now late in the Moon of the Camas. It was time for rendezvous.

Whisper had found the rendezvous along a flow of water that came to meet with the Siskadee. This place was called Ham's Fork. Here the usual drinking and laughing carried the trappers through hours of stories and games. It was always a joyous time when those who saw each other only once between winters came together.

It was Fiddler who saw her first. He hugged her like a daughter. "Pretty Lady, we've had some mighty empty camps since you left." His eyes danced. "You wait here. There's a big sandy-haired hoss over yonder who's goin' to forget about that hand game he's in when he hears what I've got to say."

"Do not tell him I am here," Whisper insisted. "Tell him you wish to show him something that will please him, maybe a horse you have won or something else, but do not tell him about me. I wish to look at his eyes when he first sees me again. That will tell me many things."

Fiddler laughed. "Don't worry about his eyes none. It's his manhood you'll have to look out for!"

Whisper waited among the cottonwoods below the many lodges and campfires of rendezvous. Here only the murmur of the river could be heard while the laughing and noise seemed distant. Soon she could hear men's voices as Jim and Fiddler walked through the trees to the place where she waited. It was hard to tell what Fiddler had said to get him away from camp, for Jim was saying it had better be something special since he had been winning at the hand game.

Fiddler pointed to Whisper. "Is that somethin' special?"

Jim's mouth dropped open. After his surprise, his eyes softened. Whisper smiled to herself. Yes, his love for her was still strong.

"It is good to see my husband again," she said. She moved over to him and put her arms around him and lay her head on his shoulder. "My nights have been long and lonely."

"I'll finish your hand game for you, Jim," Fiddler said. "I promise I won't lose." He laughed. "Or maybe you don't care now." He laughed again and hurried off toward camp.

Whisper felt Jim's strong arms around her. For a time it seemed he would never let go. Then he ran his fingers through her black hair. "How come you didn't care for yourself better?" he asked. "You've lost weight."

Whisper smiled. "You have also lost weight."

"You spoiled me," he smiled back. "I can't seem to make stew the way you can."

Then there was a silence, a questioning silence in which Jim looked deep into her eyes.

"Have I got my wife back?"

"You have always had your wife. I have never wished it any other way."

"Are you back now for good?"

Whisper took him by the hand. "Come. Let us walk a trail along the river. There are many things I must tell you about my trip to the Bitterroot."

Whisper and Jim spent the next three days together, seeing Fiddler only once in a while. Jim did not care about selling his furs, nor did he mind missing the games and contests. He wished to do nothing more than spend his time with Whisper.

They had much to talk about, for now it was more than one full moon's passing since Whisper had journeyed from the Yellowstone to the Bitterroot. She had left when there had been bad feelings between them. But those bad feelings had left Jim, and all was forgotten.

Whisper's happiness began to return. Her vision quest had eased her mind about Walking Head. She would no longer spend her days and nights with her mind on this hated enemy. When the time came, she would prepare to meet him. The time apart from Jim had shown Whisper how much she really loved this man. It was good to be with him again. There was much laughing and much lovemaking. He acted as though he was trying to make up for the time spent apart, so often did they lay with each other.

"What happened during your vision quest?" he asked her once when their love was finished. "Did you see anything? Did you learn anything?"

"I saw and learned many things, my husband," she answered. She lay on her back, looking up at the sky where an eagle soared high overhead. "There will be more things I will learn in time, for I have just begun to perceive all I was told."

"Tell me about it."

Whisper smiled. "It would be hard for you to understand many of these things. There are many things I do not as yet understand."

Jim grunted. "Why don't you just tell me you don't want to talk about it?"

"That is not it," Whisper insisted. "We have always talked about things. But how can I tell you things I do not know the true meaning of?"

"Well, I think you're just puttin' me off," Jim said with disgust. "You think I'm too dumb to understand. That's it, you're a whole lot smarter now that you've got your big medicine!"

"No! Jim, do not think those things. I would never try and fool you. Do you not understand my love for you? Can you not see this love after all our time together?"

"That don't mean you can't get a big head over learnin' what you have."

"My head is not big. It is my heart that has learned to grow. The true meaning of life has been taught to me. Many of these things you already understand, for you are a man who gives to others. You are not selfish. You do not wish for power and the right to rule other men's lives. You are not the kind who would sacrifice his honor for the things of this world, as do many of the Long Knives that come to these lands. You know me to speak with a straight tongue. This is how it has always been with us."

"What does all that have to do with your medicine?"

"My medicine is strong only if my heart is strong," Whisper explained. "I was blessed by Amótkan, chosen to see and learn things I may never be able to fully understand. But I was not changed. I did not become some special being with the power to master my own existence. No, I learned that no human being is the master of his or her existence. That can never be. Human beings can only learn what is important, and try to live the right way."

"What about Walking Head?" Jim asked. "Up to now you haven't said nary a word about him, and I haven't asked you anything. But I see a lot of paint on that shield of yours now. I'd say that means you've made some special medicine for yourself.''

Whisper pointed out toward the west, where Sun was moving closer to the horizon through a long bank of clouds. "It is true, my shield has paint. And it is painted in a sacred way: But it only means I now know the source of my power. The storm is my source of medicine. This came to me in a special way while I prayed and fasted. It is to the storm that I will pray for strength and courage when the day comes that I am to meet Walking Head.''

"I thought you told me you were staying.''

"Jim, this will be hard for you to understand. But you must understand. I know that your love for me is great, so I feel good about the faith you will need to live with me until Walking Head is dead.''

"Then you're goin' out after him?''

"Only if that is what is in the Universal Plan.''

"The Universal Plan?''

Whisper sat up and put her hands on Jim's face. "I told you this would be hard, my husband. But you wished to learn and now you must listen. The time will come when I will meet Walking Head again. I know this to be true. I know some day I will meet him in battle. I do not know when, or even where it will happen. This day will come, but only when the time is right. That is something I will learn from the signs. It is true, I will not leave to seek out Walking Head. I have learned this would not be good. I have also learned that to fight alone would not be good.''

Jim put his hands on Whisper's sides, just under her arms, and pulled her next to him. "Then I will go with you. We will fight together.''

"Yes, but only if it is in the signs. This is important. You will fight with me only if it is right. Do you understand?''

Jim threw up his arms. "You make it hard on a man to sleep at night.''

Sun was shining through the trees now, and the birds

were singing roosting songs in the branches. The light was gold, and it made their place among the trees a warm hollow. Whisper smiled and nibbled at Jim's ear. ''Why would you want to sleep when I share your bed?'' She pulled him into the cool grass where the shadow had grown dark.

''Whisper, there's more I've got to know.''

''It shall wait,'' Whisper said. Her fingers were under his shirt, skimming his chest and stomach. ''I have never known you to put talk before other things when you were in the robes with me.''

Jim laughed. He leaned over and began to nibble at Whisper's ear while she unfastened his belt. ''Those are words of wisdom, my wife.''

Whisper kissed him. ''They are words of experience, my husband. Your name should not be Jim. You should be called Man-Always-Ready.''

Whisper had not forgotten the things that gave him pleasure. He, too, held and loved her in a way no other man ever could. The grass around them was full of crickets and the standing pools of water in the river rang with the croaking of frogs. Whisper and Jim could hear nothing. Their ears were full of the warm breath from each other. The lush grass was soft and cool. When they were finished, Whisper said in a laughing way, ''We could have had a better time out in the sagebrush. The mosquitos are feasting on me tonight.''

They moved up onto a hill and watched the moon rise full over the fires of the rendezvous. Above them, in the twilight, nighthawks performed their winged dances. They swooped and dove down toward the ground from high in the sky, making a whipping sound with their wings as they cut the still night air. Off in the cottonwoods below, an owl hooted. It was the big brother of the little owl who was Whisper's guardian. It was the large owl with the feathers that looked like horns on his head. Whisper wondered if maybe this owl had come to remind her that his brother, who lived high up in the forest, was thinking of her this night.

The sounds of night moved in, and among them was the howl of the little-wolf, the trickster named coyote. He was a sly creature, witty in his ways and devious in his thoughts. He dwelled in great numbers in the valleys and plains. In many ways, the Long Knives gathered below reminded Whisper of coyote. They were a strange lot who came together for fun this one time of year, yet were at each other's throats even before the campfires were cold. They laughed and drank with one another, but still kept their eyes and ears open for ways to gain more than all others from the fur business. They thought of ways to trick one another while passing a jug of whiskey. Coyote was no more cunning than many of the Long Knives who made their own homes here.

"Where will we go to look for the beaver during these next cold moons?" Whisper asked Jim.

Jim had dug a breadroot plant from the ground beside him and was peeling the woody outer layer off the big root. "Fiddler and I have been talkin'," he answered. He cut a piece of the root and handed it to Whisper, then popped a portion of it into his mouth. "Maybe we won't look for beaver this fall."

"Won't look for beaver? Why not?"

Jim chewed on the breadroot as he spoke. "Well, we're tired of wadin' cold streams so some other nigger can cut a fat hog back in St. Louis. The way Fiddler and I see it, we can make more money and live a damn site easier by followin' suit with a few mothers out here. We plan to set up a tradin' post."

Whisper took a bite out of the piece of breadroot Jim had given her. "You mean the same kind of lodge as the Saleesh House built in our lands by the Canadians, and the place of the American Fur Company called Fort Union?"

"That's the thought," Jim nodded. "We figured the best place to build would be up in Shoshone country, maybe on the Stinkingwater where the two forks come together near the frost caves. There's still plenty of beaver up that way and we could catch a lot of brigades goin' north after rendezvous every year.''

''Would you not have trouble with the other Long Knives who are also building forts?'' Whisper asked.

Jim had dug up another root and was rubbing the dirt off so he could begin peeling it. ''Maybe,'' he said, sinking his knife into the top of the root and ripping the green stem off. ''But we've got trouble the way it is now. There ain't enough beaver to go around and there's more greenhorns fillin' these hills every day.'' Again he cut the root in sections and offered some to Whisper. Then he pointed down to the flat where the rendezvous fires burned. ''Look down there. I'd wager the hills will see more greenhorns than there is beaver to go around before many more years. They'll all need possibles—guns and traps and powder, and the like—and they'll need foofaraw for the Indian women.'' He nodded to himself. ''No doubt we'll sell more beads and mirrors and cloth than anything else.'' He stuffed more breadroot into his mouth and shrugged. ''Hell, they might as well trade their money and furs with Fiddler and me as anyone else.''

''You don't sound as if your heart is in it,'' Whisper said.

''I can't really say that it is,'' he admitted. ''I'd much rather us three—you, Fiddler, and I—have a whole valley to ourselves, and a packstring loaded with traps.'' He pointed down to the rendezvous camp again. ''But that ain't possible no more. No, not ever again. Best thing we can do is roll with the punches and let what's left of the beaver come to us, instead of fightin' over it in some stream somewhere with a pack of greenhorns.''

''It is a good plan you and Fiddler have made,'' Whisper said. ''But how will you get all the goods you wish to trade to this place on the Stinkingwater?''

''Haul them out here from St. Louis in wagons,'' Jim said. ''Or maybe take them up the river as far as the Bighorn, then pack them on up the rest of the way.'' He began to get more enthusiasm in his voice. ''You know, it wouldn't be so bad. Not when you think on it a spell. We'll have a nice spot we can stay most of the year where the Shoshones and Rotten Belly's Crows can keep the Blackfeet off us. We'll have more time for ourselves.'' A broad grin crossed his face. "In fact it will be mighty good. Fort Shoshone we'll call it. Best fort and tradin' post this side of the Mississippi."

"Yes," Whisper said, "it is a good plan. It could bring us much happiness. But there will be trouble."

"Are you talkin' Blackfeet?" Jim asked.

Whisper shook her head. "As you said, the Absaroka and the Shoshone are both our brothers. They will keep the Siksika and the Pikunis from our door. It is the evil Long Knives who worry me. There are many of them, and of them, Beeler is the worst. He will be mad that we killed Courchene and the other two in the Burning Mountains. Yes, Beeler will be trouble."

Jim threw the rest of the breadroot down in disgust. "That's been in my craw ever since Fiddler and I decided to go into this."

"Yes, something was bothering you," Whisper said. "I have never known you to like the breadroot that well when there are so many other things to eat. Maybe you could not even taste what you were eating. Maybe it was just something to settle your nerves."

Jim smiled and put an arm around Whisper. "You know me pretty good, don't you. This whole thing has been eatin' at me for a long time: all these greenhorns comin' in and spoilin' things; startin' in on a business I don't know that much about; this thing you've got with Walking Head. And then there's Beeler." He threw his hands up. "I just don't know what to make of it all."

Whisper put her arms around him. "We have each other, my husband. We have happiness. We have a good friend in Fiddler. Things are good for us. We just have to learn that there will always be new things in our lives." She took a deep breath. "It is true, not all new things are good. But we must go on living. We are meeting a power no human being can control. It is called change."

Chapter 21

THE LONG KNIFE TRADER

The walk back to the rendezvous camp took little time and, though there had been a cool breeze from the mountains blowing across the hill, it was hot down on the bottom. The added heat from the fires made the air sizzle, and sweat showed on the foreheads of both Whisper and Jim.

When they reached their lodges, Jim said, "Wonder why Fiddler hasn't made it back here by now. He told me he planned to turn in early tonight, and it ain't early anymore."

"Maybe he is still talking with Jim Bridger about the fur of the beaver," Whisper suggested.

"That's not likely," Jim said. "He was too tired to stay up just jawin' about old times."

As always, many games and dancing were going on around the fires. Many lay sprawled on the ground, sick or blacked out from the effects of the firewater. Around one fire, a group of Indian women danced naked before a crowd of laughing Long Knives. Whisper turned from the sight.

Near another fire, many men had surrounded a fight. Jim and Whisper crowded through and found Fiddler on his back, trying to keep Ed Beeler's fingers out of his eyes.

"Beeler!" Jim yelled.

The fighting stopped and Beeler looked up. All but a few in the crowd became silent. Others were too drunk and yelled, "Don't stop! Get on with it!"

Beeler quickly got off Fiddler and stood hump-backed, his eyes narrowed at Jim.

Jim already had his shirt and cap off. "Beeler, someday you'll learn not to mess with my friends."

"I've got friends too, Ayers!" Beeler spat the words out.

The crowd shouted, favoring no one in particular, but wanting more fighting.

"Sure you do, Beeler," Jim glared back. "They're at the bottom of Colter's Hell!"

Three men came out from the crowd and stood by Beeler. One said, "There's a few that ain't in Colter's Hell, Ayers."

Jim curled his lips into a snarl. "They'll soon wish they were!"

In one quick movement he slammed a fist into Beeler's face, sending him reeling backwards to the ground. Then he turned to face the others. The crowd whooped and hollered as the three came at Jim. Fiddler was up and a sharp kick to one man's ribs buckled him up in pain. Jim slammed a fist into one of the other two; the man's head jerked back, his nose crushed and pulpy against his face. The third man was a good fighter and he was big. Jim was having a hard time with him. Then Beeler came back to his feet and roared like a bear. He pulled his knife and started for Jim.

Whisper tripped him and he fell to the ground with a thud. The knife bounced from his hands and into the fire. "We shall get your knife back for you, evil one!" Whisper hissed.

Quickly she was behind him and had him by his long winter's growth of hair. He yelled and tried to swing at her, but she was strong and pulled him along the ground while those in the crowd laughed. In the next moment he was screaming and rolling in the dirt. Whisper had dragged him through the fire, and his greasy buckskins were all aflame.

The other trappers yelled and laughed. It was not a serious thing.

Of Beeler's three friends, only the good fighter was still standing. He quickly rushed over and rolled Beeler in a buffalo robe. He looked at Whisper like he couldn't believe what he had just seen. "You'd better pick better fightin' friends," Jim taunted. "Next time you might not be so lucky."

Beeler stood up and glared at Whisper. Any other man would have been nearly unconscious from the burns. "You Injun bitch!" he slurred. "I'll kill you!"

His face was welted, with puffy red streaks and blisters rising in places, and he blinked his eyes continuously.

"No, Ed!" His friend held him back. "You ain't in no shape for that."

"Let him come on," Jim said stepping forward. "It's time he goes under."

Fiddler stopped him. "That ain't the thing to do, Jim."

"What? He damn near killed you!"

"Maybe. But let's let it ride."

Jim shook his head in disgust. "It's a mistake, Fiddler."

Fiddler pointed at the drunken trappers and moved in close to Jim, talking under his breath. "Jim, it ain't healthy. Look at all these crazy hosses, brim full of whiskey. The smell of blood might just set them off. Then who's to say what would happen?"

Whisper nodded. "He is right, Jim, The firewater has robbed them of their heads. It is not a good time to fight."

Jim put his hands on his hips. "None of them stepped in against us durin' the fight."

"A man just can't tell," Fiddler argued. "It's best to play it smart." He led Jim away from the fire.

"I've got my doubts about what's smart," Jim huffed.

"If Beeler gets his way, we'll all go under. And we'll only have ourselves to blame."

Their own campfire was down to coals. Whisper rebuilt it while Fiddler worked to calm Jim down.

"I just might have got us a deal worked out with Bridger," he said. "He says he can help us get foofaraw and possibles at good prices."

"I'll bet he can," Jim said. "Just as long as he gets part of the trade. Right?"

Fiddler lit his pipe and smiled at Jim. "You must know Old Gabe pretty well yourself."

"Too well," said Jim. "It's around that he and the others in his company are up past their eyeballs in debt. I imagine he's lookin' for a way out now."

Fiddler let the smoke curl up from his mouth. "So you don't think doin' business with Old Gabe would be too good for us?"

"Do you?"

"I reckon not," Fiddler agreed. "But he knows the way out here from St. Louis like nobody else."

"So do you," Jim said. "There ain't a hoss here who knows the hills the way you do."

Fiddler frowned. "Jim, I ain't no spring chicken no more. Trips like that are for younger men."

The fire was crackling again. Whisper put a large cut of buffalo hump on a spit and sat down behind Jim. Gently, she rubbed his neck and shoulders until he finally took a deep breath and relaxed.

"Maybe you could find Fiddler and me a jug," he said to her.

Fiddler looked at Jim and puffed on his pipe. "You don't aim to get yourself riled again, do you?"

Jim shook his head and took another deep breath. "No, I'm past that stage now. I just need a snort to settle my nerves is all."

In a moment Whisper had returned with a jug from Fiddler's lodge. Jim took a long drink and handed it to Fiddler.

Before he drank, Fiddler asked, "Do you still think this tradin' post idea will pan out?"

"The more I think on it, the more I'm sure it's the best thing," Jim answered. "I thought that's the way you looked at it too."

Fiddler handed the jug back to Jim. "It's the best thing, no doubt in that. But gettin' them goods out here all the time will be one hellish pain in the ass."

Jim swirled a mouthful of whiskey before he swallowed it. "What about the river? Whisper and I talked about that earlier tonight. Hell, that's the best way as far as I can see."

Fiddler nodded and puffed some more on his pipe. "It would be a fairly easy go until we hit the Yellowstone. McKenzie owns that river you know. Nobody but Company men travel them waters without a lot of discomfort."

Again Whisper heard the name McKenzie, a name feared by all who did not work for the American Fur Company. Yes, he was a hard man to beat. He was master of the Yellowstone River, and controlled much of the Big Muddy—the river called Missouri: He had one of the Strong Lodges, a fort, where the Yellowstone and Big Muddy joined. And as Jim and Fiddler continued to talk, she knew this man had become even more powerful.

"How'll he stop us?" Jim asked.

"Hell, you've heard all the talk, Jim," Fiddler answered with a grunt. "The Company owns these mountains now. Word's out that Bridger and the others who own Rocky Mountain Fur are set to go under. You just got through tellin' me that yourself. Now why ask a silly question like how we'll get goods past McKenzie? He's got pirates all over up there."

"Maybe we can get the Crows and Shoshones to side with us?" Jim suggested.

"We might have them on our side time and again," Fiddler said. "But don't count on them to see us through any bad scrapes. Most of them go with those who've got the most liquor nowadays."

Jim blew out his breath in disgust. "I guess I knew the

river was not a good idea all along.'' He drank from the jug and handed it to Fiddler. ''Maybe we won't even have enough beaver plews to get this started. Ever think of that?''

''We've got plenty for a start,'' Fiddler assured him. ''We'll just add to it as we go along.'' He took one last drink and gave the jug back to Jim. ''This old hoss has got to get some rest. It's a long way to St. Louis.'' Then he was up and walking stifflegged to his bed.

Whisper watched him go inside his lodge and pull the flap down. The skins were pulled up a few inches all around from the ground to let the night air in. Soon Fiddler was a still form deep in sleep.

''It is truly sad to see him feel so empty,'' Whisper said. ''The coming of more Long Knives has taken his spirit from him.''

''Things are movin' too fast,'' said Jim. ''All these greenhorns are bound to spoil everything. These hills will never be the same, and Fiddler knows it.''

Then came the sound of a man walking close by. Whisper and Jim looked up to see the figure of Nat Wyeth stop in front of their fire. ''Thought I'd stop by and visit,'' he said.

Jim poked the buffalo hump. Juice oozed out and dripped into the fire and sizzled. ''Sit a spell, Nat,'' Jim said. ''There's fat cow and strong drink.''

Nat Wyeth was the Long Knife who had once owned Red Thunder. He was trying very hard to do well in this business of selling beaver fur. There was much talk of his intent to establish himself as a trader and fur buyer in the mountains. He had told many of the Long Knives at rendezvous that soon he could sell them the things they needed to trap the beaver at a much cheaper price than they were paying now. He was a man with great ambition. And he liked Jim very much.

''Quite a bunch we've got this year,'' he said as he took the jug from Jim and sat down. ''From the looks of your face I'd say you found one of those free-for-alls that seem so common around here."

"I got into a little scrape," Jim nodded. "It ain't unusual."

Wyeth laughed and took a piece of meat that Whisper had cut for him. "How's that Appaloosa of yours?" he asked.

"He grows stronger each day," Whisper said with a smile. "I am grateful to you for trading him to Jim so that I might have him. Not many men would trade such a horse."

Wyeth nodded. "He's a lot of horse, but I couldn't pass up those furs your man, Jim here, offered me." He handed the jug back to Jim and said, "I see you're still working the streams."

"Me and a whole bunch of others," Jim said with disgust. "It's gettin' so a man can't even turn around out here without bumpin' into somebody. Beaver can't last long at this rate."

"That's the truth," Wyeth agreed. "But while there's fur, there's still money in it."

"A man has to figure how to make that money," said Jim. "Sellin' to a fur company sure won't do it."

Wyeth bit off another piece of buffalo and nodded. "A fair price is seldom part of the bargain."

"I think there's a way to beat it," Jim went on. "The fur companies make a pile of profit on the furs they take to St. Louis, no doubt about that. But they make a killin' in the possibles they bring out here for rendezvous. A man loses everything he makes every year puttin' it back into gear and rotgut whiskey. Now if a man was to offer traps, guns, horse tack, and that sort of thing, at a reasonable price, he'd like as not make some money."

"Precisely, Jim," Wyeth said, taking the jug back again. "Those are exactly my thoughts. I offered you a job with me two years ago because I knew you were one of the smarter ones out here. I felt you could help me and I could help you. I still feel that way. I know you would never work directly under me; you are too much your own man for that. But if you'd care to work with me, there's money to be made.''

"Do you have a plan?" Jim asked.

Wyeth nodded. "I want to establish a trade center over on Lewis River—the one the Indians call the Snake. It would be a year-round proposition, not just during rendezvous. And it wouldn't cater to the Indian trade, as most of the older forts do. Trappers could gear up any time and pay cash, or trade furs. Either way, the profit margin is ours. We don't have to take peanuts for furs, then turn around and pay double to get outfitted for the next year. We supply possibles and make good on the furs to boot!" There was a gleam in his eye as he finished. "And most important, we will profit even more when the fur is gone!"

Jim frowned. "You mean you plan to cater to greenhorns—the traffic from the settlements."

"Exactly!" Wyeth bounced with enthusiasm. "There are already people on their way to Oregon. There will be more, many more. The trail to Oregon will pass right by my front door on Lewis River." Wyeth sat back a moment and studied Jim. Then he spoke again. "Jim, I haven't told you anything you don't already know. Why haven't you considered the same possibilities, and in the same location as me?"

"I have," Jim answered. "Fiddler and I have talked about it. But we can't see sellin' to greenhorns in wagons and bein' happy about it."

"Jim, you have to face facts," Wyeth said. "This part of the country is changing fast. People know about the West now. They'll be out here from the settlements in just a few years."

Jim was silent, but Whisper spoke for him. "Yes, this we have talked about many times. So many Long Knives will bring change to these lands. And it will be a sad thing to see."

"I'll agree with that," Wyeth said. "Maybe it won't be so good for the Indians. But your people, the Salish, are as much to blame for bringing white folks out here as any of the whites themselves.''

Whisper studied Wyeth a moment. ''This I do not understand.''

''Didn't you know your people are asking for whites to come out here?''

''No, that cannot be.''

Wyeth looked at Jim. ''I'm not trying to rile your pretty wife, Jim. Understand that. I'm just telling the truth as I see it.''

''This is truth?'' Whisper asked. ''You say the Salish are changing?''

Wyeth nodded. ''That's the way it looks to me.''

Whisper took a deep breath. ''I must hear your words. It will cause pain in my heart, but that is something I am used to. Tell me about my people, the Salish.''

Chapter 22

SHINING SHIRT

Whisper listened closely as Wyeth began telling her why he felt the Salish wanted change.

"Didn't you know that your tribe has been sending some of its people to St. Louis?" he asked her. "Didn't you know your people want to learn the white man's religion?"

"No, I did not know this," Whisper answered. "I have not been among my people for some time." She thought a moment and then added, "Why would they want to change the old ways? This I cannot understand."

Wyeth shrugged. "I can't speak for your people, but their actions make it real plain they want religion. In fact, the Little Chief is here with many of your people and many Nez Percés. They came just to meet a missionary I brought out here with me. His name is Jason Lee."

Whisper looked at Jim. "Many things have happened in the days we spent alone together here at rendezvous. I did not even know the Little Chief had come." She turned back to Wyeth. "Does this Jason Lee bring the same Christian medicine my people traveled to find in St. Louis?"

Wyeth shook his head. "Lee is a Methodist. Your people were after Jesuits. Catholics."

Whisper was puzzled. "The Catholic medicine, is it strong?"

"Your people must think so," said Wyeth with a smile. "They weren't impressed by Jason Lee. Lee didn't have many good things to say about your people, either. They wanted to see a crucifix, as proof of his medicine, and he didn't have one. The whole thing didn't go over big with either side." He laughed. "I'll bet the Jesuits make it out here before long, though. They can't stand to let the Methodists get a head start anywhere."

Jim shook his head in disgust. "I've seen this Jason Lee, and others like him. Gospel sharks is what they are." He looked at Wyeth and shook his head again. "You brought some real dandies out with you this time, Nat. They can't drink, they get sick on the food, and it scares them to death when a squaw pulls at their pants. They're worthless."

Wyeth laughed. "They're just not used to the country, or to the people."

"They'll never get used to things out here," Jim said, spitting into the dirt. "Take that greenhorn bird-watcher, Townsend, for instance. I saw him fall on his face in the river the other day chasin' some bird across to the other side. And who's that other one? Nuttall? All he does is look starry-eyed at the flowers all day. I never seen the likes of it. Like Whisper said before, they'll just ruin everything out here."

It was Wyeth's turn to get disgusted. "Those men, Townsend and Nuttall, they're scientists, Jim. They're out here to bring new knowledge to the world. There's nothing bad in that."

"Hell there ain't!" Jim barked. "They'll go back and set their tongues to waggin' about what they saw out here and soon the hills will be full of fools gawkin' at the birds and flowers. And they'll bring others that just want to come along for the ride."

While the men were talking, Whisper's thoughts had

been on her people. "I believe my people are looking for
strong medicine," she said slowly. "Yes, they must feel
this Christianity will give them more power in war against
the Blackfeet. They want the powers our ancestors had—
the powers given them by Shining Shirt." She looked to
both Jim and Nat Wyeth, to see if they agreed with what
she had finally figured out. But they were still talking about
the new Long Knives that were coming out to the West,
and they had not heard her words.

Jim and Nat Wyeth continued to argue and Whisper went
back to her thoughts. It must be true; her people were
changing. If what she had heard from the lips of Nat Wyeth
came to pass, it would mean the fulfillment of a prophecy
told to her people long, long ago. It would mean a great
change would come to the land of the Salish, and the old
ways would move aside for new ways. In her vision, the
faceless warrior had taken her through the valleys of
change. She had seen the good and the bad. She had seen
how hard it was for the human being to judge what was
bad. It seemed the human being always took what was bad
and called it good. Because of this, change was a word that
troubled her deeply.

Now it seemed her people's prophecy would come to
pass in her own lifetime. This was the prophecy of Shining
Shirt, a long ago hero of the Salish and their brothers, the
Kalispels. Whisper had heard the legend of Shining Shirt
many times as a child. Now the story came back to her as
if she were listening to it again that very day.

Shining Shirt was a man who had spoken to the spirits.
He came among the Salish in the old days, even before
they knew the horse. He had become a shaman, and later
a chief. He spoke words of great wisdom and the people
listened to him always. He told of a future time when the
lands of the Salish would know more strange men with
white skin than there were buffalo on the plains. He fore-
told they would lose their lands to these white men. The
people laughed at him, for none had ever seen any such
men with white skin. "Laugh now," Shining Shirt told

them. "But the day will come when you will all grovel at their feet."

Though this angered the people greatly, they did not harm Shining Shirt. He was a man of great medicine and had come to be their protector. He carried a charm around his neck that warded off evil and filled warriors with strong medicine during battle. It was told that there was a great battle with the Blackfeet at the place where the High Divide breaks and the buffalo trail goes through the Gate of Hell. Each Salish warrior was told to kiss the charm, which was a cross made of metal from which the figure of a dead man hung. Those who kissed the charm fought bravely and were not hurt. Those who had not believed and would not kiss the cross were injured or killed.

It was during this battle that the Blackfeet learned of Shining Shirt and his powerful medicine. As both sides fought each other, he stood upon a high rock and called down to them, holding the cross high in the air for them to see. He told the Blackfeet to stop fighting and make peace. But the Blackfeet did not listen. They laughed instead, for they were many more in number than the Salish and this was a good day for fighting. But soon these same Blackfeet looked upon Shining Shirt in awe, with their hands over their mouths. Many of their numbers lay dead or dying, while the Salish lost few. Soon they realized the medicine of Shining Shirt and hurried from the Gate of Hell into their own lands.

It was this strong medicine that made the Salish people of long ago listen to Shining Shirt. His words always proved true. He told the people that the time would come when teachers with long, black robes would come among them and change their lives forever. These Blackrobes would teach them a new way in which to live. They would change many of the old customs and bring new laws that must be obeyed. The names of the Salish people would no longer reflect brave deeds or things seen in visions, but would be names given by the Blackrobes as they poured water over Salish heads. Marriage would be different too.

A man who had married the eldest sister of a family would no longer be entitled to also take her younger sisters as wives. He would be required to live with but one wife. These things would mark the beginning of a new way of life for the Salish.

Now this prophecy of long ago was coming to pass. Whisper's eyes filled as she looked out over the singing and laughing of the rendezvous. It was the beginning of the end for all Indian peoples. Even Jim's protests could not stop this.

"Change is comin' to these hills," he was telling Wyeth. "But we don't want it!"

Wyeth shook his head. "Jim, you can't stop it. People are crowded in the east. There has to be expansion."

"Maybe so," Jim admitted. "But it still sticks in my craw."

"I don't understand you," Wyeth said. "Why don't you just take all this with a grain of salt like the rest of them do? Why do you care if you get a good price for fur or not?"

"The time will come when money will mean more than freedom," Jim said. "I see the need to start now, so I can make good by the kids Whisper and I bring up." He smiled at Whisper and gave her an affectionate pat on the leg as he continued. "There's still fur and there's still money to be made. I aim to cash in on it while the time is right."

"Where do you think you'll start your operation?" Wyeth asked.

"We're thinking up north," Jim answered. "Along the Stinkingwater maybe. We could serve everything from the Powder River and the Yellowstone clean on to the Great Falls of the Missouri."

"Good plan," said Wyeth. "But the Yellowstone is loaded with Company men."

"Maybe," said Jim. "But there's no greenhorns."

Wyeth laughed. "There's greenhorns everywhere. I'm a greenhorn."

"You learned the mountains fast, Nat. I mean those who

don't know Blackfoot sign from Sioux. They'll get a man in trouble."

"There's no way I'm going to convince you this change is in the best interests of the country, is there Jim?"

"No."

Wyeth shook his head. "Then how can you look forward to a successful business? You need people for business."

"There's good men here already who'll make it go. We don't need those who'll ask for pillows and tablecloths."

"When do you plan to start?" Wyeth asked.

"As soon as we can get geared up," Jim said. "And I think that's where you can help. You got good connections back east. You could get possibles out here for us, and we'd pay you a premium."

Wyeth nodded. "As a matter of fact, I have a goodly number of supplies on hand now I could sell you."

"Won't you be needin' them for your own business?"

"Not as many as I've got now," Wyeth said through tight lips. "I'm badly overstocked, thanks to a kind gentleman named William Sublette. I'd be willing to part with the goods at a very reasonable price."

Jim looked to Whisper with a gleam in his eye. "We could get our business rollin' this year. We wouldn't have to wait or head back to St. Louis. How's that for luck?"

Whisper smiled. "It would seem the spirits are with us."

Jim turned back to Wyeth. "I doubt if we have enough furs to take all the goods you've got to sell."

"That's no problem," Wyeth assured him. "Take what you can afford now. I'll store the rest of the stock down at my own business until you're ready to come for it."

"There's only one thing," Jim said. "I know Fiddler will be tickled pink about all this and I trust you, but I just don't know about some of the men you've got workin' for you. Namely Ed Beeler."

"I am no longer associated with Beeler. He and I had some disagreements we couldn't work out."

"I'll rest a little easier then," Jim said. "Beeler would steal me blind in a minute if he could."

"Well, I must warn you. Beeler is said to be working for the American Fur Company now. If he goes north to the Yellowstone, he could be trouble for you still."

"We'll watch out," Jim said, offering his hand to Wyeth. "We'll get all this down on paper first thing in the morning."

"Good," said Wyeth. "When do you expect to come down to the Snake and get the rest of your goods?"

"As soon as we get built up and make a little money. Maybe this fall, if all goes well for us."

"Well, I sure wish you all the luck in the world," Wyeth said. "I'll be back in the morning to finalize this." He went back toward the fire where his men were camped.

Jim turned to Whisper. "We've done it! How lucky can a man be?" He lifted Whisper into his arms and spun around in a circle, laughing.

"It makes me glad to see happiness return again to your eyes," said Whisper. "Amótkan has smiled down on us."

"We've got a lot of work ahead of us," Jim said. "But we've got something to look forward to now."

Whisper laughed. "This is the first time since we met here that your mind has been on anything but lying with me."

Jim picked her up and started for their lodge. "You're right. I knew there was somethin' we had to get done yet tonight."

Chapter 23

WAR DRUMS

The rendezvous carried on into the Moon of Service Berries—July. Jim and Fiddler were very happy, for now they looked forward to the trading post they would call Fort Shoshone. It was now a time to celebrate; their plans had become truth and soon they would follow the trails north to the Stinkingwater with a large pack train of goods.

Whisper shared in their joy. She had become more content with life since her trip to the Bitterroot. Now, during the last days of rendezvous, she won races with Red Thunder and took prizes at contests with her bow and the Hawken firestick. Once again she had both the Long Knife and the Indian peoples looking upon her in awe. Yes, the Spirit Woman was truly among them and her medicine was good.

It was during one such event that Whisper's eyes found a young Flathead brave staring at her. She had just placed an arrow through the cork from a whiskey jug at a distance of thirty paces. She had not only done it once, but three times. It was a feat unmatched by even the best warriors from her own people, as well as the Shoshone, Bannock, Nez Percé, and Iroquois, who had come from the east to the western lands with the Long Knives. It was not so much his staring that made Whisper curious about him, for others were staring as well, but something told her she knew this young brave. After she had taken her prize of a coat made from otter skin, she gave him the sign of greeting and he came over to her.

"It is you, the one called Spirit Woman," he said. "Yes, and that is a good name for you, for I saw you fight the Siksika dogs that day two winters past. You did great honor to yourself and our people that day. Then when I heard you had escaped from Walking Head, I knew you would some day become a legend among the Salish."

"Aiee!" Whisper said excitedly. "Are you of the Willow Cutters band?"

The young warrior nodded. "Yes, and I live to kill the Siksika dogs, the same ones that killed all of my family! I no longer can be warm in a lodge beside two brothers, my father and mother, and two aunts. Now there is no one who will be proud the day I have a son of my own."

"You have lost many to the Siksika," Whisper said. "You are lucky to have escaped with your own life."

The young warrior's eyes were dark with anger and his face was hard as stone as he remembered the day of the raid. "I was but a horse tender who was made to help with the escape of the women and children. It was to be the first day of my vision quest. I would have become a warrior and would have made my father and brothers proud. Instead I watched them die at the hands of those Siksika dogs!"

"Now you are alive to fight for revenge," Whisper told him.

The warrior yelled a long war cry. "Yes, and there are others who also survived and wait, as I do, for the time Siksika blood will stain our hands."

Whisper thought of her mother. No, she would not speak the name Little Grasses again. She had promised herself she would forget the past. She had told herself that to dwell on those things which had caused her great sorrow would only make her life miserable. If she asked this young warrior about those who had escaped and he did not mention the name Little Grasses, then she would surely become unhappy again. It was better not to know any more of her mother. Instead, she would talk of war against Walking Head.

"Have you completed the rites to become a warrior?" she asked.

"Yes," he nodded with pride. "I am now called Dancing Wolf. I am ready for war! I live for the day when we meet the Siksika in battle. And I would follow you. Whisper on the Water, the one called Spirit Woman. I would gladly follow you into battle, for I have seen you fight. I have seen your powers. Yes, you have strong medicine!"

Whisper nodded. "It may come to pass, if it is in the signs, that I will lead you and many other Salish warriors into battle against Walking Head. It is hard to know what lies ahead. Maybe some day the Siksika will be in our lands when you and I are in the same camp."

"Aiee, but the Siksika are here!" Dancing Wolf said quickly. "It is said Walking Head has been in these lands for many moons now. It is said he was camped on the Stinkingwater fighting Sioux and Shoshone for many moons. He is said to have crossed the Burning Mountains with his warriors into the valley where the waters of the Snake flow." He pointed to the west. "It is said he thinks the rendezvous of the Long Knives is to be there, and he knows he could then find you and take you with him."

"That dog!" Whisper raised her bow. "I will put an arrow through his heart!"

The young warrior laughed, then yelled a war cry. "Aiee, the Siksika will die!"

Whisper thought back to the dream she had had the night after her vision quest. The war cries and the fighting came back to her and it now seemed as real as it had that night. Arrows found their marks and Salish warriors waved scalps. The grass of the meadow lay flattened by horses' hooves and soaked with Siksika blood. Yes, she was lead-

ing the Salish warriors and yelling as loud as any of those
in the battle. Now Walking Head was coming down another
hill with another band of Siksika, and she was leading her
victorious warriors into battle with them. There was much
fighting and it was as hard and vicious as any the forest
had ever seen.

Was this a sign? Whisper watched the young warrior as
he danced in front of her, yelling Salish war cries. Was she
now destined to meet Walking Head and the Siksika across
the mountains in the valley of the Snake? Had the time
come so soon? Whisper thought of the warrior with no face
whose voice had told her she must not try to decide for
herself when to fight Walking Head. She remembered him
telling her that she would know when the time was right.
She would be told by signs. As the young warrior danced,
Whisper looked closely at his medicine shield. Aiee, she
had seen it before! It had been in her dream! She was sure
of it. It had belonged to one of the warriors who rode close
to her into battle against the Siksika. There was a Thun-
derbird on the shield, and the tracks of a wolf around the
bottom. Yes, it was a shield she had seen in her dream!

Now, as she was overcome with the realization that her
time had come, she began to tremble slightly. She had been
given a clear sign. But even though her memory of the
shield and the fighting was strong, something told her to
be very sure of her decision. She must read the signs cor-
rectly. She must know that what she would do now would
certainly affect the lives of many others. She remembered
the words that had come from the faceless warrior: "The
time for everything in your life comes only when it is right,
and if it is right. You cannot make things happen that do
not fit into the Universal Plan. Those things will not happen. You cannot change this. When things do happen,
maybe you will know why. Maybe you will not. Your
choice to act will govern your happiness. That is the way
it must be."

Whisper called the young warrior from his yelling and
dancing. She had made her decision.

"Are there others who wish to fight the Siksika?" she asked.

"There are many of us," Dancing Wolf answered quickly and with vigor. "It is a good day for fighting. It is a good day to die!" He yelled again.

"How many are there of you?"

"A great many. This is the day we have lived to see!"

"Why did you not go to the Valley of the Snake before this?" Whisper asked. "Why did you not lead the warriors yourself?"

Dancing Wolf's face again became hard. "The elders tell me I am not yet of age or enough honors to lead others into battle. The elders do not wish to lead themselves for they are now at peace and do not think it is wise to fight when there is no danger to our families. They believe those of us who wish to fight are fools. They say we will only leave more widows and grieving mothers among our numbers." Dancing Wolf stuck his jaw out. "The elders are quick to forget how many lodges now are empty because of our enemies, and how many of our dead are yet unavenged."

"What would the elders say if they heard I was preparing to lead a number of warriors against Walking Head?" Whisper did not care what the elders thought of her; they had forsaken her in her early hours of grief two winters past at Pierre's Hole. She asked only because she did not wish Dancing Wolf to gain disfavor among those in his band.

"There is nothing they could say," Dancing Wolf answered. "Many of them fear your powers. They do not know what to make of you, for never has there been a woman like you among our people."

Whisper thought a moment. "Would you lose honor by following me into battle?"

"A warrior would never lose honor by following one who has powerful medicine," he answered. "I will have more honor, much more honor, when they see us with blackened faces and the scalps and horses of our enemies."

"Call those warriors together who would follow me,"
Whisper told him. "And let the thunder of war drums be
heard."

Dancing Wolf returned shortly with many warriors to a
special place that Whisper had chosen for the dancing.
While a large fire was built and other preparations were
made, Whisper found Jim watching a horse race.

"Jim, I must now follow the trail of war," she told him.
"Come, there are things I must tell you."

She moved away from the noise of the race and Jim
followed her anxiously. "What?" he was asking. "What
are you telling me?"

"I have heard this day that Walking Head is in these
lands," Whisper said, pointing to the mountains to the
west. "He looks for me across the mountains in the valley
where the waters of the Snake flow. Now is the time for
me to go and finish what I have started. Now is the time
to kill Walking Head. I will leave with a young Salish warrior named Dancing Wolf. I will lead many warriors. You
must wait for my return."

"I'd planned on goin' with you when the time came."

"No, Jim, you must not. It is not in the signs. It would
not be good if you came. It could mean death for us both."

"I thought you told me I would fight with you," Jim
said with disgust. "Now you're backin' down on me."

Whisper frowned. "I told you I would not seek Walking
Head. I told you I would wait until the time was right, and
that I did not feel I would fight alone when the time came.
You were to fight with me only if it was in the signs. When
we talked, you understood this. Now that I have told you
the signs do not show you fighting with me, you say you
do not understand. Why is this?"

Jim shook his head. "All these dreams and visions. I'm
just not too sure about what the hell is goin' on around
here!"

"I do not know how long my mission will be," Whisper
said. "But it is something I know I must do. Please understand. I do not wish to leave you, but I must."

"You go right ahead," Jim said. "I think you're crazy, but don't look for me to tell you not to go."

"I feel that my time has come now," Whisper continued. "I will come to the forks of the Stinkingwater when Walking Head lies dead."

"Do what you want," Jim said coldly.

"Jim, you knew this day would come," Whisper pleaded. "I must go now; I must not wait. Time is on my side. I can only hope that it will stay on my side."

"I've never been able to talk sense into you yet," Jim said. "You go right ahead with all the warriors you can find. Maybe you don't care if you go under, I don't know. But it's gettin' hard for me to get used to you runnin' off all the time."

"Should I look for you on the Stinkingwater?" Whisper asked.

Jim shrugged. "I expect that's where we'll be."

"Do you want me to come back to you?"

Jim shrugged again. "That's up to you."

"Why should I come back to you if you do not want me?" Her eyes were flashing. "I love you, Jim, and I want to be with you. But I will not lie at your feet! I will not turn away from that which I must do!"

Jim waved an arm. "Go then! Don't let me stop you!"

"Hear my words! If you do not want me, I will leave this place and see you no more!"

Jim took a deep breath. "Whisper, you know I want you, and you know I love you. But can't you see, you're drivin' me out of my head with all this?"

"Jim, you know I must kill Walking Head before peace will come to us."

"That's crazy!"

"No! It is truth! It is the only way I can live in peace and know that my people and my baby live in the Land of Eternal Summer!" Her lips began to tremble and tears flooded her eyes.

Jim took her in his arms. His eyes, too, became wet. "You know how I feel about you," he said. "Losin' that baby was almost too much. I can't lose you too. Why do you put me through this?"

Whisper looked into his eyes. "This is the way it must be. Why is it you cannot see this? Why is it you cannot have faith? I have told you of my vision and of my dreams. I told you I did not see death for me."

"How can you really know what you saw?"

"I know I did not see death. That is important. Whatever happens, I will not die." She pushed herself away from him and looked over to the fire where the dancing had begun. "Tell Fiddler that I will soon see him again. Tell him I will bring him Walking Head's scalp."

"Why don't you tell him yourself?" Jim asked. "He's bound to be around here somewhere."

"No, I must go. I will take the things I need from our lodge and make ready for my mission." She gave him a long hug and kissed him gently. "I do wish you could be with me, for you are what is most important in my life. But I must not go against the signs."

Jim looked into her dark eyes and ran his fingers through her long hair. "You come to the Stinkingwater," he said. "I'll be there with Fiddler."

"I shall think of you all the while I am away from you, my husband," Whisper said. "For I now know a love for you I never thought possible. You will always be in my thoughts."

Again she kissed him, a long, hungry kiss that neither of them wished to end. Finally she pushed away from his arms. "I will now join the others who will follow me," she said. "I hear a sound that calls to me. Yes, I hear war drums."

Chapter 24

BUFFALO SONG

The wolves were many in number. There were four or five packs, with the count of ten or twelve in each pack. They formed a circle around the large meadow below where Salish hunters and women butchered fallen buffalo. It was a small band that had recently come over the mountains for the midsummer hunt.

Whisper led Dancing Wolf and the other warriors down the hill. The hunters were glad to see other Salish and there was talk of buffalo and war with the Siksika. Soon a fire was built for talking and smoking.

Whisper had just put Red Thunder on a picket to graze when a small group of women came across the meadow from where they had been butchering. One of them, an older woman, came over to Whisper and dropped her load of meat.

"It is you, Whisper on the Water! It is my daughter!"

Whisper's breath left her. She could hardly believe her eyes. "Mother!"

The woman took Whisper in her arms. "Amótkan has

blessed me," she sobbed. "This is a fine day in my life."

Tears were running out of Whisper's eyes. Then she was laughing for joy. "I knew you still lived!" she shouted. "I knew it!"

"Oh, my daughter, my life is once again like the blossoms of the flowers in the warm moons. I now have new life!"

After more hugging, Whisper said, "Mother, you have not changed in the time we have been apart. You are as beautiful as ever!"

"Those are kind words, my daughter, but the truth is not in them."

"No," said Whisper, "those words are truth. To me you will always be beautiful."

A broad smile broke through a face beginning to show lines of age. In her braids, white hairs showed themselves in good numbers among the black. But her eyes were bright and they danced as she spoke.

"I have spent many nights thinking of you, my daughter. They were long nights, and sleep did not come to me. I worried much about you those nights. I worried much when Sun was in the sky also. I was certain you were dead, or a slave among the Siksika. But many times these thoughts were broken by other thoughts that came to me. These thoughts told me you were not dead, nor were you a slave in the land of the Siksika. These thoughts tried to make me believe you still lived, but in another land where our people seldom go. It was hard to believe these thoughts, for my mind was full of grief and sorrow. But these thoughts kept coming back to me. They would not leave me alone. So one night I cried out loud, 'Yes, I will believe my daughter lives!' And since that time I have not dwelled on the thoughts that you were dead or a slave. I went on with my life as best I could, having no sorrow, yet no real happiness. And then today . . ." Tears again rolled down her cheeks. She wiped her eyes. "I am a foolish old lady," she laughed. "I shed tears when I am happy."

"I, too, am happy," Whisper said. "This is a happiness

I never thought I would be blessed with. I have searched these entire lands, and many other lands, for you. But from no one's lips did I ever hear the name Little Grasses.''

Her mother smiled and said, ''You have looked long for a name that is no more. I am no longer called Little Grasses.''

Whisper covered her mouth in amazement. ''What has become of your name?''

''After I escaped from our village with the others that bad day, I received a new name. I found food for those of us who survived. We were all hungry and I found a large patch of the dark blue berries that grow where it is damp. Now I am called Huckleberry Woman.''

Whisper began to laugh. ''Now you are Huckleberry Woman?''

Her mother nodded.

Still laughing, Whisper said, ''For two winters I have been looking long and hard for you. No wonder I could not find you. You are no longer long and thin and growing where the buffalo graze. Now you are big and bushy and grow under trees.''

Whisper laughed harder and her mother began to laugh with her. Tears rolled from their eyes and their stomachs began to hurt. ''You are truly a silly one,'' her mother managed to say while still laughing. ''I have not laughed so hard since I can remember.''

The feasting that night was a special time for Whisper and her mother. Much had happened to both of them since the day of the Siksika raid. Seeing each other again brought back memories of losing their family and Sun Bear Standing. But the sadness did not stay long; the joy of reunion overwhelmed them both.

''I have found a man whom I will love forever,'' Whisper told her mother. ''He is a Long Knife, but the best man in the world.''

''Your father would not have approved of a Long Knife,'' her mother said. ''But your eyes tell me your love for him is as strong as love can be.'' She gave Whisper a firm hug. "I am very happy for you, my daughter."

"He will always be good to us," Whisper assured her. "He will never tire of me, nor I of him."

Her mother smiled. "That is good. Life will send you many gifts. Maybe even children."

Whisper blinked. "Yes, maybe so."

"Children are what make life complete."

"Yes, mother, that is true. Have you gone into a warrior's lodge?"

"Pffft," her mother said through her lips. "That is a silly question, my daughter. I am no longer of childbearing age. And there are few older warriors among our people who do not already have many mouths to feed. No, I live in a widow's lodge and get my meat from those who are kind. That is why I am on this hunt. I am too old for this sort of thing."

"It is indeed fortunate that you chose to go on this hunt, though," Whisper said. "Or I still might be looking for a grass instead of a bush."

The two of them laughed again. They ate more buffalo meat and talked more of the time they had been apart. Her mother's life had, indeed, been hard. After their escape, she and a few other Salish women had become separated from the other survivors when a war party of Kainah—brothers of the Siksika—had surprised them near a river crossing. They had all been forced to scatter and hide wherever they could find cover. After that, Huckleberry Woman and the others had wandered for many suns. They had no weapons and could kill no game. Roots and berries were their only source of food until they found a small band of Salish who took them in and fed them. While her mother lived with this small band, she often wondered what had happened to those who had been separated at the river when the Kainah had jumped them. Many of them had been young men who were horse tenders. Now they were warriors, Huckleberry Woman knew, for many of them had followed Whisper into the hunting camp this very day.

She looked at Whisper closely and began to speak again.

This time her smile was gone. "There has never been a day in my life with more happiness," she said. "But now I become troubled, my daughter. I see you here without your husband, and I see you leading many Salish warriors. Why is this?"

"Jim is building a trading post where the Stinkingwater flows," Whisper answered. "He and his good friend, Fiddler, will trade with other Long Knives and the Shoshones."

Her mother nodded. "I am truly happy you have come here, and that I have found you," she said. "But why are you not on the Stinkingwater? Or why are Jim and his friend not with you?"

Whisper took a deep breath. "Mother, I have come to these lands on a mission. I have become a warrior."

Whisper told her mother of the young Siksika war chief, Walking Head, and of his desire to own her. She told the entire story of her fight with the Siksika during the raid, and how she escaped at Henry's Lake with the help of Jim.

"Many of our women have been captured and then escape," her mother said. "They do not become warriors. That is not the way of a woman."

Whisper then decided to tell her mother all that had happened. She told of her happiness with Jim, and their friend, Fiddler. She told of the baby she had conceived and how she had lost it at the hands of a Piegan war party. Her eyes filled with tears as she spoke and her body shook. Then anger overwhelmed her and she beat her fists on the ground. Her mother tried to calm and soothe her. It was all past now; new days were ahead. Still Whisper talked of fighting and vengeance, and of how all the Indian peoples knew her for the hatred she felt for Blackfeet.

"Then it is true," her mother said. "You are the one called Spirit Woman, the woman with the fighting spirit inside her."

"Yes, mother. I did not wish for all this to happen, nor do I wish to fight with paint and medicine shield as a man does. But Walking Head has caused me much grief and it is in the signs that we shall some day meet in battle.''

"What signs have you seen? That is for those who have made a vision quest.''

"I *have* made a vision quest. I saw and felt many things that day. I have had dreams and have felt many more things since that time. I know the day will come when I will face Walking Head. That is why I have come to the waters of the Snake. It is said Walking Head and the Siksika are in these lands.''

"Here?'' her mother said with concern. "Why would the Siksika come down into these lands when there are more buffalo to the north, in their own lands.''

"Walking Head looks for me, Mother,'' Whisper explained. "It is true, the Siksika should now be hunting where the waters of the Big Muddy flow. But Walking Head would rather find me than meat for his winter camps. As long as that dog follows me, I will never know peace.''

"I can see your hatred for him is deep,'' said her mother. "And I can understand your feelings, for it was my husband and your brothers who died at the hands of his warriors. But he has fought many times before, and has many honors to his name. He knows well the ways of war.''

"I, too, will learn the ways of war,'' said Whisper.

"Well,'' her mother said with a deep sigh, "then let us rejoice with one another now. I have been with you this one day in the past two winters, and it hard to know what tomorrow will bring.''

Chapter 25

STORM CLOUDS

The waters of the Snake ran shallow and wide at this place called the Valley of the Swans. There were times of the year when the large white birds covered the waters from shore to shore. But now the birds were upriver, swimming in the cooler waters of the high country, for the Moon of the Onion—August—had nearly arrived.

Sun was straight above and the day grew hot. Five suns had passed since Whisper had led Dancing Wolf and the Salish war party into the camp of hunters, where she had found her mother. Since that time there had been no sign of Walking Head or the Siksika. Now, as Whisper and Dancing Wolf sat in council with some of the other warriors, it was decided that the quest would be over with the end of this day. The warriors would travel with Whisper and her mother back over the mountains to the Siskadee, and the hunters would return to the Bitterroot.

Mid-afternoon came, and a dark bank of clouds formed in the west. The air became still and swarms of gnats came down from the sky and flew around the peoples' necks and faces. Then, from over a hill to the north, came one of the scouts. He rode hard and jumped from his horse before he had fully stopped.

"Siksika!" he announced. "There are many and they are coming fast from the north."

"Is it Walking Head?" Whisper asked.

"I did not see Walking Head among them."

"It does not matter," said Whisper. "All Siksika are dogs!" She turned to the crowd of warriors who had gathered behind her. "Put on your paint and sing your songs of war. Today we fight the Siksika!"

There was yelling and cheering as the camp came alive. Dancing Wolf clenched his fist over his heart and spoke to Whisper with pride in his voice.

"This is the day of my dreams, Spirit Woman. Yes, the time of glory for the Salish has come. And during the telling of brave deeds, your name will be on the lips of everyone who is here this day."

Whisper's mother was beside her. "Must you fight them, my daughter?"

"Mother, that is why I have come," Whisper answered. She pointed to the warriors in camp as they gathered their weapons and began their rituals. "This is the day I have waited for since the raid on our village two winters past. I only wish it was Walking Head, and not just a scouting party. There is no doubt he is traveling somewhere nearby with his main force. But he, too, will see the fury of the Salish when they avenge their dead!" Whisper started for camp to prepare herself for the upcoming battle.

Huckleberry Woman tugged at her sleeve as she walked. "Whisper, there is something I think we should discuss before you fight."

"Can it not wait, Mother?"

"It is important."

At that moment, Dancing Wolf rushed over and pointed to the hills across the river. Below the tree line was a large body of riders strung out in a long line. The Siksika had been traveling fast, as the scout had told her. And they, indeed, were many in number. Overhead, the sky began to rumble and the clouds bunched tighter. Whisper smiled as she looked across to where the Siksika sat their horses in a column and shouted war cries across the river. They were no stronger in number than her own force, and they would surely not be ready for a woman whose medicine was the storm.

"Whisper, we must talk!" her mother said.

"No, Mother, there is no time. You must take shelter in the trees along the river with the other women and their children."

Whisper rushed to her lodge and painted for war. A dark mass of black on her forehead symbolized the storm clouds, while jagged streaks of red ran from high on both cheekbones to her chin. The power of the storm, the lightning, would show vividly on her face, and all those who fought against her would know the meaning of her sign. And this day, her power would be strong. The storm was here to be with her as she fought her enemies.

Dancing Wolf and the other warriors followed Whisper out of camp, singing war songs and waving their weapons in the air. They crossed the river and spread out along the banks in a long line, facing the hill and the Siksika.

Three Siksika warriors came down from the main body, their hands raised in peace. One made the sign that he wished to talk. The rumbling in the sky grew louder and off to the west, a flash of lightning appeared.

Whisper and Dancing Wolf rode out toward the three Siksika warriors. Whisper's thoughts went back to the Battle of Pierre's Hole, now two winters past. She remembered the Gros Ventre war chief and how he had been deceived by Antone Godin and the Flathead warrior. Though war had been in the hearts of the Gros Ventres that day, they had sent the chief out to lie and to talk of peace. When Antone Godin had extended his hand in peace, the Flathead warrior had blown a hole through the chief's heart. Now maybe the Siksika felt it would be easy to capture her if they could kill Dancing Wolf first. But that would not happen.

She and Dancing Wolf stopped a short stone's throw from the three Siksika. They raised their hands in peace again, but their faces were painted for war.

One of them made signs to Whisper. "Come closer, Spirit Woman, so that we may talk."

"We can talk from here," Whisper made sign back. "What is it you wish to say to us before we make widows of your women?"

"We have come to talk, not to fight," the Siksika warrior told her. "We wish to save the lives of your people. We are many and we are all brave warriors. It is only you we come for. Walking Head travels to this place even now from the waters of the Teton. He says his heart is good and that he will not have his warriors kill the Salish dogs that travel with you, if you will come with us in peace."

"Your arrogance is matched only by your stupidity," Whisper made sign back. "If Walking Head was a man, he would be here to tell me these words himself. But he is a child and he sends children even younger than himself to speak for him. It is too bad you will not live another day to play hide and seek among the willows along the river."

The warriors straightened up on their horses in anger.

"Why is it you tell lies and expect me to believe them?" Whisper continued. "I know you and the others are but a scouting party sent out by Walking Head to find us. Now you are afraid to die like warriors. You wish to find a hole so you can tremble like the rabbit."

The three Siksika looked one to another like they could not believe that someone was speaking to them in this manner. "Walking Head does not wish to see harm come to the Spirit Woman," the leader made sign. "Nor does he wish to see her grieve at the deaths of more of her people. If you come with us in peace, none of these things will happen."

Whisper pointed to the sky, then to her medicine shield and the paint on her face. "My medicine is the storm," she said sternly. "You can see the signs on my face and on my medicine shield. Hear the sky speak, oh brave Siksika warriors. Yes, listen carefully. The Powers are telling me they are with me this day." A breeze began to blow that pulled at their hair and at the manes of the horses. The sky rumbled more and became dark as the clouds blocked out Sun. Whisper let her words sink in and continued. "Since you are no more than children, you now have the chance to run away. Go back to Walking Head and tell him that next time he should send men to find me and leave the children to play in camp."

The Siksika warrior who had been spokesman clenched both fists and pushed them out to the right and left away from him in the sign for war. "We shall see if your medicine is strong this day, Spirit Woman. For if it is not, you will surely die with the Salish dogs you call your people."

Quickly, they turned their horses and galloped off to the base of the hill to join the other warriors, who were all yelling and had their weapons raised in the air.

Whisper gathered her warriors together. They, too, were yelling war cries and chanting songs to the spirits. It was a good day to fight!

"This is the day we have all waited for!" Whisper yelled. "Today we avenge our fallen Salish brothers!"

Rain suddenly fell in short bursts between claps of thunder. Across the meadow, the Siksika were looking up at the sky and over to the Salish. Whisper smiled. The Siksika were now committed to fighting and would be too proud to give up. They would die as warriors should.

The fighting began. Whisper led the first group out from the Salish ranks toward a group that had separated from the main force of the Siksika. The Salish warriors were ready, for they knew they would get only one good chance at their enemies as they rode past each other.

Leaning low over Red Thunder, Whisper rode straight for the warrior who had been the spokesman during their talk. His eyes were wild and he had worked himself into a frenzy, but this would be his last day to fight. His trade

rifle misfired and Whisper's arrow went over his medicine
shield and into his neck. As Whisper turned Red Thunder
around to count coup, she saw him sitting up in the grass
of the meadow clutching at the arrow in his throat. Her war
club left him writhing and kicking while Dancing Wolf and
the others welcomed her back to their side with whoops
and yells.

Dancing Wolf led another group out into the meadow.
His lance found the belly of a warrior painted in solid yellow, and pushed one of his kidneys out a gaping hole in
his back. Dancing Wolf made the turn to retrieve his lance
and also came back to rounds of cheers and shouting.

Now the meadow was dotted with fallen Siksika. Every
Salish warrior had bloodied his lance or left an arrow in
the body of an enemy. Many of the fallen lay still in death,
while others sang death songs. For Whisper and her war
party, it was indeed a fine day. They had avenged many of
their people who had fallen to the Siksika in the past, while
only a few of their own warriors felt the warmth of their
own blood. And not one of those would die from his
wounds.

The Siksika came out to carry away their dead and dying.
Whisper knew this was the sign they wished for no more
fighting. But this was not to be. If they wished to run, no
one would chase them down. But they would not be allowed to leave with those who had fallen.

Whisper led the entire force out toward the remaining
Siksika. There was no fight left in them and they fell
quickly under the renewed Salish attack. More Siksika sang
death songs while the Salish exalted in victory. A few managed to escape with one who was dead or wounded, singing
songs of mourning over lost relatives or war-brothers.
Whisper knew the Salish would soon find Walking Head
and that there would be more fighting. She was ready, for
this was why she had come to these lands.

When the battle was over, the women and children from
camp came out into the meadow and committed the final
acts of vengeance. Soon the fallen Siksika were naked and

lying in pieces, just as Whisper's people had after the raids upon her village. Now these Siksika warriors would never see an eternal life of peace in their own far-away land of the afterlife. It was fitting, for the peoples of the Blackfoot tribes were the scourge of the Salish nation.

"Have you fulfilled your quest for vengeance, my daughter?" her mother asked.

"It will soon be over, Mother. Walking Head will seek vengeance and I will be waiting. Then we can live in peace."

"Tell me, my daughter," her mother asked firmly, "why is it you think so much of killing Walking Head that you do not think of yourself? You have been reading the signs of war so closely that you forget the signs of your own body."

"What do you mean, Mother?"

"I have been watching you closely, Whisper. I see that you become sick nearly every morning. Maybe you are again with child."

Whisper looked startled. She had thought the dreaming, or perhaps the tension of the mission, had caused her morning dizziness and discomfort. But now as she thought about it, she could not remember caring for herself during the woman's time each moon since her trip to the Bitterroot.

"I, too, can read signs," her mother continued. "Even if you do not know the ways of a woman during such a time, you can be certain that I do."

"Is that the important thing you had wished to speak to me about?" Whisper asked.

"Do you not think it is important, my daughter?"

"Of course, Mother," Whisper answered. "And I feel great joy, for I had believed the Pikuni war club had killed the childbearing part within me." She gently touched her abdomen. "Now I know that cannot be true."

Her mother's face was sad. "Why must you continue to fight, then? Why can't you leave it as it now is? You have taken revenge. Let us leave this place."

"We will, Mother. Soon."

"Soon? Why not now?"

"It is a strange day, Mother," said Whisper. "I have taken revenge on a hated enemy and realized I am with child, all in the same afternoon. I wish to take you with me to the Stinkingwater to tell my husband, Jim, the news. But it seems I have one last, hard journey before my happiness can come to pass.

Through the rain, Whisper could see tears on her mother's cheeks. She took her mother in her arms and held her tightly. "Mother, do not feel this way. Dry the water from your eyes and make your heart strong. I will not see death. I have a strange feeling, but it is not the darkness of death."

"Let us leave now for the Stinkingwater," her mother pleaded. "We must not allow anything bad to happen. To make war against Walking Head can mean only bad things will happen."

The sky was no longer rumbling and the rain had let up. To the west, behind the clouds, was a rainbow where Sun had found clear sky. Whisper brushed a large tear from her mother's cheek.

"I will pray to Amótkan, and to my spirit guardian, the little owl," Whisper said. "There are things that must be answered in my heart. But no matter what comes, you must be strong. I fear the times ahead will be hard for both of us."

Chapter 26

THE MEDICINE PIPE

Restful sleep did not come to Whisper that night. Again dreams filled her head and she tossed about on her robes. She was someplace she had never been before. She saw a land of rolling hills, where a wind blew constantly and where there were no forests. Buffalo filled this land, and the small coyote could be seen skulking over every hill.

Before in her dreams, she had swung the war club and loosed arrows at her enemies. Somehow this night, in these dreams, she felt as though she was bound tightly. She could not feel her arms, nor could she run on her legs. She could only see. And much of what she saw was very strange.

Lines of warriors rode trails through a land where rocks broke out into tall, pure-white cliffs. A wide river ran through these lands and on its banks was a village of many lodges. There was a large crowd of Indian people gathered at the center of the village, where they danced and sang in a ring around the center lodge. The faces of the people were hazy, and she could not make out their dress. Their songs were not Salish, but were of another Indian people. Though the songs were not familiar, Whisper could somehow sense that she knew the tribe.

Now the people broke their circle and Whisper felt herself moving forward through it, toward the center lodge. It was a big lodge, far bigger than the others. She stood near the lodge now, still unable to feel her hands and feet, and the people closed the circle around her. They continued to sing and dance around her and the lodge. The markings on the lodge suddenly became clear to her. They were large and painted all around the outside of the lodge. They were the markings of a warrior whose medicine was the weasel. Whisper choked in her sleep and struggled for breath.

"Whisper! Whisper, wake up!"

Whisper awoke with a start. It was her mother, Huckleberry Woman. In the dim firelight inside the lodge, her face showed deep concern.

"Whisper, the men on watch have become silent. They no longer call to each other in the sounds of night birds."

Whisper poked her head outside the lodge. Sun was still down below the eastern horizon, but light had broken over the rim of the mountains. She looked for Red Thunder. He paced nervously on his rope beside the lodge. All the horses had been picketed inside the circle of lodges, a tactic commonly used to discourage horse thieves while traveling through non-Salish lands. Like Red Thunder, the horses all seemed on edge.

Whisper's nerves grew taut. There was a strange silence about the camp. Though the light was still too dim to see out beyond the lodges, she knew there were other horses above the meadow.

She drew her head back inside the lodge and started for her weapons. "You are right, Mother. Something is indeed wrong."

At that instant she heard a sound at the doorflap. The painted face of Walking Head appeared in the lodge. He held a gleaming knife in his mouth. In an instant, his forearm was locked under the jaw of Huckleberry Woman and the point of his knife was at her throat.

"Do not cry out, Spirit Woman. There is but one way I can make you leave with me, and this is it."

Incredibly, he spoke to her in Salish. It was broken, but understandable.

"You send children out as sentries to watch over your camp," he said. "They died as quiet as babies."

Whisper sat frozen. Her mother appeared calm, though the knife blade had broken the skin and a bead of blood was forming in the cut.

"You look at me strangely, Spirit Woman," Walking Head told her. "Yes, I can speak the Salish tongue. You will learn more about this when we reach the land of my people. We will leave now."

"What about my mother?"

"She will travel with us for a time, then be left to go on her own."

"Then she will be allowed to rejoin those in this camp?"

"The others in this camp will die this fine day. She will be allowed to go off on her own."

"It is me you want," said Whisper. "If you want me badly enough, you will spare this woman and all those in the camp."

Walking Head's eyes were hard. "We will kill all in the camp but you. Then you will come with me to the land of my people."

Whisper shook her head. "No, that is not the way it will be, Walking Head. If you kill these people, you will have to kill me also. If you do not, I will surely cut the throat of every Siksika dog this fine day!"

Walking Head straightened up. "Then you will die!"

"It is a good day to die!"

"What is it you want, Spirit Woman?" Walking Head asked after a moment of thought.

"I have told you. I will leave only if you spare my people."

"Do you wish these Salish dogs to live? You are the only prize in this camp."

Whisper's eyes flashed. For a moment, she thought of fighting him. But it would do no good, she knew, for it would only mean death for her mother and the others in the camp. No, she must not fight now. There would be another day for that. She only wished things could have been different now. Walking Head knew this plainly from the words she spoke to him.

"The only dogs I know are Siksika! If we had been prepared to fight, this ground would have been red with Siksika blood. Our warriors are young, but they are not afraid. If you do not do as I wish, I will lead this camp against you and we will fight until the last Salish war cry is silent!"

"But now you will do as I say," Walking Head retorted. "If you value your mother's life."

"You are a fool, Walking Head, if you come into this camp and expect to leave with me alive."

"You have awakened this day with a weak mind, Spirit Woman. At this moment I have many Siksika warriors awaiting my orders to burn this camp and kill all those who are in it. There are also two who wait for me behind this lodge." He made the small squeak of a prairie mouse, which was answered by two other squeaks outside the lodge. Again the wicked smile came to his face. "Now, Spirit Woman, tell me who is a fool."

"You have won this day," Whisper told him. "I have told you I will travel with you to your lands. I will do this only because you have forced me. But do not think I will stay with you."

"You will stay with me," Walking Head spoke with confidence. "Now we will go. Quickly!" He started for the door, dragging Whisper's mother with him.

"Wait!" Whisper, ran after him. "We will smoke the pipe of peace together first. You will pledge to the Powers that your word will be kept. There will be no fighting today.

We will smoke together as a sign that this is how it will be.''

"No," said Walking Head. "I will not smoke."

"Then I will sing war songs and put on the paint of battle," said Whisper. "I must know your word will be kept."

"Your warriors will wish to fight us," Walking Head argued.

"They will listen to me. They have followed me to this camp; they will do as I ask."

After more thought, Walking Head said, "Prepare your fires and fill your pipe for smoking. You would do better in my village than to lie dead among these dogs."

Whisper turned to her mother. "Tell the camp what has happened. Tell Dancing Wolf he must listen to my words. And have the elder, Wolverine, bring his medicine pipe."

"The elder, Wolverine, will not wish for this ceremony to take place," her mother said. "This is a ceremony a man must perform, a man who is a chief or elder."

"Tell him things must be different this day," said Whisper.

Sun had now begun to creep up over the mountains. The air seemed unusually hot and sultry for the early morning hours. Though the light shone through clear skies in the east, a dark bank of clouds moved toward them from the west. Whisper smiled. This day there would be another thunderstorm.

Walking Head had sent one of the two warriors out from camp to announce what was to happen. Soon a ring of Siksika warriors approached slowly from the hills and joined together as one group. They sat their horses at the edge of camp, eager to fight but respectful of the wishes of their war chief.

"Listen to me!" Whisper told her people. Everyone had gathered in the center of camp. There was confusion, and some of the women had begun to sing their death songs. "Put down your weapons," she ordered. "There will be no fighting this day."

Dancing Wolf ran up to her. "What do you mean by shielding our enemies from us."

"Listen to my words, Dancing Wolf," Whisper said. "It is not a good day to fight. They have many in number and have prepared for battle. Though we are also many in number, there is not one among us who has painted or invoked the spirits. You must stand back and watch this day, Dancing Wolf. And tell the others to be wise and do the same. There will be another day for us."

Wolverine, the elder, stood nearby. Whisper went over to him and asked for the pipe.

"This pipe is sacred," he said with a frown. "It must be used only for sacred things. Never before has a woman touched this pipe."

"We have already lost five young men this morning," Whisper told him. "They died at the hands of the Siksika while watching the camp. Do you feel the lives of the others here are sacred? More sacred than the custom that women are not to smoke the pipe you hold?"

The elder looked to the edge of camp where the Siksika awaited the commands of their leader. Then he looked to Walking Head, whose eyes were cold and hard. He nodded and handed Whisper the pipe.

Whisper ordered that a fire be started in the center of camp for the ceremony. The medicine pipe was prepared for smoking and special preliminary prayers were offered.

Then Whisper addressed Walking Head. "The ceremony shall begin."

"You do much," Walking Head remarked, "just to save a few Salish dogs."

"Maybe it is your own life you worry about," said Whisper. "Your medicine may be powerful when you war against others, but against me, you become weakened."

Walking Head blinked, then grunted. He seated himself crosslegged at his place near the fire. He placed his articles of war beside him. Whisper sat across from him, the fire between them. She placed her war shield and her own weapons of war beside her and began the ceremony.

Whisper offered the pipe to both the earth and sky, and to the four directions—North, South, East, and West. She then sang a song invoking the Powers to hear her, and puffed on the pipe. As she again offered the pipe to the Powers, the formation of clouds that had been moving in from the West began to rumble. A slight wind began to blow, which quickly increased to a heavy breeze that pulled at their hair and set the trees to swaying. Whisper smiled. The Powers were with her.

The elder, Wolverine, took the pipe from Whisper and handed it to Walking Head. He hesitated a moment.

"Smoke," Whisper ordered. "That is a sacred pipe."

Walking Head then offered the pipe to both the earth and sky, and to the four directions. The cloud bank rolled into the sky above them and covered the sun. He smoked the pipe and handed it back to Wolverine.

Whisper pointed to the sky and to her medicine shield. She looked sternly at Walking Head. "My power is the storm. You can see the signs on my medicine shield." Her voice had a strange tone that made Walking Head tense up. "Hear the sky speak, Walking Head. The Powers are telling me they are with me this day." A gust of wind whipped the fire between them and a burning branch popped in the sudden heat of fanned flames. Walking Head jumped. "You are to live by the word you have spoken to me this day," Whisper went on. "I will live by the words I have spoken to you. I will go with you to the land of the Siksika, but you must not cause harm to any of my people here today. You will hear these words and obey them, as you have vowed to do. The Powers have heard this. Now, you will smoke again to seal these words."

When Walking Head had again finished smoking, the wind calmed. But the clouds remained and the thunder increased. The two Siksika warriors looked at the sky and then to Walking Head with their hands covering their mouths. One said, "Leave her, Walking Head. Let us go now. She is a Spirit Woman!"

"No!" Walking Head shouted, as raindrops began to

fall. "No, I must learn her medicine. Get ready to leave."

Whisper knew Walking Head had no more notions of war. He could hear the thunder and feel the rain. Yes, the Spirit Woman had invoked the Powers, and he had sworn by a sacred medicine pipe to keep peace this day. To go against his word now would surely make the Powers angry. It would mean grave misfortune for him, or even death.

"And you will not take any of the horses or belongings," Whisper ordered further. "You leave everything you did not come with."

"My vow was only against killing these Salish dogs," Walking Head said angrily. "The horses and all else now belongs to us!"

"You vowed to leave here with me only!" Whisper shouted back. "You vowed not to cause harm to any of my people. If you leave them without horses or food, you will surely be harming them."

Walking Head's eyes were alive with anger, but he did not speak. Again the sky rumbled and more rain began to fall.

"It is not a good day for you to fight," Whisper told him.

Walking Head motioned to his warriors. "Get ready to leave. Take nothing that we did not bring to this place."

Whisper handed the medicine pipe back to the elder, Wolverine. "It is truly a sacred pipe," she said.

"Never have I seen anything like this day," Wolverine told her. "You have saved the lives of many Salish people. You are Amótkan's daughter. The Powers indeed smile down on you."

Whisper gathered only a few things and led Red Thunder to the edge of camp. Higher on the slope, Walking Head and the others waited for her while she spoke in farewell to her mother.

"The storm is my strength, Mother," she said. "Do not worry about me."

Her mother's eyes were full with tears. "I fear I will never see you again."

"It is a strange day," Whisper said. "This morning I learned I am again with child and I felt I would be taking you with me to tell my husband the news. Now it seems I have one last hard journey before my happiness can come to pass." She took her mother in her arms and held her tightly.

"My heart aches so I can hardly bear it," the old woman sobbed. "Now my days will be dark again."

Whisper continued to hold her. "Mother, do not feel this way. It is only for a time; I know we will see each other again soon." She took her mother by the shoulders and held her firmly. "Dry the water from your eyes and make your heart strong. Take my weapons, which I have left in your lodge, and follow the trails north to the Stinkingwater. Find my husband, Jim, and the old Long Knife, Fiddler. Look for one with reddish-blonde hair and listen for the sound of the stringed box the Long Knives call a fiddle. You will find them where the two forks come together." She took her mother's hands in her own and squeezed them. "I love you, Mother."

There was one last, long hug between them.

"You must leave as soon as I do," Whisper said. "And hurry!"

In a moment she was on Red Thunder's back. Her mother stood looking up at her with large tears rolling down her cheeks.

"We will be together again soon," said Whisper. She bit her lip hard. "Be strong, my dear mother. Be strong."

The rain, which had ceased for a time, began again and the sky rumbled. But to the west, behind the clouds, was a rainbow where Sun had found a clear sky. Soon the Siksika had disappeared into the trails of the forest, Whisper among them, riding Red Thunder toward a land she had never before seen, except in her dreams.

Part Four

FORT SHOSHONE

Chapter 27

ABOVE THE PLAINS

The day was clear and the wind was silent. The heat that comes with the warm moons had vanished beneath the cool rain that had fallen during the past three suns. Now the sky was empty of even a single cloud this early morning, and the drops of water that clung to the grass and flowers were filled with sparkling light.

Whisper rode behind Walking Head on a horse he led with a rawhide rope. Her hands were bound tightly behind her and she wore no moccasins. Since leaving for the land of the Siksika with Walking Head, she had not been allowed to ride Red Thunder. She had been allowed to see him only when camp was made each evening, and then only under close watch. Walking Head knew if she ever got away from camp on that horse, there would be no way to catch her.

Now, in this early morning, Walking Head was taking her away from the main camp. There would be just the two of them, for he had told her he wished to have a long talk with her about the way her heart was now that she was

with him and away from her own people. They had traveled
the passing of eleven suns and Whisper had said very little
to Walking Head during this time. This was not good,
Walking Head had told her, and it was now time for her to
hear his words where no one else could hear them.

During these many suns, Whisper had thought a great
deal about her life and what she would face in the Siksika
village. It was a strange land to her, these plains, where
mountains could be found only in small groups that broke
sharply down into rolling grasslands and broken river bottoms. Never before had Whisper seen such a land. It had a
beauty all its own, not like the mountains, but vast and open
and boundless in all directions. It was a land filled with
huge herds of buffalo that covered the hills in black
swarms, and where the antelope and elk grazed in mixed
herds, ever watchful for the prairie wolves that followed
close by in large packs, their red tongues hanging from their
mouths. Though it was new and different, Whisper could
not enjoy the things she was seeing. She would rather have
been traveling with Jim and her mother, while the old Long
Knife, Fiddler, played merrily on his stringed box.

Her mind was always on the child she carried within her,
a thing more precious to her now than anything she had
ever known. The long days away from Jim and her mother
brought an echo to her mind that she would now hear always, even to her last breath of life. "Let us now rejoice
with one another," she remembered her mother saying. "It
is hard to know what tomorrow will bring."

Whisper dug her knees into the ribs of the pony and
locked her heels under his stomach. They were going up a
steep trail that would take them high above the surrounding
plains onto a giant flattopped mountain Walking Head
called Square Butte. The mountain was strange to see, sitting huge by itself over the grassy hills and badlands below.
Nearby was another mountain, smaller and round in shape,
known to the Siksika as Round Butte. At a distance from
these two lone mountains was a chain of timbered peaks
that seemed to rise straight up out of the prairie. This was

called the place of the High Wood, where trees grew all the way to the jagged tops.

At the top of Square Butte, Walking Head stopped at a place near the edge of a tall cliff. Here the trees parted and the eye could travel farther than a journey of many suns.

"This is now your land as well as mine," said Walking Head. "There is far more land out there than you have ever before seen at one time. Is that not true, Spirit Woman?"

Whisper did not answer, but looked far out over the broken hills and plains.

Walking Head pointed far down to where a sliver of water cut deep through hills and ridges steep and grey with clay earth. The land looked as though a giant had used his knife to gouge a thousand rills and gullies through a sea of grass which would have otherwise been flat.

"Those are the waters of the Arrow," said Walking Head, "where the Blackfoot tribes have come for many winters to gather wood and stone for arrow making. These waters flow to where my people have made the hunting camp along Big River, called Big Muddy by other than our own people. Soon you shall see this place and begin your life as a Siksika."

"You did not bring me so far from the others to tell me of my place among the Siksika," Whisper said. "Your desire for me shows plainly in your eyes. It is hard for me to understand why you have not simply tried to force yourself upon me before now."

Walking Head grunted. "It is true, my desire for you is strong. But, I do not wish to have my eyes clawed out and this would not make you feel for me as I do for you."

"What feelings do you have for me, Walking Head? The desire to own me is the only feeling you have. Now that you own me, your life should be happy."

"I want things to be good between us, Spirit Woman. I want our lives to be as one." His eyes were soft as he spoke, softer than Whisper thought possible for this man. "You could be a good and devoted wife to me, and I will

wait until your heart changes before I take you as a man
does a woman."

Whisper said nothing.

After a moment, Walking Head spoke again. "It is time
you forgot the past. There are many times of joy ahead for
you among my people."

"What is ahead of me? Slavery?"

"You are not a slave."

"Then why do you keep me bound at all times? Why
have you taken the moccasins from my feet? Are not these
things a sign of slavery?"

Walking Head pulled his knife and cut the ropes that
bound Whisper. He took her moccasins from a leather bag
on his saddle and dropped them at her feet. "You will no
longer be tied or watched closely. You are free to roam
among the people as you please."

Whisper rubbed the flow of blood back into her wrists
and arms. "Why do you tell me these things? Do you feel
I now have no desire to escape? If you do feel this way,
you are a fool."

"No, Spirit Woman, I believe you still wish to escape.
In time your heart will change, but you would be gone now
if I turned my back." He nodded as he spoke. "You will
now be able to leave if you so desire. But you will not ride
from here on your horse, the big appaloosa called Red
Thunder."

Whisper tightened. "What have you done with my
horse?"

"Do not fear, Spirit Woman. The horse will be well
taken care of. But he will be watched closely night and day
so that you will never be able to escape with him. I shall
see to that myself." His face was stern and his eyes hard
as he finished. "You may think you can leave anyway, then
come back and steal him later. Do not think this, Spirit
Woman. If for even one day you are not seen in the village,
I shall have the horse destroyed."

Whisper's eyes flashed with anger. "You may know
many tricks, Walking Head, but you can never change my

heart. How could you think I would ever wish to learn Siksika ways and live in your lodge?"

"There is a story you should hear, Spirit Woman," said Walking Head. "It is a story told to all the children by the elders and the grandfathers of our village. It is the story of a boy who was born Salish and became a Siksika after his tenth winter. It is my story, Spirit Woman, and you shall hear it now."

"What kind of story is this?" Whisper asked. "Lies will not change my heart."

"It is truth," Walking Head insisted. "Anyone in the village will tell you this story is truth. How do you think I came to know the Salish tongue?"

"You have not spoken to me in Salish before."

"It has taken me time to learn the words once more. A French Long Knife of the Hudson Bay Company knows the Salish tongue well. For many robes and furs he has taught me once again to speak words you can understand."

"Take me down from this mountain," said Whisper. "I wish to hear no more lies."

Walking Head's face hardened. His teeth were gritted in anger as he spoke. "Maybe you are afraid of a story that is so close to your very own, Spirit Woman. Maybe you are afraid that my words will tell your future."

"No words you could ever speak will tell my future, Walking Head. But I will hear your story."

Walking Head pointed to the west, where far out across the grasslands a range of mountains lined the horizon. "It is only on such a day as this that my story can be told," he said. "The skies are such that we may see the Backbone of the World, far to where Sun sets. Yes, I was born beyond those high mountains, in the Land of High Trees—the Bitterroot. I was taken to the War Dancers band of Siksika peoples after a raid on my people that left my entire family dead. I, like you, fought so well I was spared and taken as a captive. My heart was filled with hate for the Siksika. Though the warrior who owned me treated me well, I was bitter. His wives did many things for me, for I was to become a great warrior in time. But that did not matter to me. I thought of escape every waking hour; at night my dreams were of freedom and my return to the Salish lands.

"Finally the day came when I found a loose horse. After nearly a full moon's travel and searching, I found my village. But I was rejected. I had no relatives and though I had been known to all as a promising warrior, I was told no one would adopt me."

"My people are known for their kindness," said Whisper. "It is strange that they should turn a boy away."

"Yes, but the jealousy of some in the village was more powerful than the instinct of kindness," said Walking Head. "There was one in the village who was but a few winters older than I, and he, too, was highly thought of. He wished to some day become chief and his father wished it also. They knew I would be chosen before him if I was allowed to become a member of the band. So they told lies. They said I had come back as a spy for the Siksika. They said I was not truly Salish or I would have escaped long before. Also, they told the village I could speak the Siksika tongue better than the Salish. The others believed this and no one would look at me."

Whisper thought back on the rendezvous at Pierre's Hole and the anguish she had suffered in trying to find word about her mother. She, too, had been marked as different. No one wished to associate with her for she was feared; it was certain she would bring war with the Siksika to any band who chose to accept her. She could not blame her people for this. War had cost many sons and daughters, and more war would only mean more death. But she had been sorrowed that no one had stepped forward and spoken in her behalf. Yes, this story of Walking Head was strangely close to her own.

"I then had no people, nor any place to go," Walking Head continued. "I felt that death was surely better than living with the pain of rejection. I returned to the Siksika to face whatever punishment might be dealt. Instead I was greeted with a welcome dance and the tears of the woman

who had been my foster mother. They were the tears of a
deep love, a love like I had never known before. Her husband, the warrior who first took me as captive, told me,
'Son, it is good to have you back.' I cried. It was hard for
me to accept or understand, but I had become Siksika and
I would never again know Salish ways. This, Spirit
Woman, is also your story.''

"My story is somewhat different," Whisper told him.
"It is true, my people cannot accept me after what has
happened. But I have my own life with my Long Knife
husband. And my mother is now a part of this life. They
are no doubt looking for me even as we now speak.''

"You will forget them," Walking Head insisted. "When
you learn all I have to offer, you will forget the past.''

"No!" Whisper shouted. "This will not happen!"

Walking Head's face did not change. "We will go now
and join the others for the journey to the village. I know
what your feelings are now, Spirit Woman. But these feelings will change. You will come to love me and want me.
That is the way it must be.''

Chapter 28

DANCE OF THE WARRIORS

Walking Head appeared before the people and cheers arose from all sides. This would be a night of glory, for a dance was to be held where all the warriors would recount their war honors and the brave deeds they had performed. All would dress their finest, for the entire village would attend the homecoming feast for Walking Head and his returning warriors.

Walking Head wore his finest war-shirt and leggings. They were of tanned deerskin, colored with porcupine quills and lined with ermine tails along the arms, shoulders, and legs. He wore an elk-tooth necklace and brass armbands. He carried his shield, with bow and arrows, and held his lance, which he had lined with scalps. His face was striped with red and black paint, and his war bonnet hung heavy with eagle feathers tipped with black horse hair.

Many warriors, both young and old, joined him from all parts of the village. Many were dressed like Walking Head in war-shirts and deerskin leggings. Others were nearly naked and covered with paint and grease. Some wore otter-skin caps with tails and feathers hanging down behind. All carried their finest weapons.

Whisper watched from a place near the dancers where Walking Head had seated her. The people stared at her, as they had since her first day among them. She had been an object of much talk and finger-pointing ever since that day, three suns past, when Walking Head had proudly displayed her for all the people to see. Though all in the village thought Walking Head a truly brave leader, there was displeasure in the eyes of many elders. It was good and honorable to be brave in battle, but it was foolish to sacrifice warriors for the sake of personal pride. And this Salish woman had cost the War Dancers band of the Siksika many warriors.

For this she was hated and feared by many in camp. Already the story of how she had victoriously led a large force of Salish against the scouting party along the waters of the Snake had spread among the War Dancers. Had it not been for Walking Head's personal bravery in sneaking into the Salish camp and capturing her in her own lodge, surely many more Siksika men would have fallen before her. She was the Spirit Woman, and even though Walking Head rejoiced in her capture, she brought sorrow to many others. Her strong medicine had cost husbands and sons, brothers and close friends. The elders agreed she would only bring trouble to the village.

As was expected, trouble had first appeared in Walking Head's own lodge. Instead of returning with a slave who would perform many of the tasks and heavy chores in camp, Walking Head had brought another wife. And she was a wife who was to be treated with respect. She was not to be abused and whipped, as was the usual treatment of war captives. Instead, her place was to be one of honor in the lodge.

From the very beginning this had caused bad feelings. Walking Head's eldest wife, Songbird, had told Whisper in sign that very first day, "You may be a prize to my husband, but you are no prize to me!"

Songbird's mother, Rain Woman, scratched her grey head at the strange way Walking Head acted around this Salish woman, whom all called the Spirit Woman. It was not a good thing, for both of her daughters were wives in Walking Head's lodge. And though the younger daughter, Laughs-in-the-Morning, thought this Spirit Woman to be somewhat exciting, Rain Woman feared it would only be a matter of time before she, too, burned with jealousy.

But Whisper did not think Laughs-in-the-Morning would ever come to hate her the way Songbird did. Instead, Laughs-in-the-Morning was quick to help with the chores and even talked of the difference in customs between the Salish and the Siksika. It was clear to Whisper that Laughs-in-the-Morning had more in common with herself than she had with any of the other women in the village, for she, too, would rather ride and hunt than perform the daily tasks of a wife in a warrior's lodge. Because of this relationship between Laughs-in-the-Morning and Whisper, each day would surely bring more tension to the lodge. After only the first day, Songbird was shouting at her younger sister just for talking to the Salish woman. And later, Songbird had told Whisper in sign, "You are not to go off by yourself, but stay close to camp and do as you are told." When Whisper had made sign back, saying, "Tend to your own duties and stay out of mine," Songbird had almost been upon her. The mother-in-law, Rain Woman, had stepped in and Whisper had told her in sign, "Keep your daughter away from me. I rejoice over all Siksika scalps, be they from a man or a woman." This had put fear into Songbird's eyes, and Whisper knew there would be no more open challenges to her. But the fire between them was sure to grow ever hotter.

Whisper had told this to Walking Head and he had merely shrugged, saying, "Songbird will have to accept you, that is all."

Now, near the setting of her third sun in the Siksika village, Whisper grew more discontent. As the dancers prepared for the ceremony and the drums began, Whisper knew Walking Head would be watching her as he demonstrated his honors and brave deeds before the people. Maybe he thought that through his glory and honor he could change her heart. As she thought more about these things, Whisper grew worried. Though Walking Head had not yet tried to lay with her in her bed, she knew this night would bring the first struggle between them. This was certain; she could see it in his eyes.

The dancing began. It was a ceremony of the Kisapa—the Hair Parters society. Whisper had seen similar ceremonies among the men's societies of her own people. Each warrior's dance portrayed how he received his name, or a great deed of honor he had performed. As Walking Head danced, he made the sign for Cree, then raised his lance and shield as if fighting in battle. He lunged this way and that, thrusting his lance forward and pretending to shoot his bow at the enemy. He took a scalp from his lance and cut through the air around it, as if taking it from the head of a Cree, then held it high in the air and screamed a war cry. Whisper knew he was showing how he had achieved honor by destroying the Cree village on the Saskatchewan. She remembered the stories that had been told about this battle, which had been fought just before the last winter. Her face clouded with anger as she thought back on that time, for it had been just after this battle that Walking Head had journeyed down to find her, and she had lost her baby in the fight with the Piegans.

Other warriors danced, showing stick figures of horses if they were good at stealing, or pointing to stripes on coup sticks and scalps on their shields and weapons. Some lay on the ground, signifying wounds received in battle, while others ran by and picked them up, signifying the brave deed of rescue. Whisper watched it all in anger. She knew many of the scalps the warriors displayed were Salish.

Late that night, when the ceremony was finished, Walking Head took Whisper to his lodge.

"My mother-in-law and wives are with relatives this night, so that we may be alone," he said.

From a skin bag around his waist, he threw a handful of mixed pine and flower pollen into the air of the lodge. He sang a low chant and stretched out his arms, with upturned hands, to Whisper.

"Love charms and songs will do you no good, Walking Head," she told him defiantly. "Go back to the medicine man who made this charm for you and tell him I am Salish, not Siksika."

"You will not dishonor me this night," said Walking Head. "All the village knows we are alone here. All eyes and ears will be open this night."

"What has become of the promise you made me the day we climbed the flat-topped mountain, above the waters of the Arrow? You said then you wished for my love before you wished solely for my body. But now I see those words had no meaning."

"I thought surely your heart would have changed by now," Walking Head answered. "You have been granted every favor by me and still you do not feel for me as I do for you. Maybe it will take a night of my love to bring this change."

"There will be no change," said Whisper. "I will remain true to my husband." Then she hesitated a bit. "I wish you to hear these words, Walking Head. I could never want your love, for I am with child."

Walking Head's eyes widened.

"Yes, I carry the child of my husband, the Long Knife, Jim Ayers."

"Why did you not tell me this before?" Walking Head asked.

"Why should I have told you? Would it have meant my freedom?"

Walking Head was silent for a time. Finally he said, "Is it that you felt I would be angry? Did you fear I would do you harm?"

"It is not your child, Walking Head. Knowing this cannot be a happy thing for you."

"This is not a bad thing," said Walking Head. "You

know my feelings for you. You should know I could never wish harm to you or the child. If I accept you, I accept the child as well.''

Whisper took a deep breath. "But I cannot accept you, Walking Head. This I have told you many times, and you refuse to accept my words. It has been hard for both of us. Now, I tell you again, I will never love you nor will I ever belong with your people.''

Walking Head said nothing.

"Why can you not see this?" Whisper pleaded. "This has even brought bad feelings to the women of your lodge. Laughs-in-the-Morning wishes to be my friend and Songbird would kill me if she could. Your mother-in-law, Rain Woman, has been torn apart by these feelings and is angry with you. Also, there are many in the village who hate me as well. They know I have killed their husbands and sons. I could never be accepted here.''

"I have told my wives and my mother-in-law they must accept you. I have told all those in the village they must accept you too.''

"You cannot change someone's heart merely by telling them to do so," Whisper exclaimed in exasperation. "You have become powerful among your people and you can demand many things, but power can never gain the heart. Your commands will only fall on deaf ears.''

After a moment, Walking Head said, "We could leave this place. We could live on our own.''

"No," said Whisper, "I have my own life, as I have told you.''

"Why do you feel you could never learn to love me, Spirit Woman?" Walking Head asked.

Whisper looked at him coldly. "When I look at you, I see the eyes of my father and brothers, of lost friends who have fallen before your warriors and live no more. I see all these things and sorrow fills my heart. You, Walking Head, are the one person I could never learn to love.''

Walking Head looked saddened by Whisper's remark. The desire left his eyes and a far-away look took its place.

After a moment, he turned from Whisper and said, "There is one other thing I wished for you to have this night."

He stepped outside the lodge and returned with a vase of flowers. Their blossoms were deep lavender and their fragrance filled the lodge. It was horsemint, Whisper's favorite flower.

"I smelled this flower on you the first time we met," said Walking Head. "Your beauty is truly equal to it."

Walking Head laid the flowers at Whisper's feet and left the lodge. He had taken great pains to be sure that each flower fit just right into the arrangement. Those in the middle were cut slightly longer so that the whole group tapered in height to form a perfectly rounded bouquet.

Tears rolled from Whisper's eyes. The flowers only reminded her of Jim and the many times he had come down from a mountain hillside with a handful of blossoms for her. She longed for his arms now, and the happy fire that always burned in their lodge. She wondered about her mother also, and if she had reached the Stinkingwater. It was nearly the Moon of the Harvest of Ripe Things—September—and the time when Jim should be coming for her was fast approaching. It should not be hard for him to find the Siksika, she thought, for their fires were many and they sent smoke high into the sky. They were a bold people, these Siksika, and they seemed to fear nothing. This boldness could easily give their enemies an upper hand during an attack, for they were getting lazy about sending out sentries to watch the village. Whisper knew that any enemies in the area would know this, also. She only hoped her escape would come before these enemies attacked the village.

Chapter 29

THE BUFFALO SOCIETY

"As you watch this dance," Laughs-in-the-Morning told Whisper in sign, "you will be better able to understand why there has never been happiness in Walking Head's lodge."

Whisper, as she watched the Buffalo Society dancers make ready for their ceremony, asked Laughs-in-the-Morning, "Has their always been unhappiness in Walking Head's lodge? Even before my coming?"

Laughs-in-the-Morning nodded. "There was unhappiness long before anyone had even heard of you, long before Walking Head and his war party raided your village far over the Backbone of the World, in the Land of High Trees. There has been unhappiness as long as I can remember."

"I can see that Songbird is the reason for this," said Whisper. "Why does Walking Head stand for all the things she does?"

"He does not wish to bring disgrace to his lodge by divorcing her," Laughs-in-the-Morning explained. "She has always done the things for him that are expected of a good wife. And she has never been unfaithful.''

"Despite all those things, there has been much trouble," Whisper insisted. "Most of this trouble has been for you."

Laughs-in-the-Morning nodded. She tenderly felt the scratch marks on her face, which had been made only the night before. "Songbird is my sister, and I love her, but there is much evil in her heart at times."

Muto-ka-iks—the Buffalo Society—was made up only of women. The ceremony this day was to bring success to the hunters, among them Walking Head, who had journeyed out from the waters of the Big Muddy north to the high prairies. The dance was to be offered so that they might return with much meat.

The dancers were dressed in robes and headdresses of tanned skins. Songbird wore a Hudson Bay trade blanket of red and blue, while her head was wrapped in otter skin. Other dancers, called "Old Bulls" for what they represented, wore buffalo cap headdresses with red plumes fastened to the horns. They were all seated inside a sacred lodge erected just for this ceremony, awaiting the signal for the dancing to start.

Then a young boy, dressed in decorated skins and painted in a most sacred manner, rode a fine horse to the entrance of the sacred lodge. He was the son of Rides Kicking, a young medicine man in the band. Both Rides Kicking and the boy's mother followed their son on foot to the sacred lodge. They carried many presents for the dancers, for it was indeed a great honor to have their son chosen to take part in this ceremony.

"Walking Head is very bitter that he has no son of his own to be chosen for such honors," Laughs-in-the-Morning explained to Whisper. "He has wanted a son for a long, long time. Still there is no child, boy or girl, in his lodge. And after nearly five winters, it is believed Songbird can never bear him a child. Now you can see, Spirit Woman, why there is no happiness in Walking Head's lodge."

"What about yourself?" Whisper asked quickly.

"I do not wish to disgrace my elder sister by conceiving

before she does. I have always taken care to use the plants that prevent bearing a child."

"That is not good," said Whisper. "Does your mother know what you are doing?"

"Yes," Laughs-in-the-Morning nodded, "I have told her. She is not pleased, but she knows it is for the best. There has always been trouble between Songbird and myself, even when we were children. When Walking Head took Songbird for his wife, he was entitled to me, also. This is one custom among our people that I am sure Songbird wishes did not exist."

"And despite all this, you continue to uphold your sister's honor?" Whisper asked in disgust.

"It is a thing I must do. It is a matter of respect."

"Respect is good," said Whisper. "And it is a necessary thing among people. But it is also something that can easily be abused. For two people to know real respect, it must come from the hearts of both and not just the one."

The Buffalo Society dancers had received their presents from Rides Kicking and his wife, and were walking slowly towards the banks of the Big Muddy, like a herd of buffalo going to water. Close behind followed the "Old Bulls" dancers. Soon they were all lying along the shore like a herd that was at rest in the afternoon.

Then the chosen boy rode his fine horse to the windward side of the dancers and waved a burning buffalo chip in the air. The smoke carried to the dancers, who then slowly began to rise to their feet. They tossed their heads about, as buffalo do upon rising from sleep, and started back toward the sacred lodge. The chosen boy followed, calling out the Driving Buffalo Song, in the manner used by the Siksika in earlier times before the horse.

The dancers reached the sacred lodge and ran around the center pole, grunting and bucking, until they all fell to the ground from exhaustion. The "Old Bulls" followed, but did not run about the center pole. Instead, they walked about in the manner of a buffalo bull, slow and with a swaying motion. They bellowed and butted heads, as if fighting, and pawed the ground. Then, they too entered the sacred lodge.

"The dancers act as buffalo once did when hunted in the early days of my people," Laughs-in-the-Morning explained to Whisper. "Upon smelling the smoke, they are like buffalo being driven to a *piskun*—a high cliff they are then forced to jump over. When the dancers enter the sacred lodge and run around the center pole, they act like buffalo who have been driven over the *piskun* and are crazy from the broken legs and shoulders they have received in the fall. While they are running about, the hunters who have waited for their fall are killing them."

Whisper nodded. "Do you think this ceremony will bring luck to the hunters?"

"It has before," said Laughs-in-the-Morning.

Whisper looked around camp. "Maybe it will bring me luck, too," she said. "Most of the men are gone to the hunt, and those who chose to remain behind are watching this ceremony. I see nothing but boys who are horse tenders watching my Red Thunder. Today would be a good day to leave this place."

"Do not take that chance," Laughs-in-the-Morning cautioned. "There are those who watch you closely from the edge of camp. Songbird has seen to this. The Brave Bears, the camp guards, are watching everything closely. Nothing will escape their eyes."

"Maybe the Brave Bears will not be able to stop me," said Whisper.

"Do not chance it, Spirit Woman," Laughs-in-the-Morning pleaded. "There will be another time that is not so dangerous. Maybe Walking Head will even see fit to release you before long."

"That does not seem possible," said Whisper. "If I stay in this place much longer, I will surely lose my mind."

"If you wish to go off alone for a while, I can help," said Laughs-in-the-Morning. "If anyone asks for you, I will say we were off picking berries."

"That will mean another beating from Songbird," said Whisper.

"Maybe," Laughs-in-the-Morning remarked. "Maybe not. I have been thinking about what you said about respect. Those words are true; it is not honorable to show respect for someone who shows none for you."

"You are indeed a friend to sacrifice your own well-being for my sake," said Whisper. "I shall remember this." Then she pointed to the rock formations high above camp. "I shall journey up to those white cliffs. I had a dream about that place once. Now I shall see what that dream was truly about."

It was late afternoon when Whisper left the village. Sun had lowered himself into a bank of clouds above the western horizon, making them glow redgold.

Soon Whisper had climbed from the bottom paths up into the rocks and scrub timber of the cliffs. She wished to go high up, to reach the top of this canyon where she could see far out and know how this place joined with the lands nearby. There would be a time soon, she thought, when she would need to know the best way to journey from these lands south to the valley of the Yellowstone. From the Yellowstone she could easily find the Stinkingwater. Jim had not yet come for her and she knew there was something wrong, or he surely would have been there by this time. Now she must find a way from these lands herself. She must choose a time to leave and then go quickly. She had prayed to Amótkan each morning and night to help her, and she had also prayed that the time might come soon.

The peace among the high rocks helped to ease Whisper's tension. There was not a breath of wind, and only the cries of soaring eagles and hawks broke the silence. Swarms of swallows flew in twisting patterns from their nests along the cliffs, swooping close to Whisper, dodging her and each other at just the last second before a collision.

Whisper looked from high atop a rocky cliff out across the boundless lands below her. The day was clear and she

could see far out into the open grasslands above the broken
lands along the Big Muddy. She could see far across to the
Square Butte and the Round Butte, and to the mountains
nearby called High Wood. She knew the valley of the Yellowstone could be reached by traveling back to these two
large buttes, then turning slightly east and crossing the land
called Judith Basin. She could then reach the mountains of
the Big Snows and be close to the valley she had gone to
as a child with her people. This valley was called the Musselshell, and was filled with buffalo. She could find this
place easily, she knew, for from the mountains of Big
Snows she would be able to see the mountains of the Bulls,
where the waters called Musselshell flowed. From this
place it was but a few sun's ride down to the valley of the
Yellowstone, and a few more suns on to the Stinkingwater.

Whisper would have been excited had it not been for her
worry. Had her mother ever reached the Stinkingwater?
Maybe something had happened to her. Maybe something
had indeed, happened to Jim, as she feared. As she looked
across to the two buttes and the mountains of High Wood,
she knew her time to leave this place must come soon.

After a while, Whisper started back down for the village.
Sun was a round red ball and the clouds had drifted away.
As she followed a game trail down the hillside, she noticed
movement in a large hole in a rock cliff facing the trail.
Sun's light showed the form of an owl, the large owl with
the feather horns for ears. Whisper drew her breath. This
was not the land of the little owl and he could, therefore,
not come to hear her words. But, as brother to the little
owl, her guardian, the horned owl would hear her words
and would know the ways to help her. Now was her chance
to pray and to tell this owl those things she had wished for
so long to tell the little owl. If this owl would stay in the
rock to hear her, Whisper knew things would surely become better for her and she would see both Jim and her
mother before the moon changed again.

Whisper moved slowly off the trail and sat down on a
fallen tree where she could look into the hole in the rock. .

At first the big owl made ready to fly out, but then resettled in the hole and looked out at Whisper with large round eyes.

Whisper raised her hand in greeting to the owl and spoke. "You are the brother of my guardian, the little owl of the forest, whose home is far to the west. I cannot speak with him, for he does not live so far from the forest. It saddens my heart that he cannot hear my words; but now I have found you, his brother, and I wish to have you help me. Hear me, owl with the large feather horns for ears, hear me and know that I wish to return to my husband and mother. This place is not my home."

The owl sat motionless in the hole. His big, yellow eyes blinked from time to time while Whisper spoke.

"I am blessed with another child. I wish to see this child grow and be happy with my husband, Jim, and myself in our own lodge. I wish to see my own mother's tears at the birth of this child, and to have her share this happiness with Jim and me. I wish to see again the old Long Knife, Fiddler, who has been so good to me and who has treated me as he would his own daughter." Tears filled Whisper's eyes as she spoke further. "I must leave here soon, for something bad has surely happened to Jim or my mother. Something must be wrong at the fort on the Stinkingwater. I know Jim would be here now if that were not true. Please hear these words, owl with the feather horns. Tell Amótkan I have spoken to you, for he does not hear my words these days. You must hear me."

The big owl pushed his body out of the hole and flew out across the hillside, skimming low over the ground on soundless wings and becoming lost among a stand of yellow pine far down the hill.

Whisper took a deep breath and stared down at the pines where the owl had disappeared. "He has heard me," she said to herself with a smile. "He has heard my words."

Chapter 30

THE BRAVE BEARS

The pool was clear and deep. It sat away from the main pool used by the village for swimming and bathing, and Whisper found it to be a solitary place where she could wash and be alone.

The water was cool and refreshing. The day was hot and the flies and mosquitos were not a bother now like they would be in the morning or late evening. Whisper swam for a long time, giving thanks to Sister Water for the peace she now felt. These waters were not nearly as clean and refreshing as the lake of the Flathead, but it was still good to feel the water again.

When she had finished, Whisper put her dress back on and combed the water out of her hair. She looked out into the pool and smiled, for it was now occupied by a family of beavers whose dam building had created the swimming hole. While Whisper had been swimming, they had retreated to the safety of their mud and stick house that rose up in a mound above the water a ways from shore. All around was birdsong, for this place was quiet and secluded from the main crossings used by the buffalo and other game. Whisper lay her hands gently on her lower stomach and sang a Salish childbearing song. In this place of her enemies, she had found one source of happiness.

Then from the brush along the banks came Songbird, her mouth in a twisted smile. She made sign to Whisper.

"So, you have nothing to do but swim all day and gloat upon yourself. What is that stomach of yours? A child?"

"And you have nothing to do but crawl on the ground like a snake and peer out from the willows and brush," Whisper answered back. "Crawl back into the brush."

Whisper saw that Songbird had a black and swollen eye and one cheek was puffed out, as if a blow had landed solid upon her. No doubt Laughs-in-the-Morning had tired of Songbird's evil ways.

"You are not a guest, Salish woman," Songbird made sign in anger. "You are required to help with the chores about camp. Instead, I find you playing as a child. It is hard to know why Walking Head thinks of you as a woman."

"I am not wife to Walking Head, and I am not a slave. And I do not have to answer to you for anything I choose to do." Whisper made it obvious she was studying the wounds on her face. "I see also that there are others in this village who have tired of your troublemaking."

Songbird's eyes flashed and she took a step toward Whisper.

Whisper readied herself. "Take one step further, Songbird. I would like that. And I will tell you now, you will not be so lucky as you were with Laughs-in-the-Morning. I will see to it you make no more trouble for anyone in this village ever again. Then I will throw your body to the wolves."

Songbird shook with rage. "Save your words for the council, Salish dog, for I think you will need to explain where you have been these past few days. It is well known that you have traveled away from the village, high among the white rocks. Maybe you have been secretly doing things that would endanger this village. Like sending messages to our enemies.''

"I can go where I wish," said Whisper. "Walking Head has told me this, and he has told the entire village this."

"Yes, but Walking Head is not here to protect you now." Songbird's eyes had become slits and there was evil in her voice. "With the men off hunting, it is a dangerous time for the village. It is a time when one such as yourself could try to bring enemies upon us."

"Your enemies do not need my help to scout this village," Whisper retorted. "Any boy could do it well. Maybe it is so because the men no longer care about the fate of this village. If I had a woman like you, I would go off and die with honor in battle."

Songbird fumed. She knew she stood no chance against Whisper in a fight, and it appeared she could not outtalk this Salish woman. But she would have the last word in this matter.

"Maybe Walking Head will wish for your death when he learns you carry a Long Knife's child," said Songbird. "A half-breed child is not wanted in this village."

"It is better than no child at all," Whisper shot back. "Besides, Walking Head knows I am with child."

Songbird could not believe Walking Head would allow a woman in his lodge who carried a Long Knife child. "You are a liar," Songbird said in clear and fast sign. "You are only trying to save yourself."

"Songbird, you would not know a lie from truth. Your lips have never spoken truth."

"We shall see if you speak truth," Songbird told Whisper. "When Walking Head returns from the hunt, we shall see." Then Songbird's eyes glowed with an evil idea. "Maybe you should save yourself and leave this village now. I would say nothing about it."

"Only to the Brave Bears," Whisper retorted. "It would give you great pleasure to see trouble come to me, would it not?"

"You have made your own trouble, Spirit Woman. And

Laughs-in-the-Morning has made trouble for herself by making up stories to protect you. Yes, there is trouble ahead for you, Spirit Woman.''

A short while later, Whisper was back in camp and nearing Walking Head's lodge when she was met by a member of the Brave Bear society. He moved his horse between her and the lodge and looked down at her with a grim face. In sign he said, "You have been accused of seeking ways to destroy this village. I, as a member of the Brave Bears, must take you with me to the council lodge."

"I will not go anywhere with you," Whisper made sign back. "You should tell these things to Walking Head. Not me."

"Walking Head has nothing to do with this. Now, you will come with me."

"I will go to no council lodge until I have first spoken with Walking Head. I answer to him, not you."

"Do not speak with disrespect, Spirit Woman. I, as a Brave Bear, can take whatever action I choose to make you obey me. No one would care if I killed you. You are not highly thought of in this village."

"I do not think highly of this village either," said Whisper. "Now bother me no more."

As she started around the warrior's horse, he lashed out at her with his quirt. Whisper grabbed the quirt and wrenched it from his grip. He then pulled his war club from his belt.

"You Siksika dog!" Whisper screamed.

As he came at her with his raised club, Whisper grabbed his foot and ankle. He dropped the club and grunted in pain as she twisted the ankle sideways with all her might. Then, in a fit of rage, he lunged at Whisper from the horse.

Whisper moved aside quickly and the warrior landed on his back with a thump. In a flash, he was on his feet, and hatred turned his eyes dark. He moved toward her with his knife drawn. He limped on his left ankle, and it was to this side that Whisper moved.

Whisper had grabbed the war club, which he had lost in

the fall from his horse. She was very quick and the warrior could not keep her away from him with his lame ankle. As the village watched, Whisper slammed the war club into the warrior's temple. The skull cracked sharply and the warrior dropped to the ground, kicking and twisting in convulsions. Blood ran in streams from his eyes and ears, staining his society shirt and the ground. After a short time, he lay still with his mouth and eyes open.

Whisper quickly took the fallen warrior's bow and quiver of arrows. The camp was alive with shouting and women pushing their children into their lodges for safety. More warriors of the Brave Bear society had left their positions around camp and were assembled, talking, a ways from Walking Head's lodge. Whisper kneeled in the doorway of the lodge and fitted an arrow to the bow. Then she waited.

After more talking among the Brave Bears, one rode forward with his hand raised in peace. Whisper pulled the bowstring back and the warrior stopped his horse. She kept the bow aimed at the warrior and he finally dropped his weapons to the ground.

"What is the meaning of this, Spirit Woman?" he asked in sign.

Whisper laid the bow down and made sign back in answer. "Walking Head is gone on the hunt less than the passing of two suns and already I endure torment. The jealousies of this village will not destroy me."

"Why did you kill one of our people?"

"I will not be punished for crimes I did not commit. Speak to Songbird, the elder of Walking Head's wives. She is the one who has caused this thing to happen."

The warrior instructed the other Brave Bear members with him to search the village for Songbird. Whisper continued to plead her case.

"If I am guilty of any crime whatsoever, the accuser should wish to step forward. Is this not true?"

The Brave Bear warrior was silent, knowing Whisper's words were true. In a moment, the other Brave Bear members returned. They had not found Songbird, but Laughs-in-the-Morning had come to speak on Whisper's behalf. After talking with the Brave Bear warriors in Siksika for a time, she came over to speak with Whisper.

"They are very angry," she told Whisper in sign. "They feel you should have obeyed the dead warrior's commands to go with him."

"Yes, and I would surely have died," Whisper answered. "The people of the village would have seen to that."

"I am only here to help you, Spirit Woman," said Laughs-in-the-Morning. "I will tell the Brave Bears you have given your word to remain in Walking Head's lodge until the hunters return."

"How long will that be?" Whisper asked.

"Within a sun's passing," Laughs-in-the-Morning told her. "A messenger has already been sent to the hunting camp to tell them what has happened here. A council must be held among the chiefs and elders of the village. This is a grave matter, Spirit Woman." Laughs-in-the-Morning looked at Whisper sympathetically. "But I would have done the same thing had I your powers." Then she left to talk again with the Brave Bear warriors.

In a moment, the warrior spoke to Whisper again.

"Laughs-in-the-Morning says you have consented to stay within Walking Head's lodge until such time as a council can be formed. Is this true?"

"Yes," Whisper answered. "If you will tell me I am to be left in peace."

"No one wishes to disturb the peace here," the Brave Bear said. "It is no one's intent to accuse you until the council has listened to all and has discussed the matter."

Whisper pointed to the dead warrior. "You should have spoken these words to your society brother. He wished to take me prisoner against my will and leave me at the mercy of the village. He knew full well I could go nowhere from this lodge, and that I would not leave the village. Instead, he listened to the words of Songbird, a jealous woman. Now I only wish to be left in peace."

"Very well," said the Brave Bear. "You will be disturbed no more this fine day. The hunters will return shortly and a council will be held to judge on this matter. You are in much trouble, Spirit Woman, for killing a member of the Brave Bears is a serious offense. You will be left in peace for now, but I am certain that your peace will not last for long."

Whisper sat silent in the lodge while Walking Head's wives and mother-in-law busied themselves with the chores of evening. Songbird never looked at Whisper, but her hatred was present in every action, and on her face was a grim smile, for she knew what Whisper would soon face before the council. The village hummed with talk about Whisper and the death of the Brave Bear warrior. Already the elders were assembling for council.

Laughs-in-the-Morning waited until Songbird had left the lodge to gather wood. Then she tried to ease Whisper's tension.

"Things will turn out well for you," she said. "Walking Head is a good speaker, and he will make the council listen to his words."

A short time later, Walking Head entered the lodge and ordered his wives out. In his hand was a rawhide bridle, freshly made and painted in colorful designs. He sat cross-legged near Whisper and spoke in a low, serious tone.

"You have not tried to forget the past. Your hatred shows in your eyes, and all the people of this village can see it. Now a bad thing has happened because of your feelings."

"It was the jealousy of Songbird that caused this thing," said Whisper. "It is her hatred for me that cost the Brave Bear his life. Nothing else."

"Songbird may hate you," said Walking Head. "But she is wise in some ways. She tells me you have traveled far from camp, up among the White Cliffs high above the village. This could mean you have evil intent, that you wish to bring our enemies upon us."

"That would not help me to escape, Walking Head. I wish to leave this place, nothing else."

After a moment's silence, Walking Head placed the bridle near Whisper. "That will fit your Appaloosa," he said. "It should last you many winters."

"Why do you give me this?" Whisper asked, holding up the bridle. "Why do you continue to bring me presents when you know they do no good? You understand by now that my heart will never change, but still you try. Why do you torment yourself over me?"

"I have begun to understand some things," said Walking Head. "You know much about me, now. And you know much about the troubles within my lodge. I see Laughs-in-the-Morning is becoming a different woman, and I think it is because of you. This is good. Laughs-in-the-Morning always remained within herself before. She has always wanted my heart, but has been held back by Songbird. Now I see many things in her I had never seen before."

"She is like me in many ways," said Whisper. "I think she will grow to be herself more and more as time passes."

Walking Head was silent for a time. Finally he spoke. "Do you wish to tell me how you came to kill the Brave Bear warrior?"

"I thought surely Songbird would have told you everything by now," said Whisper. "She wishes for my death above all others."

"If only you could have just wounded him," said Walking Head. "Death is a very serious thing to the Brave Bear society. No matter what caused this thing to happen, having killed him makes it much worse."

"He would have killed me," said Whisper. "He had drawn both his war club and his knife. I had no choice."

"His relatives are demanding death," said Walking Head. "His father is Runs Kicking, a great medicine man. It was his youngest son who was chosen for the Buffalo Society ceremony. He has much say in council."

"I know who he is," said Whisper. "But his son should not have been so arrogant."

"I will be the only one to speak in your behalf," said Walking Head. "You must tell me you are sorry this has happened, so I may tell the council."

"I am not sorry!" Whisper snapped. "I could never be sorry for killing a Siksika!"

"Do you realize you face certain death for what you have done?"

"That matters not. Life holds no meaning for me in this place."

After a moment, Walking Head rose to his feet. Whisper did not look up at him, but kept her eyes to the ground.

He stood before her, as if to speak once again, but then turned, and silently left her alone.

Chapter 31

MEDICINE ARROWS

Clouds came in to fill the night sky and a slow drizzle of rain began to fall. Whisper sat uncomfortably on the ground outside Walking Head's lodge, her hands having been bound tightly behind her and her feet also bound together. Though it was late, Whisper remained awake and alert. In the center of the village, the council fires still burned and she could hear the men's voices in heated debate. During the time she had been among the Siksika, she had learned bits and pieces of their language. This night she could often hear the words "death to the Spirit Woman." When these words were used, she could then hear Walking Head's voice raised in angry argument.

Finally the rain stopped and the sky turned grey in the east. The clouds moved off to let Sun rise to a blue sky. The council fires were put out and the men returned to their lodges. Walking Head cut Whisper loose and led her to the edge of camp. His face was drawn and he looked very tired. There was sadness in his voice.

"This day will be the last I will see you, Spirit Woman.

Your medicine, the storm, came over this village last night
and turned the minds of the council. It was decided you
would be granted freedom over death. Now you must leave
quickly before something happens to change this decision.
I will see to it your horse is brought to you." He spoke
quickly to one of the boys tending the horses, then turned
to leave.

Whisper stopped him and turned him to face her. "It was
by your powers, not those of the storm, that my life was
spared. For this I am deeply grateful. I am only sorry that
our lives are so different and that things could never be
good between us."

"I have finally made myself realize I could never have
you for my own," Walking Head confessed. "And it makes
my heart sad to look upon you this day and know this is
true. But you must go now. Quickly!"

Whisper gathered the few belongings she had brought to
the village and found Red Thunder waiting outside Walking
Head's lodge. Sun had broken over the eastern rim of the
plains and the grasslands beyond the village were bathed
in gold. The village was now awake for another day and
already a crier could be seen running from lodge to lodge,
announcing the decision of the council and the news that
Whisper was leaving. Many eyes were upon her and some
voices cried out in anger against the council's decision.
Songbird's face showed disappointment. She thought surely
she would see the Spirit Woman face death this fine morning. No words were spoken, but a deep hatred filled Songbird's eyes as she watched Whisper prepare to leave.

Laughs-in-the-Morning approached Whisper with tears
in her eyes. "I do not care what they think of me," she
told Whisper. "You have been more of a friend than any
of them, including my own mother and sister. I am sad to
see you leave."

"Maybe a time will come when we will see each other
again," said Whisper. "And I do not mean during war."

"I hope so," said Laughs-in-the-Morning. "I truly hope
so."

Suddenly a rider burst into camp, yelling and pointing across the waters of the Big Muddy. Warriors ordered women and children into their lodges and began to paint themselves and sing war songs. The Brave Bear society tried to maintain order while people ran in all directions to find their weapons or safety.

"What is it?" Whisper asked Laughs-in-the-Morning. "Is the village under attack?"

"We soon will be," Laughs-in-the-Morning related rapidly in sign. "The sentry says many Crees are advancing south of the river. The Crees have found us!"

Walking Head started for his weapons and passed by Whisper without a word. She watched while he mounted his horse and led his warriors out from the village. His actions were sluggish and his war cries had no fervor in them. It was not a good day for him to fight.

"The Crees seek revenge for the raid by Walking Head just before the last winter," Laughs-in-the-Morning complained. "Their revenge will be sweet this day, for our warriors are not prepared to fight."

Whisper followed Laughs-in-the-Morning into Walking Head's lodge, where she took a bow and arrows that hung from one of the lodgepoles. There she also found the hateful eyes of Songbird and her mother, Rain Woman.

"Why do you take weapons from this lodge?" Songbird asked. "Is it not enough that you signal the Crees that we are here? Must you also fight with them against our people?"

"It is not a good day for the Siksika, and I fear for Walking Head's life," Whisper answered. "Just this past night he saved me from death at the hands of the council. Now I will try and save his life."

Songbird's face broke into a sly grin. "Maybe we shall see your death yet, Spirit Woman. The Crees are many and there are also many Siksika in this village who wish to see you dead after what has happened. No, this shall be the day when your medicine does you no good with either side."

"We shall see, Songbird," Whisper made sign back. "It

is true, there are many Crees and there is war in their hearts. But their power would surely change if someone were to kill their warriors with medicine arrows.'' She pointed to the quiver full of arrows in her hand. ''Yes, these shall become medicine arrows.''

Outside the lodge, Whisper found a large cooking fire still burning. She took the arrows from the quiver and carefully placed the steel tips among the glowing embers at the edge of the fire. Whisper smiled. She knew that very soon these arrowheads would be glowing reddish-white with heat. They would surely seem to have great medicine to those Cree warriors who would soon feel the sharp heat searing the tissues within their bodies. Maybe their cries would weaken the power of the Cree attack and keep Walking Head from meeting death this day.

The battle had already begun along the river's edge as Whisper took the arrows from the fire and jumped on Red Thunder. The Crees were advancing with a strong force and the Siksika were trying to hold them back by shooting arrows into them as they charged. But there were too many Crees, and in their eyes was a fierce hatred. They remembered well Walking Head's attack on their village, high up on the Saskatchewan, and this would be a good day to avenge their fallen people.

Walking Head then led the Siksika out into the water to try and stop the Crees from reaching the village. The battle was hand-to-hand from the backs of horses and the cries of the wounded and dying were everywhere. The Crees had waited long for this day and their warriors fought with a fierceness that made them too strong to stop. Already the women in the Siksika camp were hiding their children, for it seemed the Crees would be victorious and the village would be burned.

Whisper took a position on a dead tree that hung out over the river. She placed the arrows next to her, the steel tips glowing white-hot. Her first arrow took a Cree warrior high in the chest. His eyes rolled wide with pain and he fell from his horse screaming. He continued to scream and began to kick fiercely in the shallow water at the river's edge. Other arrows from Whisper's bow found other Cree warriors and they, too, yelled and tried to pull the arrows from their bodies while their insides burned from the heat. These arrows brought pain as no other arrows the Crees had ever known. Even when Whisper made a bad shot at one warrior and hit him in the upper leg, he acted as though he were mortally wounded, so loud did he yell.

The Crees soon saw that these arrows came from the bow of a woman whose aim was deadly. She did not dress as a Siksika, but was instead Salish. The Crees looked at Whisper with sudden fear while she continued to shoot arrows into their warriors. Where had she come from, this strange woman with the medicine arrows? She did not even seem real, for the arrows from Cree bows could not find her. It was no longer a good day for the Crees. It was no longer a good day to fight.

The Siksika then found new power in their own numbers. They shrieked war cries and fell to fighting with great strength and added courage. But even though the Siksika were holding the Crees back from their village and were fighting fiercely, it was not a good day for Walking Head. He and a group of his warriors were surrounded by Crees and were going to be killed.

Whisper took Red Thunder into the river and pushed a lance through one of the Crees. He screamed and tumbled into the water. With a war club she had picked up on shore, she rained savage blows upon the remaining Crees around Walking Head.

The Crees retreated from her in fear. She had killed many of their number with arrows that felt like fire, and now she was fighting from horseback with as much strength as any warrior they had led ever seen.

Through the fighting, Walking Head clung desperately to his horse. One arrow stuck out from his left leg, and another pierced his back near the shoulderblade. Blood trailed down his back and leg. He was growing steadily weaker, and if he fell into the river, he would surely drown.

Now the Crees were pointing at Whisper and yelling for no more fighting. They began to withdraw from the river and to collect their dead and wounded. The revenge raid against Walking Head's village that, for a time, had seemed would destroy the Siksika, was now ended. All because of a strange and powerful woman who was not even Siksika.

Now it was the Siksika's turn to fight for vengeance. They would kill as many Crees as they could before they left the river, for there were many Siksika warriors who now lay dead or wounded along the banks of the Big Muddy. The fighting would be fierce until the Crees could manage to escape up out of the river bottom and onto the flats.

As the fighting continued, a figure appeared on horseback, charging into the river at Whisper. With all the other fighting going on, no one seemed to notice that Songbird had come out from the village to kill Whisper.

Songbird may have succeeded in driving her lance into Whisper had not a stray arrow from a Cree bow caught her high in the side, just under the arm. She arched her back sideways and the lance fell from her hand into the water. A look of surprise came over Whisper as she watched Songbird fall into the water below Red Thunder. In a moment the current had carried her under and she could be seen no more.

No one else seemed to have seen Songbird's attack. All eyes were on Walking Head as they took him ashore and laid him on a pile of robes. The fighting was only here and there now, between one or two men, and both sides were caring for their fallen brothers. Only then did someone find the body of Songbird, floating near the shore. Later it would be said she died a heroic death coming to the aid of her husband.

Walking Head lay in deep sleep on a bed prepared for him by Laughs-in-the-Morning. He had received special medicines and prayers from the medicine men in the village.

Now he would rest before more prayers were said and more medicine was given him.

After the battle, Whisper had been looked upon with awe. Many in the village, both men and women, had touched her, not believing that any human could have such powerful medicine in battle. She must, indeed, be a spirit in a woman's body. The Spirit Woman was a name that truly fit her.

But even more mysterious to them was how Whisper had used her powers. Instead of joining the Crees against Walking Head, she had been the sole reason the battle had changed in favor of the Siksika. She could have gained glory for herself among the Crees, and helped them to destroy the village that had held her captive and had once left her without family and friends. Instead, she had chosen to save Walking Head's life in return for the words he had spoken to the council the night before. Now all in the village knew that the Spirit Woman had not been signaling to their enemies those times she had gone off by herself. She had, indeed, more honor than to betray the trust of Walking Head. Though she was an enemy, she was an enemy of great honor. She had saved the War Dancers band of Siksika peoples.

Now, as Whisper sat watching Walking Head sleep, Laughs-in-the-Morning came into the lodge and sat near her.

"Have you come to love Walking Head?" she asked Whisper. "Is that why you saved his life this day?"

Whisper shook her head. "My love is only for one man, the Long Knife Jim Ayers. Walking Head has been very good to me, even though I have told him often that I could never feel love for him. But he would never believe me. He thought I could someday forget my Salish past and become Siksika, as he once did. But I have a husband and a mother to fill my life with love." She patted her stomach. "And soon a child. Walking Head did not have these things. The only love he ever knew came from a Siksika lodge and not from the Salish. That is something that was meant to be, and this has hurt him deeply. I only felt he did not deserve to die this day, and I fought to save his life.''

''You are blessed with much understanding,'' said Laughs-in-the-Morning. ''You are a special person. There are not many among us who are like you.''

''Those are kind words,'' Whisper said. ''But I am not deserving of them. Because of my hate I lost a child not yet born and nearly lost my husband and a good friend. Now I will leave this village much wiser, for I now know my enemies suffer the same sorrows as I do myself.''

Laughs-in-the-Morning took a string of beads from around her neck. ''I wish to know you as a friend always,'' she said. ''I care not what blood runs inside of you. Because of you, I have found my true self, and I know that Walking Head will be happy with me as his first wife now that Songbird is gone.''

Whisper took the beads and arranged them around her neck. ''I am sure Walking Head will be pleased with you,'' she said. ''You must give him a son. That will be his first real happiness in life. And because you have been a good friend and cared deeply for my well-being, I wish also to give you a present.'' She reached into her medicine bundle and took one of the feathers that belonged to the tiny owl. ''This is a sacred thing. Place it somewhere among your most honored possessions. It will always bring you good luck.''

As Whisper left the lodge, she noticed that Laughs-in-the-Morning was still staring down at the small feather she held in the palms of her hands. It was a good gift, Whisper thought, for the owl had surely been working through her friend part of the time, or Whisper would never have been able to journey off by herself to the high cliffs. But now she must forget what lay behind in this Siksika village, for now she had a long journey ahead of her. She would need a clear mind to face what lay ahead. Something told her things were not good on the Stinkingwater.

Chapter 32

SPIRIT MOUNTAIN

The two forks of the Stinkingwater came together near the mouth of a great canyon. Steep mountains rose to high rocks on both sides, while the valley lay fresh and green where the waters flowed.

Whisper was tired from her long journey. She had ridden hard through both light and darkness for nine suns since leaving the Siksika village, stopping only to rest and to allow Red Thunder to graze. Now, as she reached the place where the fort was to have been built, she found a trail branching off toward the canyon. It was not an old trail, as the one she now traveled, but looked as though freshly made and used by travelers coming along the old trail. She became excited, for this new trail was leading toward where the two forks of the Stinkingwater came together.

As she rode along the new trail, she became troubled. She knew there would surely be a fire going at the fort and that she should be able to see the smoke clearly now. Then, at the forks of the Stinkingwater, she saw the reason there was no fire and no smoke.

What she saw was not a newly built fort, but blackened ruins. No one was anywhere near the area. Only a mass of charred logs and burned timbers remained.

A feeling of fear swept over Whisper as she got down from Red Thunder and looked among the ashes. Traps, black from flame and heat, lay in twisted piles. Barrels once filled with trade goods were now heaps of ash and rubble. The only sounds were the wind and birds in the nearby cottonwoods. No one had been anywhere near this place for many suns.

As Whisper searched through the ruins, she prayed to Amótkan that she would not find bodies. She wondered where Jim and her mother were, and if her mother had even reached this place from far over on the waters of the Snake. All this explained her bad feelings while in the Siksika village, and why Jim had not come to look for her.

Then came the boom of a Hawken, fired in the air from the hillside above her. Still holding her breath, Whisper watched Fiddler ride down the hill and over to her.

"If you ain't a sight for these sore old eyes!" he yelled. "We all thought you'd gone under or had decided to stick it out with the Blackfeet."

"Where is Jim? Did my mother come to this place?" Whisper asked both questions in one breath.

"Rest easy, Pretty Lady," said Fiddler. "We've seen better times, but we've seen a lot worse, too. Jim stopped a Hawken ball a couple of weeks back and your ma saved him, by God. She cut it out and filled him up on medicine plants. She's near as close to a full-fledged medicine man as anyone I ever saw. And your hoss, Jim, owes his life to her."

"Was it Beeler?" Whisper asked.

Fiddler nodded. "It was for a fact. But he ain't got the best of us. No, siree, we ain't licked. Not by a long shot. We've got a cache of furs and silver money, and Jim plans to get the rest of our possibles down at Fort Hall." He shook his head and laughed. "Reckon I'm talkin' your leg off, Pretty Lady. I'm right happy to see you, is all. And I know where there's a couple of other folks who'll be right tickled as well.''

Fiddler took her to a group of caves that were bunched together on the side of a mountain. "A mighty good place to hide out," he told her. "Spirit Mountain is what the Injuns call it.'' Here the gases came out from the ground, much the same as she remembered the geyser basins high in the Yellow-stone. Fiddler went on to say how they had nearly all been killed the night, two weeks past, when Beeler and his men had jumped them and burned the fort. He told Whisper they would all have burned in the fire if it hadn't been for her mother, who woke them when she felt something bad was happening. They had all run into the trees along the river and escaped harm. But Jim had been shot by one of Beeler's men and left for dead while trying to save some of the supplies from the fort. "We ain't done with Beeler over this," Fiddler told her. "I guess I should have let Jim take his hair on Green River when he had the chance last year at rendezvous.''

Now, as Whisper entered one of the caves, she met the arms of her mother. "Things are good, now," she told her mother. "I will never see a Siksika village again.''

Jim had lost weight from his wound, and awoke from sleep when Whisper's tears fell onto his face.

"Am I dreamin'?'' he asked.

"No, my love," said Whisper. "But the dreams and wishes I have carried in my heart for over a full moon's passing have this day come true for me.''

"Well," said Jim, "I guess you saw what's left of our dream down below. We'd best get to buildin' on it now that you're here to help with the cookin'.''

"There is plenty of time to build another fort," said Whisper. "Now is the time to let your side heal." As Jim started to speak to her, Whisper took a bowl of meat from near the fire. "You do less talking for a while and more eating," she told him.

Whisper took care to see that he ate well during each meal after that. Each passing of Sun took them ever closer to the cold moons and Jim grew more and more anxious to make the trip to Fort Hall for more supplies. These supplies were badly needed, for the trade with both Long Knives and Indian peoples would be very great during the cold moons.

Jim also wished to have a new fort built as soon as possible and spent much time each day cutting new logs and clearing away the burned wood and ashes. Both Whisper and Fiddler often became angry with him, for he never seemed to know when to stop working and to let his body rest.

Because of all the work, Jim's wound was slow in healing and, together with the bad back he had gotten from the Gros Ventre war club at the Battle of Pierre's Hole, Whisper worried more about him with each passing day. He was never a man to complain and would die before he called for help. His dream of owning and running a trading post had planted itself deep in his heart. Whisper knew he would fight until this dream came true.

The days went by and the grasses turned ever more a golden brown, while the leaves on the trees began to grow yellow and red. Sun shone very warm during the days, but the night brought in a coolness from high up in the mountains. Though Jim got up each morning with words about getting on the trail to Fort Hall, Whisper knew by his walk and the way he held his side that the trip would not be possible for many more suns.

The land of the Stinkingwater was a paradise and Whisper spent each day preparing for the cold moons. There was much game on the ridges and along the bottoms were beaver dams filled with speckled trout that jumped in early morning and late evening. There were always buffalo nearby, for the canyon broke out into rolling foothills and then to flats that led to the Grey Bull and the lands called Big Horn Basin. Whisper hunted often and soon there was plenty of meat drying for winter cookpots.

Jim and Fiddler talked a lot about Beeler and his men during this time. They did not know if Beeler was still with the American Fur Company, or if he had formed his own company and was trying to get rid of all the competition. There was talk around Long Knife campfires that Beeler had not been able to agree with the Company leader, McKenzie, on many things and had told him he would some day own the mountains himself. Beeler had many men who followed him, and he was a hard man to beat. He had caused Jim and Fiddler much hardship, and had cost them precious time and money.

Then, late one evening, it was learned he had become trouble to everyone in the mountains.

"How's for a meal?" A group of trappers called out. "It's been a hard day."

Jim and Fiddler put down their axes and welcomed the five free trappers, all old friends.

"Fire's hot and there's buffalo hump to be roasted," said Jim.

The men talked of old times and the price of beaver. Good trapping grounds were a thing of the past and the days when a brigade roamed a river bottom by itself all winter would never happen again. Fights with Blackfeet had been common. Good friends had gone under and still others were marked for life where a lance or an arrow had cut muscle or bone. The Sioux and Crees to the east had taken their share of men. Even the Crows, who thought more of horses than scalps, had started to tear up camps and kill from time to time. "Too many greenhorns rilin' them all up," one man said. "Them Injuns get nervous when the woods are full of whites."

"And now the whites are all agin' one another," the same man said. He pointed to the ruins of the fort. "This hoss don't hold with the likes of a man who'll do a thing like that to another. To me that's lower than a snake will crawl."

"Beeler will get his in good time," said Jim, his mouth full of meat. He took a swallow from a jug that was being passed around. "He's up on the Yellowstone and thinks he's safe as a babe. But he ain't. I aim to settle up."

"I should have known it was Beeler," said the trapper. "He's a mean one. But he ain't up on the Yellowstone."

Jim looked up from where he was cutting another piece of meat off the roasting hump. "You say he ain't up on the Yellowstone?"

"No," said the trapper. "We run into him and his bunch down on the Snake. He was headed south, for sure. Maybe to try and burn out Fort Hall, same as he did here."

Jim stopped chewing and looked over to Fiddler.

"Wyeth's got a passel of men," said Fiddler. "Beeler would be a fool to try Fort Hall."

"He's a crazy one," said one other trapper. "He wants these mountains himself. He'd try anything."

"How far down the Snake you see him?" Jim asked.

"Below the *Tetons*," the trapper answered. "They didn't seem to be in no big hurry. Just the same, they asked a lot of nosy questions, like, who's at the fort and how many men. Questions like that."

Whisper watched Jim as the night wore on. He grew more and more restless and when all others had gone to sleep, he tossed and turned in his robes.

As she lay next to him, Whisper sensed his increasing unease and asked, "Do you feel you must go to Fort Hall soon?"

"Real soon," he answered. "I'm figurin' on goin' just as soon as I can get things packed tomorrow."

"Fort Hall is far ahead of us, Jim, and your wound is not yet fully healed."

"The wound is fine," said Jim.

"It will do you no good to die. I do not want a dead husband."

"I won't die, and it won't do you no good to worry about it. Don't you want to see us make it here?"

"Yes," Whisper answered. "But it is a long and a hard journey to the waters of the Snake. It would be hard for a man who had all his strength. You do not have all your strength."

"No use to argue," said Jim. "I'm goin'. I've got to."

Whisper took a deep breath. "I will go with you. It would not be wise for you to go alone, and Fiddler would be of more help here with my mother."

"Then first thing, we can catch what horses and mules Beeler didn't run off," said Jim. "We'll have to make good time to stop Beeler if he figures to jump the fort down there. By God, I haven't worked for all this just to watch it go up in smoke!"

Whisper lay back in the robes, thinking. It was not a good trip for her to make with the baby, but she had no choice. She could only hope that she and Jim would reach Fort Hall and get their supplies before Beeler and his men destroyed everything.

She felt Jim's arms around her and his lips against her cheek.

"I love you, Whisper," he said. "You know I only want the best for us."

"I also love you," she said. "And we shall have the best."

Chapter 33

FORT HALL

The mountains sat blue in the distance and the peaks had begun to shine with a new whiteness in Sun's light. Early storms had again come to the high country, leaving snow among the rocks and jagged peaks above the timberline. The cold moons would soon be coming to all the lands.

The last eleven suns of their journey from the Stinkingwater had brought little sleep, for Jim had worried and talked much about his fear that Beeler and his men would beat them to Fort Hall. But there had been no sign of Beeler during the journey and now Fort Hall stood before them along the waters of the Snake.

The bottoms were flat and open. Scattered herds of horses and mules had grazed the brown grass completely off the ground for a long distance on all sides of the fort. Here and there were rings of rocks where lodges had stood. Soon the rocks would be used again, by Nez Percés, Shoshones, and maybe even Flatheads, but now was the time for the fall buffalo hunt.

Long Knives, with Hawkens ready, opened the gates and eyed Whisper and Jim closely before deciding they brought no trouble. Here and there were other Long Knives, sleeping off the effects of the firewater they called whiskey or loading supplies for their fall beaver hunts. Other Long Knives stood guard along the high walls, watching Whisper and Jim for a few moments before they finally looked back out to the open country. If Beeler came, he would surely meet with men who were ready for that kind of trouble.

"The name's Evans," the clerk inside said. "Wyeth left me in charge here. I been expectin' you, except long before this."

"We had some trouble up north," Jim explained. "A man named Beeler and his men burned our fort. I heard he was headed down here with the same thing in mind."

Evans had a grin on his face. "I heard he was camped a ways out, up on the Portneuf. Maybe he's that big a fool, I can't say. But there's a passel of men here and we'll blow him clean across the flats."

"I wish we'd been ready," Jim said. Then he added quickly, "But for now, we'd best get our gear and march north. It's a far piece back up to the Stinkingwater."

"A man can't help but admire your spunk, Ayers," Evans said as he led Jim and Whisper to a log building and showed them a cache of supplies. "There ain't a lot of men who'd try this business, what with the Company goin' strong like it is and men like Beeler around. It's hard enough even when you have men and money."

"Got any mules or horses to spare?" Jim asked.

"Take your pick off the flats," Evans said. "There's more out there than I feel good about. It brings Injuns around here with thievin' on their minds. Maybe you'd take a shot of whiskey. Wyeth says you're a drinkin' pal of his."

"I could use a wettin' down," said Jim. They went back into the main store and Jim asked, "Where is Nat these days?"

"He's headed for the Columbia. He wants to build another fort out there. You know him, always pushin' his way into things."

"That's Hudson Bay country," said Jim. "He's liable to bite off more than he can chew."

"He already has," said Evans. "He's got too many things goin' at one time to my way of thinkin'. He's got this ship, the May Dacre, and he thinks he can haul fish back east from them salmon waters in Oregon country to pay for his trappin' supplies out here. He thinks of it all, and gets them fat eastern dandies to back him to boot. I never seen the likes of it."

"He's got big plans," said Jim. "I hope they work out for him."

Then the door burst open and a trapper yelled inside, "Evans! We got trouble!"

Just inside the gates, two trappers were helping a third down from his horse. The shaft of an arrow stuck out from his stomach.

"He needs doctorin' bad," one said. "He took a Blackfoot arrow through the guts and ain't neither of us knows how to go about gettin' it out."

"Blackfeet?" said Evans. "Where?"

"Just north of here. We was headed back up the Snake and ran into them. They didn't seem like they was itchin' for a fight none, but that fool Beeler opened fire on them. Then, I hope to tell you, we was just lucky we was on fast horses and close to the fort."

Jim eyed the trapper a moment and asked, "Did you say you was ridin' with Beeler?"

"He's crazy," said the trapper. "He never should have started shootin'. Them Blackfeet wasn't even painted." He turned back to Evans. "Ain't there nobody around who knows nothin' about doctorin'?"

Jim swung him around by the shoulder. "I asked you if you was one of Beeler's men!"

"Ayers!" Evans yelled out. "This ain't the time for trouble."

"I don't cater to no skunks who burned my fort," said

Jim, eyeing the trapper coldly. Then he turned to Evans. "Why don't you ask him if he didn't come down here with Beeler to watch Fort Hall burn?"

The trapper looked to Evans and licked his lips. "Look, we just come to find some doctorin' for a dyin' man. That's all."

"Take your man inside," Evans ordered him. He turned to Jim. "We don't need no trouble here, Ayers. We got enough problems around here as is."

"Well, I see I ain't got a choice," said Jim, looking around at the men who were watching him closely. "We'll be gone first light tomorrow," he told Evans. "But you'd better keep them three tucked under your wing until then."

Later that night, Whisper lay with Jim in their robes near a fire inside the fort. Other fires burned brightly within the walls and there was much drinking, and laughing. Earlier, the wounded man had died and the other two had left the fort, eyeing Jim and Whisper as they rode out. Whisper felt somehow that they had not seen the last of these two Long Knives.

"Beeler's still in this country," said Jim, letting out a deep sigh. "Now there's Blackfeet, too. If it ain't one thing, it's another."

Whisper thought a moment and said, "There are many trails that lead to the north and back to our own lands on the Stinkingwater. Maybe we could journey east over the mountains and into the valley of the Siskadee."

"There's bound to be trouble over there, too," said Jim. "The whole damn country's either got Blackfeet after hair or other trappers lookin' to rob a man of his gear." He was silent a moment. Then he nodded and said, "But if we took the trail that leads northwest across the desert to the Twin Buttes, I'll bet we wouldn't meet up with a soul."

"That is a dangerous trail with so many horses and mules," said Whisper. "There is little water in those lands and that means losing animals and supplies. Maybe even our lives."

"We've got to chance it," said Jim. "In two days we'll

reach the Twin Buttes, then we'll cut off northeast on the trail that comes in at the crook in the Snake. We'll be travelin' the desert no more than four days at most. And there's water here and there. We'll find it.''

Whisper heard the doubt in Jim's voice. He knew it was a very dangerous trail to travel. And with so many supplies, they would have to travel very slow in a land where Sun beat down with a fire that burned hot even this close to the cold moons. But Jim's mind was made up and as Whisper turned to try and find sleep in the robes, she could already see the endless desert.

Before them lay a vast, open land that had seen heat for an endless time. The grey medicine bush the Long Knives called sagebrush stood ragged, pointing skyward with limbs like a many-fingered hand that had pushed up out of the hot sand. Overhead the sky was blue and cloudless. And far, far away to the west was the hazy blue of the mountains above the Big Lost River, or Godin's Fork as the Long Knives called it.

Whisper felt Sun's fierceness beating down upon the thin piece of blanket she used to cover her head. Like the hood of the Long Knives' capote that shielded the face from snow and wind during the cold moons, her piece of blanket would do the same against the harsh heat of the desert. Sun had crossed the sky nearly twice now since they had left Fort Hall and the heat had taken much of their strength. In the near distance stood the Twin Buttes, the strange mounds that the desert had pushed up so that all who traveled these burning lands could see them. Soon they would find the trail that would lead them back towards the waters of the Snake, where the land once again knew the freshness of rain and the flowers pushed their blossoms between the lush blades of grass.

Jim turned and said to her, ''Are you keepin' your eyes to our backtrail?''

Whisper nodded and he turned in his saddle to face the trail ahead. When they had left the fort and crossed the waters of the Snake, she had told Jim of the worry she had about the two men who had left the fort the night before after their companion had died. She well knew they had waited for her and Jim so that they might tell Beeler about the supplies they carried. She had known this to be true for she had pointed out a rider on a far hill watching them as they traveled out into the desert. And, as Whisper now looked across the desert behind them, a cloud of dust appeared.

"Damn the luck!" Jim yelled. "We can't run the stock in this heat. We'll have to fort up."

As Jim took supplies down for them to fight behind, Whisper fixed an arrow to her bow and sang a Salish war song. Soon the cloud of dust grew large and from it Beeler appeared with nine men, among them the two who had left the fort.

"They are many more than we," Whisper said. "But there are those among them who will sing death songs this fine day."

"Looks like you and your squaw are in a fix, Ayers," Beeler laughed. "I thought for sure you'd gone under when we burned your fort. Guess I'll finish you now."

Jim leveled his Hawken and spoke down the barrel. "You just goin' to talk, Beeler, or fight?"

Beeler laughed again. "Right spunky for a man in your fix. We got you in a hole, Ayers. Might just as well make it easy on yourself and come on out."

"Not a chance, Beeler," Jim yelled. "Let's see you and that pack of nit-pickin' scum with you come in and get us."

Beeler and his men dismounted and spread out in the sagebrush. Whisper knew she could be most effective by using her bow after Jim had fired his Hawken. For a time all was silent. Then Jim saw one of them dart a ways out and took quick aim.

The Hawken boomed loud and a scream came from one of the men as he jumped up and doubled over at the middle, then fell squirming into the sand.

"Gut shot," said Jim. "He'll yell for a while and maybe give the others a thing or two to think on."

As Whisper knew they would, the others got up and quickly rushed forward, knowing it would take Jim time to reload. Whisper was ready and arrows whistled through the hot air. Two men fell and kicked in the sand and a third struggled back to cover with a wooden shaft through his upper leg.

Jim laughed and yelled, "You think we ain't ready for you, Beeler? Just come on like that again."

But Beeler and his men had learned how foolish they had been. Now they were upon their horses and were preparing to make a rush at Jim and Whisper. They clung to the far sides of their horses and leveled their Hawkens under the horses' necks, in the fashion of Indian warriors.

"That won't do them no good," Jim laughed. "They can't shoot straight like that."

As they came, Jim cautioned himself over and over, "Hold! Hold! Wait until they get closer!" Then, as Beeler's horse was nearly upon them, he fired.

Beeler was thrown headlong into the sand as his horse collapsed with a bullet through the head. The other horses behind cut off to both sides and an arrow from Whisper's bow found one of the men, the one who had spoken to Jim at Fort Hall, and he fell twisting from his horse.

As Jim hurried to reload, one of the others fired and the ball whizzed between Whisper and Jim. Then the rider who had fired jumped his horse over the barricade of supplies and dived off onto Jim.

Whisper heard Jim yell in pain as the trapper came down hard onto Jim's wounded side. The pain made Jim a wild man and he quickly overpowered the trapper and rammed his knife into him again and again.

"Jim, do not hurt yourself worse," Whisper told him.

Jim stood up and yelled out, "Get back here and fight, Beeler!"

During the fighting, one of the others had picked Beeler up onto his own horse. Now those who were still alive were in a group talking. Then Beeler pointed to the desert behind Whisper and Jim.

"We don't need to do nothin' more, Ayers," he yelled. "You can't go nowheres without a horse. The desert'll get you now."

Whisper and Jim looked to see their horses and mules scattered out behind them over the desert. The fighting had scared them and even Red Thunder was running with reins flying wild.

"Oh, God," Jim said under his breath.

Beeler laughed again. He yelled out to Whisper and Jim, "Hell, we won't bother you no more now. You ain't got a lick of water and it's a full two days walk back to the Snake. You'll make the buzzards mighty happy."

Whisper and Jim were helpless as Beeler and his men rounded up the mules and horses. Whisper felt rage inside her as she watched Red Thunder being led behind one of the trappers. Soon they were specks in the distance, moving in a long line along the trail that came in to the northeast along the waters of the Snake.

"Well, there ain't a lot of choice left for us," Jim told Whisper. "We'd best get started." He held his side and the pain lined his face.

Whisper looked out across the desert. "We must move quickly," she said. "We must travel at as fast a pace as possible. We cannot live for more than two suns in this land."

They checked Beeler's fallen horse and found his water-bag had been split open in the fall. It would be of no use for them to look further for water here. All that remained now were dead men.

Whisper started off at a trot with Jim behind her. He gripped his side but kept up with her pace. Fear crept into Whisper, for she knew there would be less than two suns for Jim. He was hurting inside and this would take much of his strength. And beyond lay only desert and Sun that went forever.

Chapter 34

THE NIGHT CAMP

The night was still, with the light of a cut moon casting shadows over the desert. The sand crunched underfoot and distance had taken on a meaning only of vastness and unending direction. To go on and on and on was all they could do now. To keep moving and push forward, though all around were only the high tops of the medicine bushes looking black and eerie in the shadowed night. The night air seemed to bring back some of the strength that Sun had taken during the day. But even the cool darkness could not help their burning throats.

Time had no meaning now and the mind brought out those things which Whisper knew to be most important: her baby—the child within her that must surely be crying out for water also; her mother, whose face had shown so much sadness that day she had left with Walking Head; and Jim, who now struggled behind her with rasping breaths.

They had moved on through the night, Whisper keeping her pace and Jim working to stay with her. His pain was greater with the passing of time, but he was a strong man, stronger than any other Whisper had ever known, and he would not stop. He would not even speak of his great agony. Only the grimacing looks that showed when the moonlight hit his face and the heavy breaths full of groans told Whisper that he had never hurt so much in his life.

For a time they had traveled with only the sounds of their feet in the sand. But now, as the moon continued to move across the sky, there came the howls of wolves, which grew ever louder. After a time, Whisper stopped and pointed across the desert. The light of a fire burned in the distance and the shadows of men could be seen around it.

Jim caught his breath and said, "It's them damn Blackfeet. I'd bet good money on it."

"Why would they travel these lands?" Whisper asked. "There is nothing to hunt and few war parties find the strength to fight in this heat."

"It's hard to tell. Maybe we're closer to the Snake than we thought."

Whisper shook her head. "It is far yet to those waters. It is strange that they are in these lands."

"Maybe they plan to reach Godin's Fork. You can't ever tell about Blackfeet."

It was hard to see if the camp was indeed Blackfeet. But Whisper was sure they were Indian peoples. The howling of the wolves had not been wolves, but sentries posted to keep watch over the camp.

"We must get around them," said Whisper. "We must not be seen or heard by them."

Jim nodded. "I'd rather die of a dried up craw than be butchered by them, no doubt about that."

Crouching low to keep their backs below the level of the sagebrush, Whisper and Jim began moving slowly around the camp. It would be foolish to try and tell them she was the Spirit Woman and that she had saved Walking Head's life far to the north along the Big Muddy, Whisper thought, for even if there were those who believed her, there would be others who would wish to kill her. No, it would not be a good thing to try, even though it could mean the taste of water and life itself.

Time seemed to move slower now than at any other time Whisper could remember. The desert was still, without even a wisp of wind, and every breath seemed to roar in her throat. Every light crunch of sand or sagebrush underfoot seemed to fill the night with sound. Nearby were the sentries, still howling that all was well while voices and laughter from the camp grew ever louder. Soon Whisper could hear pieces of conversation. Jim had been right, these warriors were Siksika.

Then from behind came the sound of a bush cracking. Whisper turned to see Jim lying twisted in the sand, holding his side. She went quickly to his side.

"My guts," Jim hissed into her ear. "They cramped up on me. I couldn't keep from doublin' over." He groaned.

"Come," said Whisper. "We cannot stay here. We must move a ways away. Then you can rest."

Whisper helped Jim to his feet. They quickly moved further away and lay close together under a large sagebrush plant. They could dare not make a sound now. It would mean their lives.

When Jim had fallen one of the sentries had barked, as does a wolf in alarm. Now the night was silent. Whisper knew that there would soon be the sounds of Siksika feet moving over the desert sand as they looked for the reason the twig had snapped.

Now was a time of great danger and Whisper knew that even breathing could be heard by Siksika ears when they listened carefully. Beside her, Jim's face was all sweat and pain as the fire of his wound shot through his side. The feeling of thirst had become ever stronger now that they were lying still.

Nearby came the sound of footsteps. The footsteps came closer and the sagebrush where they lay rustled and dried leaves fell into Whisper's face. The footsteps stopped for a moment and Whisper felt her lungs heaving within her as they cried out for air. Still she refused to breath. Then the footsteps began again and traveled away from them.

For a time that seemed forever, Whisper and Jim lay silent. There were no more footsteps, but the howling did not begin again. It would not be safe until the sentries again took up their watch and worried no more about the noise they had heard in the night. Whisper could remember from her childhood among the Willow Cutters band of Salish that any time danger was felt, the warriors of the village would look until they found what had caused the alarm. It was no different among the Siksika.

After a time, Whisper heard laughing. She sat up and wiped the sweat from her face and eyes. A ways off the sentries had gathered and were laughing among themselves. One held up a rabbit he had killed with an arrow.

Slowly, Whisper and Jim moved away from the camp until the fire and the voices became lost in the distance. When Jim spoke, he had shame in his voice.

"I just about got us killed back there," he said. "Maybe you'd do better to move on and let me fend for myself."

Whisper took Jim by the arms and looked closely into his face. In her voice was much anger. "I do not ever want to hear words such as those from your lips again," she said. "We have far to go and it is not wise for you to stop me to say something I will never listen to, not as long as there is life in my body."

When Sun came and made the eastern sky red, a wind began to blow off the sand. Whisper and Jim continued on with baked faces and swollen tongues. This day would be the hardest of any day that Whisper or Jim had ever known. There had been the hard days of travel in the cold lands of the Yellowstone when snow lay deep and the air stung the face. And there had been the pain of wounds in battle. But never before had there been the feeling that death was so near as in this place, where the heat never quit and the senses left the body.

From out of the flats grew broad lakes, and the sagebrush grew to be all tall cottonwoods green with life. "No!"

Whisper would tell herself. "The desert lies!" Her steps grew heavier and the sand grew hotter under her feet. Overhead was the screeching of the big black bird that found those who could go no further. Death birds. The ugly birds that Amótkan had fashioned to tear the rotting flesh from the bones of the fallen. There were many of them, and Whisper could remember their crooked beaks and long, curved necks, for she had seen them many times beside the bodies of buffalo or other fallen game. And once near fallen Long Knives her people had found while hunting. She could remember the terrible birds and how the flesh hung from their beaks.

It seemed the death birds were growing in number and that they were coming to the ground just a short ways further in the desert. "Do not wait for me to fall," Whisper said to herself. "You will not taste my flesh!" But as she came closer, she could see what the death birds had found. She turned and saw that Jim was also watching, and that his eyes could not believe what they saw.

"My God!" he said.

There, in the sand, were men buried up to their necks with only their heads showing. Some were dead, others still living. All had been scalped.

The death birds squawked and flapped away, landing clumsily nearby. Whisper and Jim looked at the men, still not believing. Pieces of torn flesh hung from their faces and eyes were missing where the death birds had started their feasting. Those still alive could only moan in low tones, for screaming had long since passed their lips.

Jim knelt down in the sand and looked into a face that was barely recognizable.

"Beeler? Can you hear me?"

The eyes that slowly opened in the face were dull and glassy. The top of his head showed a bloody uneven circle and a patch of skull shone bare and white in the sun where his hair had once grown. His face was covered with rip marks from the beaks of the death birds, and ants and flies were crawling in and out of the wounds. His lips, split open from the heat, moved slowly. But no sound came from them.

Jim looked up to Whisper. "It must have been those Blackfeet we saw last night."

Whisper nodded. It had seemed to her, as she and Jim had made their way past the Siksika camp, that there had been many more horses than there were warriors. A warrior takes as many as three extra ponies on the hunt or warpath, but Whisper had known from the sounds she could hear nearby that there were very many horses in this Siksika camp. But there had been no time to worry about it then, and there was no time now. They would have to keep moving or they too would become a feast for the death birds.

Whisper helped Jim back to his feet. "We must go on, or die ourselves."

"Beeler can tell us what happened to our supplies."

Whisper shook her head. "His lips will never speak again."

Chapter 35

THE SPIRIT DREAM

The day grew steadily hotter and the thirst within Whisper burned like a raging fire. Nowhere was there any sign of water, nor would there be until they reached the waters of the Snake. Forever ahead lay sand and the grey medicine bush, the sagebrush that wavered before her eyes now like ghosts moving across the desert.

Behind her was Jim's labored breathing. He had said nothing since they had left Beeler and his men buried in the desert sand. Jim's eyes showed he knew little about where he was or what he was doing. His eyes were on Whisper's back all the time, and it was getting harder and harder for him to keep up with her.

The day wore on and Sun moved straight above. Whisper pushed on, fighting the urge to stop and rest. Close behind came Jim, and he now had nearly reached the breaking point. He often cried out for her to stop and she would tell him, "We cannot. To stop is to die!" She knew his side was ready to explode with pain. But if he stopped, he would surely fall. And he would not be able to rise again.

Finally, as Sun crossed further toward the west, Whisper heard Jim stumble behind her. She turned and saw him fall. His breathing was harsh and labored, his eyes nearly swollen shut.

"Get up, Jim!" Whisper tugged on his arm. "Get up. We must go on!"

He looked up at Whisper and caught his breath. "Damn. You're still the prettiest woman I ever saw. You know, I sure wish Fiddler was here to play us a tune. And your ma. She saved my life, she did. Pulled me through. Funny about her and Fiddler. Her face lights up when that old coon pays mind to her. Old Fiddler. I think maybe your ma and him feel good together. Damn! Wish them two were here now."

"Jim, you must get up. I will help."

"Wait. Whisper, wait. Oh, God, my side."

"Jim, get up!"

"We've had some good times, Whisper. You and me. And I wanted us to see them oceans. God, but I love you. Do you figure God will take me in? He must care about me some or He'd never have sent you."

"Jim!" She shook him hard. "Get up!"

"Can't."

"You'll die! Do you not wish to see your child born? Must I leave you here and send your son back to find his father's bones. What should I say to him? Must I tell him his father was too weak to survive?"

"Child?"

"Your child, Jim. Your son. If you stay here, you will not see him born."

Jim grunted and came to his knees. Whisper helped him up and he stumbled. She steadied him, then shouted into his ear.

"Forget your wound," she said. "Forget your pain. Remember your child, your son!"

Jim started to walk.

"You must catch me. If you don't, you are not a man!"

"I am a man."

"You must catch me!"

Whisper started trotting again. She steadied herself, for a sudden dizziness came over her. Behind her, Jim had started trotting again. Somehow, he had found a new strength.

Whisper continued to yell back at him, "Catch me! Catch me! You let a woman out run you?"

The day wore steadily on. Sun moved farther in the sky. Death birds circled overhead and called out to each other that soon they would feast. In a short time there would be meat for their bellies. "Do not slow down!" Whisper would yell. "Catch me!"

But Jim's steps became slower and slower. He groaned in pain, holding his side. His mouth hung open and dry. Blood oozed from cracked lips and a parched face. Then, again, he fell.

"Get up! Get up!" Whisper shook him again. She yelled as loud as she could, but her voice would not rise above a hoarse whisper. "Jim, get up!"

Jim shook his head feebly. "You go ahead; save yourself and the child. You can make it."

Tears came into Whisper's eyes. "No! Jim, get up!"

"I've had the best with you a man can ask for," Jim went on. "I love you more . . . more than anything else in the world." He reached for her. "Let me touch the child." He put his shaking hands on Whisper's stomach. "Take care of my son. Tell him I love him." He settled back and closed his eyes.

Whisper rubbed her tears away and shook him with as much strength as she could find.

"Listen to me! Listen!"

Jim's eyes came open.

"I will not tell this child that you love him. I will tell him you were weak. I will tell him that you gave yourself up to the desert because you were a weak man." Then she shook him again. "No, I will not even tell the child about you. I would not want him to know someone as weak as you fathered him. He would not be proud of such a father."

Jim's eyes grew dark and he forced himself up to his hands and knees.

"What? What are you tellin' me?"

"I should have stayed with Walking Head," Whisper went on. "At least he was not weak. *He* would not have given up and died." She got to her feet and looked down at Jim. "It is right that you should stay here and become meat for the death birds. It is right for the weak to leave their bones in the desert." Then she turned and started off across the desert, not looking back at him.

"What?" he yelled hoarsely. "You can't talk to me like that!"

Jim stumbled to his feet and took a deep breath.

Whisper continued on. She heard him yell behind her, "Wait, damn it all!" But she went on and his slurred cussing mixed with the scrape of his tired feet through the sand, and she knew he had started out again.

The day went on and the heat seemed to have no end, just as the desert had no end. Whisper pushed on, though she herself had begun to grow very weak. She could not imagine the pain Jim must be feeling with the wound as well as his thirst for water. But neither must stop now, for they would have no strength to begin again.

Movement was only the body forced on and on while the mind floated separately. Whisper knew her feet were going forward, but the feel of the sand was gone and even the big grey medicine bushes called sagebrush seemed hazy and unreal. Like Jim had told her a ways back, there had been better times. There had been happy times together, when Whisper felt the strength of him as a man as he lay with her and held her close amid the mountain breezes and the sounds of water trickling nearby. They had shared the days of spring, when the grass once again turned green and Earth brought forth new life. Now these things seemed not to exist, for the mind was beyond them and into a land where all was hazy and the colors were bright and mixed. They heard the sound of rushing wind and every living thing moved silently and off the ground. All things took strange shapes and animals and bushes appeared to have the heads of men.

Then, in this strange land, there came the sounds of men's voices and a column of riders that circled in front of her and stopped. Whisper saw them get off their horses and come toward her. She stopped and quickly looked in all directions. The riders were everywhere.

Jim had fallen again and Whisper found her way back to him while the men continued to come toward her. She tried to yell at them, but could not. They were Indian peoples, these men, and there were many of them. Again she tried to shout at them, to tell them to leave her and Jim alone. They must be evil spirits, these men. Surely they were from the land of death and they had come for her. She tried to sing a death song, a song that Amótkan would hear. She stood over Jim and, again, tried to yell. They would not take them. She was not ready to die and did not want to see these spirits. One of them reached out to her and his hand was so close. She jerked back and fell backwards over Jim. The sand was hot against her skin. Still the man, the evil spirit, came toward her. His words were hard to hear and she did not want to hear him. She tried to crawl away in the sand, but she had no strength. She saw that many of them were near Jim. They had him! They were taking him! One of them was bending over her. She wanted to cry out, "No! Leave and do not take us! We do not wish to die!" But her lips would not move and her mouth was so swollen that not a sound would come out. All was spinning before her; then all was black.

"Drink slowly. Do not take too much at a time."

Whisper felt the cool freshness of water in her mouth. Her face smarted from the wetness against burned lips and skin. The water went down and sickness came on. Slowly, she took more water. The blackness left and hazy dizziness took its place. Then, in a short time, her eyes once again came into focus. She was looking into the face of Walking Head.

"Your mother, and the old Long Knife, Fiddler, told us you had traveled to these lands."

Whisper sat up. It was late evening and the air was much cooler.

"You are a woman of very strong medicine. The waters of the Snake flow only a short ways away. If we had not come, you would surely be there now."

Whisper looked around. Siksika warriors were gathering wood for a fire while others cared for the horses. At her shoulder was Red Thunder, nudging her with his nose. Beside her was Jim, his face smeared with bear grease.

"Last thing I expected was to have my hide saved by a Blackfoot," he said with a grin. "Especially this one."

Walking Head pointed at Jim. "I wish to meet this Long Knife who is such a man that you cannot forget him."

"He is indeed a man," Whisper said of Jim. "He has come all this way across the desert with a wound in his side."

"We both came across the desert," said Jim. "And this hoss would be bones now if you hadn't drug me halfway."

Whisper turned to Walking Head. "Why have you come to these lands?"

"I was told in a dream to come to this place," Walking Head answered. "I had a spirit dream while I lay sick from my wounds. I lay for many days not knowing if I would live or die, for the Cree arrows had taken much blood from me. Laughs-in-the-Morning sat near me all this time and told me the story of how you saved my life and our village. Then one night a dream came to me. After that I became stronger and was able to get up from my bed in just three more suns.

"In my dream was a desert, and death birds filled the air. I stood looking across the desert while a warrior with no face pointed far out and showed me two people walking. Then he pointed in another direction where many horses and mules were being led along a trail by Long Knives. One of the Long Knives rode your Appaloosa horse, Red Thunder. I then knew the two people walking were you and your Long Knife husband. 'Those two people walking need your help,' the faceless warrior told me. 'They are good people and one of them has been good to you. One of them has saved your life, for you will not die now. You will become strong and lead your people for many more winters. But you must travel to this desert land, for what you see here will come to pass before this moon is full.' This I heard clearly in my dream.

"I was strong enough to travel when Sun had crossed the sky but five times. I told the elders of my dream, and there were many warriors who wished to follow me. When we reached the Stinkingwater, your mother and the old Long Knife, Fiddler, were afraid. But I smoked the pipe of peace with them and they told me you had journeyed to these lands. Then I knew my spirit dream was soon to become real."

"We passed your camp in the night," said Whisper. "We did not know it was your camp. We knew only that it was a Siksika camp, and that meant enemies."

"Yes," said Walking Head, "and I wondered then if it was not you who had alarmed the sentries. But I did not know for sure until we came to the place where you killed the Long Knives."

"It was a hard fight," said Whisper. "But they were many and we lost our horses. It is good that you had the spirit dream. I thought surely Jim and I had met death this fine day."

"No," said Walking Head. "Death is not strong enough to overpower someone such as you. The faceless warrior told me you were a chosen being and that I had become a chosen being by defending your life at the council fires after you had killed the Brave Bear warrior. He also told me that I would be wise in the future to think less about the warpath and more about the happiness in my lodge. That happiness has now come, and Laughs-in-the-Morning is truly a good wife. This is something I could not see before. The faceless warrior is a man of wisdom."

Whisper nodded. "I know the faceless warrior well," she

said. "For I, too, have had spirit dreams such as yours. And this day has taught me much about the Universal Plan."

Walking Head beckoned to one of his warriors, who brought over a small otter-skin quiver with a small bow and arrows.

"A son such as the one you will bear should learn the ways of a warrior early in life," said Walking Head. "Tell him he will have a friend always in the Siksika war chief Walking Head."

Whisper took the bow and arrows. "And if it is a girl?"

"Then she shall be as her mother."

Whisper and Jim shared meat with Walking Head and his warriors that night and for three nights after. Soon their strength had returned and they were both happy to be on their way back to the Stinkingwater. Now, as Sun rose once again for another day, a fire was built in the center of camp, a ceremonial fire over which Walking Head himself said many prayers.

"Now is the time for our leaving," said Walking Head to Whisper and Jim. "This day I will journey over the mountains to the land of the Three Forks, and further to the Big Muddy to tell my people that my dream has been fulfilled. And you will journey to the Stinkingwater, where you will live in peace. I remember the day, Spirit Woman, when you made me smoke the pipe of peace with you. This day we shall, the three of us, smoke again so that our hearts may know peace for each other always."

When the ceremony was finished, Whisper said to Walking Head, "You now have a happy lodge to return to, for Laughs-in-the-Morning awaits your return and wishes to make you proud of her. I am sure you, too, will soon have a son that will be chosen to join in the sacred ceremonies. Go in peace, and may your life be filled with much happiness."

Walking Head nodded. Then he was on his horse, leading his warriors toward the mountains. Sun shone brightly on his war-shirt and headdress, as well as on those of the other warriors. They were a bright array of color and their ornaments sparkled in the light. They moved in a long column and Whisper remembered well the day she had been riding with them, that day not long ago when she had left her mother to go with Walking Head to the land of the Siksika. That day had been one of sorrow. But this day was one of great happiness, for now she and Jim could live together with no more fear of war.

As she and Jim crossed the waters of the Snake, she saw the golden leaves falling from the trees into the water. Her mother had seen leaves falling the day Whisper had gotten her name. "They fell so gently that it made me think of you as I held you in my arms," she remembered her mother saying. "Like the soft voice of life; a whisper. Whisper on the Water."

Now happiness was with Whisper. And as she followed Jim along the trail that would take them to their new homeland, she felt this happiness would last forever.

EPILOGUE

The days passed quickly now, so quickly that Whisper could hardly count each one. The skies were clear with the cool nights that settled in over the forest. The wild geese made long V's in the sky as they once again journeyed south to the warm lands. The trails from the mountains were now used by elk as they came down from the high country to those areas where they could find food when the snows fell. Along the foothills and out on the flats, the buffalo were moving to their winter grounds. The bulls had left the herds and would not return until the warm moons came again. The rabbit was once again white, and ice lined the banks of the waters. Though Sun shone brightly this day, the wind was from the north and a bank of white clouds was coming in.

Whisper was in good spirits and did not care if snow would soon cover the land. She watched Red Thunder graze from where she sat at the edge of the clearing, high up in the forest. She looked down on a land that she had quickly come to love and to call home. The valley of the Stinking-

water. Far below, smoke curled up from the chimney above
the fort. Jim said it was even larger and built better than
the first one. Now other Long Knives who looked for the
beaver came through often and stopped at the fort for supplies. It was going to be a good trading post.

The old Long Knife, Fiddler, played his stringed box
often. Whisper was glad that he and her mother had decided
to live as husband and wife, also. The two of them had
come to love each other and it was a good thing for them.
It made Whisper happy to see her mother once again enjoying life and rejoicing in each new day.

Life had come to be a great pleasure to Whisper now. It
gave her great happiness to see the faces of their family,
as they now called themselves, as they all sat around a fire
telling stories and filling their mouths with buffalo meat.
There was no worry now and each night brought sleep.
Jim's wound had healed and he was as strong as ever. There
would always be happiness now, and even the cold moons
would not change this.

Whisper's greatest joy came when she pressed her hands
to her stomach and felt the life of the child within her. "It
shall be a boy-child," her mother told her often. "You
carry him low inside of you, as a woman always carries a
boy-child. He will become a handsome man."

He would indeed become a handsome man, Whisper
thought. And he would have a pretty young sister to play
with, and maybe a brother, also. Life had certainly changed
for her and she was glad. Peace was a much better way to
live than war.

As Sun fell lower, Whisper sang her evening songs and
said prayers of thanks to Amótkan for the happiness she
now knew. She had learned many things in the past two
winters, and had become a better person. Those who traveled to the fort still talked of her as the Spirit Woman.
Whisper knew she would always be known by this name,
for she was now a legend in the forest. It was even said
that the Blackfeet did not cross the mountains to war as
much now, because they feared revenge by the Spirit

Woman. Yes, and there would be more stories, Whisper knew, for campfires make things seem bigger than they really are. She remembered the song she had heard at the rendezvous in Pierre's Hole:

> *See her walk among the lodges,*
> *Spirit Woman, medicine woman.*
> *She comes among us with her power*
> *And mighty warriors watch her pass.*
> *Oh, Spirit Woman, medicine woman,*
> *Keep the Blackfeet from our lands.*

But Whisper's weapons would stay in her lodge. She would go on no more vision quests and would no longer lead Salish warriors into battle.

Whisper stood up and looked across the valley. The storm was coming and it was time to go back to the fort and to see once again the happiness in Jim's eyes, a happiness that would never leave now that Whisper was beside him forever. She, herself, felt this same happiness, for her life was now complete.

She turned Red Thunder onto the trail that led down into the valley of the Stinkingwater. And above her, where Sun shone the final light of this day on tiny branches of an old dead tree, a little owl flew on tiny silent wings and disappeared into the forest.

Westerns available from

Available by mail from

1812 • David Nevin
The War of 1812 would either make America a global power sweeping to the Pacific or break it into small pieces bound to mighty England. Only the courage of James Madison, Andrew Jackson, and their wives could determine the nation's fate.

PRIDE OF LIONS • Morgan Llywelyn
Pride of Lions, the sequel to the immensely popular *Lion of Ireland*, is a stunningly realistic novel of the dreams and bloodshed, passion and treachery, of eleventh-century Ireland and its lusty people.

WALTZING IN RAGTIME • Eileen Charbonneau
The daughter of a lumber baron is struggling to make it as a journalist in turn-of-the-century San Francisco when she meets ranger Matthew Hart, whose passion for nature challenges her deepest held beliefs.

BUFFALO SOLDIERS • Tom Willard
Former slaves had proven they could fight valiantly for their freedom, but in the West they were to fight for the freedom and security of the white settlers who often despised them.

THIN MOON AND COLD MIST • Kathleen O'Neal Gear
Serving in the trenches as a Civil War Confederate spy, a woman of the West makes her way alone towards the promise of the untamed Colorado frontier—until her new life has room for love.

SPIRIT OF THE EAGLE • Vella Munn
Luash, a young woman of the Modic tribe, tries to stop the Secretary of War from destroying her people.

THE OVERLAND TRAIL • Wendi Lee
Based on the authentic diaries of the women who crossed the country in the late 1840s. America, a widowed pioneer, and Dancing Feather, a young Paiute, set out to recover America's kidnapped infant daughter—and to forge a bridge between their two worlds.